Praise for *Strawberry Fields*

"An effervescent comedy, beneath which lies a more somber look at the costs of globalization." —*The New Yorker*

"Of course, it's more than just funny. It's also sad and wise and tender and generous and even sexy. . . . It is to the author's credit that her satirical impulse never disguises the terrible sadness of her characters' lives. If anything, the comedy and drama draw from the same source: the gap between dreams and numbing reality. I didn't know whether to laugh or cry. . . . One way or another, these strawberry fields are forever." —*The Washington Post*

"Absolutely splendid." —*The Boston Globe*

"*A Short History of Tractors in Ukrainian* introduced [Lewycka's] comic genius. She is, as *Strawberry Fields* confirms, more precisely a mistress of the tragicomic, seamlessly welding humor and pathos into realistically zany episodes. . . . *Strawberry Fields* contains bushels of food for thought." —*San Francisco Chronicle*

"In Lewycka's hands, these migrants emerge as dreamers and searchers, and their travels along the UK's economic underbelly leave them wiser if not richer. . . . As in her bestselling debut *A Short History of Tractors in Ukrainian*, Lewycka blends satire and slapstick with melancholy realism, creating a big-hearted fable that's punchier than many a political polemic." —*Bloomberg*

"A comedy in the Shakespearean sense . . . If you've read Lewycka's previous novel, *A Short History of Tractors in Ukrainian*, you'll know that she has the uncanny ability to pluck diamonds of comedy out of the blackest pits of affliction. . . . A riotous pilgrimage in quest of the modern versions of redemption—work and money, and the adventures along the way blend the awful with the absurd in a grisly sort of slapstick: Dante's *Inferno* as interpreted by the Simpsons. . . . Marina Lewycka is a spirited and inventive writer and one of the surprises of English literature. . . . Had Penguin Books not taken a chance on *A Short History of Tractors in Ukrainian*, we might never [have known] her boldly satiric voice, which sounds like Jonathan Swift in its savage indignation and rip-roaring instinct for the outrageous. In *Strawberry Fields* Lewycka confirms her position as a master of *la comedie humaine*, which aims to expose the secret world of folly and greed and machination beneath the surface of middle-class comfort." —*The Buffalo News*

"Marina Lewycka follows her phenomenally funny *A Short History of Tractors in Ukrainian* (nominated for both the Booker and the Orange prizes) with the socially astute, fundamentally satirical *Strawberry Fields*. . . . This is a stunning

novel. . . . *Strawberry Fields* stands along the best of Zadie Smith and Monica Ali. It is sometimes outrageous, sometimes bawdy and constantly entertaining."
—*The Seattle Times*

"A hard-hitting reprise of the many horrors that starry-eyed immigrants face in the West. . . . At a time when volcanic shifts in the global economy are creating new fissures between peoples and societies, *Strawberry Fields* should be compulsory reading for anyone who wishes to delve into the human stories trapped within the cracks."
—*St. Petersburg Times*

"A darkly comic trip through rural England told by migrant workers on a strawberry farm. . . . *Strawberry Fields* deftly portrays both the kindnesses of the workers to one another and the harsh realities of migrant life. . . . With immigration taking a primary place in the daily news, it's important to have novels like this, putting a face on the faceless with heart and humor."
—*BookPage*

"UK-based Lewycka, a Booker and Orange Prize nominee for 2005's *A Short History of Tractors in Ukrainian*, follows up with a Chaucer-inspired tale of migrant workers trapped at a global capital's thuggish bottom. . . . Captivating . . . Many of the characters are complex and multifaceted. . . . As a send up of capitalism's grip on the global everyman, Lewycka's ensemble novel complements Gary Shteyngart's *Absurdistan*."
—*Publishers Weekly*

"[T]he voices are real and strong. Yola, the group's nattering, overbearing, self-appointed supervisor, is funny and sharply sketched. Letters from Emmanuel, an orphan from Malawi, to his sister, are both amusing—filled with inadvertent double-entendres—and strangely beautiful, written in twisted, Latinate English and marked by genuine wonder and deep religious feeling. Lewycka also skillfully communicates the hopes and yearning of a Ukrainian girl named Irina."
—*Los Angeles Times*

"Readers of Lewycka's first book will find themselves on familiar terrain. . . . We are treated to the best malapropisms money can buy, along with some demented soliloquies. It would be wrong to call this broken English—it is merely scuffed, chipped and idiomatically cracked. . . . The author's ambition is laudable. So is her skill in creating characters that flirt with ethnic commonplaces and then transcend them. . . . Even the cartoonish secondary players have a springy sort of life to them. Amid the malaprops and bathroom jokes, some of which suggest a more genteel Borat, the author makes a plea for tolerance, dignity and elementary kindness."
—*Newsday*

"An uplifting and laugh-out-loud read."　　　　　　　　　　—*InStyle*

"A jolly romp."　　　　　　　　　　　　　　—*The London Review of Books*

"Marina Lewycka has pulled off another story with a big heart."　　—*Daily Express*

"A sweet, quirky tale."　　　　　　　　　　　　　　　—*Elle*

"Immensely appealing . . . [*Strawberry Fields*] all but sings with zest for life, could hardly be more engaging, shrewd and winningly perceptive about the waste inflicted by prejudice and injustice."　　　　　　—*The Sunday Times*

"As in her bestselling first novel, *A Short History of Tractors in Ukrainian*, Marina Lewycka's talent for comic writing is apparent from the beginning. . . . [*Strawberry Fields*] is a funny and charming novel."　　　　　　—*The Observer*

"The combination of charm and savagery make [*Strawberry Fields*] a piquant and disturbing read—the fictional equivalent of chocolate laced with chili."
　　　　　　　　　　　　　　　　　—*Sunday Telegraph*

PENGUIN BOOKS

STRAWBERRY FIELDS

Marina Lewycka is the author of *A Short History of Tractors in Ukrainian*, which has been translated into thirty languages, has sold more than 750,000 copies worldwide, and was nominated for the Booker and Orange prizes. She is married, with a grown-up daughter, and lives in Sheffield, England.

strawberry fields

marina lewycka

PENGUIN BOOKS

PENGUIN BOOKS

Published by the Penguin Group

Penguin Group (USA) Inc., 375 Hudson Street, New York, New York 10014, U.S.A.
Penguin Group (Canada), 90 Eglinton Avenue East, Suite 700, Toronto,
Ontario, Canada M4P 2Y3 (a division of Pearson Penguin Canada Inc.)
Penguin Books Ltd, 80 Strand, London WC2R 0RL, England
Penguin Ireland, 25 St Stephen's Green, Dublin 2, Ireland (a division of Penguin Books Ltd)
Penguin Group (Australia), 250 Camberwell Road, Camberwell,
Victoria 3124, Australia (a division of Pearson Australia Group Pty Ltd)
Penguin Books India Pvt Ltd, 11 Community Centre,
Panchsheel Park, New Delhi – 110 017, India
Penguin Group (NZ), 67 Apollo Drive, Rosedale, North Shore 0632,
New Zealand (a division of Pearson New Zealand Ltd)
Penguin Books (South Africa) (Pty) Ltd, 24 Sturdee Avenue,
Rosebank, Johannesburg 2196, South Africa

Penguin Books Ltd, Registered Offices:
80 Strand, London WC2R 0RL, England

First published in Great Britain under the title *Two Caravans* by Fig Tree,
an imprint of Penguin Books Ltd 2007
First published in the United States of America by The Penguin Press,
a member of Penguin Group (USA) Inc. 2007
Published in Penguin Books 2008

1   3   5   7   9   10   8   6   4   2

PUBLISHER'S NOTE
This is a work of fiction. Names, characters, places, and incidents are either the product
of the author's imagination or are used fictitiously, and any resemblance to actual persons,
living or dead, business establishments, events, or locales is entirely coincidental.

THE LIBRARY OF CONGRESS HAS CATALOGED THE
HARDCOVER EDITION AS FOLLOWS:
Lewycka, Marina, date.
Strawberry fields : a novel / Marina Lewycka.
p.   cm.
ISBN 978-1-59420-137-0 (hc.)
ISBN 978-0-14-311355-3 (pbk.)
1. Agricultural laborers—fiction.   2. England—fiction.   I. Title.
PR6112.E895S77   2007
823'.92—dc   22 2007001932

Printed in the United States of America
Designed by Stephanie Huntwork

TO DAVE AND SONIA

But that I praye to al this compaignye,

If that I speke after my fantasye,

As taketh not agrief of that I seye;

For myn entente is nat but for to pleye.

—GEOFFREY CHAUCER,
  Prologue to the Wife of Bath's Tale,
  The Canterbury Tales

strawberry fields

two trailers

There is a field—a broad south-sloping field sitting astride a long hill that curves away into a secret leafy valley. It is sheltered by dense hedges of hawthorn and hazel threaded through with wild roses and evening-scented honeysuckle. In the mornings, a light breeze carries up over The Downs, just enough to kiss the air with the fresh salty tang of the English Channel. In fact so delightful is the air that, sitting up here, you might think you were in paradise. And in the field are two trailers, a men's trailer and a women's trailer.

If this were really the Garden of Eden, though, there ought to be an apple tree, thinks Yola. But it is the Garden of England, and the field is full of ripening strawberries. And instead of a snake, they have the Dumpling.

Sitting on the step of the women's trailer, painting her toenails fuchsia pink, petite, voluptuous Yola watches the Dumpling's Land Rover pull in through the gate at the bottom of the field, and the new arrival clamber down out of the passenger seat. Really, she cannot for the life of her understand why they have sent this two-zloty pudding of a girl, when what is clearly needed is another man—preferably someone mature, but with his own hair and nice legs and a calm nature—who will not only pick faster, but will bring a pleasant sexual harmony to their small community, whereas anyone can see that this little miss is going to set the fox among the chickens, and that all the men will be vying for her favors and not paying attention to what they are really here for, namely, the picking of strawberries. This thought is so annoying that it makes Yola lose concentration on her middle toe, which ends up looking like a botched amputation.

And there is also the question of space, Yola broods, studying the new girl as she makes her way past the men's trailer and up through the field. Although there are more women than men, the women's trailer is smaller, just a little four-berth tourer that you might tow behind when you go off on holiday to the Baltic. Yola, as the supervisor, is a person of status, and although petite she is generously proportioned, so naturally she has a single bunk to herself. Marta, her niece, has the other single bunk. The two Chinese girls—Yola can never get the hang of their names—share the fold-out double bed, which, when extended, takes up the whole floor space. That's it. There is no room for anyone else.

The four of them have done their best to make their trailer seem bright and homey. The Chinese girls have stuck pictures of baby animals and David Beckham on the walls. Marta has stuck a picture of the Black Virgin of Krakow beside David Beckham. Yola, who likes things to smell nice, has set a bunch of wildflowers in a cup, hedge roses, campion, and white-gold honeysuckle, to sweeten the air.

A particularly charming feature of their trailer is the clever storage space: There are compact cupboards, cunning head-level lockers, and drawers with delightful decorative handles where everything can be hidden away. Yola likes things to be neat. The four women have become skilled at avoiding one another, skirting around each other in the small space with womanly delicacy, unlike men, who are defective creatures, prone to be clumsy and to take up unnecessary room, though of course they can't help it and they do have some good points, which she will tell you about later.

This new girl—she skips right up to the trailer and drops her bag down in the middle of the floor. She has come from Kiev, she says, looking around her with a smile on her face. Irina is her name. She looks tired and disheveled, with a faint whiff of chip fat about her. Where does she think she is going to keep that bag? Where does she think she is going to sleep? What does she have to smile about? That's what Yola wants to know.

"Irina, my baby, you can still change your mind! You don't have to go!"

Mother was wailing and dabbing at her pinky eyes with a tissue, causing an embarrassing scene at the Kiev bus station.

"Mother, please! I'm not a baby!"

You expect your mother to cry at a moment like this. But when my craggy old Papa turned up too, his shirt all crumpled and his silver hair sticking up like an old-age porcupine, okay, I admit it rattled me. I hadn't expected him to come to see me off.

"Irina, little one, take care."

"*Shcho ti*, Papa. What's all this about? Do you think I'm not coming back?"

"Just take care, my little one." Sniffle. Sigh.

"I'm not little, Papa. I'm nineteen. Do you think I can't look after myself?"

"Ah, my little pigeon." Sigh. Sniffle. Then Mother started up again. Then—I couldn't help myself—I started up too, sighing and sniffling and dabbing my eyes, until the bus driver told us to get a move on, and Mother shoved a bag of bread and salami and a poppy seed cake into my hands, and we were off. From Kiev to Kent in forty-two hours.

Okay, I admit, forty-two hours on a bus is not amusing. By the time we reached Lviv, the bread and salami were all gone. In Poland, I noticed that my ankles were starting to swell. When we stopped for fuel somewhere in Germany, I stuffed the last crumbs of the poppy-seed cake into my mouth and washed it down with nasty metallic-tasting water from a tap that was marked not for drinking. In Belgium my period started, but I didn't notice until the dark stain of blood seeped through my jeans onto the seat. In France I lost all sensation in my feet. On the ferry to Dover I found a toilet and cleaned myself up. Looking into the cloudy mirror above the washbasin I hardly recognized the wan dark-eyed face that stared back at me—was that me, that scruffy straggly-haired girl with bags under her eyes? I walked around to restore the circulation in my legs, and, standing on the deck at dawn, I watched the white cliffs of England materialize in the pale watery light, beautiful, mysterious, the land of my dreams.

In Dover I was met off the boat by Vulk, waving a bit of card with my name on it—Irina Blazkho. Typical—he'd gotten the spelling wrong. He was the type Mother would describe as a person of minimum culture, wearing a horrible black fake-leather jacket, like a comic-strip gangster— what a *koshmar*!—it creaked as he walked. All he needed was a gun.

He greeted me with a grunt. "Hrr. You heff passport? Peppers?"

His voice was deep and sludgy, with a nasty whiff of cigarette smoke and tooth decay on his breath.

This gangster-type should brush his teeth. I fumbled in my bag, and before I could say anything, he grabbed my passport and Seasonal Agricultural Worker papers and stowed them in the breast pocket of his *koshmar* jacket.

"I keep for you. Is many bed people in England. Can stealing from you."

He patted the pocket and winked. I could see straightaway that there was no point in arguing with a person of his type, so I hoisted my bag onto my shoulder and followed him across the car park to a huge shiny black vehicle that looked like a cross between a tank and a Zill, with darkened windows and gleaming chrome bars in the front—a typical mafia-machine. These high-status cars are popular with primitive types and social undesirables. In fact he looked quite a bit like his car: overweight, built like a tank, with a gleaming silver front tooth, a shiny black jacket, and a straggle of hair tied in a ponytail hanging down his back like an exhaust pipe. Ha ha.

He gripped my elbow, which was quite unnecessary—stupid man, did he think I might try to escape?—and pushed me onto the backseat with a shove, which was also unnecessary. Inside, the mafia-machine stank of tobacco. I sat in silence looking nonchalantly out the window while he scrutinized me rudely through the rearview mirror. What did he think he was staring at? Then he lit up one of those thick vile-smelling cigars—Mother calls them New Russian cigarettes—what a stink! and started puffing away. Puff. Stink.

I didn't take in the scenery that flashed past through the black-tinted glass—I was too tired—but my body registered every twist in the lane, and the sudden jerks and jolts when he braked and turned. This gangster-type needs some driving lessons.

He had some potato chips wrapped in a paper bundle on the passenger seat beside him, and every now and then he would plunge his left fist in, grab a handful of chips, and cram them into his mouth. Grab. Cram. Chomp. Grab. Cram. Chomp. Not very refined. The chips smelled fantastic, though. The smell of the cigar, the lurching motion as he steered with one hand and stuffed his mouth with the other, the low, dragging pain from my period—it was all making me feel queasy and hungry at the same time. In the end, hunger won out. I wondered what language this gangster-type would talk. Belarusian? He looked too dark for a Belarus. Ukrainian? He didn't look Ukrainian. Maybe from somewhere out east? Chechnya? Georgia? What do Georgians look like? The Balkans? Taking a guess, I asked in Russian, "Please, Mr. Vulk, may I have something to eat?"

He looked up. Our eyes met in the rearview mirror. He had real gangster-type eyes—poisonous black berries in eyebrows as straggly as an overgrown hedge. He studied me in that offensive way, sliding his eyes all over me.

"Little flovver vants eating?" He spoke in English, though he must have understood my Russian. Probably he came from one of those newly independent nations of the former Soviet Union where everyone can speak Russian but nobody does. Okay, so he wanted to talk English? I'd show him.

"Yes indeed, Mr. Vulk. If you could oblige me, if it does not inconvenience you, I would appreciate something to eat."

"No problema, little flovver!"

He helped himself to one more mouthful of chips—grab, cram, chomp—then scrunched up the remnants in the oily paper and passed them over the back of the seat. As I reached forward to take them, I saw something else nestled down on the seat beneath where the chips had been. Something small, black, and scary. *Shcho to!* Was that a real gun?

My heart started hammering. What did he need a gun for? *Mama, Papa, help me!* Okay, just pretend not to notice. Maybe it's not loaded. Maybe it's just one of those cigar lighters. So I unfolded the crumpled paper—it was like a snug, greasy nest. The chips inside were fat, soft, and still warm. There were only about six left, and some scraps. I savored them one at a time. They were lightly salty, with a touch of vinegar, and they were just—mmm!—indescribably delicious. The fat clung to the edges of my lips and hardened on my fingers, so I had no choice but to lick it off, but I tried to do it discreetly.

"Thank you," I said politely, for rudeness is a sign of minimum culture.

"No problema. No problema." He waved his fist about as if to show how generous he was. "Food for eat in transit. All vill be add to your living expense."

Living expense? I didn't need any more nasty surprises. I studied his back, the creaky stretched-at-the-seams jacket, the ragged ponytail, the thick, yellowish neck, the flecks of dandruff on the fake-leather collar. I was starting to feel queasy again.

"What is this, expense?"

"Expense. Expense. Foods. Transports. Accommodations." He took both hands off the steering wheel and waved them in the air. "Life in vest is too much expensive, little flovver. Who you think vill be pay for all such luxury?"

Although his English was appalling, those words came rolling out like a prepared speech. "You think this vill be providing all for free?"

So Mother had been right. "Anybody can see this agency is run by crooks. Anybody but you, Irina." (See how Mother has this annoying habit of putting me down?) "And if you tell them lies, Irina, if you pretend to be student of agriculture when you are nothing of the sort, who will help you if something goes wrong?"

Then she went on in her hysterical way about all the things that go wrong for Ukrainian girls who go west—all those rumors and stories in the papers.

"But everyone knows these things only happened to stupid and uneducated girls, Mother. They're not going to happen to me."

"If you will please say me what are the expenses, I will try to meet them."

I kept my voice civilized and polite. The chrome-bar tooth gleamed.

"Little flovver, the expense vill be first to pay, and then you vill be pay. Nothing to be discuss. No problema."

"And you will give me back my passport?"

"Exact. You verk, you get passport. You no verk, you no passport. Someone mekka visit in you Mama in Kiev, say Irina no good verk, is mek big problem for her."

"I have heard that in England—"

"England is a change, little flovver. Now England is land of possibility. England is not like in you school book."

I thought of dashing Mr. Brown from *Let's Talk English*—if only he were here!

"You have an excellent command of English. And of Russian maybe?"

"English. Russian. Serbo-Croat. German. All languages."

So he sees himself as a linguist; okay, keep him talking.

"You are not a native of these shores, I think, Mr. Vulk?"

"Think everything vat you like, little flovver." He gave me a leering wink in the mirror, and a flash of silver tooth. Then he started tossing his head from side to side as if to shake out his dandruff.

"This, you like? Is voman attract?"

It took me a moment to realize he was referring to his ponytail. Was this his idea of flirtation? On the scale of attractiveness, I would give him a zero. For a person of minimum culture he certainly had some pretensions. What a pity Mother wasn't here to put him right.

"It is absolutely irresistible, Mr. Vulk."

"You like? Eh, little flovver? You vant touch?"

The ponytail jumped up and down. I held my breath.

"Go on. Hrr. You can touch him. Go on," he said with horrible oily enthusiasm.

I reached out my hand, which was still greasy and smelled of chips.

"Go on. Is pleasure for you."

I touched it—it felt like a rat's tail. Then he flicked his head, and it twitched beneath my fingers like a live rat.

"I heff hear that voman is cannot resisting such a hair it reminding her of men's oggan."

What on earth was he talking about now?

"Oggan?"

He made a crude gesture with his fingers.

"Be not afraid, little flovver. It reminding you of boyfriend. Hah?"

"No, Mr. Vulk, because I do not have a boyfriend."

I knew straightaway it was the wrong thing to say, but it was too late. The words just slipped out, and I couldn't bring them back.

"Not boyfriend? How is this little flovver not boyfriend?" His voice was like warm chip fat. "Hrr. Maybe in this case is good possibility for me?"

That was a stupid mistake. He's got you now. You're cornered.

"Is perhaps sometime we make good possibility, eh?" He breathed cigar smoke and tooth decay. "Little flovver?"

Through the darkened glass, I could see woods flashing past, all sunlight and dappled leaves. If only I could throw myself out of the vehicle, roll down the grassy bank, and run in among the trees. But we were going too fast. I shut my eyes and pretended to be asleep.

We drove on in silence for maybe twenty minutes. Vulk lit another cigar. I watched him through my lowered lashes, puffing away, hunched over the wheel. Puff. Stink. Puff. Stink. How much farther could it be? Then there was a crunching of gravel under the wheels, and with one last violent lurch the mafia-machine came to a halt. I opened my eyes. We had pulled up in front of a pretty steep-roofed farmhouse set behind a summery garden where there were chairs and tables set out on the lawn that sloped down to a shallow glassy river. Just like England is supposed to be. Now at last, I thought, there will be normal people; they will talk to me in English; they will give me tea.

But they didn't. Instead, a pudgy red-faced man wearing dirty clothes and rubber boots came out of the house—the farmer, I guessed—and he helped me out of Vulk's vehicle, mumbling something I couldn't understand, but it was obviously not an invitation to tea. He looked me up and down in that same rude way, as though I were a horse he'd just bought. Then he and Vulk muttered to each other, too fast for me to follow, and exchanged envelopes.

"Bye-bye, little flovver," Vulk said, with that chip-fat smile. "Ve meet again. Maybe ve mekka possibility?"

"Maybe."

I knew it was the wrong thing to say, but by then I was just desperate to get away.

The farmer shoved my bag into his Land Rover and then he shoved me in too, giving my behind a good feel with his hand as he did so, which was quite unnecessary. He only had to ask and I would have climbed in by myself.

"I'll take you straight out to the field," he said, as we rattled along narrow winding lanes. "You can start picking this afternoon."

After some five kilometers, the Land Rover swung in through the gate, and I felt a rush of relief as at last I planted my feet on firm ground. The first thing I noticed was the light—the dazzling salty light dancing on the sunny field, the ripening strawberries, the little rounded trailer perched up on the hill and the oblong boxy trailer down in the corner of the field, the woods beyond, and the long, curving horizon, and I smiled to myself. So this is England.

The men's trailer is a static model, a battered old fiberglass box parked at the bottom of the field by the gate, close to a new prefab building where the strawberries are crated and weighed each day. Stuck onto one corner of the prefab is the toilet and shower room—though the shower doesn't work and the toilet is locked at night. Why is it locked? wonders Andriy. What is the problem with using the toilet at night?

He has woken early with a full bladder and an unspecific feeling of dissatisfaction with himself, his trailer mates, and trailer life in general. Why is it, for example, that although the men's trailer is bigger, it still feels more cramped than the women's trailer? It has two rooms—one for sleeping and one for sitting—but Tomasz has the double bed in the sleeping room all to himself and three of them are sleeping in the sitting room. How has this happened? Andriy has one of the seat-beds and Vitaly has the other. Emanuel has made himself a hammock from an old sheet and blue bale twine, skillfully twisted and knotted, and slung it across the sitting room from corner to corner. He is lying there breathing deeply with his eyes closed and a cherubic smile on his round brown face. Andriy recalls Emanuel's look of astonishment and horror when the farmer suggested he should share the double bed with Tomasz.

"Sir, we have a proverb in Chichewa. One nostril is too small for two fingers."

Afterward, he took Andriy to one side and whispered, "In my country homosexualization is forbidden."

"Is okay," Andriy whispered back. "No homosex, only bad stink."

Yes, Tomasz's sneakers are another insult—their stink fills the trailer. It is worst at night when the sneakers are off his feet and stowed beneath the bed. The fumes rise, noxious and clinging, and dissipate like bad dreams, seeping through the curtain that divides the bedroom from the sitting room, hovering below the ceiling like an evil spirit. Sometimes, in the night, Emanuel rolls silently out of his hammock and places the sneakers outside on the step.

Another thing—why are there no pictures on the walls in the men's trailer? Vitaly keeps a picture of Jordan under his bed, which he says he will stick up when he finds something to stick it with. He also keeps a secret stash of canned lager and a pair of binoculars. Tomasz keeps a guitar and a pair of Yola's panties under his bed. Emanuel keeps a bag full of crumpled papers.

But the worst thing is that because of the slope, and the way their trailer is positioned, you can only get a view of the women's trailer from the window above Tomasz's bed. Should he ask Tomasz to move over so he can take a look and see whether that girl is still around? No. They'd only make stupid remarks.

In the women's trailer they have been up since dawn. Yola has learned from experience that it is better to rise early if they don't want the Dumpling knocking on the door and inviting himself in while they are getting dressed, hanging around watching them with those hungry-dog eyes—doesn't he have anything better to do?

Irina and the Chinese girls have to get up first and fold away the double bed before there is room for anyone to move. They cannot use the lavatory and washroom until the Dumpling arrives with the key to the prefab—what does he think they're going to do? Unroll the toilet paper at night?—but there is a handy gap in the hedge only a few meters away, though Yola cannot for the life of her understand why there always seem to be faces grinning at the window of the other trailer whenever any of the women slips behind the hedge. Don't they have anything better to do down there?

There is a cold-water tap and washing bowl at the side of the women's trailer, and even a shower made from a bucket with holes in the bottom, fed from a black-painted oil drum stuck up in a tree. In the evening, after it has been in the sun all day, the water is pleasantly warm. That nice-looking boy Andriy, who is quite a gallant despite being Ukrainian, has erected a screen of birch poles and plastic sacks around it, disregarding the protests of Vitaly and Tomasz, who complained that he spoiled their innocent entertainment—really those two are worse than the children at nursery school, what they need is a good smacking—and now they can no longer see the shower, they spend all their time making comments about the items on the women's wash line. Recently a pair of her panties has disappeared in mysterious circumstances. Yola cannot for the life of her understand how grown men can be such fools. Well, in fact, she can.

It was Tomasz who stole the panties, in a moment of drunken frivolity one night last week. They are made of white cotton, generously cut, with a pretty mauve ribbon in the front. He has been looking out ever since for the right moment to return them discreetly without being caught— he wouldn't want anyone to think he is the sort of man who steals women's underwear from wash lines and keeps them under his bed.

"I see Yola has washed her undies again today," he says morosely in Polish, peering through Vitaly's binoculars from the window above his bed. "I wonder what is the meaning of this."

The white panties dangle in the air like a provocation. When Yola recruited him to her strawberry-picking team, there had been a twinkle about her that had seemed to suggest she was inviting him to . . . well, more than just pick strawberries.

"What do you mean, *what is the meaning*?" asks Vitaly in Russian, mimicking Tomasz's Polish accent. "Most of what women do is completely meaningless."

Vitaly is vague about his origins and Tomasz has never pressed him, assuming he is some kind of illegal or Gypsy. Despite himself, he is impressed by the way Vitaly can slip easily between Russian, Polish, and Ukrainian. Even his English is quite good. But what use are all those languages if you have no poetry in your soul?

"In the poetry of women's undergarments, there is always meaning. Like the blossoms that fall from a tree as the heat of summer approaches. . . . Like clouds that melt away . . ."

He can feel a song coming on.

"Enough," says Vitaly. "The Angliskis would call you a soiled old man."

"I am not old," protests Tomasz.

In fact he has just turned forty-five. On his birthday he looked in the mirror and found two more gray hairs on his head, which he pulled out at once. No wonder his hair is beginning to look thin. Soon he will have to surrender to the grayness, to cut his hair short, put away his guitar, exchange his dreams for compromises, and start worrying about his pension. What has happened to his life? It is just slipping away, like sand through an hourglass, like a mountain washed to the sea.

"Tell me, Vitaly, how has life turned you into a cynic at such a young age?"

Vitaly shrugs. "Maybe I was not born to be a loser, like you, Tomek."

"Maybe there is still time enough for you."

How can he explain to this impatient young man what it has taken him forty-five years to learn—that loss is an essential part of the human condition. That even as we are moving on down that long lonesome road, destination unknown, there is always something we are leaving behind. He has been trying all morning to compose a song about it.

Putting down the binoculars, he reaches for his guitar and begins to strum, tapping his feet in time to the rhythm.

> *There once was a man, who roamed the world o'er.*
> *Was he seeking for riches, or glory, or power?*
> *Was he seeking for meaning, or truth or . . .*

This is where he gets stuck. What else is that wretched man seeking? Vitaly gives him a pitying look.

"Obviously he is looking for someone to fuck."

He picks up the binoculars, turns the knob to focus, and gives a soft whistle between his teeth.

"Hey, black man," he calls to Emanuel in English, "come and see. Look, it's just like the little panties that Jordan is wearing in my poster.

Or maybe . . ."—he adjusts the binoculars again—". . . maybe it is one of those string nets they use to package salami."

Emanuel is sitting at the table, chewing a pencil for inspiration as he composes a letter.

"Leave him, leave him," says Tomasz. "Emanuel is not like you. He is . . ." He strums a couple of chords on his guitar as he searches for the right phrase. "In this box of fiberglass, he is searching for a gem."

"Another loser," snorts Vitaly.

Dear Sister

Thank you for the money you sent for with its help I have now journeyed from Zomba to Lilongwe and so on via Nairobi into England. I hope these words will receive you for when I came to the address you gave in London a different name was written at the door and nobody knew of your wherebeing. So being needful of money I came into the way of strawberry picking and I am staying in a trailer with three mzungus here in Kent. I am striving with all my might to improve my English but this English tongue is like a coilsome and slippery serpent and I am always trying to remember the lessons of Sister Benedicta and her harsh staff of chastisement. So I write hopefully that you will come there and find these letters and unleash your corrections upon them dear sister. And so I will inform you regulally of my adventures within this rainstruck land.

From your beloving brother Emanuel!

The women's trailer is already in sunshine, but the sun hasn't yet reached the bottom of the field, where Andriy is standing at the kitchen end of the men's trailer trying to light the gas to make some tea. The coarse banter from the sleeping room irritates him, and he doesn't want the other three to notice the agitation that has come over him since yesterday. He lights another match. It flares and burns his fingers before the gas will catch. Devil's bum! That girl, that new Ukrainian girl—when their eyes met, did she smile at him in a particular way?

He replays the scene like a movie in his head. It is this time yesterday. Farmer Leapish arrives as usual in his Land Rover with the breakfast food, the trays of empty boxes for the strawberries, and the key to the prefab. Then someone steps out of the passenger door of the Land Rover, a pretty girl with a long plait of dark hair down her back, and brown eyes full of sparkle. And that smile. She steps into the field, looking around this way and that. He is there standing by the gate, and she turns his way and smiles. But is it for him, that smile? That's what he wants to know.

He made a point of sitting next to her at dinner.

"Hi. Ukrainka?"

"Of course."

"Me too."

"I can see."

"What's your name?"

"Irina."

He waited for her to ask—"And yours?"—but she didn't.

"Andriy."

He waited for her to say something, but she didn't.

"From Kiev?" he continued.

"Of course."

"Donetsk."

"Ah, Donetsk. Coal miners."

Did he detect a hint of condescension in her voice?

"You been to Donetsk?"

"Never."

"I came to Kiev."

"Oh yes?"

"In December. When demonstrations were going on."

"You came for demonstrations?" A definite condescending lilt.

"I came to demonstrate against demonstrations."

"Ah. Of course."

"Maybe I saw you then. You were there?"

"Of course. In Maidan Square."

"In demonstration?"

"Of course. It was our Orange Freedom Revolution."

"I was with the other side. White and Blue."

"The losing side."

She smiled again. A flash of white teeth, that's all there was to it. He tries to picture the face, but he can't get it into focus. No, there was more to it than teeth; there was a crinkling around the nose and eyes, a little lift of the eyebrows, and two infuriating dimples winking below the cheeks. Those dimples—he can't get them out of his mind. Was it just a smile, or did it *mean* something?

And if it *means* something, does it mean I've got a good possibility here? A good possibility of a man-woman possibility? Should I take things further? Or should I just play it cool? A girl like that—she's too used to men running after her. Wait for her to show the first card. But what if she's shy—what if she needs a bit of help with that first card? Sometimes a man must act to bring about a possibility.

But then again, isn't this the wrong time and place, Andriy Palenko, to be involving yourself with another Ukrainian girl? What about the blond-haired Angliska rosa you came all this way to England for, the pretty blue-eyed girl who is waiting for you, though she doesn't know it yet herself, loaded with high-spec features: skin like smetana, pink-tipped Angliski breasts, golden underarm hair like duckling down, et cetera. And a rich Papa, who at first may not be too happy about his daughter's choice because he wants her to marry a banker in a bowler hat like Mr. Brown— what father would not?—but when he gets to know you will soften his heart and welcome you into his luxurious en-suite-bathroom house. For sure he will find a nice little job for his Ukrainian son-in-law. Maybe even a nice car . . . Mercedes. Porsche. Ferrari. Et cetera.

Yes, this new Ukrainian girl has some positive features: nice looking, nice smile, nice dimples, nice figure, nicely rounded, plenty to get hold of, not too thin like those stylish city girls who starve themselves into Western-type matchsticks. But she's only another Ukrainian girl—plenty of those where you came from. And besides, she's a bit snobbish. She thinks she's better than you. She thinks she's a high-culture type with a superior mentality, and you're a low-culture type. (And so what if you are? Is that something to be ashamed of?) You can tell by the way she talks, being so stingy with her words, as if it's money she's counting out. And the ridiculous plait, like that crow Julia Timoshenko, fake-traditional Ukrainian. Tied with an orange ribbon. She thinks she's better than you because she's from Kiev and you're from Donbas. She thinks she's better than you, because your dad's a miner—a dead miner, at that.

Poor Dad. Not the life for a dog let alone a man. Underground. Down below the mushrooms. Down with the legions of ghost miners, all huddled up in the dark, singing their eerie dead-men's songs. No, he can't go down there anymore, even if it's the only way he knows how to live, how to put bread on the table. He'll have to find another way. What would his father have wanted him to do? It's hard enough living up to your parents' expectations when you know what they expect. But all Andriy's father ever said to him was, "Be a man." What is that supposed to mean?

When the pit prop gave way and the roof fell in, Andriy was on one side of the cave-in and his father was on the other. He was on the living side; his father was on the side of the dead. He heard the roar, and he ran toward the light. He ran and ran. He is still running.

I AM DOG I RUN I RUN FROM BAD MAN CAGE I HEAR DOGS BARK ANGRY DOGS GROWL ANGRY DOGS BARK THEY WILL FIGHT THEY WILL KILL I SMELL DOG RAGE MAN SWEAT MAN OPENS CAGE MAN PULLS COLLAR MEN SIT SMOKE TALK DOGS BARK LIGHT TOO BRIGHT BIG ANGRY DOG SNARLS SHOWS TEETH HAIRS BRISTLE ON HIS BACK HE WILL KILL I AM NOT FIGHTING DOG I AM RUNNING DOG I JUMP I RUN I RUN TWO DAYS I EAT NO MEAT HUNGER PAINS IN BELLY MAKE ME MAD I FEEL HUNGER I FEEL FEAR I RUN I RUN I AM DOG

The women's trailer was small, but so cozy. I fell in love with it straight-away. I put my bag down and introduced myself.

"Irina. From Kiev."

Okay, there was some unpleasantness upon my arrival. Yola, the Polish supervisor, who is a coarse and uneducated person with an elevated view of her own importance, said some harsh words about Ukrainians for which she has yet to apologize. Okay, I was a bit dismayed at the overcrowded conditions, and I may have been a little tactless. But then the Chinese girls very kindly told me I could share their bed. I wished I hadn't finished the poppy-seed cake, for a small gift can go a long way in these circumstances, but I still had a bottle of home-made cherry vodka for emergencies, and what was this if not an emergency? Soon we were all firm friends.

We ate our dinner sitting out on the hillside all together, drinking the rest of the vodka and watching the sun set. I was pleased to discover there's another Ukrainian here—a nice though rather primitive miner from Donetsk. We chatted in Ukrainian over dinner. Poles and Ukrainians can understand each other's language too, though it's not the same. But of course I have come to England mainly to improve my English before I start my university course, so I hope I will soon meet more English people.

English was my favorite subject at school, and I had pictured myself walking through a panorama of cultivated conversations, like a painted landscape dotted with intriguing homonyms and mysterious subjunc-tives: *would you were wooed in the wood*. Miss Tyldesley was my favorite teacher. She even made English grammar seem sexy, and when she recited Byron she would close her eyes and breathe in deeply through her nose, trembling in a sort of virginal ecstasy, as though she could smell his pheromones wafting off the page. Please, control yourself, Miss Tyldesley! As you can imagine, I couldn't wait to come to England. Now, I thought, my life will really begin.

After dinner I went back to the trailer and unpacked my bag. On a patch of wall below the head-level locker I put up my picture of Mother and Papa standing together in front of the fireplace at home. Mother is wearing pink lipstick and a ghastly pink scarf tied in what she thinks is a stylish bow; Papa is wearing his ridiculous orange tie. Okay, so they wear terrible clothes, but they can't help it, and I still love them. Papa's arm is around Mother's shoulder, and they're smiling in a stiff uncertain way, like people whose hearts aren't in it, who are just posing for the camera. I looked at it while I drifted off to sleep, and a few pathetic tears came into my eyes. Mother and Papa waiting for me at home—what's so sad about that?

The next morning, when I woke up, the trailer was flooded with sunlight and everything seemed different. The gloomy thoughts and fears of yesterday had fled like ghosts into the night. When I went out to the tap to wash, the water splashing on the stones caught the sunbeams and broke them into hundreds of brilliant rainbows that danced through my fingers, cold and tingly. In the copse behind me, a thrush was singing.

As I bent toward the tap, the orange ribbon slipped off my plait, swirling in the water. For a moment I remembered the orange balloons and banners in the square, the tents and music, and my parents, so excited, gabbing like teenagers about freedom and other such stuff. And I did feel a stab of sadness. Then I picked up the wet ribbon, shook it out, and hung it over the washing line. As I looked down over the valley, my heart started to dance again. I took a deep breath. This air—so sweet, so English. This was the air I'd dreamed of breathing; loaded with history, yet as light as . . . well, as light as something very light. How had I lived for nineteen years without breathing this air? And all the cultured, brave, warm-hearted people that I'd read about in Chaucer, Shakespeare, Dickens—okay, I admit, mostly in translation—I was ready to meet them.

In fact I was particularly looking forward to meeting a gentleman in a bowler hat like Mr. Brown in my *Let's Talk English* book, who looks supremely dashing and romantic with his tight suit and rolled-up umbrella, and especially with the intriguing bulge in his trousers' zipper area, which was drawn very realistically in black ink by a previous owner of that textbook. Who wouldn't want to talk English with him?! Lord Byron looks romantic too, despite that bizarre turban.

English men are supposed to be incredibly romantic. There's a famous folk legend about a man who braves death and climbs in through his lady's bedroom window just to bring her a box of chocolates. Unfortunately, the only Englishman I have met so far is farmer Leapish, who doesn't seem to fit into this category. I hope he is not typical.

Please don't think I'm one of those awful Ukrainian girls who come to England only to ensnare a husband. I'm not. But if love should happen to come my way, okay, my heart is open and ready.

The kettle starts to whistle. Andriy pours the water onto the teabag, adds two spoonfuls of sugar, and, cradling the hot cup in his hands, wanders down to the gate, where he sometimes stands when he has an idle moment, observing the passing cars and looking out for his Angliska rosa. Leaning on his elbows, he drinks slowly, enjoying the heat in his throat, the cool breeze blowing up The Downs, and the noisy chatter of birds doing their early-morning stuff. The sun has come up over the hill and although it isn't yet eight o'clock, he can already feel its warmth on his skin. The light is as sharp as crystal, marking out the landscape with hard crisp shadows.

He likes to come down here, to look out at this England, which, despite being just beyond the gate, still seems tantalizingly out of reach. Where are you, *Let's Talk English* Mrs. Brown, with your tiny waist and tailored polka-dotted blouse? Where are you, Vagvaga Riskegipd, with your bubble gum and ferocious kisses? Since he came to England two weeks ago he hasn't met a single Angliska rosa. He has seen them drive past, so he knows they exist. Sometimes he waves, and once one of them even waved back. And yes, she was blond, and yes, she was driving a red Ferrari convertible. She was gone in the twinkling of an eye, before he could even vault over the gate to see the rear spoiler disappear around the bend in the lane. But for sure she lives somewhere nearby, so it is only a matter of time before she reappears. Okay, so his last girlfriend Lida

Zakanovka went off with a soccer player. Good luck to her. There are better women waiting for him over here in England.

He blows on the hot tea to cool it down and thinks about his last visit to England. How long ago was that? It was about eighteen years, so he must have been seven years old. He was accompanying his father on a fraternal delegation to visit the mine workers' union in the city of Sheffield, which is twinned with his home town, Donetsk. Learn, boy, his father had said. Learn about the beauty of international solidarity. Though it didn't do him much good when he needed it. Poor Dad.

He doesn't remember much about Sheffield, but three things stand out in his memory from that visit. First, he recalls, there was a banquet, and a sticky pink dessert, of which he ate so much that he was later horribly, messily, pinkily sick in the back of a car.

Second, he remembers that the renowned visionary ruler of the city, who had welcomed them warmly with a long-long speech about solidarity and the dignity of labor (the speech had so impressed his father that he repeated it many times over), who had sat next to them at the banquet and kindly pressed more and more of that treacherous pink dessert on him, and in the back of whose car he had later been sick—this man was blind. The man's astonishing blindness, the fearsome all-excluding wall bricked up behind his visionary eyes, had fascinated Andriy. He had closed his eyes tight and tried to imagine what it would be like to live behind that wall of blindness; he went around bumping into things, until his father slapped him and told him to behave himself.

The other thing he remembers is his first kiss. The girl—she must have been a daughter of one of the delegates—was older and bolder than him, a long-legged girl with white blond hair and a sprinkle of freckles on her nose. She smelled of soap and bubble gum. While the fraternal speeches droned on and on in the hall, the two of them had played a wild game of chase along the echoing corridors of the vast civic building, racing up and down stairs, dodging in doorways, shrieking with excitement. She had pounced on him at last and wrestled him down on the stone stairs, pinning him to the ground, pressing her strong body on top of him. They were both out of breath, panting and laughing. Suddenly she had swooped down on him with her lips and kissed him—a wet, insistent kiss, her tongue pushing against his mouth. It was a kiss of subjugation. He'd been too young and too astonished to do anything but surrender. Then she'd given him a bit of paper with her name scrawled on it, the "i"s dotted with little hearts. Vagvaga Riskegipd. An incredibly sexy name. And a telephone number. He still has it, tucked into the back of his wallet like a talisman. At school, when the other boys chose to study Russian language or German, he chose English.

He tries to conjure up her face. Fair hair. Freckles. The smell of bubble gum is vivid in his memory. An incredibly sexy smell. Does she still remember him? What does she look like now? She would be in her early thirties. What would she do if he suddenly appeared on her doorstep?

They say Angliski women are incredibly sexy. According to Vitaly, who knows these things, Angliski women are as cold as ice to touch, but once they start to melt—once the passion heats them and they melt inside—it's just like a river bursting its banks. There's no stopping these Vagvaga women; these Mrs. Brown women. A man has to keep a cool head or he could drown in the torrent of their passion. But getting them to the melting point—there's a real skill in that, says Vitaly. The Angliska woman is attracted to dashing men of action, men who are bold enough to make hazardous journeys and climb in through bedroom windows bearing boxes of chocolates, et cetera. This type of behavior melts the Angliska woman's icy heart. Will strawberries be okay as a substitute for chocolates? For all other acts in this drama he's prepared. He's ready for anything. He feels the lifeblood pulsing through his body, and he wants to live—to live more sweetly, more intensely.

"Be a man," his father had said.

One of the annoying things about my mother is the way she always classifies people according to their level of culture. It's as if she carries a perfectly defined hierarchy of culture in her head.

"It doesn't cost anything to be cultured, Irina," she says, "which is just as well, because if it did, teachers would be among the least cultured people in Ukraine."

The worst thing is, I seem to have picked up her habit, even though I know you shouldn't judge people by appearances. But sometimes you can't help it. Take us strawberry pickers, for example.

Although they are Chinese, the Chinese girls are definitely cultured types. One is a student of medicine and one is a student of accounting. I can't remember which is which, but medicine is more cultured than accounting. The Chinese Chinese girl has her hair cut short like a boy's, and she's quite pretty, but her legs are too thin. The Malaysian Chinese girl is also pretty, but she has a perm, which looks stupid on that type of hair. Maybe it's the other way around. They are friendly toward me, but they talk and giggle together all the time, which is annoying when you don't know what they're giggling about. Their English is terrible.

Next come Tomasz, Marta, and Emanuel. Tomasz is some kind of boring government bureaucrat, though he has taken a leave of absence from his job because he says he can earn more money picking strawberries—stupid, isn't it? He claims to be a poet, which of course is extremely cultured, though there is little evidence of this, unless you count those dreary songs he sings whenever Yola is around. And, besides, he is quite ancient—he must be in his forties—and he has a pathetic little beard and hair almost down to his shoulders like a hippy. *Koshmar!* And there's a dire smell about him.

Marta is educated, and she even speaks a bit of French, but that Roman Catholic–type education is full of rules and mysteries and lacks practical content—like Western Ukrainians. Anyway, Mother says that Catholic is less cultured than Orthodox. Marta is nice and friendly, but she has a big nose. Probably that is why she's still unmarried at the age of thirty.

Emanuel is adorable, but he is not quite eighteen and also a Catholic, though he appears to be an intelligent type, and he wears a horrible green anorak even when it's not raining. Of course he is black, but this does not make him any less cultured, because as any cultured person knows, black people are just as cultured as anybody else. He often sings as he picks strawberries in the field, and he has a beautiful voice, but he only sings religious songs. It would be nice if he sang something more amusing.

Vitaly is mysterious. He never gives you a straight answer. Sometimes he disappears; no one knows where he goes. He is clearly intelligent because he speaks good English and several other languages, but his manner is rather coarse and he wears a gold chain with a silver penknife dangling around his neck. His eyes are dark and twinkly with cute curly eyelashes, and his hair is black and curly. In fact he is not bad looking in a flashy curly sort of way. I would give him seven out of ten. Though he is not my type. Maybe he is a Gypsy.

Near the bottom is Ciocia Yola (strictly speaking she is only Marta's aunt, but we all call her Ciocia). She is a vulgar person with a gap between her front teeth and obviously dyed hair. (My mother's hair is dyed too, but it's not so obvious.) She claims she was once a nursery school teacher, which is not a proper teacher at all, and she also claims to be the supervisor and puts on airs which are unwarranted and extremely irritating. She likes to sound off about her opinions, which are generally not worth listening to.

Right at the bottom is Andriy, the miner's son from Donbas. Unfortunately miners are generally primitive types who find it difficult to be cultured, however hard they try. When he works in the field, I can smell his sweat. He takes his shirt off when it gets too hot and shows off his muscles. Okay, they may even ripple a bit. But he is definitely not my type.

As for me, I'm nineteen, and everything else about me is still-to-be. Fluent-English-speaker-to-be. I hope. Romantically-in-love-to-be. Are you ready, Mr. Brown? World-famous-writer to-be, like my Papa. I have already started to think about the book I will write when I get back home. But you have to have something interesting to write about, don't you? More interesting than a bunch of strawberry pickers living in two trailers.

Yola's eyes narrow as she watches the Ukrainian girl wander along the strawberry rows as if she had all the time in the world to fill those boxes. Out in the strawberry field it's the hierarchy of the check-in that matters. Several times a day, the farmer counts the trays of boxes, checks them in, stacks them on pallets in the prefab, and notes down who has earned what. The women generally earn less. The men earn more. The supervisor of course earns the most.

Yola is both the gang mistress and the supervisor. As a former teacher, she is a person of natural authority and a woman of action. It is her belief that maintaining a pleasant sexual harmony within the picking team is the key to success, and for this reason she encourages the men to take their shirts off in the sun.

She doesn't want any griping or unpleasant comments behind her back, especially from those Ukrainians, now that there are two of them. Not that she has anything against Ukrainians, but it is her belief that the high point of Ukrainian civilization was its brief occupation by Poland, though the civilizing effects were clearly quite short-lived and superficial. To be fair, this Ukrainian boy Andriy is quite a gentleman as well as a good picker, but he is inclined to moodiness, and he thinks too much. Thinking is not good for a man. He is quite nice looking, though of course he is much too young for her, and she isn't the type of a woman to seduce a boy half her age, though she knows some who would in Zdroj, which she will tell you about later.

Yes, if only there were more good pickers like that. Nobody understands the problems she faces, for her pay depends not just on her own efforts but on the performance of the good-for-nothing team she supervises in the field. She tells them—but will they listen?—to pick strawberries just right. Too white and farmer will reject. Too ripe and shops complain. And you have to handle correctly, and drop gently—don't throw—into boxes. She tells them, and they just carry on exactly the same as before. Really, she is getting too old for this game.

This is her second summer as a supervisor, her seventh summer in England, and the forty-seventh summer of her life. She is beginning to think she has had enough. During those seven summers she has picked almost fifty tonnes of strawberries for the Dumpling, and the income from this, added to the extra sums paid for additional services of a private nature, have allowed her to buy a pretty three-roomed bungalow on the outskirts of Zdroj with half a hectare of garden that leads down to the Prosna River where her son Mirek can potter around to his heart's content. She has a photo in her purse of Mirek in the garden sitting on a rope swing that hangs from the branch of a cherry tree in full blossom. Ah, those little smiling eyes! When he was born, she had to make a difficult choice—give up her job or put him in an institution. Well, she has seen those institutions, thank you very much. Then someone at the school said they were recruiting strawberry pickers for England, and her sister said she would look after Mirek for the summer, so she seized the opportunity. And what woman of action but of limited choices would not do the same?

Last autumn she invested some of her strawberry money in a pair of Masurian goats and this year there are two snow white kids running about in the garden, bleating, jumping over each other, nibbling at the dahlias, and generally causing mayhem. She was thinking of those kids as she lay on the straw in the back of the Dumpling's Land Rover last night looking up at the swaying roof, while he toiled and puffed away above her. And she smiled to herself and let out some delightful bleating noises, which the Dumpling mistook for cries of pleasure.

Usually Yola brings a team of pickers she has recruited locally in Zdroj, for there were always people desperate for a bit of cash since they closed the millinery factory, but this year nobody wanted to come, because now Poland is in Europe Marketing why should they work for that kind of money when they can earn better money legally? Three friends who were supposed to be coming let her down at the last minute, and she has brought only Marta and Tomasz to England with her. The Dumpling has had to find additional labor through other agents of a more shady character, and has even hinted that he will not renew her contract. Just let him dare—we will see what the wife has to say.

Being a supervisor is not as easy as you might think. You have to deal with all types of personalities. That Tomasz, for instance, has been hanging around making eyes at her; well, that is in itself not so surprising, as she is generally thought to be an attractive woman, but at the end of the day he has come to England to pick strawberries, not for any activities of a more carnal nature, for which there are plenty enough opportunities back in Poland, Lord help us.

Or take Marta, her niece—her religious airs are enough to put anyone off sainthood.

"Are you okay, Ciocia?" she asked, the first time she saw Yola lying on the ground with her shapely legs stretched out in front of her, breathing deeply with her eyes closed.

"I am letting the sun enter my body to warm me from inside like a good husband. Why don't you do the same, Marta?"

"Why would I want the sun for a husband?" Marta said sniffily. "I will let the spirit of the Lord warm me from inside."

Probably her excessive piety is not her fault. She could only have learned it from her mother, Yola's sister, who although very kind when it comes to looking after Mirek, can be extremely irritating. Well it's one thing to go to church and ask for forgiveness for your own sins, but quite another thing to rub other people's noses in theirs.

And while we're on the subject of noses, it is of course not Marta's fault that hers is so big, but maybe it is why she has so little discrimination when it comes to men, for she seems to be drawn to the most unsuitable types and obvious sinners, like Vitaly, for example. Yes, Yola has observed the way Marta's eyes follow him around the field, and she doesn't want the poor girl to be taken advantage of. She knows that type of man. She was married to one, once.

As for this new girl, Irina, she is far too free and easy with that dimply smile of hers, and Yola has noticed the way the Dumpling's eyes linger on her longer than is strictly necessary. She picks strawberries that are more white than red, and answers back when Yola politely draws this to her attention, and sniffs when Yola tries to teach her the correct handling technique, which is like this, you have to cradle them in your palm from below, never more than two at a time, like a man's testicles. Don't squeeze them, Irina!

Okay, I admit I wasn't the fastest strawberry picker, but I didn't need that bossy Polish auntie to point it out to me in that vulgar way.

This was my fourth day here, and I still couldn't believe the pain in my back and knees every time I bent down to strawberry level. When I stood and straightened up, my bones creaked and groaned like an old woman's.

The Ukrainian boy would slip fruit into my boxes when the men's rows and the women's rows came together, which was nice of him, but I wished he wouldn't stare at me like that. Once when I sat down for a rest, he came and sat beside me and popped a strawberry in my mouth. Well, I could hardly spit it out, could I? But he'd better not start getting any ideas, because I haven't come all this way to spend my time fending off the advances of a miner from Donbas.

I had enough of it fending off advances from the boys at school. They were generally primitive types who just wanted to grab all the time—not very romantic—and they had no idea whatsoever about tender words and gallant gestures. In my opinion, everyone should read *War and Peace*, which is the most romantic book ever written, as well as the most tragic. When Natasha and Pierre come together at last, it gives you a feeling inside that is quite fiery in its intensity. That's the sort of love I'm waiting for—not a quick thrash behind the bushes, which is what all the boys seem to be interested in.

"Love is like fire," Mother used to say. "A treasure, not a toy." Poor Mother, she is getting very middle-aged. Her mouth would pucker up in a disapproving lipsticky pout when we passed those girls on Kreshchatik wearing skirts that were just a little strip of cloth between their navels and their knickers, laughing with their mouths open as the boys splashed them with beer. Although it is more romantic if a girl saves herself for *the one*, still there was something unsettling, something knowing about those open-mouthed smiles. What was it they knew and I didn't? Maybe here in England, away from my mother's prying eyes, I would be able to find out. Watching the ripple of that miner's arms as he lifted the pallets of strawberries got me wondering about all that again. *Just wondering, Mother. Nothing more.*

There is a pull-off further up the lane that forks to Sherbury Down, sheltered by a row of poplars, from where you can look down over the field through a gap in the hedge. From this vantage point Mr. Leapish the farmer sits in his Land Rover and surveys the rustic scene with satisfaction. The men, he observes, like to race one another along the strawberry rows, while the women are attentive to each other, and don't want anyone to get left behind. Mr. Leapish is mindful of this difference and has given the men new rows to pick, while the women he assigns to go over the rows that have already been picked by the men. The women earn less, of course, but they are used to that where they come from, and they don't complain. Thus by working with the grain of human nature, he maximizes both productivity and yield. He is pleased with his skill as a manager.

Today is Saturday, payday, and he will have to fork out for their wages later, so his mind is particularly focused on issues of arithmetic. Eight boxes per tray, half a kilo per box, eighty kilos per picker per day on average, six days a week, over a twelve-week season. His brain ticks over effortlessly in mental arithmetic mode. When this field is picked out, they'll move on to another one down in the valley, then back up here again after the plants have reberried. Pickers are paid 30p a kilo, before deductions. And each kilo sells at £2. Not bad. All in all, it's not a bad little business, though he doesn't make as much as that newcomer Tilley up the road with his acres of polytunnels. He could get more if he sold to the big supermarkets, but he doesn't want the inspectors poking around in his trailers, or asking questions about the relationship between Wendy's business and his business. The beauty of it is that half of what you fork out in wages you can claw back in living expenses. And he's helping these poor souls make a bit of money that they could never get their hands on back where they come from. So that's a bonus.

At one o'clock precisely, he will drive up to the gate and honk the horn and watch the strawberry pickers pick up their laden trays of boxes and make their way down the field. He should really pick up the trays more often in the warm weather, and get the fruit into cold storage. That's what you have to do to sell at £2.50 a kilo to the big supermarkets. But the local petrol stations that are his outlets don't ask questions.

Maybe the Ukrainian boy will already be down there, waiting to open the gate. Keen. Good picker. Hard worker. Wish they were all like that. This new girl seems a bit of a dead loss, but maybe she'll speed up a bit when she picks up the rhythm. Nice looking, but not very forthcoming— at his age, he needs someone who knows what she's doing to get the old motor started. Don't know why Vulk sent her—he'd asked for another man. Now Vulk wants her back. Maybe he'll put her to work in another of his little businesses. Well, he'll have to see how she performs at the check-in. If she's useless, he might have to let Vulk take her off his hands.

After the check-in he'll let the poor souls have half an hour for lunch, which he has brought in the back of the Land Rover. As always, it's sliced white bread, margarine, and cheese slices. Today he's particularly pleased because he's found a new supplier that sells a white sliced loaf for 19p. He was paying 24p a loaf before. Eight loaves a day—two for breakfast, which they eat with jam, two for lunch, which they have with cheese slices, and four for dinner which they eat with sausages—over several weeks—it all adds up. The new girl is small, and he reckons she won't eat much, so he hasn't deemed it necessary to increase the provisions, except for an extra loaf of bread. This feeding regime, he has calculated, provides a perfectly balanced diet at minimum cost, with carbohydrates, proteins, sugars, and fats, all the essential energy-giving nutrients they need. The fruit-and-vegetable requirement is present in the strawberries, which they eat naturally during the course of the day, and which also help to keep them regular. Some farmers let their workers buy their own food and don't let them eat the strawberries, but Leapish reckons his system is more cost-effective. They soon get sick of the strawberries. Yes, even with the commission he pays Vulk for living expenses, he reckons he can still make money on it.

Each worker pays £49 per week for food, including tea, milk, sugar, and as many strawberries as they can eat (where else could you live like a lord for less than fifty quid a week?), and £50 per week rental for their trailer bunk, which in this part of the country and at the height of the summer holiday season is extremely reasonable. In fact maybe too reasonable. Maybe he should be charging £55. At least, in the men's trailer. The women's trailer, admittedly, is rather small. But it has a special place in his heart.

He looks at it, perched there at the top of the field like a fat white hen, and his eyes go a bit misty. This is the trailer that he and Wendy went off in for their honeymoon, more than twenty years ago—a Swift Silhouette, latest model, with lots of storage space, built-in furniture, and a fully equipped kitchenette complete with two neat gas rings, a miniature stainless-steel sink and drainer with a lift-off worktop, and a compact gas-powered fridge—how Wendy had loved it. That trailer park above the cliffs at Beachy Head. Spaghetti bolognese. A bottle of Piat d'Or. They had certainly given that fold-out double bed some hammer.

When they had gone into the strawberry business, seven years ago, Wendy had been in charge of the trailers. She had set up a separate company to provide the accommodations, food, and transport for the pickers—that's how you get around the red tape that restricts how much you can deduct from wages. This is what's crippling the country, in his humble opinion—red tape—as though making a profit is a dirty word—he has twice written to the *Kent Gazette* about it. Yes, it had been more than a marriage, it had been a real partnership. Of course things were different now. Pity, really, but women are like that. Jealous bitches.

Anyway, not his fault. What man wouldn't do the same? No point in being sentimental about it. Yes, it was a good size for two people, could fit four at a pinch. Five? Well, they'd managed all right, hadn't they? But the men's trailer—it's a static Everglade in pale green, the sort you can hire ready-sited in scores of windswept trailer parks on cliff tops overlooking the English Channel—that had once been an abode of great luxury, with ruched pink satin curtains and quilted velvet seats, now admittedly more brown than pink, and propped up on bricks since one of the wheels had gone missing. Probably those New Zealand sheep shearers, though heavens only knows what they wanted a spare trailer wheel for. Acres of room in it. An extra £5 each—that would bring in £20 per week. He needn't tell Vulk. And that would be £20 a week nearer to achieving his dream.

Yes, although Mr. Leapish is a practical man, he too has a dream. His dream is to cover this whole sweet south-sloping sun-bathed strawberry hillside with polytunnels.

At six o'clock the shadows were lengthening across the field. When the horn of the Land Rover sounded again down by the gate, I picked up my tray of strawberry boxes and carried it down to the prefab.

"How many you got, Irina?" asked Ciocia Yola, sticking her nose into my tray. Okay, I admit I had only filled twelve trays all day. Marta had filled nineteen. Yola and the Chinese girls had filled twenty-five each—you should see the way they go at those berries. Anyway, they're smaller than me, and they don't have to bend so far. The men had filled fifteen trays each that afternoon, and another fifteen in the morning. Each tray carries about four kilos of strawberries. I could see that the farmer was annoyed. His face was red and lumpy like a strawberry. Or maybe, according to Yola, like a testicle. Anyway, I kept my face absolutely expressionless as he told me that today I'd earned fourteen pounds, barely enough to cover my expenses, and I was going to have to do better. He spoke slowly and very loudly, as though I were deaf as well as stupid, waving his hands about.

"NO GOOD. NO BLOODY GOOD. YOU'VE GOT TO PICK FASTER. ALL FILL UP. FULL. FULL." He swept his arms wide, as if to embrace all his pathetic boxes. "DO YOU UNDERSTAND?"

No, I didn't understand—the shouting was flustering me.

"OTHERWISE YOU'RE DOWN THE ROAD."

"Road?"

"ROAD. DOWN THE BLOODY ROAD. YOU GET IT?"

"I get blood on road?"

"NO, YOU SILLY COW, *YOU* GET ON THE ROAD!"

"I get silly cow on road?"

"OH! FORGET IT!"

He slammed my tray onto the pallet, dismissing me with both his hands in a way that was quite uncivilized. I could feel tears pricking at the back of my eyes, but I certainly wasn't going to let him see that. Nor Yola, who was standing behind me in the queue with her full tray and her smug gap-toothed smile. And behind her was Andriy, gawking at me with a grin. Well he could go to hell. Nonchalantly, I sauntered up the field to the women's trailer and sat down on the step. They could all go to hell.

After a while, I heard the farmer's Land Rover pull out of the gate and putter away down the lane. A pleasant stillness descended on the hillside. Even the birds were taking a break. The air was warm and sweet with honeysuckle. An evening like this is a gift to be treasured, I thought, and I wasn't going to let anything spoil it. The sky was pale and milky, with shining streamers of silvery clouds over in the west—a real English sky.

Vitaly and Andriy were relaxing on the backseat of Vitaly's car enjoying a can of lager—apparently the rest of the car is disintegrating in a hedge somewhere on the Canterbury bypass. Typical Vitaly. Tomasz had disappeared into the next field to check his rabbit traps. Emanuel was sitting on a crate outside the men's trailer with a bowl of strawberries beside him, writing a letter. The Chinese girls were curled up on Marta's bunk, reading their horoscopes. Marta had already lit the gas under the pan of sausages, and our little cabin was filled with a smell that was both mouth-watering and disgusting at the same time. Yola was taking a shower. I stretched out on her bunk for just a moment. I was feeling so tired, every muscle in my body was aching. I would just have a little rest before dinner.

I AM DOG I RUN I RUN I KILL RABBIT I EAT ALL I LICK BLOOD GOOD BLOOD MY BELLY IS FULL GOOD BELLY-FULL FEELING I FIND RIVER I DRINK GOOD WATER I DRINK SUN IS ON ME WARM I REST I LAY MY HEAD ON MY PAWS IN THE SUN I SLEEP I DREAM I DREAM OF KILLING I AM DOG

It is Marta's belief that our daily food is a gift from God, to be prepared with reverence, and that eating together is a sacrament. For this reason she always tries her best to make a pleasing evening meal for the strawberry pickers, but tonight is Emanuel's eighteenth birthday and she has made a special effort to rise to the challenge of the unpromising ingredients provided by the farmer.

In the pan, the sausages have already turned bright pink and a grayish gelatinous fluid is oozing out of them and soaking into the bread, which Marta has cut up into strips and put to fry with the sausages and some potatoes that Vitaly found by the roadside. There are some wild ceps, and some green leaves of wood garlic waiting by the side of the pan, which she will stir in at the last minute. The remainder of the bread she has pressed into dumplings with a sprinkling of mauve thyme flowers and a pair of pigeon's eggs, which Tomasz found in the woods. They are boiling merrily in a pan. Marta is cooking up all the sausages—the men's as well as the women's. Why? Because Polish women are proper women, that's why.

Ciocia Yola is taking a shower, preparing herself for another sinful night of love with the farmer. The sun must have warmed the water in the barrel to a pleasant temperature, for Ciocia Yola is singing as she rubs herself with perfumed soap, a tuneless wordless song. Ciocia Yola is not a good singer.

Then there is a tap-tapping on the side of the trailer and a man's voice speaking in Polish. "Lovely ladies, I have here a small offering with which you may enhance our supper." It is Tomasz, with the bloodied body of a rabbit in his hands. "Maybe the lovely Yola would accept this small token of my affection."

"Leave it on the step, Tomek," Ciocia Yola calls from the shower. "I'll be ready in a minute."

"Maybe you would like me to skin it for you?" He looks hopefully toward the shower. There are some holes in the plastic screen, but they are in the wrong places.

"It's okay. You can leave it. I know how," says Marta.

She takes the dead rabbit from him with a sigh and strokes its fluffy fur. Poor little creature. But she has already worked out a nice recipe in her head to send it to the next world. Tomasz is still hovering on the doorstep, and a moment later is rewarded by the sight of Yola emerging from the shower, wrapped only in a towel.

"Go away, Tomek," she says briskly. "Why are you hanging around here like a bad stink? We will tell you when dinner is ready."

He slopes off down the field.

In Marta's opinion, her aunt would be better off with a decent serious chap like Tomasz, even if he does have some oddities, than with some of these ex-husbands and would-be husbands she seems to go for. But Ciocia Yola has her own ideas about men, as about everything else.

Marta picks up the rabbit and with a sharp knife makes a deft slice up the creature's furry belly. She skins it and cuts it up into small pieces which she tosses in the pan with some fat from the sausages and some leaves of wood garlic and wild thyme. A delicious aroma floats down the field. At the last moment, she throws in the fried sausages, ceps and potatoes, and adds a can of Vitaly's beer to make a mouth-watering sauce. She tastes it on the tip of her tongue, and closes her eyes with sheer good-Polish-woman pleasure.

Andriy and Emanuel have built a fire in a grassy spot at the top of the field. Although there is plenty of dry wood in the copse, and small twigs for kindling, it still seems to take them a lot of huffing and puffing and flapping of branches to get it going. When it has caught, and the smoke has drifted away, they arrange a circle of logs and crates and the old car seat to sit on. The Chinese girls have set out the plates and cutlery (there are only six sets, so some people will have to share or improvise). Emanuel has picked a huge bowl of strawberries, and Marta sets them to marinade in cool tea, with sugar and some wild mint leaves. She finds she is increasingly having to modify or disguise the taste of the strawberries to make them more palatable to the pickers. These she will put into a bowl lined with slices of white bread, and this will be turned out onto a dish as a birthday pudding instead of a cake for Emanuel, of whom she is especially fond. There are no candles, but later there will be stars.

Emanuel is watching as Tomasz tunes his guitar. Then Tomasz passes him the guitar and starts showing him some basic chords. Vitaly gets out his stash of lager and his cash box. Ciocia Yola has put on her clean mauve-ribboned knickers from the wash line, a short frilly skirt, and a low-cut blouse. No doubt this is all for her lover's benefit. Marta doesn't know what her aunt sees in the farmer. Dumpling, she calls him. He is more like a suet pudding. If you're going to commit fornication with a man, you may as well choose one who is nice looking. But no doubt God will forgive her. He's good that way.

Then Chinese Girl One bangs the side of a pan as though it were a gong, and they all take their places around the fire in anticipation of Marta's feast.

Down in the valley, a summery haze shimmers over the treetops and shadows are already gathering. The cut-crystal brilliance of the light becomes soft and muted, as though shining through layers of silk. The silver streamers of clouds have turned to pink, but the sky is still bright, and the sun has an hour or so to go before it touches the treetops. It is almost midsummer. A thrush sits on the branch of an ash tree in the copse, singing his heart out, and from the far side of the copse his mate calls back. It is the only sound to break the stillness, apart from the sound of a dog barking in the woods far away.

An evening like this is a gift from God, thinks Marta, as she gives thanks and prepares to celebrate.

Only Irina is missing. Andriy goes to look for her and finds her still curled up asleep in the trailer. Her hands are folded under her chin, and two circles of color have fallen like rose petals on her cheeks. Her lips are slightly parted. Her orange ribbon has come loose and the stray strands of dark hair are streaming on the pillow. He gazes for a moment. Really, for a Ukrainian girl, she has some quite positive features.

"Wake up. Dinner's ready."

He has it on the tip of his tongue to say, "Wake up, sweet one." But why would he want to say a thing like that? Fortunately the words get stuck in his mouth before they can emerge to embarrass him. Irina yawns, stretches, and rubs her eyes. She rolls off the bunk, still a bit wobbly from sleep. He takes her hand to help her step down from the trailer, and she rests her weight on him briefly before drawing it away.

The strawberry pickers have seated themselves in a circle and are passing around the steaming plates of food: dumplings, rabbit-and-sausage stew with fried bread, garlic, mushrooms, and potatoes. The delicious smell of each dish strikes him like a miracle; his body shivers with readiness; he is incredibly hungry. After Marta has said grace, Vitaly sells everyone a can or more of excellent lager at a special discounted price. At first they all eat in silence, listening to the birdsong, watching the magical shifts of light as the sun slips toward the horizon. After a while, conversations break out in a babble of languages.

He is sitting next to Irina on a low log, watching her from the corner of his eye. He likes the way she eats, tucking into the food with enthusiasm, only stopping from time to time to flick back her long hair when it slips down over her face.

He leans and whispers into her ear, "Have you got a boyfriend back home, then?"

She turns her head, giving him a hard look.

"Yes I have, of course. He is two meters tall and he is a boxer."

"Really?"

"Of course."

"What is his name?"

"His name is Attila."

She doesn't look the type to have a boxer boyfriend, but women are notoriously unpredictable, and he has heard that sometimes the most refined types are drawn to the roughest of men. So maybe he stands a chance with her after all.

To his left, Tomasz is trying a similar approach. He sits close to Yola on Vitaly's car seat and murmurs, "Is there someone waiting for you back in Poland, beautiful Yola?"

"What business is it of yours?" Yola replies briskly.

"Only that if there is, he is a lucky man."

"Not so lucky as you imagine. What do you know about luck?" she snaps. "Better to keep your mouth shut, Mr. Poet, unless you know what you're talking about."

On the other side, Emanuel and Chinese Girl Two are each trying to find out where the other comes from. Emanuel discovers that she is not from China, which seems odd, while she discovers only that he is from Africa, which everyone knows already. Then Vitaly presses another can of beer on them and Marta intervenes, chiding him gently for taking advantage of Emanuel, who is too young and has clearly had enough already. Chinese Girl Two starts to giggle uncontrollably, and soon they are all giggling, even Marta.

Now Tomasz takes up his guitar and starts to sing a terrible rhyming song he has composed himself about a man who sets out to find the woman of his dreams. Yola tells him to shut up. Andriy turns to Irina.

"Will you sing something for us, Ukrainka?"

She gives him another hard look.

"Why don't you ask Emanuel?" She sinks her teeth into a piece of rabbit. Hm. He doesn't seem to be getting anywhere with this girl.

Dear Sister

I wish you were here for in Kent the strawberries are even more delicate than the strawberries of Zomba.

Today being my eighteenth birthday we have enjoyed an outstanding party. My mzungu friend Andree and I made a big bonfire which we lit upon much fevered flapping and smoking and there was a delicate feast prepared for us by a good Catholic Martyr though she is not yet ascended and after feasting we sat upon the hillside to behold the beauteous sunset (though not as beauteous as the sunsets of Zomba) with the sun setting like a firey disk and the first star of the ferment twinkling like a diamond in the sky and the hills cool in their darkening. And when our hearts were opened everybody began to sing.

The Poland mzungu named Toemash has a guitar which is of extreme interest to me and he sang a ballad of a man with a tamborine and his many jangly followers. Then the two China girls sang in high soprano an ineffable song of great beauty. The Ukraine girl also sang sweetly with choral accompaniment from Andree who eyed her eagerly. Then the Catholic Martyr sang a song of praise with assistance from her auntie. And I sang my song Oh come Oh come Emanuel which I learned from Sister Theodosia. And at the end everybody sang Happy Birthday Dear Emanuel and it came to pass that this outstanding song is available not only in English but also in Ukrainian Polish and Chinese!!! And so united in song we enjoyed the Radiance of the evening.

I had drunk two cans of lager, which is more than I'm used to. Whenever anyone poured a drink, Mother always used to put on her preachy voice and say, "Irina, a drunken woman is like a blighted rose." In fact everyone, even Marta, had drunk too much. Marta was doing the dishes now. Yola was supposed to be helping, but she had disappeared. The Chinese girls had drunk two lagers each and had gone back inside the trailer— they are very sensitive to gnats. Emanuel had drunk eight and had fallen asleep, stretched out in front of the embers. Tomasz had drunk six, moaning all the while that he would much rather have a good glass of Georgian wine, and now he was strumming another miserable dirge about how much the times are changing. Vitaly was gathering up the empty cans and counting his earnings for the evening. Andriy had drunk at least eight, I noticed, and when I pushed his hand away from my knee he wandered off a bit unsteadily down through the field. A drunken miner is not very appealing.

As the sun went down the air started to turn cool, nipping my bare arms and legs, so I went back inside the trailer to find my jumper and jeans. Yola was sitting there, combing her dyed hair and daubing on cheap pink lipstick in preparation for her date with that pudgy farmer. She kept jumping up to look out the window like an overexcited poodle. Suddenly she yapped, "Look at that, girls. We have a visitor."

She pointed out the window. Instead of the farmer's Land Rover, a huge black mafia-machine was pulling up at the bottom of the field. My heart thumped. It was like a fist punching my chest. The car door swung open and a bulky black-clad figure emerged. Even at that distance I recognized him.

Vulk looked around, then he started walking clumsily up through the field, treading on the clumps of strawberries. I didn't stop to think, I jumped up and dashed out the door without looking behind me. I slipped through the gap in the hedge into the copse. My heart was thumping away. Keeping my head down, I crept along the other side of the hedge, away from the trailer and back into a thicket of trees. Behind a dense evergreen bush I crouched down and listened. I could hear voices, men's and women's, but I couldn't hear what they were saying. The blood was beating so loud inside my head I couldn't hear my own thoughts. It was like one of those bad dreams where the beating of your own heart wakes you up. Thump Thump. I dug my nails into my palms, but the pain was real. After a while, Yola came out into the field and called my name.

"Irina? Irina? Come, girl, there is a handsome-man visitor for you."

That woman is so dire. Why doesn't she go off with Vulk herself if she likes him so much? He's probably just her type. I sat motionless, holding my breath, until Yola gave up and went back to the trailer. Then I let my breath out. But still I sat tight. This was a waiting game between us, him and me. On a branch, a few inches from my nose, a spider was spinning its web, working away furiously. I watched as it dropped down onto a lower twig, then clambered back up its silky ladder, heaving its fat body on its spidery little legs. Then it sat in the center of its web and waited for its prey to pull at the threads.

After some time I heard Vulk's voice. He was by the hedge. He started calling, "Little flovver! Come, little flovver! Come!"

That sludgy voice. My stomach turned. I couldn't see from my hiding place, but I could imagine the ponytail flicking from side to side.

"Come! Come!"

I breathed in and held my breath. My heart was thumping so loud I was sure he must be able to hear it as he wandered up and down beside the hedge, his footsteps heavy on the ground. Crunch crunch. "Little flovver! Little flovver!"

Then a horrible familiar smell hit my nostrils. He had lit a cigar. He must be standing in the field by the hedge, smoking. Puff. Stink. I couldn't see him but I could smell him nearby. My whole body was tense, my breathing fast and shallow, like when you're trying to run in a nightmare but your limbs are locked. I couldn't tell how much time had passed. The light was fading from the sky. After a while the smell of the cigar faded too. Was it safe to come out? I was just about to move when I heard voices again. He was back at the trailer. I strained my ears. I couldn't catch what he said, but I heard Yola's vulgar laugh, then after another eternity the sound I'd been waiting for—the engine of the mafia-machine starting up.

The gate closed with a *clack*, and the engine noise dissipated into the stillness.

It was twilight when I finally dared to emerge from my hiding place, back into the brightness of the trailer.

"Oh, here you are!" cried Marta. "I was so worried."

"Here you are!" Yola's voice had a scolding edge. She looked me up and down and winked in a vulgar way. "You hev secret lovver." She said it in English, for the benefit of the Chinese girls. "Good-looking man looking for you."

"Not so good looking." I wrinkled my nose.

The Chinese girls laughed.

"Good-looking enough," said Yola. "Not a baldie. Plenty good hairs."

"Too long. Looks like woman hairs," said Chinese Girl One. "Like Toh-mah." They both giggled like mad.

"He had flowers," said Yola.

"Flowers? What for?" The thought of him bringing me flowers made me feel sick.

"A flower in hand for you. Hee hee." Chinese Girl Two cupped her chin in her hands laughing with glee. "Pink flower. Pink. Flower of love." As though pink would make all the difference. They all thought it was a big joke.

"I do not want those flowers," I said nonchalantly. I was still elated at my escape, and the last thing I wanted was to remember that terrifying journey, the cold chips, the nausea, the fear. "The man is not only old, but he is rather ugly, with minimum culture."

"We are all God's creatures," said Marta reproachfully. I suppose no one has ever given her flowers, on account of her large nose. She is a very kind person, but sometimes I think she takes her religion too far.

Andriy has drunk at least eight cans of lager, and now he has his back toward the field and is concentrating on the pleasurable sensation of aiming a warm torrent of piss at a stubborn nettle growing out of the hedge. It wavers under the stream, but bounces back. He takes aim and hits it again. It bends but doesn't break. Its sharp leaves glisten cheekily as he zips up his fly. I'll be back to get you later, he promises the dogged little plant.

As he heads back to the trailer in the fading illusory dusk, his eyes light on a vision of incredible beauty. Is he drunk or dreaming? Generously proportioned, sensuously curved, beautiful yet mysterious, ferocious yet pliant, monstrous yet perfectly crafted. He stretches out his hand, his fingers trembling to touch. Yes, she is real. He strokes the gleaming body of black and chrome. He walks around her. Yes, from every angle, she is perfect.

And inside? He tries the passenger door. It is not locked. He climbs in, clambers across to the driver's seat, sinks into the soft but firm tobacco-fragrant leather. What height. What power. He fondles the leather-encased steering wheel. He runs his hands over the dashboard. What an array of controls. He depresses the clutch. He shifts through all the gears. The transmission glides like butter. He tries out the brake and accelerator pedals. They are firm but yielding. He searches for the ignition key. It is not there. He tries the glove compartment. He feels inside. Something is there—something bulky and cold. Not keys. A gun. Devil's bum!

He takes it out, holds it, turns it over in his hands. His fingers close around it. Its menace is palpable. He opens it up—why are there only five bullets in the barrel? What happened to the sixth? Not quite knowing why, he takes the gun and slips it into the pocket of his trousers. The weight pulls against his belt. He likes the feeling of its presence, close to him but out of sight. He climbs down from the vehicle and quietly closes the door.

By the time he gets back to the bonfire, he finds that all the women have gone into their trailer. Emanuel is asleep. Vitaly has disappeared. Tomasz is still singing sadly to himself. He decides to have one more go at that wretched nettle before turning in for the night. He is standing in the shadow between the hedge and the men's trailer when he sees the owner of the black four-by-four come down through the field and climb into the driver's seat. Even in the dusky light, Andriy can see that he is an unprepossessing man. What a waste. And then there's the little matter of the gun—what does he need a gun for?

The events that follow take place so quickly, and in such a confusion of dazzle and darkness and too much lager, that afterward, he is never quite sure exactly what happened.

Just as the twilight swallows up the taillights of the four-by-four, the sound of another engine rips through the stillness of the valley. At first he thinks it is the farmer's Land Rover running rough, but the sound is louder, deeper, with an exciting throbbing underbeat. He steps out, hoping to catch a glimpse as it races by. But the engine stops at the gate, the gate swings open, and in roars the red Ferrari, top down, headlights blazing. He feels his head start to spin. Twice in one night. This must be a dream. And then out of the Ferrari steps the blonde.

She is perhaps more mature than he imagined, but the confusing light can play all sorts of tricks. She is tall too, taller than him, with blond hair pinned in an untidy nest on top of her head. She is wearing tight white trousers that catch the gleam of the headlights, revealing a shape that is not as shapely as he'd dreamed, maybe more sedan model, but still definitely the blond blue-eyed Angliska rosa. She steps forward without noticing him lurking by the trailer and strides up into the field.

"Lawrence!" she shouts, in a voice that is sharp and resonant with fury. "Lawrence, where are you? Come here, you bastard!"

Her words echo around the valley, and are met with silence.

Despite his initial disappointment, Andriy thinks he should seize the moment, if only for the sake of the Ferrari. This is after all a night of magic, in which two amazing things have already happened, and all sorts of mysteries and transformations may be possible. He steps out of the shadows opening his palms in a gesture of appeasement.

"Lady . . ."

She swings around to face him.

"And who are you?" she barks. Really, her voice is not as he had imagined it either.

"Lady . . ."

Suddenly his English deserts him. So stepping forward he does something he has seen older men do in Ukraine but has never done before in his life, something that would normally make him cringe with embarrassment to think of; but now it just seems the right thing to do. He takes her hand, lifts it to his lips, and kisses it.

The effect is instantaneous. The Angliska rosa grabs him in both her arms and kisses him ferociously on the mouth. This is a pleasant surprise. He knows he is quite attractive to women—well, he's had some successes in the past—but never before has the magic been so immediate. Leaning back on the hood of the Ferrari, she pulls him down on top of her and kisses him vigorously. Her lips are warm and taste of whiskey. Her body, like the upholstery of the four-by-four, is firm but yields to his touch.

"You'll do, puppet." She rips open the buttons of his shirt. What's going on here? Is this a typical English display of passion? He notices with another small stab of disappointment that the sports car is not a Ferrari at all but a Honda (still, it *is* a sports car, and a red one) and her Angliska rosa mouth is insistent and dominating in a way that reminds him strangely of . . . yes, his first kiss. Vagvaga Riskegipd sitting astride him on the steps of Sheffield City Hall, forcing her determined little tongue between his lips. These Angliski women!

Then he hears the engine-roar of another car pulling into the field, but when he tries to take a look, she yanks his head down firmly, his mouth on hers. Her tongue is working hard. The next thing he hears is Yola's voice, yelling from the top of the field,

"Dumpling! Dumpling! Watch out!"

Fighting back against the blonde's embrace, he lifts his head and sees the farmer standing by the Land Rover, staring back at him. He doesn't look very pleased. Pinned to the hood of the sports car in the grip of the blonde, Andriy is starting to wonder whether it was wise to surrender to the passion of this unpredictable Angliska rosa.

"What the hell . . . ? You bitch! You bloody bitch!"

The farmer strides toward them. The Angliska rosa looks up over Andriy's shoulder and with her free hand, not the one that is fumbling with his fly zipper, she gestures at the farmer with two fingers. Andriy tries to seize the moment to escape, but the blonde holds him fast, and now the enraged farmer runs forward with a roar and flings himself onto Andriy's back. Holy whiskers! This is not turning out at all according to plan. He is trapped between the two of them like the meat in some crazy sandwich. The farmer's weight is crushing the breath out of him. As the farmer thrashes about, his rough hands grappling with Andriy's throat, the blonde wriggles out from underneath them, clambers back into the sports car, and turns the engine on. The car lurches forward and the farmer slides off the hood onto the ground with a thud.

"Watch out, my Dumpling!"

Andriy, still hanging onto the hood, hears Yola's shriek at the top of the field, and looking around he sees her tottering down between the clumps of strawberries in her flimsy high-heeled sandals. The farmer sees her too as he picks himself up.

"Go back, Primrose!" He waves her away.

The car reverses, revs up a bit, then suddenly accelerates forward. There is a horrible crunch. The farmer falls writhing to the ground. The car reverses and revs up again. Andriy is hanging onto a windshield wiper with one hand and hammering on the glass with the other.

"Stop! Stop!"

"My Dumpling!"

He hears Yola's cry behind him, but he can't quite see what's happening. As the car lurches forward again, he flings himself off and lands on top of the farmer, who is rolling on the ground twisted up in agony, his mouth open as if in a scream, though only faint gurgling noises are coming out. Andriy disentangles himself shakily and stares in horror. The bones of the farmer's left leg are sticking out all over the place. The car is reversing and revving up again.

"My poor Dumpling!" Yola stumbles down through the field and, diving forward, tries to drag the farmer free. But he is too heavy for her. The car is heading at them. Andriy staggers to his feet and the two of them manage to heave the writhing farmer out of the way, missing by inches the front bumper of the car, which has picked up some speed, the blond Angliska rosa grinning like a maniac behind the wheel.

Crash! With a horrible rip of metal, it plows into the rear end of the men's trailer, which topples off its pile of bricks and lands at a crazy angle on its axle.

The Angliska rosa gets out to inspect the damage to her car. Then she walks over to the farmer squirming on the ground in the glare of the headlights, and gives him a kick.

"You sleazy bastard. Next time it's curtains."

"Wendy," he groans, "it was nothing. Just a bit of slap and tickle."

Yola has been keeping out of the blonde's way, but self-control is not her strong point.

"Slapping ticker! What is slapping ticker? Eh?" She lays into him with her fuchsia-tipped toes. "I am primrose, not slapping ticker!"

"Yola, please. . . ." Andriy struggles to restrain her, but she breaks free and takes a run at the farmer.

"Get off him!" shouts the blonde. "He may be a sleazeball, but he's my sleaze, not yours!" She dives at Yola, catching her off balance with one foot poised for a kick, and grabbing her around the waist she wrestles her to the ground. They are both panting and tearing at each other's hair.

"You all sleazes!" Yola writhes and thrashes, but the blonde is bigger and stronger than she is. "Let me go!"

"Stop! Please! Be calm!" cries Andriy, grabbing the blonde and holding her tight in his arms. "Lady, please. . . ."

Seizing the moment, Yola scrambles away and takes cover in the men's trailer. Andriy grasps the blonde's hand, which is clenched into a fist, and tries to raise it to his lips, but she wrenches it free, swings wide, and lands it on his jaw with a crack.

Stars appear in the black space behind his eyes.

The Chinese girls are staring out of the window, trying to work out what is going on in the field below. Shifting between the blaze of headlights and the pools of darkness, the action is disjointed and confusing. They see the car reversing and driving forward. They see Yola launch herself at the body on the ground. They hear the smash as the car plows into the trailer. They see Irina standing with Marta, a little ways below the trailer, watching the events at the bottom of the field. At some point in all the chaos, Vulk's four-by-four pulls in through the open gate and drives silently up around the margin of the strawberry rows to the women's trailer, headlights off. Irina looks around and sees him appear out of the darkness. She screams and makes a dash for the copse, but this time he chases and catches her. The Chinese girls witness the abduction, but they are unable to stop it. Vulk bundles Irina struggling and yelling into his vehicle, and drives off into the night.

bye-bye strawberry. hello mobilfon

i screamed and screamed. I could see the Chinese girls and Marta turn and run toward me. I could see their terrified faces, white in the blaze of the headlights. I felt the clamp of Vulk's hand on my shoulder, the grip of his arm across my throat. Then I blacked out.

When I came to, I was jolting and swaying about in a vehicle, pounding along a road in the dark. I could smell the familiar horrible tobacco stink of the leather upholstery pressed against my cheek. My stomach twisted up with horror and despair. How had I let this happen? *You fool Irina. Stupid. Careless idiot. Drop your guard for one moment and you've had it. You might as well be dead. Better to be dead. Better dead than . . . No, don't think of it. Blank it out. Blank.*

My shoulders were shaking. My hands and feet were icy cold. *Mama, Papa, please help me. I am your little Irina. A treasure not a toy. Don't be angry. Help me. Surely someone will help me. This is England.*

"Little flovver okay?" That sludgy voice! I was crumpled up on the floor in front of the passenger seat, my legs folded awkwardly under me, my face resting on the leather seat. A few inches from my face was the tattered bunch of flowers.

"Little flovver think she can running from Vulk. Little flovver think she clever. But Vulk everywhere more clever. I vait. I come back. Houp! I catch. I make possibility."

Stop. Think. There must be some way . . . The car door—maybe it will open. The car is going fast. You'll be hurt—maybe killed. Better dead than . . . No. Stop. Think. Talk to him. Trick him with words. Think of something, quick. Mama Papa, help me. Make a plan. The car door opens. No, the door is locked. No, the door opens. You fall, you roll. You are hurt but you are alive. You run. Someone will help you. This is England. You run. He runs after you. He has a gun.

Vulk shoved the battered bouquet at me so that the stems caught my hair.

"You like it, flovver?"

I shut my eyes and kept quiet. I could hear the creak of his leather coat as he leaned over me. I could smell tobacco and tooth decay. He touched my face. I felt his rough fingers tracing the line of my cheek and my jaw. The car lurched. I kept my eyes shut. The fingers played down my neck. I felt them pressing and lingering in the hollow of my collarbone, creeping down under my blouse.

"Beautiful flovver. You like it, flovver?"

Think. Speak. You are clever—use your wits. The right words could save your life. Say something.

I couldn't say anything. My throat went into a spasm. I started to retch violently. A dribble of lumpy fluid trickled out of my mouth onto the car seat. I felt the car slow down, swerve, and bump over rough ground. He must have pulled off the road. He leaned over and opened the car door on my side. We were on a shadowy track that seemed to lead into some woods. He pushed my head out of the door.

"You sick outside."

I retched again and again, my head hanging over the side of the car into the darkness. Vulk waited.

Now. Now's the time to run. Jump. Run for it. Into the wood. Duck behind the bushes. Vanish into the shadows of the trees. Lie still. Hide.

My eyes adjusted to the darkness. My body tensed. And as though he could read my thoughts, Vulk said, "You run, I shoot with gun."

Better dead than . . . Blank. Dead. Blank.

I jumped.

I AM DOG I RUN I RUN I SMELL EARTH AND WOOD AND WATER TREES BUSHES BRAMBLES I SMELL FOX I SMELL RABBIT BUSHES TOO CLOSE TEAR SKIN I BLEED I RUN SHARP STONE PAW PAIN BLOOD LICK BLOOD PAIN I RUN FAR AWAY ANGRY DOG BARKS FAR AWAY MAN SHOUTS SILENCE IS CLOSE NIGHT-BIRD CALLS NIGHT-BIRD REPLIES BIRD-LOVE TALK SILENCE TREES BUSHES HEDGE LONG FIELD SWEET GRASS MOONLIGHT I RUN I RUN I AM DOG

"You'd better beat it," says Wendy. She is dialing something on her mobilfon. In the half light, her face looks ashen and crazy. Andriy stares at her, wondering what had possessed him.

"Beat?"

"Beat it. Before the police come."

He understands "police come."

"But I . . ."

"You rammed him with my car, didn't you? Dispute over wages."

"But . . ."

Andriy looks at the farmer, but he seems to have passed out.

"Who do you think the police will believe? Here," she tosses him a car key.

His heart leaps. But the key is not for the sports car, it is for the Land Rover. "You can take that bloody strawberry tart too." She gestures toward the top of the field. What does she mean? He pockets the key and steps forward to embrace her. She backs away.

"Just go."

He climbs into the Land Rover and tries the key. It starts up instantly. The pedals and gear movements are rough. The last car he drove was his father's Zaporozhets. His first thought is to drive out through the gate and put his foot down, but his passport and two weeks' wages are tucked in an old sock under his mattress. And there is something else that holds him back—that girl, her dark hair spread on the pillow, waking from sleep. He won't go without saying good-bye to her. Good-bye and God be with you? Or good-bye and see you again? That's what he wants to find out.

He turns off the engine and goes back to the men's trailer, which is leaning crookedly on its one wheel. Yola is there, sitting on Tomasz's sloping bed, shaking and crying uncontrollably, and Tomasz is comforting her.

"I'm going," says Andriy. He retrieves his passport and money and starts to stuff his other belongings into his bag. "Before police come."

Yola looks up, startled.

"Police coming?"

He nods. She jumps up, pushing Tomasz out of the way.

"I go too. I get my bag." She makes her way toward the door. "Wait. Please wait."

Tomasz pulls his bag down from his locker and starts to pack too.

"I come with you."

Emanuel is sleeping on Vitaly's bunk, but he opens his eyes and raises himself up on one arm, shielding his eyes from the light with the other and mumbling something in his own language.

"We're going. Good-bye, my friend." Andriy closes the door quietly and returns to the Land Rover with his bag.

He drives the Land Rover around the edge of the field, overtaking Tomasz, who is running straight up through the strawberry clumps, his bag and his guitar bouncing on his back. The second gear on the Land Rover keeps slipping and the steering is loose. He'll have to drive carefully.

He knocks and opens the door of the women's trailer. Inside is hysteria and chaos. Yola is trying to gather her possessions by the light of an oil lamp and at the same time to calm Marta and the Chinese girls, who are sobbing uncontrollably.

"Where's Irina?" he asks.

"Man take it," says one of the Chinese girls, trembling, and the other chimes in, "Woman hairs man take it."

"Man in gangster car has taken Irina," Marta explains in Polish.

Blood swims before Andriy's eyes. How has this happened? How has he let this happen? What kind of man would let his girl (is she his girl?) be snatched away like that? He feels faint and sick.

"Which way?"

The girls point vaguely down the field. His heart shrinks at the uselessness of it. What a fool he's been. The blonde. The Ferrari. What a stupid useless idiot.

"Let's go. Let's go."

He grabs Yola's bag, and Marta's, because she wants to go with her auntie, then the two Chinese girls start shrieking and wailing.

"We no stay. We come. We go. Bad woman hairs man come again."

"You pack up quick quick," says Yola. They are all scrabbling about, shaking hysterically, and Tomasz is getting in the way, clunking them with his guitar each time he moves. Andriy thinks he sees a flash of blue lights between the trees down in the valley. Suddenly he realizes what to do. He jumps into the Land Rover, maneuvers around, backs up, and hitches the trailer to the towing bracket. There is even a socket into which he plugs the connector. It hardly takes two minutes. Then he is off.

As he bounces along the edge of the field, a small figure in a green anorak stumbles out in front of him, seeming still the worse for eight cans of lager. He slams on the brakes. The trailer lurches and almost leaps off the towing bracket. Hm. He'll have to remember not to brake so sharply.

"Get in," he yells. Emanuel clambers into the back of the Land Rover and settles into the hay.

At the bottom gate, Wendy is still crouched over the prone body of the farmer. She looks up briefly as they drive off and Andriy thinks he catches the flicker of a smile on her face, but it could be just a trick of the light.

He can't get up into third, and it keeps slipping out of second, and trying to control the rebellious sway and tug of the trailer hitched to the back with the steering so loose is no joke. And there, wailing up the valley, are the flashing blue lights. Holy bones! He's only gone a few kilometers and they're after him already.

How has this happened, Andriy Palenko? Fifteen minutes ago, you had a Land Rover, money in your pocket, the open road, a childhood sweetheart waiting for you. Now you have six passengers, an unruly trailer, and the police on your back. Why didn't you just say no?

Ahead of him, on the left, is a turning—a grassy track that seems to lead into a wood. He veers off the road. After a few meters the track widens into a parking place with an old picnic table. He pulls to a halt and jumps out. In the back of the Land Rover Emanuel is asleep on the hay. Andriy sticks his head in the door of the trailer.

"Everything okay in here?"

The four women and Tomasz are crouching in a huddle on the floor. Marta has been sick.

"Where are we?" asks Tomasz.

"I don't know. I don't know where we are or where we're going. We stay here. In the morning we decide."

He sits down on the floor next to the others, resting his head in his hands. He realizes his knees are shaking. He is covered in sweat. If the police come, he will just explain everything. He will tell them it was all a mistake and take the consequences like a man. This is England.

Yola definitely has nothing to apologize for. Definitely not. When your lover betrays you and insults you with slapping ticker, if you are a woman of action, you have to act. There was that big dolt Andriy, trying to make everybody calm. What use is calm in a situation like that? Naturally the wife would try to put the blame on her. All lies. But try telling that to a policeman. She knows the mind of the policeman—she was married to one once. And the way the policeman thinks is this: The guilty person is one who has a motive. Does Andriy have a motive to run over Dumpling? No. Does she have a motive? Yes.

So best thing is to keep out of police's way. Back to Poland. Quick quick. But this beetroot-brain says he can't drive anymore, he wants to sleep. And you can see from the way he is looking at bed that he thinks he should be allowed to sleep here in women's trailer. And that underwear thief Tomasz (he thinks she doesn't know, but she does) has taken off his shoes. Pah! What a stink! All the girls start to shriek and cover their noses. She folds her arms across her bosom and says firmly,

"This is women's trailer, for women only."

But will this pig-headed beetroot-brain listen?

"Yola," he says, "you may have been queen of strawberry field, but here on road, I am boss. And if I am going to drive to Dover, I need good night's sleep."

Yola explains patiently that in the absence of the farmer, for which, by the way, she denies all responsibility, she is the senior figure, and she will decide about sleeping accommodations.

"I am mature and respectable woman, and I cannot be expected to share my sleeping quarters with any man."

Well, his reply is so uncouth that she will not repeat it, except to say that it referred to her age, her underclothings, her country of origin, and her relationship with farmer, which being pure business arrangement, and moreover one conducted in foreign country, has no relevance to any discussion of her character, a nuance which is probably too subtle for a Ukrainian.

"Andriy, please!" Tomasz intervenes, in a very calm and dignified way. "Is no problem. You can sleep in Land Rover, and I will stay here on floor."

"No! No!" cry all the girls in chorus. "No room on floor!"

"Well then, we will all sleep in Land Rover. Somehow we will manage."

Well, they did manage. Somehow. So that's that.

Andriy really let rip at Yola, and now he feels better. Out in the cool predawn, the sky is already growing lighter and the stars have disappeared. Tomasz has taken off his sneakers once more, placed them on the hood, and stretched himself out on the front seat of the Land Rover, his feet sticking out of the window, perfuming the breeze with his socks.

Andriy wonders where Irina is spending this night. The thought makes his stomach clench unpleasantly. He crawls into the back, fitting himself around and on top of Emanuel, who has slept through everything, curled up knees to chin on the sweet-smelling hay. There is an old blanket on the floor that he pulls up over them. Although the air is chilly, the silence of the wood, the breathing of earth and roots and sap at last put him into such a deep sleep that he doesn't wake until the morning sun strikes through the silvery tree trunks.

I AM DOG I RUN I RUN ALONE FIELD HEDGE ROAD ALL DARK I SEE BLUE LIGHT FLASH FLASH I SNIFF LISTEN I HEAR BAD WHEELIE NOISE WHOO WHAA WHOO WHAA I RUN FIELD RIVER I DRINK SMALL ANIMALS SCUFFLE SMELL OF GRASS AND EARTH DEAD THINGS ROTTING ANIMAL SMELLS FRESH PISS BADGER FOX WEASEL RABBIT I RUN ROAD FIELD WOOD ROAD WOOD STOP SNIFF SNIFF I SMELL MAN FEET GOOD STRONG FEET SMELL I GO SEEK MAN FEET SMELL I RUN I RUN I AM DOG

I jumped.

I fell. The ground was soft. I rolled, picked myself up, and I ran. *Mama, Papa, help me, please. I am little Irinochka.*

I was thinking—the trees—I must get into the trees. I scrambled up the bank into the woods, dodging between low branches. Here I would have a chance. If I was lucky, the trees would stop the bullets. I braced myself for the shots as I ran, flinching, waiting for the bang that would tell me I was dead. There were no shots. All I could hear were footsteps, his and mine, crashing through the undergrowth and dead branches on the ground. Crash. Crash. *No shots. Why no shots? Maybe I was dead already.* It was so dark. Dark like the cupboard under the stairs. Dark like a grave. Before, there'd been a faint glimmer from the headlights, but now I was past that, running into pitch blackness. It was too dark to run. Too many obstacles, shadows that turned into trees, branches that hit you in the face, tree roots that grabbed at your legs, terrors invisible. No moonlight here. On one side, I thought I could see the edge of the woods, the gray gleam of sky through the trees.

I veered right, slithered down the bank back onto the track, and sprinted silently along the grass. I could still hear him behind me in the woods. Crash. Crash.

Now there was a bend and the track climbed steeply uphill, with a jagged hedge on one side. Above the hedge I could see the sky, stars, breathless, skipping up and down as I ran. I stopped, panting for breath. My chest was exploding. Blood was pounding in my ears—boom boom boom boom—*Keep going. Don't stop now. You are younger and fitter. You can outrun him.* I tripped on a tree root, fell, picked myself up, and ran on—boom boom boom. When I couldn't run any longer, I stood still in the lee of a tree trunk and listened. My breath was coming in great gulps. I could still hear the crunch of footsteps in the woods, I couldn't tell how far behind me. So he hadn't given up yet. I ran again, wildly, stumbling and tripping. *Slow down. Take care. If you fall, you are finished.*

This is how a hunted animal feels, I thought, gasping for breath, terror rushing in through all your senses, drowning in your own fear. I found a gap in the hedge and squeezed through, the thorns grabbing at my clothes. On the other side was starlight, a long plowed field. I was breathing wildly, panting, choking. I tried to run, but the furrows were impossible, so I walked for a bit, breathing slow mouthfuls of air, stumbling in the ruts. Then I stopped, crouched, and listened. Silence. No footsteps. No gun. Nothing.

A bit farther up I cut back onto the track and ran again, more slowly now. My heart was banging about like a wild bird in a cage. *Is it finished?*

Has he gone? How will you know? Last time, he waited until you thought he'd gone, then he came back.

As I climbed the hill, the sky grew lighter. When I couldn't run anymore I carried on walking. I didn't stop for a long time. At last I found a hollow where a big tree had been uprooted. I made a bed of dry leaves and pulled some branches over for shelter, so I would be invisible from the track. I lay there, keeping quite still, waiting for my heart to slow down—boom boom—watching the dawn breaking, pink and peachy, with little clouds like angels' wings.

Andriy is the first to wake, conscious of something warm and heavy on his legs. He thinks at first it is Emanuel who has rolled over onto him in the night. He gives him a gentle shove and comes up against warm fur covering solid muscle. Holy whiskers!

The creature is huge and hairy and it snuffles in its sleep. He sits up and rubs his eyes. The dog sits up too and gazes at him with what he can only describe as adoration in its soft brown eyes. It is a big, handsome dog, short-haired and mainly black, with some white hairs around its muzzle and belly, which give it a mature, distinguished air.

"Woof!" it says, beating its sturdy tail against the side of the Land Rover.

"Hey, Dog!" says Andriy, rubbing its ears. "What are you doing here?"

"Woof!" says Dog.

Emanuel wakes next, to the sound of the tail thumping rhythmically against the side of the Land Rover, and he seems less pleased to see the dog.

"Is okay, Emanuel. Is good dog. No bite."

"In Chichewa we have a saying. *Where the dog pisses, the grass dies.*"

"Woof," says Dog. Andriy can see that despite himself Emanuel is quite taken with the enthusiastic tail wagging and the tongue hanging out, wet and pink, between the sharp white teeth.

But the most passionate meeting is between Tomasz and Dog—such a foot-nuzzling, face-licking, tail-beating, jumping-up, rolling-on-the-ground frenzy. Finally in a snuffling ecstasy Dog finds Tomasz's sneakers on the hood of the Land Rover, and though Tomasz tries to stop him he runs off with one in his jaws and chews it completely to pieces. Well, this is quite a splendid dog, thinks Andriy, for the sooner those sneakers disappear the better. And a dog with such a good sense of smell may help you find a missing person.

I AM DOG I AM HAPPY DOG I RUN I PISS I SNIFF I HAVE MY MEN THEY GO TO PISS IN THE WOOD MAN PISS HAS GOOD SMELL THIS MAN'S PISS SMELLS OF MOSS AND MEAT AND HERBS THIS IS GOOD I SNIFF THIS MAN'S PISS SMELLS OF GARLIC AND LOVE HORMONES THIS IS ALSO GOOD BUT LOVE HORMONES ARE TOO STRONG I SNIFF THIS MAN'S PISS SMELLS TOO SOUR BUT HIS FEET SMELL GOOD I SNIFF IN THIS WOOD ARE OTHER MAN SMELLS VOMIT MAN-SMOKE WHEELIE OIL I SNIFF NO DOG SMELLS I WILL MAKE MY DOG SMELL HERE I RUN I PISS I AM HAPPY DOG I AM DOG

Yola feels the dog is showing far too much enthusiasm, sticking its nose up her skirt on any excuse, in a way that reminds her of . . . No. She is a mature and respectable woman, and there are some secrets she is not going to share with any nosy-poky book readers.

It also shows a great interest in urine. When the women wake up, about an hour after the men, it tries to accompany each of them in turn as she goes to urinate in the woods and has to be driven off.

"Where is this dog from?" asks Yola. "It should go to its home." But nobody seems to know. Then it looks at her with such tender appeal in its eyes that her heart melts instantly, for she is a soft-hearted woman, and she takes Irina's orange ribbon and ties it under the dog's chin in a charming bow.

Marta observes that the dog's paws are scratched and bleeding, as though it has run some distance, and she applies some excellent Polish antiseptic ointment. They even share some of their bread with it, which is all they have for breakfast, but this is unnecessary, as it disappears into the woods and comes back later with a rabbit in its mouth.

After eating, it stretches itself out at Tomasz's feet, its head resting on its paws and one ear cocked, to listen to their discussion. For now it seems they must engage in endless discussions about where to go, which is completely unnecessary, because Yola had already decided they are going to Dover.

Doubtless they will even find the Ukrainian girl there. She wasn't such a bad girl after all, but probably she brought this disappearance upon herself by too much indiscriminate smiling. Once these gangster types get an idea into their heads, what can you do? And the flowers were a nice gesture.

As far as Yola is concerned, everything is clear. Andriy, who to his credit has apologized in a gentlemanly way for his outburst last night, got them into this jar of pickles from flirting with the farmer's wife, and now he must get them out of it, quick quick, before police come.

"When police is involved, one small thing may go on forever. Everything unnecessarily tied up in paper." She knows from experience just how bureaucratic a bureaucracy can be. She was married to a bureaucrat once. "Meanwhile poor Mirek is waiting for us in Zdroj. Mirek; Masurian goats; plums ripe in garden. Time to go home." She wipes a dramatic tear from her eye.

"Who is Mirek?" whines the hippy-hair Tomasz, with a face like a belly ache.

"Mirek is my beloved son."

"Beloved also of God," adds Marta, rolling her eyes heavenward. "One of God's special ones."

Why does Marta always go on about the poor boy's difficulty, unnecessarily broadcasting it to the whole world? She has already scared off at least two potential husbands with her pious mewlings. Yola gives her a discreet kick.

"And his father? Is his father also waiting?" Tomasz persists.

"His father is gone." Yola fixes Tomasz with her steely eye. "Why you asking so many questions, Mr. Stinking Feet? You got enough problems of your own without sticking your nose into mine."

Now everybody wants to have their say.

"We go London," says one Chinese girl. "In London is plenty Chineses. Plenty money work for Chineses. Better than in strawberry."

"I have an address for a man in England. Wait, please, thank you." Emanuel starts to shuffle through his papers. Shuffle shuffle. "Outstanding good man. His name is Toby Makenzi, and with his help I hope I will recover my sister's wherebeing."

"Emanuel, why you not coming to Poland with us?" says Yola kindly. That boy needs a mother, not a sister, she is thinking. Maybe even a little brother. And Tomasz says, "Emanuel, if you come in Poland I will teach you to sing and play the guitar."

In Yola's opinion, Emanuel is already a much better singer than Tomasz.

"I wonder where Vitaly is," Marta says. Yola noticed Marta earlier looking at Vitaly out of the corner of her eye, in a way that can only mean one thing, and she thinks it ironic, to say the least, that someone so religious should be attracted to someone with such an air of sin about him. But it is often the way.

Then Tomasz starts up again, giving her that doggy eye.

"I will go to Dover with you. From there to Poland. Boat, bus. We go all together. Maybe your boy needs a father? What you say, Yola?"

Yola smiles noncommittally. "First you get new shoes."

Hair too long. Bad smell. Not her type.

"Andriy? What is your plan now?" she asks

Andriy says nothing for a few minutes, and Yola is about to ask him again, when he says in a quiet voice, "I will first find Irina."

The others all fall silent. Marta starts to cry.

I must have fallen asleep. I woke up when a beam of sunlight struck the hollow where I was curled up. My limbs were stiff from the cold damp ground. My whole body was aching. I stood up, stretched. Then I remembered. Vulk. The woods. Running. Was he still out there waiting for me? I crouched down again. It was too soon to celebrate, but I was alive, unharmed, and it was a new morning.

The sun must have been up for a few hours. The air was still fresh and misty, that soft mistiness that promises a warm day to come. You know how some mornings you wake up and you're full of happiness just at being alive? I could hear birdsong and the bleating of sheep and another sound, farther away, a sweet, joyful sound. Church bells. It must be Sunday. In Kiev on Sundays you hear bells ringing out like this all over the city, and you see all the country women coming in wearing their best clothes with their headscarves tied over their ears and their gold teeth flashing, and crossing themselves as they come out of church, and Mother makes curd cake with raisins, and even our cat Vaska gets cream for a treat, then he licks his paws and rubs them behind his ears—will you remember me when I get home, Vaska? Will I ever get home? Suddenly, my eyes were full of tears. Sniff. Snuffle. *Stop it. You must keep a clear head and keep your eyes open. Make a plan.*

Below me, I could see the track between the field and the woods along which I had run last night. I remembered my terror. My thumping heart. The stars jumping above the jagged hedge. In daylight the path looked so nice and rustic as it wound its way innocently up the woody hill. In the other direction, it curved away below the contours of the land and disappeared from view. Where was I? How far did we come last night? How long did I black out for?

I scanned the fields one by one; maybe from here I'd be able to see the strawberry field. I'd recognize it from the two trailers. The landscape seemed familiar, but I soon realized that all fields look much the same, like a pattern of brown and green handkerchiefs, sprinkled with parsley. Do they sprinkle handkerchiefs with parsley? Maybe not. There was a lane rising between tall hedges, a row of poplars. I counted them—one, two, three, four, five. Were they the same poplars? Not far away was a cluster of trees that could be the copse at the top of the strawberry field. But where was the trailer? Over in the west I saw a strange white field that gleamed like a lake. But the edges were too square. It looked more like a field covered in glass or plastic. Were there any such fields nearby? I couldn't remember. I couldn't see any houses at all, just a stubby church spire rising from a clump of trees over near the shining field. Maybe there was a village there, hidden by the fold of the land; maybe over there were church bells and people walking to Sunday worship.

Down below, where the bottom of the track must reach the road, something was glinting—I could glimpse a flash of sunlight on metal through the leaves. It must be a parked car. My heart started up again— boom boom. My stomach twisted. Was he still down there waiting for me? Would he come looking for me? I lowered myself silently back into the hollow and pulled a branch down to cover me from view. This time, he wouldn't get me. However long he waited, I would wait longer.

If Andriy found driving forward with the trailer difficult, reversing it is even worse. It seems to have ideas of its own. It is late morning by the time they are ready to leave. Emanuel stands watch, waving him on as he backs out of the woody picnic spot onto the lane. Yola, Marta, and the Chinese girls are in the back of the Land Rover, with Dog at their feet. Tomasz is in the trailer, trying to catch up on his sleep.

Once they are on the main road, the driving is easier. It is quite interesting to tow something so heavy, he thinks, you have to plan ahead to avoid sudden maneuvers. He has started to get a feel for it by the time they get to the Canterbury bypass, when suddenly he spots a police car up ahead and two officers checking the passing cars. Holy bones! Are they on to him already? He makes a sharp left turn, puts his foot down, and now finds himself heading on a one-way road into the city center, the trailer swinging along behind, and the others all shouting different directions at him from the back. The shouting is pointless. It just distracts him. There is nowhere to go but straight ahead.

He finds himself in a maze of narrow streets; cars parked all over the place; pedestrians wandering around without looking. What a nightmare! This left-side driving business is no joke. How can he get back on the beltway? He takes a right turn and squeezes the trailer through a narrow archway, which might have had a no-entry sign on it, but too late now, when suddenly Marta shouts,

"Stop! Stop!"

He slams the brakes on. The trailer bucks and jolts. Remember not to do that again, Palenko. Gentle pumping action next time. From the trailer, there is a crash and a shout, and a few moments later Tomasz stumbles out in his socks and underpants, rubbing the sleep from his eyes.

"What's happening? Why have we stopped?"

"I don't know," says Andriy. "Why have we stopped?"

"Look!" says Marta, pointing.

He clambers out and stands on the pavement with the others. They are all gazing upward. In front of them, a towering creamy mass of carved and weathered stone, arches upon arches of strange intricately patterned tracery, the stone as delicate as paper, soars higher and higher into the sky, and the solemn figures of long-dead saints gaze back down at them from their pedestals.

He has seen the golden-domed cathedrals of Kiev, the skyline miracle of the Lavra, but this is different—yes, this is quite something. No paint or gilt. The beauty is all in the stone. What would it have been like to work up here in the sky, chipping and carving away at this luminous stone with a hammer and chisel, instead of hammering at the coal face in the dark underground? Would he have become a different kind of man— closer to the angels?

He bows his head and crosses himself in the Orthodox way, just in case. No one speaks. Marta closes her eyes and crosses herself too. Yola pulls down the hem of her skirt below her knees and crosses herself with both hands. Tomasz goes back into the trailer and puts his trousers on. The Chinese girls just stare.

Emanuel whispers to Andriy, "What are these beastings and goblins? Why have they put symbols of witchcraft upon a Christian church?"

"Don't worry," he whispers back. "It's okay."

Dear Sister

Today I was blessed with a visitation of Canterbury Cathedral which is an outstanding Ediface built completely of stone and miraculously carved with fearsome fiends and hobgoblins sitting outside gaping open-mouthed. But the inside is filled up with mysterious Peace for in this Cathedral are many wondrous window glasses such as I have never seen even in St George's on Likomo Island that deepen sunlight into red and blue and stories of Our Lord and His Saints are told in colourful artistry.

And a priest came upon us and asked if we would pray and I was afraid to partake of the protestant faith but the Catholic Martyr whispered that all such Cathedrals belonged formally to our Good Religion and were stolen from us by mindless protestants. So we went into a small prayersome chapel beauteous in stillness and light and we asked the Lord to deliver our sister Irina who was seized by the Spawn of Satan and nobody knows her wherebeing. After the prayers everyone said Amen even the dog I wish you could see this dog it is outstanding in piety. And I also prayed for that godless fellow who has slipped through the fishing net of Love. For in this silent glimmery chapel I felt the Presence of the Lord standing close beside us listening for our prayers and I felt His breathing in the cool stony air.

Then I heard Organ music and a choir was singing Sheep May Safely Graze which stirred me up for this Cathedral is named after Saint Augustine. Then good Father Augustine of Zomba knocked on my memory door and his kindly ways which watered my eyes with rememberances of home.

Andriy feels better, more at peace, after their prayers in the cathedral. It isn't until they are back at the trailer that he notices Emanuel is missing. He goes back to the chapel to look for him, but he has disappeared. Somewhere in the cathedral, an organ is playing and a choir is singing. Drawn by the music, he follows the sound along a stone aisle where the ancient glass throws pools of colored light on the floor. A service is in progress, and there in the front row of the congregation is Emanuel.

His eyes are shut, so he can't see the odd looks the others are giving him, but his mouth is open, startlingly pink in his youthful brown face, and he is singing aloud in a sweet high voice, along with the choir. And as he sings, tears are pouring down his cheeks. There is something so vulnerable and yet so powerful about the closed eyes, the open mouth, the tears and the music, that it makes Andriy catch his breath. Who is this young man? Andriy feels an urge to put his arm around him, but he holds back, as you would hesitate to wake a sleepwalker, for fear that the sudden shock of reality would break his heart.

A flash of memory comes to him—a circle of enraptured faces at a secret Orthodox service down in a woody ravine, where his grandmother took him as a child. The priest sang the litany and sprinkled them with holy water, promising forgiveness for their sins and solace for the grinding daily hardship of their lives. "Kyrie eleison. Lord have mercy."

His father said that religion was the opium of the masses and it was a shame that his mother, who was a good woman in every way and a good communist, should believe such nonsense.

In the silence at the end of the music, he goes up to Emanuel and touches his arm. Emanuel opens his eyes, looks around him, and smiles.

"Ndili Bwino, my friend."

Her prayers have made her feel pleasantly righteous, and after righteousness it is natural to feel hungry and thirsty. So as far as Yola is concerned, their first priority when they get to Dover is to have some lunch.

Unlike in Canterbury, where all the shops were open, in Dover everything is very closed. At last down a back street they find a small, gloomy shop with two narrow aisles, smelling of spices and something musty and not very nice. The shopkeeper is a plump Indian woman about Yola's age, dressed in a green sari, with a red spot on her forehead. Yola studies her curiously. She is not unattractive in an Asiatic sort of way.

The red spot seems to be in the wrong place. Surely it should be on her cheeks.

Yola as the supervisor is naturally in charge of the shopping, but in the interests of harmony she lets everyone have a say. They agree on five loaves of white sliced bread (better than coarse Polish bread and quite inexpensive), margarine (more modern than butter, and also cheaper), apricot jam (Tomasz's favorite), teabags and sugar (they have been drying out and reusing their teabags, but there is a limit), bananas (Andriy's choice, typical Ukrainian), salted peanuts (a special request from Emanuel), a large bar of rum-and-raisin chocolate (Yola's own little luxury), two large bottles of Coca-Cola for the Chinese girls, and a tin of dog food. Tomasz lingers in the off-license section, studying the labels, but his request for a bottle of wine is firmly rejected by Yola. Unnecessary. Too expensive. Andriy is also hanging around in the off-license, looking at the beer.

"Did you see the markup Vitaly has been making on the beer he has been selling us?" he says grumpily. Typical Ukrainian.

Marta has stayed in the Land Rover with the dog, and Yola cannot remember her special request.

The Indian shopkeeper tut-tuts as she puts all this through the till.

"You are not eating a balance diet."

"Not balance?" It is Yola's responsibility to see they eat properly.

"Protein. You must have a protein. If you eat all this you will be feeling sick."

Yola looks at their pile of shopping and realizes that she is right. Just looking at all this stuff is making her feel a bit unwell.

"What can you recommend?"

The shopkeeper hms and ruminates.

"Pilchards." She points down the aisle. "Fishies. Good for you. Cheap. In tin over there."

Yola thinks the fishes in the picture on the tin look plump and appealing and she is pleasantly surprised by the price. They take two tins.

Between the waist of the shopkeeper's sari and the bottom of her blouse is a soft bulge of brown flesh. In civilized countries this area of a woman's body is normally concealed, but Yola notices that the Ukrainian is staring at it fixedly.

"Madam," he says, very politely, "I wish to ask, from where you learn such wisdom?"

What a flatterer that beetroot-brain is, almost like a Pole. (Of course Polish men are renowned throughout the world for being flirtatious, on account of their habit of hand kissing, but sadly this does not make them good husband material, as Yola has discovered to her sorrow.) The shopkeeper laughs modestly and points at a picture above the counter of a smiling wrinkled old woman dressed in bright blue, with a triple string of pearls and a stylish blue hat.

"This lady is my inspiration."

Everyone gathers around to look. The old woman in the picture looks back with a cheerful smile and a wave of her gloved hand. Yola thinks that to have both a veil and little blue feathers in a hat is unnecessary: One or the other would have made a sufficient statement.

"She is a lady of extreme age and wisdom. In her long years, which unfortunately are now over, she gave many cheery indications of the important things in life. To have friends come from afar is a pleasure—this is one of her great sayings." The shopkeeper folds her arms on the counter with a friendly smile. "You not from around here. I think you all come from afar, innit?"

"You are right, Madam." Tomasz smiles ingratiatingly. "We have come from all the corners of the world—Poland, Ukraine, Africa, China."

He too is staring at the brown bulge. Really, what can you do with men?

"And Malaysia," adds Chinese Girl Two.

"Well, have a lovely time, my dears, and bon appetit." The shopkeeper beams at them over the counter. "That is another of her sayings."

"This is a great saying," says Emanuel. "I will commit it to memory."

But Chinese Girl One whispers to Chinese Girl Two, "I think that saying attributed to the old lady in blue is in fact a saying of Confucius."

And Chinese Girl Two points at the red spot in the middle of the shopkeeper's forehead and whispers, "I think it is a bullet hole."

They giggle.

I AM DOG I AM GOOD DOG I SIT WITH MY MAN I EAT DOG FOOD MEAT MAN EATS MAN FOOD BREAD FISH WE ALL EAT WE ALL SIT ON SMALL SMOOTH STONES NEAR BIG WATER SUN SHINES HOT THIS WATER IS NOT GOOD TO DRINK BAD TASTE BIG WATER RUNS AFTER DOG DOG RUNS AFTER BIG WATER BIG WATER HISSES AT DOG SSSS DOG BARKS AT BIG WATER WOOF DOG SNIFFS BIG WATER SNIFF SNIFF NO DOG SMELL NO MAN SMELL ONLY BIG WATER SMELL EVERYWHERE STONES WOOD WEEDS WASTE DOG FINDS MAN-SHOE BESIDE WATER WET SHOE GOOD MAN-SMELL SHOE DOG BRINGS WET SHOE TO SOUR-PISS-STRONG-FEET-SMELL MAN HE IS HAPPY GOOD DOG HE SAYS I AM GOOD DOG I AM DOG

Andriy feels quite queasy by the time he's finished his lunch. Those pilchards in tomato sauce—they were good, but perhaps he shouldn't have eaten so many. While the others set out on foot to the ferry terminal, he spreads his towel on the pebble beach and stretches out in the sun with Dog beside him. The slow pull and surge of waves down at the water's edge is soothing. Dog falls asleep almost instantly, hissing and snoring as rhythmically as the sea. Andriy is incredibly tired, but each time he is on the point of sleep the fluttery panicky feeling starts up and wakes him. *I did not do it.* The left-side driving, the excitable passengers, this self-willed trailer, the argument with Ciocia Yola, and a niggling unspecific anxiety which swirls around in his head like a mist without taking any fixed form, all have tired him out yet left him unable to relax.

He must have started to drift away at last, when he is brought back abruptly by a thunderous crash just a few feet from where he is lying. His blood freezes; his heart begins to pound. Half asleep, as if waking from a nightmare, he listens to the dreadful sound—a long crescendo, a terrible

reverberation, a slow fading rumble. It is the long-drawn-out growl of
the earth crying in pain. It is the roar of the coal face collapsing in the
darkness below ground.

He sits up, rubs his eyes. There is nothing. Nothing but the waves
pounding on the pebbles a few inches away from his feet. The tide has
come in. And yet, in that moment of waking, he relived the terror of
looking into the fuming blackness of noise and dust and knowing his
father would never emerge alive.

That sound—no, he will never be able to work underground again. He
cannot go back down there. In fact he had never wanted to be a miner in the
first place. He would have stayed on at school and studied to be a teacher or
an engineer. But when he was sixteen, his father had shoved a pick into his
hands—they were long past the time of power tools—and said,

"Learn, son. Learn to be a man."

He had replied in that clever sixteen-year-old way that makes him
wince now to remember, "Is a man someone who grubs about like a beast
under the ground?"

And his father had said, "A man is someone who puts bread on
the table, and puts his comrades' safety before his own, and doesn't
complain."

In Donbas, there is only one way to put bread on the table. When
they said the pit was uneconomic, international solidarity couldn't help,
the mine workers' union couldn't help. So they had gone back underground and helped themselves. Well, you have to live, don't you? When
the roof fell, Andriy had lived, and two others. Six had been killed. The
story didn't even make the headlines beyond Donbas.

But why him? Why did he live, when the others died? Because a voice
in his head insisted, if you want to live, run—keep running. Don't
look back.

He watches a bank of gray clouds massing up on the horizon.

And why Sheffield? Because Sheffield is the place where the puddings
are pink and the girls put their tongues in your mouth when they kiss.
And there was something about the blind man, the gentleness of his

voice when he spoke of the welcome that awaits strangers in his city, the way he clasped your hand and seemed to look right into your heart, even though of course he wasn't looking at all. Yes, now you remember, Vloonki was his name.

And once you get to Sheffield? He hasn't thought that far ahead. Tomorrow he will look for Irina, and when he has found her, he will be on his way.

However long Vulk waited for me, I would wait longer.

From my leafy hiding place, I watched as the sun carved its slow arc from the wooded hills in the east, up over the rolling patchwork of green and gold fields, and down to the other horizon. It was strange, because although I could see the sun moving, I felt inside as though time were standing still. I was waiting—waiting and trying not to think about why I was waiting, because those thoughts were so horrible that if I let them creep into my mind, I might never be able to chase them out again. *"You like flovver . . . ?"*

When I get back to Kiev, I thought, I will write a story about this. It will be a thriller, following the adventures of a plucky heroine as she flees across England, pursued by a sinister but ridiculous gangster. Thinking of my story made me feel better. When you write a story, you can decide how it ends.

As the sun moved across the sky, a spume of streaky clouds that unfolded in its wake started to thicken and turn heavy. Strange how I had never noticed before how expressive clouds can be, like people, changing, ageing, drifting apart.

At some point I must have fallen asleep, because suddenly I opened my eyes to find the sun had disappeared and what I had thought was a line of hills, blue in the distance, was in fact a long bank of clouds that had swallowed up the sky. It was going to rain. I was incredibly hungry. I thought if I didn't eat something soon, I would faint. I squeezed myself out of my hollow and peered down the track. Where I had caught the gleam of sunlight on metal before, there was nothing now but leaves. Had he gone, or was it just that the sun had moved around? Was he hiding, waiting for me? Maybe everywhere I go from now on, he'll be hiding, waiting. *Stop. Don't think those thoughts. If you think like that, you will be his prisoner all your life.*

I knew I had to find food. I looked around me. There were trees, bushes, grass, leaves. Were any of them good to eat? I pulled a handful of grass—well, if cows eat it, it must be okay. I chewed on it, but I couldn't bring myself to swallow. There were some red berries on a shrub with a vivid toxic luster. *Mama, Papa, you know about this sort of thing. Don't be foolish, Irina. You know you shouldn't eat berries or mushrooms unless you are absolutely sure. How many times do I have to tell you that?*

Even as I was turning these thoughts over in my head, I had already started to walk back down the track. In the daytime, it seemed no distance. I crawled through and walked down the other side of the hedge to keep out of view. At the bottom, the track widened and there was an old wooden table with benches on each side, though some of the planks had been pulled off. There was no vehicle in sight, but the ground was gashed with tire marks. Either he'd been back, more than once, or there'd been other vehicles. I looked more closely. There, in one of the wheel-ruts, I spotted the stub of a cigar. My heart started up—boom boom. I remembered he had a cigar last night, but was it the same cigar? Or had he been back? Had he been sitting in his mafia-machine, smoking a cigar and waiting for me? *"Little flovver . . ."* I stamped on the stub and ground it into the grass. And there was another strange object, something gray and rubbery. It looked like part of a shoe. What a stink! But Vulk's shoes were shiny black.

Then I noticed, beneath the broken table, a screwed up bundle of paper. I knew at once what it was. Another stroke of good luck! I picked it up. That smell! I couldn't help myself. I was salivating like a dog. I unwrapped the bundle and counted them. One, two, three . . . There were lots! I stuffed them into my mouth. My stomach growled with pleasure. They were cold and stiff, like dead men's fingers. They were absolutely delicious. And something else was buried there beneath the chips, something golden and crispy. I broke off a piece and put it on my tongue. It was like manna. It was . . . It was all gone.

Then I thought, what an idiot you are, standing here by the roadside where anyone passing could see you, stuffing yourself with somebody's thrown-away leftovers. If Mother could see you . . . *Well, she can't, can she?*

Somebody's leftovers. . . . Whose leftovers? Did he have some chips in the car last night? No, I would have noticed the smell. So they must be someone else's. Or maybe he went and bought some chips, and came back here, and sat in the car and waited for me to return. Waited for me so he could . . . *Stop! Don't think that thought. Every time you think of him, he possesses you.*

The ferry terminal is almost deserted, and silent apart from the wailing of a small, tired, chocolate-smeared girl tugging at the skirt of her equally tired mother. Marta remembers the bustle and excitement of their arrival, only a few weeks ago. Now everyone seems so despondent. Andriy stayed at the beach. Emanuel has gone to look at the boats. The two Chinese girls are outside eating ice-cream cones. Yola and Tomasz are wandering around looking for the office where they can get their tickets exchanged. Yola's face is red: maybe from stress, or maybe from too much sun earlier on the beach, when her hat blew away, and the bad language that followed was appalling. Tomasz is wearing one smelly sneaker and one sneaker that is wet and two sizes too large for him. He too got sunburned on his nose. Marta can't really concentrate on what everyone else is doing because she is desperate for a bathroom.

While Yola and Tomasz go off in search of the ticket office, which is in another part of the building, Marta follows the signs to the restroom. She is just making her way back when she catches sight of a young man lounging near the coffee bar, talking on his mobile phone. He seems to be looking for someone. He is quite tall and smartly dressed, with a gold chain around his neck and a glittering jewel in one ear. His shaved head gleams shiny brown, and he is wearing black sunglasses, which give him a slightly sinister air. There is something familiar about him. She tries to get another look without staring too obviously. Suddenly, he grins and waves. Should she wave back? Then he takes off his dark glasses and she recognizes him at once: It is Vitaly.

He slips the mobile phone into his pocket and saunters over to her.

"Hi, Marta. How's things?"

"Okay." She hesitates. So much has happened since their last supper together. "Well, to say the truth, Vitaly, not good. We had to leave the strawberry place. The farmer was injured and Ciocia Yola is worried about police."

"Hm. Police is not good."

"They are trying to change tickets at this moment."

"They are going back to Poland?"

"We are all going, as soon as possible. And you, Vitaly, what are you doing? You look so smart. Are you finished with strawberry?"

"Bye-bye strawberry. Hello mobilfon." He smiles mysteriously, then he lowers his voice. "Recruitment consultant," he says in English.

"Vitaly!" Marta is impressed. "What is that?"

"Dynamic employment solution. Cutting edge fwhit fwhit"—he does a quick double slicing movement with the edge of his hand—"organizational answer for all your flexible staffing need." His fluency is breathtaking.

"You have become a businessman, Vitaly! English-speaking VIP."

She stares, feeling a little embarrassed at her own shabbiness. Already the curly-haired, smiling, strawberry-picking Vitaly with his appealingly wayward air has dissolved into this new smoothly confident businessman who slips effortlessly between Polish and English.

"It is a pity you have to go back so soon. I can find you an excellent employment in this area. High wage. Comfortable living situation."

"Oh, Vitaly, how you place temptation! I would stay, but I think Ciocia Yola wants to go home. She misses her son." She catches the sinful twinkle in his eye and thinks how pleasant it would be to lead him back to the path of righteousness.

At that moment, Yola and Tomasz reappear with thunderous faces. They have not been able to exchange their tickets. The office is closed. They have been told by someone—they are not sure who—that they must come back tomorrow or go to the office in town and queue for a possible cancellation. Now they are arguing about who it was who gave them this information and what exactly she said. Yola says she was the office cleaner or maybe another disgruntled passenger and her word is not to be trusted. Tomasz says she was an official from the port authority and it is unfortunate that Yola sent her away with a wasp in her ear without listening to what she had to say.

"Why could they not simply put a notice up, instead of making us run around like idiots in this heat?" Ciocia Yola fumes. "Where is toilet? Did you find toilet, Marta? Who is this?" She stares. "Vitaly?"

Vitaly extends his hand and shakes hers warmly.

"I hear you are thinking of returning to Poland, Yola."

"Who has told you this?"

"Ciocia, I told him," says Marta in her most soothing voice. "Don't be cross. But Vitaly says he can find us excellent high-wage work in this area. Vitaly, tell Ciocia what it is you do."

"Recruitment consultant. Cutting edge fwhit fwhit dynamic employment solution consultant with advance flexible capacity for meets all your organizational staffing need." He seems to be picking up speed as he repeats it.

"My God!" says Yola. "Vitaly, you have become somebody."

He lowers his head modestly.

"I am working for British company. Nightingale Human Solution. I have been on *training seminar*."

"Trenning semeenar—what is this, Vitaly?" Marta cannot conceal the wonder in her voice.

"Oh, is nothing," Vitaly smiles modestly. "Anyone can do it. You only have to learn some words in English. And of course contacts. The main thing is to have contacts."

"You have contacts, Vitaly?" asks Yola. Despite her previous status as supervisor and gangmistress, she too is awestruck by this newly transformed Vitaly.

"He has mobilfon," whispers Marta.

Only Tomasz seems unimpressed.

"We are not seeking new employment, thank you, Vitaly. We are planning to return to Poland as soon as we can change our tickets."

"Ah, changing tickets is impossible. You will have to buy new tickets. You will need money for this."

"This excellent employment you talking about," Yola pursues. "What is this high wage?"

Vitaly pauses for a moment as though performing mental arithmetic.

"It will be in region of five or six hundred pound a week. Depends on performance. Maybe even more."

They all gasp, even Tomasz. It is three times what they were earning in the strawberry field before deductions.

"And you can say good-bye to trailer. You will be staying in luxury hotel."

"And so this employment—what will we do?" asks Marta.

"Poultry." Vitaly slips back into English. "You will be contributing to the dynamic resurgence of the poultry industry in the British Isles. Or as we say in Polish," he winks at Marta, "you will be feeding chickens."

Marta pictures herself surrounded by a happy flock of plump brown birds who cluck and strut as she scatters handfuls of grain among them. Her heart melts.

But Tomasz whispers to Ciocia Yola, "Think of Mirek. Remember the police."

"Yes," Ciocia Yola looks dejected. "We want no trouble. Better we go back. If we can find some way with these idiots who are running ferry-boats these days. We will try again tomorrow. What do you say, Marta?"

Before Marta can say anything, Vitaly intervenes.

"I have heard, through my contacts, that as the farmer is not killed, merely injured, is no problem with police."

"But even if he is injured," says Tomasz, "they must make inquiries."

"It will be only formality. It would be pity, I think, to pass by this opportunity to earn plenty good English money. Think of investments you made in your fare for coming here. Think what luxuries you can buy for your son with this money, Yola."

"Mm," says Yola. Marta can see the thoughts passing across her face.

Suddenly, there is a burst of loud merry music by her ear. Di di daah da! Di di daah da! Marta jumps. It is Vitaly's mobile phone.

"Please excuse me!" he whips it out of his breast pocket and starts jabbering in a language that is not English, nor Polish, nor Ukrainian, nor Russian, waving his free hand in the air. He is getting very agitated. An argument seems to be developing. At one point, he covers the phone with his hand, and whispers to the others, "I'm very sorry. Forgive me. Urgent business matter."

Marta tries to catch some words, but he is talking too fast. Yola and Tomasz are conferring together, weighing up the joy of chickens against the joys of returning to Poland, when suddenly the Chinese girls appear, clutching their well-licked stubs of ice-cream cones. They stop in mid-lick and start to giggle when they recognize Vitaly. They too are amazed at his transformation.

"He has become a . . . what are you, Vitaly?"

Vitaly beams, stows his phone in his pocket, and puts his dark glasses back on.

"Dynamic employment cutting edge fwhit fwhit recruitment consultant for all you flexible solution."

He performs a small bow. The Chinese girls giggle even more, but Vitaly quiets them with a dramatic hand gesture and continues in his astonishingly fluent English. "If you ladies are also seeking a new employment, I have number of interesting possibilities which I would be happy to present for your consideration."

They exchange glances that are both nervous and excited.

"I may be able to find good position for you in Amsterdam. Have you been to Amsterdam? It is a city of extraordinary beauty, built entirely on water. Like Venice, but even better."

"I have see pictures," says Chinese Girl Two. "Is more beautiful than Kuala Lumpur."

"But no doubt you have boyfriends waiting for you back in China? You girls get up to all sorts of tricks, eh?" Vitaly's voice has become suddenly low and sweet like honey. "You naughty Chinese girls sometimes sleeping with boyfriend, eh? Make nice love?" This is more like the old smilingly-sinful Vitaly than the new businessman Vitaly, thinks Marta, though she is rather surprised by his questions.

"Not boyfriend," says Chinese Girl One. Chinese Girl Two just shakes her head sadly.

"No boyfriends. That is very good news. Well," he consults his mobile phone again and presses a few buttons. "I think there may be good position for you looking after children in family of diplomat. Chinese diplomat based in Amsterdam. He has six children, three boys and three girls, and you will look after three each, so that is why two persons are required. They are very intelligent children, so great care and patience is needed. You must never beat them or shout at them. Do you think you will be able to do this?"

"Yes, yes," they exclaim. "But . . ."

He catches Chinese Girl Two's eye and quickly adds, "Temporary job. Three months only. Regular nannies are on vacation. Hey, don't be afraid, you know me. You can trust me—I am your friend, I look after you." He winks. "You will live with this family in their large luxurious house in the heart of Amsterdam's old city. You will have your own elite apartment, and you will travel everywhere by boat. It is very prestigious position with high level of responsibility, and pay will be commensurate. You will be in euros." He glances once more at his phone. "Five thousand euros per month."

They gasp; it sounds like a lot, even though they have no idea of the exchange rate from euros to pounds to yuan or ringgit. "I need to make some telephone calls to ascertain full details and see whether this job is still available. I will meet you here tomorrow at midday. Bring your bags with you. And passports."

"I too would be interested in such a job looking after children," says Marta.

Suddenly, the fluffy brown chickens seem much less appealing. Vitaly looks at her, studies her for a moment, focusing his gaze on her nose, and smiles kindly.

"I think looking after chickens is better for you."

After his disagreeable doze on the beach, Andriy decides it is time to take a look around Dover. Dog, still wearing his orange ribbon under his chin, comes with him, padding along at his side, sometimes going off to follow an interesting scent, then racing to catch up.

The sky has turned heavy and the light has a grayish, dirty hue. His head is aching from sleeping in the sun, and a cloud of pessimism has settled over him. He had felt so sure earlier that he would find Irina in Dover—a feeling based partly on a hunch, and partly on the fact that he too came into England via Dover, though with a different agent. But now he doesn't know where to start. He finds the streets of Dover depressing: shops closed, houses and hotels run-down, people sullen with tight faces. It feels like a town whose heart has died. In fact it reminds him of Donetsk, idlers with no work hanging out on the streets, drinking, begging, just staring. Too many strangers like himself, looking for something that isn't there, waiting for their luck to change. And all the time the dismal grating noise of the sea in the background, and the miserable wail of gulls.

As he wanders through the streets, the impossibility of his task grows on him. Where should he start to look? And why is he even looking for this girl? What happened to her has happened, and although of course you would have prevented it if you could, really she is not your responsibility. Her boxer boyfriend should be looking after her. Bye-bye, end of story.

Retracing his footsteps to the beach, he passes a young man with a bucket and a fishing rod. He looks Ukrainian, with his round face and dark eyes, but it turns out he's Bulgarian. He says, in a mixture of broken English, Bulgarian, and Russian, that he has been fishing off the pier—he points vaguely beyond the beach—and the fish are for sale. Andriy buys a small mackerel and two other unspecified fish for fifty pence, and starts to feel more cheerful.

The others are already at the trailer by the time he gets back. The Chinese girls are sitting inside poring over their horoscopes and whispering with suppressed excitement. Tomasz has found an old piece of tarpaulin and some blue rope in the lorry park on the way back, for which he has amazing plans. Yola and Marta are eating ice cream, and Marta has brought some back for him. Emanuel has had the foresight to fill up the two empty Coca-Cola bottles with clean water from the public toilets.

Andriy feels a prickle of annoyance when they tell him about their encounter with Vitaly. Bye-bye strawberry, hm? Hello mobilfon? The others are talking excitedly about their new employment prospects. Will his pride allow him to ask Vitaly to find something for him? And if he does, will it be like the markup on the cans of beer—a business opportunity disguised as a favor?

"Come, Andriy," says Marta. "It will be the last night we will all spend together. We must celebrate." And suddenly Dog comes bounding up with a partly frozen chicken in his jaws.

Dear Sister
Our small strawberry family is at an end. The Polish mzungus are to undergo chicken employment and the Chinese girls are designed for Amsterdam. Only Andree and I and the Dog will endure in the trailer. For our celebration Toemash has induced a bottle of Italian wine and we found a field near Dover which is blessed with an abundance of carrots which Martyr confronted with eagerness. The Dog also has bestowed a frozen chicken upon us.
While Martyr was knifing the carrots Andree and I went about to collect firewood and so we fell upon a shaded hollow where we came upon

Toemash and Yola walking together and talking with solemn voices. And when they came back to the trailer Yola was holding the hand of Toemash and in the other hand a pair of woman's underwearings.

Then Toemash and Andree constructed a tip-top tent from the tarpaulin and blue rope collected by Toemash and I was given to sleep on my own in the back of the Land Rover befitting my small size.

The feast prepared for us by Martyr was outstanding and also Toemash's wine and soon it was time to sing. Toemash has composed an outstanding song about a band of travellers and their stories of love and misbehaviour which he sang with the companionship of his guitar and I would be very interesting to learn to play a guitar for Toemash has already taught me some chords. On my turn I sang the Benedictus from the B Minor Mass of Bach which Sister Theodosia taught to me and we gave thanks for the Friendship we have enjoyed together in the strawberry place. And in my heart I prayed once more to be reunited with you dear sister and for the speedy deliverance of Irina for I knew a storm was coming for the red sun went down through an angry swelling of white and grey and clouds which obscured the rising of the moon.

When I had finished the chips, I licked the scraps off the paper. Then I licked the grease off the paper. Then I considered my options.

If I turned right, I would be heading toward the row of poplars and the gleaming white field. If they were the same poplars, that way would take me back to the strawberry field, where I could collect my bag and the bit of money I'd saved, and the others would look after me and help me get away. If I turned left, it would probably take me toward Dover. I'd go to the police and they would send me back to Kiev, where my mother would be waiting for me with tears in her eyes. "I warned you, Irina, but you wouldn't listen!" she'd say, sniffling all over me. And I'd hang around in the apartment, just me and Mother and the cat, getting on one another's nerves, wishing Papa was there, and dreaming of coming to England.

I turned right.

The sun had gone down and the light had started to fade, and now an annoying wind had sprung up. I'd better keep moving or I'd freeze to death.

I started to walk, swinging my arms briskly by my sides for warmth because I only had a light jumper. Lucky I'd put my jeans on over my shorts the other evening, when the gnats started to bite. The lane wound around between tall hedges, so most of the time I couldn't see where I was going, sometimes climbing a bit, sometimes dropping down again. Nothing looked familiar. The row of poplars had disappeared from view altogether.

I lost track of how far I'd walked. A car passed, its headlights blazing, but it didn't stop. Then it started to rain. I didn't mind at first, because I was thirsty, and I stuck my tongue out to catch the water. Then my jumper started to get soaked through and I was shivering, with the wind tugging at my wet clothes and lashing the rain into my face. This was dire!

I started to run, my head bowed into the rain, my hands stuffed down into the pockets of my jumper. Another car passed and I waved my hand, but it had already whooshed away in a cloud of spray. Just as I could feel the rain penetrating through to my skin, I came upon an old shed or garage made of corrugated iron, set back from the road. I pushed the door and it creaked open. Inside it smelled of oil, and a hulk of some old motor was rusting in the corner under a plastic sheet. There was even a chair. That was a bit of luck! I sat down. The chair wobbled. It only had three legs. Well, there was nothing for it but to sit and wait until morning.

Snug in the warmth of her bunk, Marta listens to the rain pattering on the curved roof of the trailer, a soft, intimate tapping sound, like a friend asking to be let in. She is thinking about Irina. On the other single bunk, Ciocia Yola is muttering in her sleep, engrossed in some nocturnal argument. Even in sleep, her aunt usually finds someone to berate. The raindrops get louder, more insistent. A brisk wind has picked up, rattling the lightweight panels of their fragile home and blowing through the checked curtains that are drawn across the opened windows. The Chinese girls in their double bed are wide awake too, huddling close together. Ciocia Yola wins her dream argument with a final snort and gets up to close the windows. Marta puts the kettle on and spreads some slices of bread with margarine and apricot jam, and the inside of the trailer is soon warm and steamy. They all sit on the edge of the double bed in their nightclothes, eating bread and jam, and talking in whispers for no particular reason.

Then there is another louder tapping sound outside, and men's voices. Marta opens the door. Andriy and Tomasz are standing there looking like two wet socks on a wash line. Their awning has blown away. Although this is a women's trailer for women only, Ciocia Yola relents when she sees how bedraggled they are.

"Come in. You can shelter from the storm."

They towel themselves dry and sit on the edge of the bunk too. Marta pours them steaming mugs of black sweet tea. Then she hears Dog barking softly—snoof! snoof!—and there is another knock on the door. Dog and Emanuel have come to join them. They are not wet—it was dry in the back of the Land Rover—they just want company. *To have friends come from afar is a pleasure*, says Emanuel, wiping his feet on the mat as he comes in.

Somehow all seven of them squeeze in, Andriy perched on a stool, Tomasz, Emanuel, and Dog sitting on the floor, the women huddling up on the double bed, drinking tea, eating the rest of the bread and jam, and listening to the rain hammering on the roof. I will always remember this night, thinks Marta. Friendship like this is a gift from God.

After a while, when they start to feel sleepy, Tomasz and Andriy stretch out in the single bunks and Emanuel curls up on the tiny floor space in between. Marta and Yola squeeze into the double bunk with the Chinese girls, and Dog goes underneath. Marta, who is in the middle, has to nudge off her aunt and the nearest Chinese girl with her elbows. The girl's weight, when she rolls down onto Marta, is surprisingly firm and warm. She wonders which of the two it is. Even though she never got to know very much about the Chinese girls, the closeness of their trailer life has made them somehow intimate.

As she drifts between sleeping and waking, Marta rehearses last night's meal over in her head. Really, it was a masterpiece. First she fried Andriy's fish in margarine with wild garlic leaves and some mushrooms that Tomasz brought back from the field. She used just a splash of wine to make a delicious sauce for the chicken, which was cut into small pieces and simmered slowly in herbs and tea. It was unfortunate that their earlier shopping was so limited, she said to her aunt, with a note of reproach in her voice, but there was still some stale bread left, which she cut into delicate croutons and fried lightly with a sprinkling of fresh roadside marjoram to make a tasty accompaniment. The carrots were chopped into fine julienne strips then boiled and served with a margarine-and-apricot glaze. She regrets the theft of the carrots, which she knows is a sin, but prays that their owner will be rewarded in heaven, for when we feed the poor, we feed Our Lord. And although there was only a small teacup of wine each, it was enough for them to raise a toast in honor of their friendship and a happy reunion in the unspecified future.

"To all trailer dwellers everywhere!" Tomasz said, raising his cracked cup.

In fact nobody gets very much sleep that night. They lie awake listening to the storm outside, and talking in low whispers, until at last the wind drops, the rain patters away, and the sky grows light.

Vitaly is waiting for them at the ferry terminal the next day. He is talking on his phone again and looking around with an edgy, anxious air. Marta notices for the first time the restlessness in his eyes, and it makes her feel uneasy. After the intimacy of last night, his brash cell-phone patter seems to strike a false note. But he smiles with delight when he sees them.

He has a companion with him, a young man with the same shaven head and a complexion as dark as his own, but older, with slightly coarser features and a scar across his left cheek which has caught the tip of his lip, whom he introduces as Mr. Smith.

"Mr. Smith will be your escort," he says to the Chinese girls. "He will accompany you to Amsterdam and introduce you to family of distinguished diplomat. Is this not so, Mr. Smith?"

Mr. Smith smiles, and the scar on his upper lip pulls tight against his teeth.

"Ladies. Please come with me. You have your passports?"

He leads them through the crowd to a large silver car that is parked outside.

"Good-bye," they say, waving their hands through the darkened glass.

Song Ying, known to the others as Chinese Girl One, comes from Guangdong Province in southern China. Her father works in a new bank in a large industrial town and is a person of some standing in the local community. Her mother is a teacher. Song Ying is their only child, and they dote on her, sparing no expense, so she was raised with rather an elevated expectation of what her life will be like. She was a bright girl, and they have paid for her to have private lessons. At nineteen, she passed the entrance exams to be accepted into the prestigious Beijing University Business School. Her parents have saved up enough money for the fees. Her courses start in the autumn. Or at least that's when they were due to start.

Sixteen months ago, her mother became pregnant. The authorities had become lax about the one-child rule, and she thought she might get away with it, but recently, in one of their periodic bouts of orthodoxy, they have been tightening up again. She is summoned to the provincial council and given the choice of aborting the fetus or paying a substantial tax. Song Ying's mother uses some of her savings to have an ultrasound scan done privately. The scan tells her that she is carrying a boy. Song Ying's parents discuss the choice facing them late into the night. Her father urges her mother to have the abortion, but her mother weeps so much that in the end he relents. They go ahead and have the child, and they pay the tax.

The tax takes up all the money they have saved for Song Ying's education and more, leaving them in debt. The baby is beautiful. He is spoiled by all the members of the family and grows fat very quickly. Song Ying's mother is happy and hardly notices Song Ying anymore, except to tell her, "Look, you have a beautiful brother. Isn't that enough?" Song Ying's father takes a promotion to help pay the extra tax, and another night job in a restaurant. "Don't worry," he tells his daughter, "I will find you a good job in the bank even without a university degree." Song Ying cries into her pillow at night, but nobody hears.

Then Song Ying learns of a college in England where for a modest fee overseas students can enroll and get a student visa, without having to attend any classes. With a student visa, she can come to Britain to study, and still work part-time. No one will check how many hours she is working. The college will gladly confirm that she is attending classes, so long as she pays the fees. They will even help her find a job. She can work all the hours she likes, and so favorable is the exchange rate with the yuan that, even after paying for the airfare and the college fees, the money she earns will more than fund her first year at the university in Beijing—she does the calculations carefully, for she cannot afford to make a mistake. Then she applies to the college, is accepted, and signs an agreement to pay for her airfare and her fees from the wages she will earn.

The college is not what she expected—it is just some rooms above a betting shop in a shabby street miles from the center of London. There are only four classrooms. Most of the students, like herself, have not come to study. Her job in a busy restaurant often leaves her feeling too tired to concentrate on the few English classes she does attend. Through the college, she meets Soo Lai Bee, a Malaysian Chinese girl, who has enrolled for an English language course (the college does run some genuine courses alongside its other activities). For Song Ying, having grown up without brothers or sisters in the intensely protected environment of her parents' home, to have the company of another girl her age is delightful. They speak the same language, and they have so much to talk about. Soo Lai Bee is sympathetic to her troubles and has problems of her own to share. They become inseparable. When the college puts out information about the strawberry-picking job, and offers to provide (for a fee, of course) the requisite papers declaring that they are students of agriculture, they both decide on the spur of the moment to give it a try.

Although the college found Song Ying the strawberry-picking job, she has not yet earned enough to pay her college fees, let alone saved enough for the university. However, she is hard-working, intelligent, and ambitious. Surely she will find a way to achieve her dream?

To be Chinese in Malaysia you have to be twice as clever and work twice as hard to get anywhere, that's what Soo Lai Bee's father told her. Even then, it's not always enough. So when Soo Lai Bee, known to the others as Chinese Girl Two, got five straight A's in her STPM exams and still failed to get a place in medical school, while a number of Bumiputra Malay students with lower grades got quota places, her hopes were dashed. It's because the Chinese are too successful in Malaysia, her father muttered darkly. If the majority Bumiputra population gets resentful, there will be riots against the Chinese. Look at Indonesia. Even so, it rankled. Her parents, who were ambitious for her, agreed that she should study in England.

Yes, it would cost a lot of money. But her father had funds, having built up a successful family construction business. If you're Chinese in Malaysia, the only way to do business is to team up with a Bumiputra company. They get the contract, under regulations that restrict granting of contracts to non-Malays, then you buy the contract from them. They get the business, you do the work, the law is observed, and everybody is happy.

In fact Soo Lai Bee's father got on quite well with his Bumiputra business partner, Abdul Ismail, who had made his millions selling on Bumiputra-quota car-import permits to the Chinese, and dabbled in construction contracts as a sideline; they even met socially sometimes. It was at one of these gatherings that Soo Lai Bee met Zia Ismail, his son. It was partly the fact that he was Bumiputra that attracted her to him; it was partly the fact that she was not Malay that attracted him to her. It is the privilege of young people to fall in love with the wrong person, and they did.

Abdul Ismail was furious. He gave his business partner an ultimatum: Break up the relationship, or break up the business partnership. Soo Lai Bee wept and wept, but really, there was no choice. Her mother and two older sisters put pressure on her. Her father warned that without the business partnership, and the lucrative public sector contracts, there would be no fees to fund her English university education. Don't worry, I'll wait for you, said Zia Ismail.

Her English medical school place was conditional on her achieving a Grade 7 in the International English Language Test, and her parents thought it best to get her out of the way at once. She signed up with a college for overseas students in London. Within two weeks of her departure for England, Soo Lai Bee learned that Zia was engaged to someone else.

At first she was sad, then she was furious, then she was glad to be away from home and in a new country where nobody cared what race you were. At the college, she made friends with Song Ying, another Chinese girl, who wasn't even studying but just needed a work permit. They talked for hours about mothers, fathers, boyfriends, brothers, sisters, Poles, Ukrainians, Malays, and Englishes. They laughed and cried together. They went off to pick strawberries together. They went off to Amsterdam together.

buttercup meadow

The Majestic Hotel in Shermouth might have been considered luxurious in the 1950s, compared with hotels on the Baltic, but it has seen little by way of refurbishment or even basic maintenance since then. Among its many discomforts are the fact that the lift is broken (Yola and Marta's room is on the fifth floor), the water in the communal bathrooms is turned off after nine p.m. (en suite? You must be joking), and it is infested with cockroaches. They do, however, have a very nice view of the sea.

But the worst thing about the Majestic Hotel is that inside its massive redbrick-Gothic-cockroach-crawling walls are housed some two hundred people, not travelers or holidaymakers, but people trying to live their lives here—migrant workers like themselves, asylum-seekers from every strife-torn corner of the world, homeless families from city slums in England—stacked one above the other like souls in hell, jostling in the queues for the filthy toilets, stealing each other's milk from the mouldy communal fridges, keeping each other awake with their arguments, celebrations, and nightmares.

There are no communal meals and "guests" have to take their meals in cafés or forage for themselves and eat in their own rooms—nice for the cockroaches. And though there is no birdsong, neither is there ever silence; for even in the dead of night there is always someone getting up for an early-morning shift or returning from a late one, playing music or having a fight or making a baby or comforting a crying child, so that the only way to stay sane is to cut yourself off, to block out the crush of humanity pressing in through the walls, the floors, and the ceilings. Yola sums it up in three words: "Too many foreigners."

If this were really Hell, though, there should be devils with pitchforks, thinks Yola. Instead, they have been assigned to share a room with two Slovak women, who are not particularly welcoming to the newcomers, having previously had it to themselves, and who have spread their stuff out and hung their wet underpants to dry all over the place, making the room steamy as well as cluttered. Of course they are not to be blamed that the hotel has no proper laundry facilities, but even worse, in Yola's opinion, is the type of panties they choose to wear, which are of thong design. The uncontrolled way these Slovak women's hefty buttocks bounce around beneath their thongs is deplorable, and Yola cannot for the life of her understand why any woman should choose to inflict such discomfort on herself when generously cut underpants of the white cotton style are universally available, inexpensive, and known to have hygienic advantages, and moreover, contrary to what might be supposed, are considered to be extremely seductive by men of a more refined nature, of whom, she can only suppose, there are precious few in Slovakia.

Marta also views the thong underpants with abhorrence, though for different reasons.

When Yola and Marta were dropped off at the hotel, Tomasz was told to stay in the van, as he was needed at the Sunnydell Chicken Farm and Hatchery in Titchington. He protested vehemently that he only wanted to be with Yola and he didn't care about this new job, he would be happy just to sit with his guitar and sing to her. But the van was already on its way, Yola and Marta waving and disappearing through the rear windows.

"No worry. Not far," said the minibus driver. "You come back when you have good pay in you pocket, then you make good possibility. Heh heh."

For some reason, all the seats of the minibus had been taken out, so the passengers had to squat on the floor. From this position, he couldn't see much of the surroundings, but there were fields, woods, and at one point a glimpse of the sea. Then they were negotiating speed bumps on a long tarmac drive, and they had arrived.

The minibus pulled up in front of a pair of small brick semidetached houses standing in a ragged overgrown garden behind a wooden fence. They should have been charming but, even at first sight, Tomasz felt there was something seedy and forbidding about them. The curtains were drawn, although it was late morning, and there were several overflowing black rubbish bags by the front doors, which tainted the air with a vile smell.

"Here," said the driver, indicating the house on the left. "You stay here." Then, as if to reassure him, he pointed to the house on the right. "And I am stay here."

Tomasz picked up his bag and slung his guitar across his shoulder. Well, to stay in a house at last would be a good change, he thought, and at night at least he could close his eyes and close the door.

"When you ready, you go to office there."

The driver pointed across to a double gate behind which was a wide yard and a low redbrick building with a few vehicles parked outside. Beyond that, up another drive, were several huge green hangar-like buildings, some twenty meters apart. That, Tomasz realized, was where the smell was coming from.

I AM DOG I AM SAD DOG MY GOOD STRONG-FEET-SMELL MAN IS GONE MY PUT-OINTMENT-ON-FOOT FEMALE IS GONE MY GOOD-UNDER-SKIRT-SMELL FEMALE IS GONE ALL GONE AWAY GOOD-BYE DOG THEY SAID GOOD-BYE GOOD DOG I AM GOOD DOG I AM SAD DOG I AM DOG

The smell from the farmyard was bad enough, but Tomasz was not at all prepared for the stench that would hit him when he opened the front door of the little house: It was a smell of dead air, sweat, urine, feces, semen, unwashed hair, stale breath, bad teeth, rotten shoes, dirty clothes, old food, cigarettes, and alcohol. It was the smell of humanity. And even though he himself was more immune than most to these smells, still it made him gasp and cover his nose and mouth with his hand.

There were two rooms downstairs. One, which had its door open, had six chairs around a table on which the greasy remains of a meal were waiting to be cleared away. The other room was at the front, and Tomasz opened the door to a wave of hot, stinking breathed-out air. Inside were six—no, there were seven—sleeping figures curled up on mattresses on the floor, surrounded by their pitiful possessions spilling out of holdalls and carrier bags—a jumble of shoes, clothes, bedding, papers, cigarette packs, bottles, and other human debris. There was a gentle chorus of snoring and snuffling. He backed out quickly and closed the door.

Upstairs was the same. In one room, the smaller of the two, there were four mattresses laid out on the floor, so close that you had to walk over them to get to the other side of the room, and on each mattress was a prone sleeping figure. In the other, larger room, there were six mattresses and six sleeping figures. No—one mattress over in the far corner was unoccupied, and Tomasz realized with a terrible sinking feeling that this was the mattress allocated to him.

He went back downstairs into the dining room, pulled up a chair, and with a feeling of despondency so intense that it was almost pleasurable, he got out his guitar. So this was to be his condition now. What was he but a fragment of broken churned-up humanity washed up on this faraway shore? This was where his journey has brought him.

There must be a song in this.

I was woken up by birdsong, so sweet and close that for a minute I thought I was back at the trailer. I opened my eyes and looked around.

Where was I? Sunlight was streaming in low through a dusty window. Then I remembered: At some point in the night, I'd abandoned the three-legged chair and rolled myself into the plastic sheet on the floor. I must have slept like that. My clothes were still damp. No wonder I felt stiff. I stood up and stretched myself, straightening each arm and leg painfully. *Ujjas!* What a night. I remembered that I'd had a dream—one of those terrifying dreams where you're running and running, but you can't move. One of those dreams that makes you glad to wake up to a sunny morning.

My stomach was rumbling again—the effect of yesterday's chips had worn off. I eased the door open and stepped outside. The rain had passed and the sky was clear, but there were still puddles on the ground. In Kiev, when it rains in the night you wake up to see all the golden domes of the churches washed clean and glittering in the sunlight, and the potholes in the roads full of water. "Mind the puddles, Irina," Mother would say as I set off for school, but I always got splashed.

I was in somebody's garden. The old garage was at the bottom of a long graveled drive. At the end, behind a screen of trees, I could see the chimneys of a big house. My feet crunched on the gravel and somewhere not far away a dog started to bark. Was it on a chain? Was it fierce? I stood still and listened. The barking stopped. Then faint and far away I heard another sound—the drone of a car engine, getting closer.

A few minutes later, I saw the vehicle. It was a white van. I stepped forward and waved. The driver slowed down and waved back. Stupid man—couldn't he see I wasn't just waving for fun? I jumped directly in front, so he had no choice but to screech to a stop. The driver wound his window down and yelled,

"You crazy? What you doing?"

That homey accent! That round face! That dire shirt! I could tell at once that he was Ukrainian. For some stupid reason, I felt tears pricking at the back of my eyes.

"Please," I said in Ukrainian. "Please help me."

He opened the passenger door.

"Get in, girl. Where you want to go?"

I tried to speak, but I found myself sniffling, which was pathetic, because after all I was alive and nothing terrible had happened.

"Okay, girl. You don't cry," said the van driver. "You can come with us."

As the van moved forward I heard voices in the back. I turned in my seat and saw there were about a dozen people, men and women, crouching or squatting on the floor. They were all young. Some were chatting quietly. Some seemed half asleep. They looked like students—they looked quite like me, in fact.

"Hello," I said in Ukrainian. There was a chorus of hellos, some in Ukrainian, some in Polish and a couple of other Slavic languages I couldn't place.

"Strawberry pickers," explained the driver.

"Ah, that's lucky! Me too."

I started to explain about the trailers and the strawberry field, and then suddenly there it was, just flashing past on the right, the little copse, and the gate, and the lovely, familiar south-sloping field. But what had happened to our trailer?

"Stop, please!" I cried. The driver pulled to a halt, shaking his head.

"Stop. Go. Stop. Go. Typical woman."

"Wait. Please. Just one moment!"

I ran back down the lane and opened the gate. The women's trailer had gone—vanished completely. Only the shower screen was still standing, the black plastic flapping forlornly. The men's trailer was there, leaning at an angle. I tiptoed up and peered through the window. It was empty. No one was around. The field was full of ripe strawberries. At the top of the field, I could hear the thrush still sitting there in the copse singing its early-morning song.

I climbed back into the van.

"Stop? Go?" said the van driver.

"Let's go."

After the Chinese girls have gone with Mr. Smith, and Vitaly has taken the Poles to their rendezvous with the van driver (whom he refers to as the "transport manager"), Andriy, Emanuel, and Dog go off for a consolatory ice-cream cone to get away from the heat. They arrange to meet Vitaly later at a pub in town.

Andriy hopes that Vitaly, with his new mobilfon wealth, will stand them a round of drinks, but when he comes back it turns out that unfortunately he has no cash on him, so from what is left of his two weeks' wages, Andriy has to pay for two small beers for himself and Emanuel and a double scotch with Coke for Vitaly.

They take their drinks through a door marked Beer Garden into a dank courtyard full of empty beer barrels, where the sun barely peeps above high brick walls that are covered with dismal, sooty ivy. They are the only people there. Dog finds the remains of a sandwich wrapped in a paper napkin under one of the tables, and gobbles it up, spreading crumbs and shreds of paper everywhere. Emanuel and Andriy sip their beers slowly to make them last.

At once Vitaly wants to know what has become of Irina, and there is an annoying presumptuousness about the way he talks, moving seamlessly between Russian and English.

"I thought you and she would be making possibility by now. I could find her very nice job in London. Dancing. Can she dance? Good pay. Luxury accommodation."

When Andriy tells him about the night-time abduction, he whistles between his teeth.

"That Mr. Vulk is a no-no-good. He brings bad reputation to profession of recruitment consultant."

"He is recruitment consultant?"

"Yes of course. But not same like me. Not employment solution consultant with capacity for advance meeting flexi. He is more interested to make overseas contact. My contact is to find work for people when they arrive on ferry. Dynamic cutting solution to all organization staffing."

"And he is living here in Dover?"

"In some hotel, not far away, I think."

"Can you take me to him?"

"Aha! I see you are still thinking of making possibility with this Ukrainian girl."

Andriy gives a studied shrug. "Well, of course I would be interested to know where she is. But she already has boyfriend, I think. Boxing champion."

Vitaly gives him a funny look. "Boxing? This is unusual for high-class girl. Angliski?"

"Maybe. I think so." He too has his doubts about this boyfriend.

He feels unaccountably furious with Vitaly. Where did he get these clothes, these sunglasses, this phone? And how all the women were dancing around him at the ferry terminal! It couldn't have been just the markup on the beer at the trailer, could it? And why did he keep it all to himself? The strawberry pickers shared everything, but Vitaly had been secretly keeping something aside for himself all the time. And how quickly this transformation from equal to superior had taken place. Devil's bum! It had happened overnight. Of course he had lived through a time like this in Ukraine—one day they were all comrades, next day some were millionaires and the rest had . . . coupons. How had it happened? No one knew. It left a bad taste in the mouth.

And what can you do with coupons? You can't eat them. You can't spend them. All you can do is sell them. But who will want to buy? Suddenly, the millionaires were all billionaires, and the rest had enough for a load of coal to see you through the winter and that was it, bye-bye, end of story. Now the whole country was run by mobilfonmen.

And this Vitaly—if he finds this Irina, will he ring you on mobilfon and say, hey, Andriy, my friend, come and make possibility? Unlikely. And what would she think of this new recruit-consult mobilfonman Vitaly? She considers herself so superior—the new high-spec Ukrainian girl—maybe the new Vitaly will just be in her category. Hello, mobilfon businessman—this is Irina calling—can we make a possibility? And if she makes a possibility with Vitaly, what does it matter to you, Palenko? Now he feels irrationally, fumingly angry with Irina as well as with Vitaly.

"And I have an Angliska girl," he adds pointedly to Vitaly. "Vagvaga Riskegipd. In Sheffield. I am on my way to find her."

Vitaly gives him another odd look.

"Listen, my friend, if I see Vulk, I will ask him what happened to this Ukrainian girl."

He almost hopes that Vitaly will offer him a job—good pay, luxury accommodation, et cetera—just so that he can have the pleasure of turning it down. But he doesn't, and Andriy's pride won't let him ask. They arrange to meet in the same pub at the same time tomorrow. As Vitaly strolls away, he takes his mobilfon out of his pocket and starts to talk, waving his free hand up and down for emphasis. Andriy tries to make out what language he is speaking.

The sun is blazing at full heat, cutting short hard shadows onto the cracked pavements. He wanders back toward the trailer with Dog and Emanuel, still feeling irritable and resenting the money he spent on Vitaly's double scotch. Worse than that, he feels shabby, poor, and unattractive. Is he jealous of Vitaly? How shameful it is to be jealous of someone who is inferior in every way, except that he has a mobilfon and better trousers. This is what Vitaly has done to him. This is what Vitaly and Irina between them have done to him. Yes, he thought Vitaly was his friend, and all the time he was taking a bit on the side. Well, here are his true friends. Hey, Dog! But Dog is off on a trail of lamp posts. Hey, Emanuel! Emanuel has found a half-full packet of smoky-bacon flavored chips in the beer garden, which he shares with Andriy, shaking out the last bits into his hand. The artificially flavored salt dissolves on his tongue, tasty and toxic.

"Hey, Emanuel. You like fishing? Maybe we have big luck."

"Sikomo. Fishing is very interesting. But where will we attain good nettings?" Emanuel starts to sing, "*I will make you fishers of men.*"

They stroll down to the pier together. The Bulgarian lad who sold him the fish yesterday said this was the best way in town of making quick money. Down a side street, in a maze of car and lorry parks not far from where they left their trailer, they find the entrance to the Admiralty Pier. It must have once been quite a grand structure, but now the ornate cast iron is decrepit and grimy, covered in pigeon droppings, and a few dead pigeons fester where they have dropped behind the barriers. The stench hits you when you walk in.

A couple of men are hanging around at the entrance with a selection of rods and buckets, some blue, some yellow.

"You wanna buy or rent?" asks the older of the two, who is wearing a black woolly hat pulled down over his ears, despite the heat, and a black vest that reveals arms and shoulders covered with an incredible array of tattoos. "Rent is five quid a day. Or you can buy it for twenty-five quid. Superior tackle. Great investment. Pays for itself in five days, and from then on it's sheer profit. Are you gonna be here for a few days?"

The man is talking too fast. It is stretching Andriy's English to its limit. What is the price? he wonders.

"What it is?"

"Quality tackle. As used by all the top competitive fishermen. Fella caught a twenty-five-pound cod off of here the other day. Got fifty quid for it. Cash in hand." He looks Andriy and Emanuel up and down, as if appraising their fishing potential.

"Put food on yer table every night, and the surplus you can sell to us. A quid a kilo. Easy money. No tax. No questions asked. Yours to spend as you wish. Just five quid for the day. Try it out."

Andriy picks up a rod and examines it. He hasn't been fishing since he was a kid, but it can't be so difficult—that Bulgarian lad didn't look particularly bright.

"Five quids? Five pounds?"

"That's it, mate. Big shoal of mackerel coming in with the tide. You'll cover the cost in no time, and then all the rest's yours to take home to the missus."

Andriy hands over his five pounds. The man gives him a rod and a blue bucket.

As the Ukrainian driver pulled in through the gate, I saw the gleaming white field that I'd spotted from the hillside yesterday. It had looked as though it were covered with plastic, and it turned out to be just that—rows upon rows of tunnels made out of polythene sheeting stretched over metal hoops. Down the center of each tunnel was a row of straw bales, with bags of compost on them, planted with strawberries. It was like a whole garden under cover. The air was humid and warm, sweet with the scent of ripe strawberries, and another sickly chemical smell that clung to the roof of my mouth. Despite the smell, I was so hungry I couldn't help myself—I reached out and started cramming the strawberries in my mouth. The others laughed.

"You can't be a real strawberry picker, Irina! We're not allowed to eat them. They'll sack you if they catch you," said Oksana, who seemed to have taken me under her wing. Oksana was from Kharkiv, a bit older than me, and nice, though not very cultured—but all that seemed much less important now.

The supervisor, Boris, was also Ukrainian. He was a bit fat, and not too bright, with a thick Zaporizhzhia accent. He kept looking at me and saying if I proved myself today he'd put in a good word for me and sort out my paperwork when we got back to the office. He was sure they'd take me on, because the warm weather has caused the strawberries to ripen early and—this was the third time he'd said this, what was the matter with him?—he'd put in a good word for me.

When he told me the wages, I couldn't believe it. It was twice what we got at the other place, and I started thinking about all the things I would buy—some lovely scented soap, nice shampoo, new underpants—little sexy ones that Mother would detest—a massive bar of chocolate, some strappy sandals, and I needed a hairbrush, a new T-shirt, maybe two, a warmer jumper, and don't forget a present to take back for Mother. And the picking was so easy; no bending, no lifting. Yes, I thought, I'm lucky to get this chance, and I'd better make the most of it, so I picked like crazy, because I had to prove myself.

At the end of the shift, when we went back to the strawberry farm, Boris came up and said it was time for me to prove myself. Then he pushed himself up against me in a disgusting way and kissed me on the mouth, with wet slimy kisses. I wasn't frightened—Boris just seemed stupid and harmless—so I made myself go limp and let him kiss me, because I really really wanted this job. His gaspy breathing on my face made me feel cold inside. On the scale of sex appeal I would give him a zero. Okay, it's a transaction, nothing more, I told myself. I tried to imagine Natasha and Pierre kissing, lost in each other. Were men different in those days? When he'd finished, I wiped my mouth on my T-shirt and followed him up the stairs to the office.

Andriy walks down the Admiralty Pier with his rod and blue bucket in his hands and Emanuel at his side. The pier is a bleak span of concrete almost a kilometer long, reaching like a crooked dog-leg out into the sea, and every meter seems to be occupied by a fisherman, bucket at his feet, rod or line pitched over the water, staring out over the waves. In some of the buckets there are a few small fishes, but nothing to speak of.

About halfway along the first leg, Andriy and Emanuel come across the Bulgarian lad who sold Andriy the fish. He introduces his two friends, who are Romanian and Moldovan.

"Usually two or three of us here," says the Bulgarian. "Next few meters is Baltics. Fish fryers. Up there"—he points for Andriy's benefit—"Ukrainians and Byelorussians. Beetroot eaters. Over there"—he points for Emanuel's benefit—"we even have Africa. God knows what they eat. Down that end are Balkans—Serbs, Croats, Albanians. Best steer clear of those. Too much fighting."

"And Angliski fishermen?"

The Bulgarian lad points to the end of the pier.

"That's where all Angliskis go. Right up to end. Past Balkans. You can tell which is Angliski. Every one wears woolen hat. Even women. Pulled down over ears. Even in summer. Very good at fishing."

"You get good fishing?"

"Plenty. Plenty fish everywhere. Easy money."

Andriy glances down into the lad's bucket. There are a few minnows. Who does he think he's kidding?

"How long you been doing this fishy thing?"

The lad looked shifty. "Few days."

"Where you get this fish line and bucket?"

"Man by pier. Same like you. Easy money."

"Easy for him."

The Bulgarian lad looks away and fiddles with his fishing rod. Andriy feels like thumping him, but what's the point?

"He says plenty plenty mackerel coming this morning," the lad calls plaintively to Andriy's disappearing back. Poor mutt, doesn't even realize it's the afternoon.

"I go find Africa!" Emanuel heads off toward the two black figures hunched over their rod near the angle of the dog-leg. Andriy picks up his bucket and rod and goes off to find the Ukrainians. They are two thin-faced youths, one with a shaven knobby head, one with a sticking-up Klitschko–style crew cut.

"Hi lads."

"Hi mate."

"Any luck?"

"Not much."

In fact, judging from the content of their buckets, none at all.

"Where you from?"

"Vinnitsa. You?"

"Donetsk."

Andriy positions himself in the small gap beside them and takes a look at his rod—he's paid for it, so he'd better try to get his money's worth. Then he realizes he didn't get any bait. He asks the lads if he can borrow some.

"No need for bait. Just stick feather. Mackerel go for feather. They think it's fish," says the knobby-headed one.

"Must be bit stupid."

"Yeah. Huh huh huh," the lad snickers.

"Does anyone ever catch anything?"

"Yeah. 'Course. They must do."

"I mean, enough to pay for rod and bucket?"

"Yeah, I reckon somebody must. Why d'you get blue bucket?"

He notices their bucket is yellow.

"Blue, yellow. What's the difference?"

"Blue is you rent. You give back at end of day. Yellow is you keep. Use every day."

"You mean I give back bucket at end of day? Even if I catch nothing?"

"Maybe you are his fish, and he has caught you." The knobby-headed lad grins. "Not even with any feather. Huh huh huh."

"Devil's bum!"

Andriy looks up and down the pier. There are mostly yellow buckets, a few blue ones, and some buckets of other colors, red, green, black, gray. Really you've got no one but yourself to blame, Andriy Palenko, for listening to that moon-faced cretin. He counts the yellow and blue buckets and tries to calculate how much profit Mr. Tattoo has made in a day. Easy money.

Over in Africa, Emanuel seems to have been abandoned by the others and left in charge of their fishing gear. What's going on? There is something about Emanuel that brings out a protective impulse in Andriy: He too is an innocent soul lost in this mobilfon world. Andriy gives him a thumbs-up sign, but Emanuel doesn't notice. He is staring intently at the sea.

Andriy also stares down at the waves, their dismal, unpromising churning, their slap and gurgle against the concrete, the obscure and disgusting-looking bits of debris that come to the surface from time to time. The sea is very overrated, he thinks.

The next time he catches Emanuel's eye, Emanuel is looking agitated and beckons him over. He seems quite distressed.

"Africa Mozambique men say please look after our fishy things, we go for toilet. One hour. Two hour. Still not coming back."

What on earth is he talking about?

"No problem, friend." Andriy lays a soothing hand on his arm. "Everything normal."

This is strange, he thinks. Why is this bucket red?

After a couple of hours, the Mozambicans have still not come back and the two Ukrainian lads, having caught four fish between them, are celebrating with a rolled-up cigarette and a bottle of beer and then a few more bottles. They offer him a bottle, but he shakes his head. He likes a beer as much as the next man, but there's something desperate about the way these lads are drinking. He's seen it on the Donets often enough—a lad has a beer, then a few more, then for a laugh he jumps into the river to cool off, and that's it: bye-bye, body never found, end of story.

A cool breeze has sprung up, and those that have brought jackets zip them up; those that haven't, including Andriy and Emanuel, start to shiver. The slap and gurgle of the sea gets stronger, and sometimes a spray of water splashes over them. The tide has come up. At one point there is a ripple of excitement along the pier. A shoal of mackerel has been spotted and is definitely on its way. But it never seems to arrive.

As evening approaches, most of the fishermen are ready to call it a day. There have been a few bigger fish caught up at the Angliski end; the Balkans, too, have had a run of luck, and a fight has broken out over who gets what. Andriy still hasn't caught anything.

"Hey, pal," says the Klitschko—crew-cut Ukrainian, "you should keep on to that rod and bucket. Why give it back to Mr. Tattoo? Then at least you get something for your money. Five quids is robbery. Better get yellow like us next time. Investing for future."

Hm. There seems to be some logic in what the Ukrainian is saying.

"But Tattoo man waiting for us at end of pier?"

"You can get past him easy. Look, Ukrainian boy, we help you a bit. We put your blue bucket inside our yellow one." He takes the bucket and with a quick slop transfers the four little fishes. "See? We take one rod each. We meet you at pub—over there." He points. "You buy us pint of beer, and rod and bucket will be for you to keep." He gives a big toothy grin. "Okay?"

"Okay."

Andriy wonders if there's a catch, but if you can't trust a fellow Ukrainian, who can you trust?

Suddenly he hears a shout from the Africa sector of the pier.

"Reel it in! Turn the reel!" A big man in a woolly hat is instructing Emanuel, who is wrestling with a rod that is bent right over into an arc. He starts to turn the reel, but it seems stuck and he starts to tug and jerk.

"Steady steady," says the woolly-hat. "Wind her in gently."

Emanuel starts to wind again; then something great and silver breaks the surface of the water, thrashing and splashing against the waves. There is a stir of excitement from the other fishermen, and suddenly everyone has gathered around to watch. The creature is massive, wild, and fighting for its life. Carefully, Emanuel reels it in, then with an incredible flip lands it on the pier, where it bucks and slaps against the concrete.

"Get it in the bucket!" someone shouts, but it is too big for the bucket.

"Haven't you got a net?" someone else shouts.

"Or a knife? Get a knife to it!"

"No!" cries Emanuel.

He puts the still-trembling fish into the Mozambican's red bucket, nose down in a few inches of water, its huge tail bent sideways and quivering above the rim. Andriy pushes through the crowd to pat him on the back.

"Good job, my friend. We sell this fish make good money."

Several woolly-hats have arrived on the scene, and everyone is talking excitedly about how much the fish will weigh, with the highest bid coming in at twelve kilos.

Mr. Tattoo is waiting at the exit, stopping people with blue buckets as they come out. His sidekick has a spring scale and they are weighing the puny catches and doling out puny amounts of money. His eyes light up when they see the giant fish in Emanuel's bucket.

"Nice bit of cod you got there, mate. Big as a nigger's dick," says Mr. Tattoo. "Unusual for this time of year. Want to stick it on the scale?"

"This fish is not for selling. Is for me," says Emanuel with emphasis. "I catch. I keep."

Mr. Tattoo's eyes narrow. The mermaid on his bicep seems to frown.

"Fair enough, mate. Catchers keepers. It's a free country. But you got to give your rod and bucket back now."

He reaches for the rod. Emanuel grips it tighter.

"No! This is rod and bucket of Mozambique Africa men."

A small crowd has gathered. Andriy loiters on the edge of the crowd, trying to make himself invisible.

"What about the gear we rented you?" Mr. Tattoo can't take his eyes off the fish. "You got to give it back now, chum. Givee backee bucketee. Or givee fishee. Comprenday?" He has raised his voice.

"No!" Emanuel is getting flustered. "This bucketee is of my Mozambique friends go toilet."

Mr. Tattoo grimaces. "Yuk! That's disgusting. Don't you black-boys get potty-trained? There's toilets at the end of the pier."

Pleased with himself, he looks around the crowd for approval. Andriy is keeping his head down. He is waiting for the moment to melt away and get out of the quay unnoticed, but the sidekick spots him and makes as if to grab him.

"There he is. That's him what got the gear off of us."

"That was not me. That must be other Ukrainian." Andriy sidesteps quickly. "The one that was with dog." He wants to make a run for it, but he can't abandon Emanuel.

From the corner of his eye he can see that the other Ukrainians have cleared the quayside and are making their way over the intersection, his blue bucket cunningly concealed inside their yellow one.

Another woolly-hat fisherman steps forward from the crowd and challenges Mr. Tattoo.

"Let him have the fish, Bert. A fisherman's got to keep his catch."

"You keep out of it, Derek," says Mr. Bert Tattoo. "The bugger's trying to nick off with me tackle. And he's been using the bucket for a toilet."

He looms over Emanuel menacingly and grabs the handle of the bucket.

"Give me the tackle or give me the fish. Tidge, sort him out."

Tidge steps forward menacingly.

"Hang on a minute, Bert. That ent your bucket. It's a red one. It must be one of Charlie's."

The Bulgarian lad, who has been waiting for his catch to be weighed, is getting impatient, and now he pushes forward and tries to slip his three measly minnows on the scale. But Mr. Tattoo is having none of it.

"Dogfish. No use to me. I told you yesterday. Are yer thick, or what? Eat 'em yerself. Or give 'em to the dog."

As if summoned, suddenly Dog appears across the road, wagging his tail.

Andriy sees Dog. He also sees that the two Ukrainians have walked right past the pub and are heading off up the road. They have broken into a trot. Devil's bum! The thieving rat-faced scoundrels!

He breaks out of the crowd, grabs Emanuel's fish out of the bucket, and starts to run after them.

"Here, give me that fish!", yells Mr. Tattoo, dropping the bucket and lunging forward. He grabs hold of its tail. It slithers out of Andriy's hand, and then, as if alive, it skips out of Mr. Tattoo's hand too and slides across the ground flapping its tail. A dozen hands reach for it at once.

"Let the fisherman keep his catch! It's a lawful size!" shouts Derek.

"That red bucket must be one of Charlie's. Before 'e kicked it. God rest his soul!" cries another woolly-hat.

Bending and shoving like a rugby scrimmage, they try to grasp the fish, which is still thrashing about between their feet. Dog watches with interest from the sidelines. It seems as though Mr. Tattoo has it at last, but he can't get a grip on it. Then suddenly, like the cavalry charging in, Dog launches himself from the edge of the action, makes a low tackle between the legs, grabs the fish in his jaws, and he's off.

I AM DOG I RUN I RUN WITH FISH FOR MY MAN BIG LIVE FISH FLAP FLAP I HOLD IT TIGHT IN MOUTH TAKE CARE NO BITING GOOD DOG MY MAN LIKES FISH I WILL BRING THIS FISH TO MY MAN I RUN MEN RUN AFTER ME BIG PISS-ON-TROUSER MAN RUNS AFTER ME HE SHOUTS I RUN FASTER I RUN ON ROAD I RUN ON SMALL STONES BESIDE BIG WATER RUNNING MEN ARE FAR BEHIND HERE IS ONLY BIG WATER I SLOW I TURN I WALK I WILL BRING THIS FISH LIVE TO MY MAN I WALK BESIDE BIG WATER THIS WATER IS BAD IT JUMPS AT ME WITH SNAKE NOISE SSSS FEET WET I BARK WOOF OFF I BARK MOUTH OPEN FISH JUMPS OUT OF MOUTH INTO BIG WATER FLAP FLAP SSSS WOOF FLAP SSSS BIG WATER SWALLOWS FISH ALL GONE I HAVE NO FISH FOR MY MAN I AM SAD DOG I RUN HOME I RUN I AM DOG

Andriy is sitting on the step of the trailer by the beach waiting for Emanuel and Dog. His forehead is covered in sweat. He is drinking water out of a bottle and brooding darkly on the events of the afternoon. He caught those lads; he ran all the way up the hill after them, and he caught them and asked for his gear back. And they just laughed at him. Rat-faced thieving Ukrainian scum. And when he made a grab for the bucket, the lad with the Klitschko crew cut drew a knife on him. Well, he backed off, of course. He wasn't going to risk his life for a stolen blue bucket. But the incident left him feeling depressed. What's happening to his country? What's happening everywhere? His dad is dead and all his dreams and ideals are dead with him: solidarity, humanity, self-respect. All the things he believed in have turned to dust, and the new world is run by mobilfonmen.

Later, when Emanuel comes back with the Mozambicans' rod and bucket, he brightens up a bit.

Dear Sister

I am now in Dover. All the mzungus expecting Andree have departed and in place of picking strawberries I am now a fisherman. This stirs me up with memories of our happy childhood days beside the Shire River and I wonder what has become of you my sister and whether we will ever meet again. If my letters receive you please come to Dover where you will find me always on the pier for I have become like one of the Disciples of Our Lord at Galilee but our fishing here is not with netting but with rods. When we came upon the pier we met a mzungu who had an outstanding tattoo on his arm it was a picture of a woman who was half a fish combing her hair and looking in a mirror shaped like a heart. The fulsome wavings of the woman's hair obscured her nakedness and down below were modest fish scales which glimmered as the mzungu moved his arm. And a story fizzed into my memory told by some fishermen who adventured on the Mozambican shore of our lake of a beauteous woman whose bottom half is fish who sits on a rock and lures sailors to their deaths. Could this be the same one!!!

And on this pier I fell into the company of some Mozambican fishermen who were friends of our cousin Simeon's brother-in-law in Cobue. And after some chatter they confided their rod and bucket to me and went away. When they did not return I was confounded for I could not leave their things having in memory the Chichewa saying a man's rod is his dearest treasure and I prayed for their return. After some whilings a great fish came upon my rod which made me tremble for this fish resembled the beauteous woman of the story and it was an outstanding big job to lift her from the sea with all the mzungus crowding round and shouting in their languages. As her flappings became weaker I put her in a bucket of water for she was tormented in breathing and I wondered again about the

Mozambicans was she my fish or theirs??? For she was the most respelendent fish I have ever met and reminded me of the woman in the story.

And this question was subtly resolved by the dog who grabbed the fish in his jaws and put her back in the sea. And every day since then I have come to the pier with the bucket and rod of the Mozambicans but neither they nor the fish have ever returned.

The office was through a door across the courtyard. Tomasz thought at first that there was no one there, then a tall skinny man with a terrible rash of acne on his cheeks popped up behind the desk. He looked delighted to see Tomasz.

"Yes, mate, right. You've come at the right time. I'm Darren Kinsman, the foreman. We've got another bloody supermarket promotion starts next week—buy one get one free—and we're short of hands for the catching team. We usually do it at night, but the team's got another job at Ladywash and they've got to get going. It's easy. All you got to do is catch the birds and load them onto the lorries. Nothing to it. My boy Neil'll show you the ropes. Start in half an hour."

"No problem." Tomasz wondered when would be the right moment to raise the question of his accommodations.

"Then all you have to do is scrub out the barn for the next crop. Nothing to it."

"How many chicken?"

"Plenty. Forty thousand."

"Ah." Tomasz tried to imagine forty thousand chickens, but his imagination failed.

"Where you from, pal? Ukraine? You got papers? SAWS? Concordia?"

"Poland."

"Poland, eh? You won't need papers then. Don't get many from there now. Not since they joined Europe. Listen, pal—what's your name?" He glances down at the passport Tomasz has pushed across the desk. "Tomasz?—you work for the agency, not for us, if anybody asks you, okay?

You get six quid an hour, but for every hour you work you do another voluntary, okay?"

"So is six quids for one hour, or two hour?"

"No, six quid an hour. The other hour is voluntary, like I said. You don't have to do it. There's always plenty that do. Ukrainians, Romanians, Bulgarians, Albanians, Brazilians, Mexicans, Kenyans, Zimbabweans, you lose track. Jabber jabber jabber around here. Day and night. It's like United bloody Nations. We used to get a lot of Lithuanians and Latvians, but Europe ruined all that. Made 'em all legal. Like the Poles. Waste of bloody time. Started asking for minimum wages. Chinesers are the best. No papers. No speekee English. No fuckin' clue what's goin' on. Mind you, some folks do take advantage. Like them poor bleeders down at Morecambe. Jabber jabber jabber into the mobile phone, tide comin' in, and nobody's got a clue what they're on about. What's the point of having foreigners if you got to pay 'em same as English, eh? That's why we went over to the agency. Let them take care of all that."

Darren finished the paperwork and with a flourish thrust the passport back across the desk to Tomasz. Tomasz understood from this that he was now in some oblique way employed by Vitaly. He was getting a bad feeling about this job.

"And accommodation is provided?"

"By another agency. Well, it's the same, really. They'll deduct that from your wages, so you don't have to worry about it. Health. Tax. Insurance. Transport. They take care of all that for you."

"And the house is this one. . . ." he pointed across the road.

"That's it, pal. On the left. Didn't Milo take you there?"

"Yes, I saw. It was very full."

"Don't worry about that. They'll all be gone by seven o'clock. They're the night shift. We bus 'em off to Shermouth."

"I'll put a good word in for you, Irina." Boris led me up the steps to the office at the Sherbury strawberry farm. Obviously he thought I'd proved myself sufficiently. Next time he tried anything, I'd put a knee in his gut.

The first thing the woman at the desk asked was, "Have you got your papers? I need your passport and a valid Seasonal Agricultural Worker's certificate."

I explained that all my papers had been stolen. She raised her eyebrows, if you can call them that, though they were really just two little arches drawn in pencil.

"The agent who brought me here. He tried . . . He wanted . . . He took me. . . ."

I didn't know the English words to explain the horror of it. "He kept my papers."

The woman nodded. "Some agents do, though they're not supposed to. We'll have to sort it out if you want to work at Sherbury. We don't do illegals here. Some supermarkets get a bit funny. Leave it to me. I'll have to make some phone calls. Do you remember the agent's name?"

"Vulk. His name was Vulk." Just saying it made me shudder.

"I think I've heard the name. And the farmer?"

"Leapish. Not far away from here."

The little bald eyebrows bounced up again. In my opinion, people should leave their eyebrows alone.

"The one who was run down by his strawberry pickers? Did you have anything to do with that?"

"Oh, no. I had no idea. It must have happened after I left."

Okay, so it was a lie, but only a small one.

"So why did you leave?"

"Not enough ripe strawberries to pick. I wanted to earn more money."

Okay, two small lies. The woman nodded. She seemed happy with my answer.

"You'll earn good money here. After expenses." That word again! "Mind you, I wouldn't be surprised if they used a crooked agent. There was some funny goings-on on that farm." The woman dropped her voice.

"They say that Lawrence Leapish was having it off with one of the pickers, and Wendy Leapish had a Moldavian toy boy."

What on earth, I wondered, was a Moldavian toy boy?

"They say that after her husband came out of hospital, she sat him in the wheelchair and let him watch their carrying-ons. Can you believe it—here in Sherbury?"

"That also must have happened after I left."

The arch-eyebrowed woman scribbled some notes. I have seen a number of eyebrow disasters in Ukraine, including Aunty Vera's, but these were among the worst. She gave me a temporary number, until my paperwork was sorted out, and assigned me to an empty bunk in trailer thirty-six, with Oksana. There were two other Ukrainian girls there too, all ex-factory workers from a closed footwear factory at Kharkiv that used to supply boots to the Soviet army, and they all had certificates from the same nonexistent agricultural college as me.

"Welcome to the crazyhouse," said Lena, who was the youngest of the four, with very dark sad eyes and hair cropped like a boy's. She produced a bottle of vodka from her locker and passed it around. I was going to say "No thanks," but instead I said "What the hell" and took a large gulp.

See, Mother, Papa? I'm okay. Everything's okay. As soon as I could get to a phone, I'd ring them. I wondered what had happened to the picture of them that I'd stuck on the wall of the trailer. I wondered what had happened to the trailer, and the people—the Chinese girls whose bed I'd shared; Marta who was so kind; the nice-looking Ukrainian miner from Donetsk. Would I ever see them again?

Tomasz had found it hard to imagine what forty thousand chickens would look like, and even after he has seen them with his own eyes, he still can't quite believe what he has seen.

When Neil opens the door of the barn for him to look inside, a wave of heat and stench hits him, and in the half darkness he sees just a thick carpet of white feathers; then as Neil turns up the light, the carpet seems to be moving; no, crawling; no, seething. They are so tightly packed you can't make out where one chicken ends and the next begins. And the smell! It hits him in the eyes as well as the nose—a rank cloud of raw ammonia that makes his eyes burn, and he coughs and backs away from the door, his hand over his mouth. He has seen paintings of the damned souls in hell, but they are nothing compared to this.

"Plenty of chickens, eh?" says Neil, who has been assigned to look after him. He is Darren's son, seventeen years old, skinny and tall like his father, and with the same acne problems. "So that's all you got to do—grab 'em by the legs, four or five at a time, and stuff 'em in these cages. That's all there is to it." He slams the door of the barn.

"Plenty. Too much plenty."

"Yeah, too much plenty. Heh heh heh." The lad chuckles. "That's good. It's because they grow too fat. They start off as little yeller chicks, and in six weeks they're like this—too fat to walk around on their own two feet. Mind you, you see people like that, don't you? Fat bastards. Did you read about that woman who had to have two seats on a plane and they charged her double fare?"

"Double fare?" Tomasz wishes the lad wouldn't talk so fast.

"You can get some overalls at the office."

"But this is normal?"

Tomasz still cannot take in what he has seen. Just in the area in front of him—in about a square meter—Tomasz counted one, two, three . . . twenty chickens, all jostling together, desperate to get out of the way of the men. Yes, they call them chickens, but their bodies look more like misshapen ducks—huge bloated bodies on top of stunted little legs, so that they seemed to be staggering grotesquely under their own weight—those of them that can move at all.

"Yeah, they breed 'em like that to get fat, like, quicker." Neil pulls a pack of cigarettes out of his pocket, puts one between his lips, and offers one to Tomasz. Tomasz shakes his head. Neil lights the cigarette with a match, puffing lots of smoke out, and at once starts coughing and sputtering. "It's the supermarkets, see? They go for big breasts. Like fellers, eh?" Cough cough. "Did you see that woman on *Big Brother*?"

"Who is big brother?"

"Don't you know *Big Brother*? What do they have on telly where you come from? It's where they lock 'em all up together in a house, and you can watch 'em."

"Chickens?"

"Yeah, yeah, just like chickens. I like that." The lad chuckles again. Actually, he's quite a nice lad, thinks Tomasz. Friendly and talkative. About the same age as Emanuel, with the same gawky innocence. "And there's this voice that's, like, telling 'em, like, what they've got to do. And they're not supposed to have sex, but one of 'em did—that one with the big, like, knockers I was telling you about."

"Big like knocker?"

"Yeah, massive."

"But how can they walk when the breasts are so large? How can you tend so many?"

The lad gives him an odd look.

"Is that like . . . what 'appens . . . like . . . in your country?"

"In Poland everybody—"

"Poland?" There is a note of awe in the lad's voice. "Wow. Never been there. So the women've all got big knockers?"

"Yes, many people has. Keep it in shed at side of house."

"Oh, you mean chickens." A flush of enlightenment creeps over his youthful face.

"Of course. We have to look after it."

"Oh, it's all taken care of, in here." The lad looks oddly disappointed. "See them pipes? That's where the water comes in, see? And the food comes in down there. As much as they can eat, 'cause they want to fatten 'em up fast. Fast food, eh? Geddit? They keep the lights on low, so they never stop for a nap—just keep on feeding all night. Bit like eating pizza in front of the telly. The low lights calm 'em down. That's why they usually catch 'em at night. It's all scientific, like."

"But so many together—this cannot be healthy."

"Yeah, it's all taken care of. They mix the feed with that anti-bio stuff, like, to stop 'em getting sick. Better than't National Elf, really, everyfink provided. Best thing is, when you eat the chicken, you get all the anti-bio, so it keeps you elfy too, if you fink about it. Prevention is better than cure, as my nan says. Like Guinness."

"And cleaning up mess?"

"Nah, they don't do that. Can't get to the floor. Too many birds. Can't get in. Just leave it. They just have to walk about in it. Chicken shit. Burns their arses, and their legs. Who'd be a chicken?" As he talks, he is zipping himself into blue nylon overalls. "You don't want to get it on your shoes. Go right over the top. Burn yer socks off. After they've gone, that's when you go in to clean it all out, ready for the next crop."

"Crop?"

"Yeah, it's what they call 'em. Funny, innit? You'd think it was vegetables or somefink. Not somefink alive. But vegetables is alive, ent they? Are they? I dunno." He scratches his head and takes another drag on his cigarette. "Vegetables." Cough, cough. "One of life's great mysteries."

Then he stubs out the cigarette and carefully returns the unsmoked half to the pack. "I'm just taking it up, like, steady, a few puffs at a time," he explains. "Building up to full strengf. Anyway, you'll need some overalls, pal. What's your name?"

"Tomasz. My friends call me Tomek."

"Tom—Mick . . . whatever. Mind if I just call you Mick? You'll need some overalls, Mick. Let's go see if there's any left."

They walk across to the office. At the back is a storeroom, and there is a pair of blue nylon overalls hanging on a peg above a bench on which is scattered a jumble of male clothing.

"We're in luck," says Neil.

Tomasz zips himself in. The overalls are too short in the leg and nip around the crotch. Neil looks him up and down critically.

"Not bad. Yer a bit big for 'em. Here, you'll need these." He passes Tomasz a ragged pair of leather gauntlets, and puts a pair on himself. "And some boots."

There is only one boot left, a green one, though fortunately it is the right size.

"One's better than none," says Neil. "Count yer blessings. . . . D'you remember that song? My nan sings that all the time. When she's not singing hymns. She's very, like, Christian, my nan. Always says a prayer for the chickens. But she likes her Guinness. You'll have to meet her."

"I would very much like to."

Neil hunts around and eventually finds a black Wellington boot under the desk in the office, which is a smaller size. This is becoming quite a regular thing with me, thinks Tomasz, stowing his odd-sized sneakers under the bench and putting on the odd-sized boots. Maybe it is a sign of something.

He walks back to the barn stiffly because of the tightness in the left boot and crotch.

"Ready?" says Neil. "You'll soon get the hang of it. We'll have a practice before the team gets here. In we go."

He opens the barn door and they wade into the roiling sea of chickens. The chickens squawk and screech and try to flap out of their way, but there is nowhere for them to go. They try to flutter upward but their wings are too weak for their overgrown bodies and they just scramble desperately on top of one another, kicking up a terrible stinking dust of feathers and feces. Tomasz feels something live crunch under his foot and hears a squawk of pain. He must have stepped on one, but really it is impossible not to.

"Grab 'em by the legs!" yells Neil, through the inferno of screeching and feathers and flying fecal matter. "Like this!"

He raises his left hand, in which he is holding five chickens, each by one leg. The terrified birds twist and flap, shitting themselves with fear, then they seem to give up and hang limply.

"See, it calms 'em down, holding 'em upside down."

There is a snap, and one of the five flops and sags, its thigh dislocated, its wings still beating. At one end of the barn is a stack of plastic crates. Neil slides one out, thrusts the birds in, and pushes it shut. Then he wades into the melee for another five.

Tomasz steels himself and reaches down into the seething mass of chickens, holding his breath and closing his eyes. He grabs and gets hold of something—it must have been a wing—and the bird struggles and squeaks so pitifully in his hands that he lets go. He grabs again, and this time he gets the legs and hoists the poor creature up into the air, and not wanting to risk losing it, stuffs it straight into a cage. Then another. Then he manages to get two at a time, and then three. He can't hold more than that, because he cannot bring himself to hold them by just one leg. After about half an hour he has filled one cage, and Neil has filled four.

"You'd better get a move on," says Neil, "when the catching team gets here."

As if on cue, the barn door opens and the rest of the team arrives— they are four short dark-haired men who are speaking in a language that Tomasz can't understand. They spread out along the length of the barn, and now the screeching and flapping intensifies and the whole vast barn is a storm of feathers and dust and stench and din as they work furiously, grabbing the chickens five at a time and bundling them into the cages.

"Portugeezers," shouts Neil to Tomasz above the racket. "Or Brazil nuts! Respect!"

And he raises a gauntleted hand. Tomasz does the same. What is the lad talking about? Fired up by the other men's example, he grabs at the chickens with a renewed energy, and even manages to get four in one hand, holding them each by one leg. And again. And again. And again. It is exhausting work. Inside the hot nylon shell of his overalls, he feels his skin running with sweat. His eyes are burning. His hair is stiff and matted with excreta. Even his nose and mouth seem clogged with the disgusting stuff.

The cages are filling up; the captive chickens, exhausted with terror, tremble and cluck hopelessly, covered in the excrement of the newly captured birds still flapping and struggling above them. After a couple of hours enough of the chickens have been caged that they can begin to see the floor of the barn. It is a reeking wasteland of sawdust, urine, and feces in which injured and ammonia-blinded birds are staggering around.

At his feet he sees a bird with a broken leg dragging itself through the muck, squawking piteously, weighed down by its monstrous breast, and he realizes with a stab of remorse that it was probably he who broke the creature's leg by stepping on it.

He reaches down for it, and gets it by both legs and hoists it into the air, and as he does so it swings round and he feels the other leg break, and the bird hangs there limply from its two broken legs staring at Tomasz in terror.

"I'm sorry, little chicken," whispers Tomasz in Polish. Should he put it in a cage? He catches Neil's eye.

"Yeah, don't worry, Mick. They're always doing that." He moves around toward Tomasz, waving four chickens in the air. "Brittle. No strengtf, see? They can't move around to build their legs up. Should get 'em playing football, eh? Chicken football. Of course some of 'em do, but the chicken's the football. Who'd be a chicken, eh?" Tomasz picks up the broken bird and puts it into a cage where it collapses beneath a pile of other chickens that scramble on top of it. He is beginning to feel sick.

"Time for a break, pal," says Neil.

Outside in the sunshine, they take deep gulps of air and splash themselves with water from a tap at the side of the barn. Then they slump in a line on the ground along the wall. Neil takes out his half cigarette and has a few puffs, coughing away with a determined look on his face.

"Getting there, getting there," he says.

The Portuguese, or the Brazilians, light up cigarettes too. They have unzipped their overalls, and Tomasz can see that they are wearing nothing but underpants underneath. In fact one of them doesn't even seem to be wearing underpants. That is sensible, he thinks. Then he thinks about the too-tight-in-the-crotch overalls that he is wearing. Who wore them before? He turns to the young man who is sitting next to him. He is a bit shorter than Neil, and probably about the same age, with curly hair and beautiful teeth.

"Portuguese?"

"Yes," says the young man.

"Brazilian?"

"Yes."

Tomasz points at himself.

"Polish. Poland."

"Ah!" The young man beams. "Gregor Lato."

"Pele," says Tomasz. They shake hands.

"You like football?"

"Of course," says Tomasz, for the sake of friendship, even though it is not strictly true, as he finds all sports tedious, but if anything would prefer to watch Juvenia Krakow play rugby. It is one of those little areas of dissent he has carved out for himself, like drinking wine instead of beer and listening to foreign music.

"Later we play." The young man's teeth flash in a smile.

"Later we play bagpipe." The other man sitting next to him has a mad glint in his eye.

"Scottish?" Tomasz asks.

He winks at Tomasz. "Scottish."

As they are finishing their cigarettes a huge lorry trundles up, and the four men jump to their feet and go across to talk to the driver, who also seems to be Portuguese. Or Brazilian.

"They are from Portugal or Brazil?" Tomasz asks Neil.

"Yeah. One or the other. Some are Portugueezers pretending to be Brazils. Some are Brazils pretending to be Portugueezers."

"They pretend to be Brazil?"

"Yeah, mad, innit? Yer see Brazils are illegal, so they get in by saying they're Portugueezers. But the Portugueezers are legal now, wiv that Europe, like, marketing fing, and some of 'em've been making trouble, so nobody wants to take 'em on anymore. That's what me dad says."

"They making trouble?"

"Yeah, trade unions. Minimum wage. Elf and safety. Brazils don't cause trouble, see, 'cause they're illegal. So if the Portugeezers want a job, they have to pretend to be Brazillers—Portugueezers pretending to be Brazillers pretending to be Portugueezers. Mad, innit? It's a mad mad mad world. Did you see that film? Went to see it with my nan at Folkestone. Best film I ever seen."

"Very." Tomasz shakes his head.

"You ever been to Folkestone? My nan used to take me there when I was little. They call it Folkestone Pleasure Beach. Pleasure my ass. I wrote it on the road sign. If you go to Folkestone you'll see it. Pleasure Beach my ass. Yeah, I wrote that."

"Interesting."

"Yeah, I made my mark."

"What is minimum wage in UK?"

"I dunno. Not much. Do you have that where you come from? Poland?"

"We have one very famous trade union. Is name Solidarnoszc. You know it?"

"Sounds like something you could get yer teeth into. Solid-er nosh. Heh heh. Geddit? Yeah, I reckon I'm going to Brazil." He throws in this bit of information so casually that Tomasz, who is still thinking about trade unions, almost misses it. He looks at the lad with renewed interest.

"So you make voyage of discovery?"

He had been like that at his age, always looking for a way out. Of course, when he was seventeen, that had been in communist times, and the only journeys to be made were the inward ones. He remembers how one of his friends had got hold of a pirated tape of Bob Dylan and they had sat, four of them, in his father's car, locked inside the garage, the windows misted up with their spellbound breath, listening to the music as though it were the chimes of freedom. In every life there is a moment when you can break free of taken-for-granted situations and strike out in a different direction. That evening had been a turning point in his life. He had taught himself English in order to understand the words, and a few months later he bought a second-hand guitar from a Czech Gypsy who happened to be passing through Zdroj. And he made himself a promise: One day he would come to the West.

"Voyage of discovery? Heh heh. I like that," said Neil. "One day, when I save up enough, I'm going to Brazil. It's my dream. Everybody's got to have a dream. That's why I'm learnin' to smoke." He looks across at the four Portuguese-Brazilians, who have zipped up their overalls and are making their way back to the barn. "Maybe their dream was coming to England. Come to England and work up to yer ankles in chicken shit. Funny dream, eh?"

The four Portuguese-Brazilians have started to load the crates of chickens onto the back of the lorry. They beckon to Tomasz and Neil, who reluctantly go across to join them. They have made a line and are passing the cages along to the truck, the tightly packed chickens screeching with panic as they fly through the air and land on the back of the truck with a thump. It is amazing how many cages they have filled, and yet the number of chickens in the barn hardly seems to have diminished.

After the lorry has gone, it's back into the barn for more catching and caging. The day drags on, tedious, dirty, and grueling. Tomasz's arms are aching so much he thinks they will drop off. His legs and forearms are bruised from the pecking and thrashing of the struggling birds. But worse, his soul is bruised. He is already losing his sensibility of the chickens as living sentient creatures and, through the same process, of himself also. At one point he finds himself thrusting five birds at a time into a cage with such force that one of them breaks a wing. What is happening to you, Tomasz? What kind of a man are you becoming?

By the end of the afternoon, the floor is littered with dead and dying birds, some trodden into the sawdust and excrement, some still flapping and struggling to stay alive. Tomasz feels his own soul is like a dying bird, fluttering in the mire of . . . of . . . Maybe there is a song in this, but what chords could be plangent enough to express such desolation?

"Did we kill so many?" he whispers to Neil.

"Nah, don't worry pal," says Neil. "Most of them was dead already. See if they break a leg, or if they're a bit weak, they can't make it to the feeding line, so they die of hunger. Mad, really, when there's all that food there for 'em, but they just can't get through to it. Anyway, they only live six weeks from hatchin' to catchin'. Six weeks! Not much time to develop a personality, eh?"

"Personality?"

"Yeah, that's what I'm trying to develop—a personality."

Another lorry arrives, and trundles away into the leafy lanes with another load of screeching misery. It is time for another break. Neil carefully smokes another half cigarette. The Portuguese-Brazilians race to the tap and splash around, laughing and wrestling one another's heads under the water. Tomasz drinks gulp after gulp from the tap, then washes his hair and face under the cold running water. To have longish hair and a beard in this situation is definitely a disadvantage. If only he had some of Yola's nice scented soap.

"Uh-oh." Neil looks over toward the Portuguese-Brazilians, who are becoming increasingly raucous. "Bagpipes. Yer'd better not look at this, Mick."

But Tomasz is transfixed.

One of them, the one with the manic eyes, has seized a bedraggled broken-legged chicken, and, tucking it under his arm, its head poking out backward behind his elbow, he is sneaking up on his friend, who is bending down to close a cage. As he straightens up, the other man squeezes the chicken hard with his elbow, like a bagpipe, and a torrent of excrement flies out of the chicken's tail end and hits the man in the face. The chicken squawks and struggles to free itself, excrement still dribbling from its behind. The victim bellows in fury, wiping his face with his hands, which just spreads it around even more. Then he grabs another chicken, sticks it backward under his arm, and squeezes it hard at his friend with a rough pumping action. The chicken lets out a long screech of pain. Excrement flies. The older man comes rushing across, shouting at the other two to stop, skids in the slime, and ends up wallowing on the ground in all the muck. The fourth man just stands and watches, clutching his sides and weeping with laughter. Neil also stands and laughs, whooping hysterically, tears pouring down his face. To his horror, Tomasz finds that he is laughing too.

The foreman pulls himself up and fires off a stream of abuse in Portuguese. Sulkily, they resume their work. There is an edge of barely suppressed excitement as the number of birds diminishes, and catching the remaining ones becomes more challenging. It is incredibly hot, the shit on the floor steaming like a manure heap, but they still can't leave the doors of the barn open. These last few chickens are the survivors, the tough ones. The men are all having to run around more, shouting and swearing, as they skid in the muck trying to corner and grab the birds.

In the end, there is just one chicken left, a large canny bird that dodges and sidesteps with amazing skill as they try to close in on it. Then one of the Portuguese-Brazilians—the football enthusiast with the beautiful teeth—catches the fleeing chicken with the tip of his boot, sending it up into the air. Its wings are too weak to carry its weight, and as it flops down the second Portuguese-Brazilian runs up and gives it a mighty kick, sending it up into the air again. It is spinning and screeching. Feathers are flying everywhere. The older man is shouting to them to stop, but the game is too exciting. The first one boots it right across the feeding trough and raises his arms in the air shouting, "Goal! Goal!" The bird, dazed and disheveled, picks itself up and starts to run again, limping. It is running toward Tomasz. Suddenly it stops and looks at him, its strange round eyes blinking. He looks back. They stand and face each other, man and bird. Then, with a quick swoop, he bends down, grabs the bird, and holding it in both hands, dashes across the barn, opens the door, and runs outside. Still holding the chicken against his chest, he sprints through the yard to a low wire fence beyond which is a dip and a hedge at the bottom. He leans and puts the chicken down on the other side of the fence. It stands there, bewildered, blinking in the bright light. He leans over, gives it a shove, and whispers in Polish, "Run, chicken, run!" The bird hesitates for a moment, then suddenly it dashes toward the hedge as fast as its stunted little legs will carry it, and disappears into the undergrowth.

The others have followed him outside, with puzzled looks on their faces.

"What yer doing, Mick?" asks Neil.

Tomasz turns to face them with a crazy grin.

"Rugby. I score."

By the time they have finished, he is so burned out with exhaustion that he longs for that filthy mattress with five other sweaty exhausted bodies stretched out alongside. The four Portuguese-Brazilians have gone off somewhere with the lorry driver. Tomasz is too tired to go with them and decides instead to stretch his legs and walk down to the village to see whether he can buy something to eat. Their pair of houses is on the outskirts of Titchington, which turns out to be no more than a cluster of quaint steep-gabled cottages with gardens full of roses, clustered around a pretty medieval church. He wonders whether the villagers know the horror that is happening on their doorstep. It was said that the villagers who lived near Treblinka had only a hazy idea of what was happening behind the barbed-wire fence a few kilometers away. They, like the villagers of Titchington, must have been bothered by the smell when the wind blew in a certain direction.

There is no shop or pub. He realizes with dismay that he has nothing to eat, and there is nowhere to buy anything. When he gets back to the house, it is empty. The sleepers have all disappeared—there is nothing but their lingering smells and their shabby holdalls and overflowing carrier bags lined up against the walls to remind him they were there. He hunts around in the cupboards and finds some slices of stale bread and a tin of tomatoes. In a drawer in the kitchen there is a can opener. He eats the tomatoes just like that, out of the tin, mopping out the juice with stale bread. At the end, he still feels hungry. If only there were some pilchards. Or some chocolate biscuits. And a nice glass of wine. Chianti. Rioja. He wonders where Yola and Marta are, and what they are eating. Rabbit maybe. Or fish. He imagines he can smell the dish, fragrant with herbs, and Yola, smelling of soap, passing a plate to him and smiling. *Come, eat, Tomek.*

Then there is a knock on the door, and, without waiting for him to open it, Neil walks in. He has changed out of his overalls into jeans and a black leather jacket, and he has a motorcycle helmet under his arm. In his other hand, he is holding something in a paper bag.

"Here, Mick. I got this for you. Solid-er nosh."

The bag is warm. Tomasz opens it. Inside, in a foil container, is a small chicken-and-mushroom pie.

"Thank you." He starts to unwrap it. The smell is penetrating and delicious. It must be the tiredness, or all the pent-up horror of the chicken barn, or maybe just loneliness that makes the tears spring into his eyes. "Thank you. You have saved me from desolation row."

"Desolation row." Neil nods. "That's good. Is it a film?"

"It is song."

"I like that."

"And good luck with your voyage."

"Yeah," the lad shuffles his feet backward toward the door. "Yeah. I'm getting there."

There is a full moon that night, which shines in through the open curtains of the upstairs bedroom, lighting up the five sleeping figures curled up on their mattresses on the floor—five strangers, who arrived at half-past midnight and made such a noise when they came in that they woke Tomasz, who had gone to bed three hours earlier. Now, despite his weariness, he can't get back to sleep. He listens to their deep, rhythmic breathing and stares at the moon. He is thinking about the chicken— the one that ran away. Is it sleeping in the hedge tonight, under the moonlight? Is it enjoying its freedom? What is freedom?

"Yer'll be on chicken-shit cleanup for a few days. Then they're sending yer to the slaughterhouse," Darren had said, and Tomasz had shuddered.

"Is there not another job I could do?"

"Nah, pal. Yer've got to go where they send yer."

"Where black is the color and zero is the number."

Darren gave him a funny look.

Is he freer here in the West today than he was in Poland in the years of communism, when all he dreamed of was freedom, without even knowing what it was? Is he really any freer than those chickens in the barn, packed here in this small stinking room with five strangers, submitting meekly to a daily horror that has already become routine? Tormentor and tormented, they are all just damned creatures in hell. There must be a song in this.

Yola was in a foul mood. She had discovered that morning, don't ask how, that the Slovak women who shared their hotel room had no pubic hair. How could this be permitted? Presumably they were not born this way—well, presumably they were, but acquired it in the natural course of things, and had taken unnatural steps to remove it. There are many bad things that can be said about communism, but one thing is certain, in communist times women did not abuse their pubic hair in this way—a practice that is unnatural, unsightly, undignified, and, without being too specific, potentially dangerous.

Brooding on the abuses that women perpetrate on themselves and each other, Yola arrived at Buttercup Meadow Farmfresh Poultry near Shermouth already spoiling for a fight. And her mood darkened even more when she discovered that she, a woman of action with two years of supervisory experience and an advanced knowledge of the Angliski way of life, and of life in general (which she will tell you about later), was not immediately appointed to a supervisory post within the plant. Instead, the supervisor of her section was a rather coarse and disagreeable Romanian woman called Geta, who spoke appalling English and had difficulty in communicating with her workforce, who were mostly Slavs and who had no conception of the importance of sexual harmony in maintaining a pleasant atmosphere in the workplace. She had a distasteful habit of spitting on her fingers as she reached for the chicken pieces coming down the line, and Yola supposed it could only be her blond hair, which anyone but a fool could see was dyed, and her shameless bosom, which was clearly held up with latex foam and underwiring (an abomination about which Yola also has some strong opinions, which she will tell you later), and her Diploma in Food Hygiene from the Polytechnic Institute at Bucharest, which anyone but a fool could see was a forgery, which had secured for her this enviable position.

Anyway, this underwired fake-diploma fake-blondie starts trying to show Yola how to put two pieces of chicken onto a polystirene tray, which anyone would think from the way she goes on you would need a polytechnic certificate for, when all you have to do is grab two bits of breast from the conveyor belt, which has all kinds of chopped up chicken meat on it, and you don't have to spit on your hands like that fakie-Romanian does, and when Yola points this out to her she gets huffy and says, you Polish women now you legal you think you know everything but you don't know anything, and you put your two bits of breasts on tray like this, and you tuck all loose bits of fat and skin underneath to make breasts look nice and plump, which when you think about it is just what latex foam does to fake-blondie's underwired bosom, in fact fake-blondie discloses that these chickens also have water, salt, pork meat, and other stuff injected in them to make them look plump, which is even worse than latex when you think about it, because you have to eat it, which you don't with latex—though things some men do nowadays, nothing would surprise her—and then you just cover them with bit of cling film from this big roll, and then you send them down belt to women who do weighing and stick labels on, yellow labels for one supermarket, blue labels for another, and so on. You don't need certificate for that, do you?

Marta's job is even less challenging.

When she arrived at Buttercup Meadow she made it clear that the job she wanted was feeding the chickens. But her supervisor, a nice, friendly Lithuanian chap who had no front teeth, but in spite of—or maybe because of—this spoke quite good Polish, explained that there was no longer such a job, because the feeding of chickens was now completely automated on account of the mixture of hormones and antibiotics they get, and in any case the poultry barn is very smelly and is not a suitable place for a young woman of her sensitivity.

Instead, she was assigned to the part of the plant where chickens are graded. They come through from the slaughterhouse on a belt, and all Marta has to do is examine the chickens, select those which are plump and undamaged, and place them on another belt—these are the ones that will be packaged and sold as whole birds. The birds that are a little bruised, or just have, say, a leg broken, or ammonia burns on their hocks, are left on the line, and they go through to another part of the plant where they are chopped into chicken pieces and then go through for packaging, where Ciocia Yola is doing her bit. The chickens that are very badly bruised and mangled go into a huge plastic tub, from which they will be taken and processed for the catering industry—for pies, restaurants, chicken nuggets, and school lunches.

At first, Marta is too engrossed in spotting and selecting the whole and undamaged birds to think very much about the process, and she doesn't question why so many birds are coming through those folding rubber doors in such a terrible state. The chickens she selects, although unfortunately dead, have a pleasant and peaceful look about them as well as good plump breasts, and she passes the time thinking up delicious recipes through which they could pass into the next world with dignity. For instance, they could be stuffed with oatmeal, tarragon, lemon, and garlic, or with cranberries, brown sugar, and belly pork—that is her mother's favorite—or with breadcrumbs, butter, and dried fruits, or with chestnuts and . . . actually chestnuts are quite nice by themselves. And they can be coated with a tasty marinade of paprika and yogurt, or honey and horseradish, but not too much horseradish, that can be a bit strong, maybe just pepper, cracked black peppercorns that crunch when you bite, and a sprinkle of marjoram, which is always nice with white meats.

She would like to ask the supervisor, who is quite nice for a Lithuanian, whether she could take a chicken home with her one day, to try out that horseradish recipe—of course she would pay for it—but then she remembers that they are no longer in the trailer, and there is nowhere to cook in their cramped hotel room. Well, that is one more thing that will have to wait until she gets home.

She finds that when she is not thinking of recipes or the deeds of the saints, which can get rather repetitive after a while, she is thinking increasingly of her home in Zdroj, of her older brother, who is still living with them, her mother, who is a teacher, and her father, who works at the town hall and is a colleague of Tomasz's—what, she wonders, has become of him?—and little Mirek, who is often part of their family too, when Yola is in pursuit of a new husband. And though Yola's ways are sometimes rather sinful, it is not for us to judge her, because none of us is without sin, and who knows what we would do in that situation, and it was a disgrace that the baby's father left her, walked out and left her with a Down's syndrome baby to bring up on her own.

"When are we going home, Ciocia?" Marta asks Yola, as they stand in the sunshine outside the plant, counting their first week's wages.

"When? When we are millionaires." Yola smiles grimly at her niece. Surely there has been a mistake. The wages are about a quarter of what Vitaly promised. There is a slip of paper in the envelope with them, with all kinds of incomprehensible letters and numbers. There was never any of this nonsense with old Dumpling. Just cash in hand.

"Deductions—what is this mean?" she asks Geta, who is standing nearby, also counting her wages, which look considerably more than Yola's, even though she does nothing but strut around and stick her nose into everything. At least when Yola was a supervisor she set an example through her own hard work.

"Deductions is everything what you paying," squawks Geta in her appalling English. "See—transports, accommodations, taxes, superannuations, Nis."

"Nis?"

"In England, everybody paying. Is law."

"And this one—TR. What is this?"

"This is mean trenning ret. You no skill you must hevva trenning."

"Trenning? What is it?"

"Trenning is learn. You must learn how to do this job."

"This job every idiot can do. How I am learn?"

"I teach, you learn. I teach you to put chicken on tray."

"And for this I pay?"

"After two week will be normal ret."

"And you are pay more?"

"Of course. I supervisor ret."

Yola feels a red-hot pressure building up inside her as though she is about to explode, and Marta has to hold her back, and who knows what might have happened at this point were it not for the intervention of an incredibly handsome young man with long blond hair and muscles in his calves the size of prize-winning marrows such as most women can only dream of—and yes, he is wearing shorts, which most men cannot get away with but in this case it is acceptable, in fact it is excellent, because the legs are suntanned and covered with fine blond hairs, and have muscles the size of—yes, we know that already. Anyway, this godlike man steps forward and says,

"Do you need any help with your payslip?"

Well, in this situation, what woman would not?

And marrow-legs explains everything, how the superannuation is for her pension when she retires, but since she will be retiring in Poland not in England she will not see a penny of this, and she will probably not see a penny anyway because these bloodsuckers will not pay the money into any pension fund, but will put it into their own pockets to spend on Rolls-Royce cars and luxury yachts, and yes, since she has mentioned it, probably they will also buy uncomfortable underwears for their sluttish wives, and the same is with this National Insurance, and maybe the tax too—if the taxman sees any of it he will be lucky, and the deductions for transport and accommodations are not strictly illegal, but they are excessive, and he will look into it if she likes. And at the end he asks her whether she would like to join the Poultry Workers' Union. Well, in this situation, what woman would not?

Tomasz too has been recruited to the Poultry Workers' Union by a young man wearing shorts who accosted him on the way in to work, though the young man's legs were not a factor in persuading him—it was a deep unaccountable anger with Vitaly, and everything that he represents. That Vitaly, he is too impatient—he is so much in a hurry to get rich that he has forgotten the basics of how to be a human being. And Tomasz felt angry with himself too: He should never have gotten involved in Vitaly's schemes. He had come to England to hunt for some rare Bob Dylan recordings and see a bit of the world before he got too old, and yes, maybe even find love if it should come his way. Yet somehow he had allowed himself to be degraded to the point where he could inflict suffering on other living creatures without so much as a quiver of sentiment. He had become a pawn in their game.

It was only seven o'clock in the morning, and already two terrible things had happened to him today. When he had gone down at dawn into the squalid eating room of the house to stuff his mouth with a few slices of bread, margarine, and jam—yes, he had invested in some apricot jam—before the white van came for him at six o'clock, he sat down to work on the song which he had been composing in his head during the night. And that's when he discovered that his guitar was missing. He couldn't believe it at first. He hunted everywhere, under the table with its debris of food scraps and crumpled wrappings from last night's meals, in the mouldy kitchen cupboards, through the bedrooms still clogged with the over-breathed air of exhausted sleepers, in the grimy understairs cupboard. That was it. There wasn't anywhere else to look. Someone had stolen it. One of these desperate anonymous men from some impoverished or war-blasted region of the world had stolen his guitar, and by now had probably traded it for—for what? A bottle of vodka? A chicken-and-mushroom pie?

This time he didn't even cry. What was the point?

Milo let him sit up front in the passenger seat of the van, because he was the first to be picked up. As he climbed in, he remembered with a stab of regret that he hadn't even said good-bye to Neil, his only friend. He was being taken to new accommodations in a seaside boarding house on the outskirts of Shermouth, closer to the slaughterhouse of the processing plant where he was due to begin work at six thirty. If he'd been sitting in the back, he probably wouldn't have seen it; but up there in the front seat, he couldn't miss it: there, right on the bend in front of them, the squashed remains of a white chicken that had been killed on the road. So that's where its freedom had ended. Milo put his foot down and ran right over it. There must be a song in this, thought Tomasz; then he remembered about his guitar.

But if there was one thing that brought home to him how much he and the chickens really had in common, it was what happened later that morning: the incident of the Chinese slaughterman's thumb.

When the chickens arrived at the slaughterhouse, Tomasz's job was to hang them up by the feet in shackles suspended from a moving overhead conveyor, where they dangled, squawking hopelessly, especially those with broken legs (though by now he was immune to the squawking) as the conveyor dispatched them, headfirst, through a bath of electrified water, which was supposed to stun them, before their throats were cut with an automatic blade. But just in case the water didn't work or the blade missed, which was often enough, there were a couple of slaughtermen standing by to slit their throats before they were sent through to the steam room, where they were plunged into a scalding tank to loosen their feathers. Then they were mechanically defeathered and defooted before being eviscerated by another team of slaughtermen.

The slaughtermen were Chinese, skilled with the knives, but they were a bit short for the height of the overhead belt, so they couldn't always see what they were doing; and it just so happened that one of them grabbed at a bird that had gotten stuck in the automatic foot-cutter, and somehow managed to slice off the end of his thumb, just above the first joint. At first you couldn't even hear him screaming because of the noise of the chickens. Tomasz stopped the line and rushed off to find the supervisor, who immediately got onto his mobile phone and started shouting for another slaughterman to be sent, while the rest of them hunted around for the bit of thumb among the blood, droppings, and feathers on the slaughterhouse floor; but it had disappeared, and all the while the man was yelling and moaning and clutching his hand in a fist to try and stop the bleeding. In the end, they gave up on finding the piece, and somebody just drove him to the hospital to be stitched up as best they could.

Then the supervisor started shouting at Tomasz for stopping the line: "We're losing money, yer twat, just get the bloody line moving, so we can get some bloody chickens coming through. What d'yer think this is, bloody Butlins?"

He looked only a few years older than Neil, without the acne, but also without the charm.

"Here." He handed Tomasz the slaughterman's knife, still covered with blood, though whether it was his or the chickens' he couldn't tell. "You'd better take over, 'til the replacement gets 'ere."

If I were to lose my finger, Tomasz thought, I could no longer play the guitar.

"Gloves. I need leather gloves."

The supervisor looked at Tomasz with narrowed eyes.

"Are you some kind of troublemaker?"

"Same gloves we had in chicken catching. Without such gloves this work is dangerous." For some reason, he still felt angry not so much with the supervisor, nor the owners of the plant, but with Vitaly.

"Listen, mate, people been doin' this work without gloves for nearly two years."

"And?"

"We've only lost three fingers. Well, four if you count this thumb."

"Without gloves I will not do it."

"Where're you from?" asked the supervisor.

"Poland." Tomasz smiled, knowing it was not the answer the man wanted.

"Oh, I should've guessed. Effin troublemakers. You'll be wantin' bleedin' maternity pay next. Here, wait. You keep shacklin' while I find some friggin gloves."

"No," said Tomasz. "Even for shackle work is need gloves."

The supervisor went a horrible purple color.

"Listen, yer bloody Polish big girl's blouse, next time I get any lip from you, it's down the road. It's only because we've lost this chuffin' Chinaman, else yer'd be down the road now."

But he went and found a pair of gloves.

Tomasz pulled them on slowly, pensively, one finger at a time. There was another phrase that nasty supervisor had used that got him thinking about Yola: Where was she? What was she doing? Was she thinking of him?

In the rest of the plant, the sudden stillness of the conveyor belt created a welcome break. Yola sighed and looked around. She hadn't realized how noisy that conveyor was until it stopped. The narrow windows of the packing room were too high to look out of, but shafts of sunlight were angling in up there, with their bright reminder of summer. How had she become trapped in this place? The pressure in her bladder was becoming more insistent, but the thought of asking Geta's permission to use the lavatory was just too humiliating. She held on. All around her people were taking the opportunity to relax, chat with their neighbors. Two of the Slovaks even tried to nip outside for a cheeky fag break, and Geta rushed out after them yelling, "No smok! No fudh fudhijjin!"

Yola thought this would be a good time to sneak out through the door unnoticed, but Geta spotted her and insisted on accompanying

her, claiming it was her responsibility to make sure that the toilet opportunities were not abused, especially by Poles and Ukrainians, the devil
only knows what they get up to in there, sometimes you could see the
smoke coming out from under the door. How can you be expected to
relax and enjoy a nice toilet break when this underwired harridan is
standing outside and trying to hurry things along by rapping on the
door and telling you to get a move on? Yola stayed firmly locked in for
an unnecessarily long time, and made all kinds of toilet noises, just to annoy her.

"And don't forget to wash hand after," snapped Geta.

"Why you say this to me?" hissed Yola, from behind the still-locked
lavatory door. "I am a teacher not a piggy."

"I am fudhijjin qualify you not," squawked Geta.

"I piss on your certificate."

"Not certificate, diploma."

"I defecate on your diploma."

She farted noisily.

Marta, meanwhile, went around and chatted to the young women on the
other side of her belt, who turned out to be Ukrainians from the west,
and one of them had been to Poland though not to Zdroj. So, like many
people all around the plant, she was away from her position when suddenly the belt started up again with a judder, and she had to race around
to catch the first chickens going through. She picked them up off the line;
there was something repulsively solid and wooden about them—in fact it
was just as if they had been cooked—boiled—complete with their feet
still on and their innards inside them. While she was wondering what to
do with these horrible whole-boiled birds, another bird came through
that was definitely not boiled alive, in fact, though it had lost most of its
feathers, it seemed fairly intact, as though it had bypassed foot-cutting
and evisceration altogether. As she reached for it, the poor, limp, featherless thing started to struggle in her hands. It was still alive. Then the

next one came through, and to her horror, it was alive, too. Or half alive. And then another. The line had picked up speed now and was going at its usual pace. What should she do?

She grabbed the three half-alive birds off the line, and started to scream.

The Lithuanian supervisor was the first to arrive. He laid a soothing arm around her shoulder and offered her a handkerchief. Geta, having abandoned her thankless toilet vigil, was next on the scene. The live birds had by now recovered from their shock and were scuttling around on the factory floor. The boiled birds had moved on down the line, and there were more half-alive birds coming through, faster and faster. Geta started shouting at Marta, and at the featherless chickens that were scurrying here and there between everybody's legs, and at the Lithuanian supervisor, who shouted back that Marta was a sensitive type and should not be upset.

"Polish is not sensible, is lazy bastard!" Geta shouted, which was too much for Marta, who burst into tears. Then one of the chickens made a dash through the door, which Geta had left open, and the others followed, straight through into the packing room. At the far end of the packing room another door opened, and Yola, having realized that the live audience for her toilet noises was no longer listening, was sauntering back into the plant. Seeing the chickens darting toward her, she naturally held the door open for them. And they were gone.

"Sack! Sack! You sack!" shouted Geta, her face blotched with fury, and gave Yola a little shove.

"Sack youself!" Yola shouted, and shoved her back.

Yola was not without friends in the breast area, and friends of friends in drumsticks and thighs, and Marta was not going to stand by and let her aunt be insulted, so Geta suddenly found herself surrounded by an angry crowd demanding that she apologize and reinstate Yola at once.

Meanwhile, news of the Chinese slaughterman's thumb had spread like wildfire around the plant. In the evisceration room, it was his whole thumb that had been cut off; by the time it reached drumsticks and thighs, the poor man had lost his whole hand; and in weighing and labeling, he had had to be amputated above the elbow. The Chinese were marching around stamping their feet and chanting incomprehensibly, their pockets bulging with chickens' feet, while others were unshackling the chickens, which were tumbling dead and half-dead onto the belt and the floor.

All at once several doors of the plant flew open and out into the bright sunshine of the yard poured the workforce. The three naked chickens were still there, clucking around and wondering what would happen next.

Tomasz noticed that the blond man with the impressive calf muscles who had recruited him to the union was still hanging around by the gate. He looked as though he had been about to get on his bike and call it a day but turned back when he saw the commotion in the precinct. Then Tomasz spotted Yola. She came bursting out of one of the doors, rushed up to the union man in a dramatic manner, and threw her arms around him. So Tomasz's joy at finding her was tempered with desolation at finding her in the arms (well, almost) of another man.

"She say sack! She say, you sack!" she was wailing.

"Hold on, hold on." The union man's voice was calm, but with a nervous edge. "Let's establish a procedure. Is anyone from management here?"

Geta came forward at once. "Is Polish no good working. Too much toilet. Chicken run away."

The three liberated chickens clucked wildly, as though to prove her point.

"Hold on," said the union man, his voice now sounding more nervous than calm. "Let's just get the facts. What chickens are we referring to here?"

Now the slaughterhouse supervisor, the one who had argued with Tomasz about the gloves, pushed his way through the crowd.

"Listen, mate, I don't know who you are or what you're doing here, but you can bugger off. Okay?" He turned to Geta. "Shut up. Don't talk to him. This wanker's a nobody. We don't want him on the premises."

"Hold on. I'm the representative of—"

"Bugger off or I'll call the police."

Suddenly the Chinese men from the evisceration room arrived on the scene, and they were still carrying their fearsome-looking knives. They started shouting and waving the knives in the air, and though no one could understand what they were saying, you could see that they were pretty mad. The supervisor got his mobile phone out, but one of them knocked it out of his hand onto the ground and stamped on it again and again until it was completely smashed.

"Hold on!" The union man held up his hand. "No violence, comrades. I'm sure we can resolve this through peaceful negotiation."

The supervisor looked only fleetingly grateful.

"Listen, matey, the only negotiation I'm interested in is getting these idle buggers back to work."

"Hold on. Hold on. First we must hear their grievances."

There was a clamor of voices and squawks. Everybody seemed to have a grievance, even the chickens.

"Every minute that line's stopped, we're losing money. It's all very well sayin' hold on friggin' this, hold on bleedin' that, but the soddin' supermarkets don't hold on, do they? Buy one get one free, mate. That's what we got to give 'em. By Friday. Otherwise we lose the supermarket contract and it's bye-bye Buttercup Meadow, and all these friggin' wankers that's shoutin' for workers rights can say bye-bye to their bleedin' jobs."

"Well, all the more reason to resolve matters speedily. Now—"

"Okay, tell 'em if they get back to work now we'll meet all their demands."

Tomasz could see that this union man was getting nowhere, and that the supervisor was out to trick them. He jumped onto an upturned crate and cupped his hands around his mouth.

"This is no matter for negotiation! It is violation of human dignity! And chicken!"

Yola spun around. "Tomek!"

One of the annoying things about men, Yola has observed, is that you spend years looking for a good one, then two come along at once. This blond-haired man with calf muscles like prize-winning marrows would be any woman's dream, and those blond hairs on his legs, what woman wouldn't like to . . . But let's be realistic, he is in England and probably you will not be able to persuade him to come to Poland, and even if you did, what would he do there? Only make trouble. And this Tomasz, although he has certain defects he is getting better, and she is confident that if she could scrub him down with bit of nice-smelling soap and get rid of those socks, which are probably nylon, and replace them with some nice wool or cotton ones, which are more comfortable and don't make your feet sweat unnecessarily—whoever invented nylon socks should be castrated—and get rid of those sports shoes which do nothing for a man, and replace them with some nice leather shoes—there are many excellent shoes made in Poland and quite wide-fitting—then problem would be all but solved, and a pleasing sexual harmony might develop.

And she can see that he is a kindhearted man, and he has already expressed some interest in becoming a father to little Mirek. And although she has not yet told him of Mirek's difficulty, and she wishes her God-prattling niece would shut up and not let the cat out of the bag too soon, she is sure that when he sees him there in the flesh and sees what a darling he is, what a little darling, he won't just walk away—like the last one did.

And, besides, now this Tomasz is becoming quite a hero. See how he jumps up and shouts in a big manly voice, "How many years must these persons exist before they learns to be free?"

"Hold on, hold on," says marrow-legs, with a panicky sound in his voice, "we must concretize the demands."

Really, these men, even the nice ones, do talk some rubbish.

And now a large silver car arrives, exactly like the Rolls-Royce that marrow-legs has described, and a middle-aged man with silver hair, a

very respectable-looking type, could even be a doctor, definitely not a
type to have wife in sluttish underwear—mistress maybe—comes over to
find out what is going on, and marrow-legs explains that one man had to
have his arm amputated and a woman was wrongful dismissal for spending too long in toilets. Rolls-Roycie says, "Hm. Hm," and rubs his chin,
and marrow-legs says she must be reinstate and the man must getting
compensation, then that bossy Romanian cow butts in unnecessarily and
says they are all taking advantage, especially no-good Polish, who think
now they in Europe they can do what they like, and Rolls-Roycie says,
"Hm. Hm" again. Then the senior supervisor, an inferior type given to
unnecessary bad language and degenerate behavior, who pinches the
girls' behinds and says they must make sex with him if they want to have
a job ("No one wants to make sex with you, you poky-penis dog," said
Yola), this supervisor arrives and says that Polish man with long hair is
troublemaker—could it be Tomek he is referring to? Everyone looks for
Tomasz but he is disappeared, and where is Marta? She is disappeared
too, though nobody could say that Marta is troublemaker. And then they
have another thing to worry about because suddenly whole yard is full of
chickens running and flapping everywhere, except some which have broken legs can only crawl, really these chickens are in very poor condition,
and one of them makes poopie-poo on Rolls-Roycie's shoe, and he says,
"Where did these fucking birds come from?" Really it is quite surprising
when gentleman of such refinement uses a bad language. But where did
these birds come from? It is mystery.

Andriy and Emanuel turned up for their meeting with Vitaly at the pub
and spent an hour and a half sitting there drinking their half pints of
beer, but Vitaly didn't arrive. What should they do? Emanuel wants to
head for Richmond, near London—he has found his friend's address—
but Andriy still feels reluctant to leave. That girl—maybe she is here, and
Vulk, who knows where she is, is definitely here. And Andriy has heard
what can happen to Ukrainian girls in England. So even if there is

definitely nothing between them, and even if he has definitely decided that he will go and search for Vagvaga Riskegipd, is it not his responsibility first to find this girl and return her to her parents? Because if he doesn't do this, who will? Not those other good-for-nothing Ukrainians who think only of looking after themselves and drinking beer; no, he is not that type of man.

They agree to spend a few more days in Dover, parking their trailer up at the carrot field and traveling in daily by Land Rover. Emanuel says he wants to develop his fishing skills, now that he has established his rights over the red bucket, and the Mozambicans have vanished without a trace—the rumor on the pier is that they have been deported—and though he never repeats his luck of the first time, he manages to provide dinner every day, and even to sell some to Mr. Tattoo, who seems to have completely forgotten about their previous disagreement.

Andriy spends his days combing the streets and hotels of Dover. One day he finds the shop with the Indian shopkeeper. Now her sari is blue, and she seems to have gotten shorter and plumper since his last visit. Although he has only a little money left from the two weeks' wages he earned at the strawberry farm, and he really must put petrol in the Land Rover, he buys some more bread and margarine. He considers buying some pilchards too, but he doesn't want to offend Emanuel, who takes his fishing role very seriously.

"You are not eating balance diet," she chides gently.

"Yes, yes. Also we eating fish."

"You must have vitamin. Otherwise you will be getting diseases of poor nutrition. Lemon is good. Here, on your right. Not expensive. After you cook fish you squeeze some drops."

He takes a lemon.

"And you need roughage to establish a good bowel habit. You must eat vegetable."

"We eating plenty carrot. Every day carrot."

"Carrot is a first-class source of roughage and essential vitamin A. Make sure you wash it good."

"Thank you, lady, for your advice." He tries not to stare too obviously at the appealing brown bulge at the top of her sari. Really, plump women can be rather sexy.

"You know in this town is too many poor people eating bad diet. Drunken sailors. Out-of-work miners. She"—she points to the picture of the lady in the blue hat above the counter—"is perfect example of how with good diet you will ripen into old age."

He learns from the Indian shopkeeper that here too, not far away, there were once coal mines, which closed after the great strike of 1984. Now he understands why this town has a feel of the Donbas about it. Although he was only five years old, he remembers vividly the solemnity with which his parents donated their gold wedding rings to buy food for the British miners. What happened to all that money? The Ukrainian miners could certainly do with it now.

"I am looking for man named Vulk. Gangster type. Dressed up in black."

The shopkeeper shakes her head. "In this town now is too much gangster. But I am pleased to say none of it has ever come into this shop, for if it did I would chase it away."

"And one Ukrainian girl. Long dark hair. Very . . ." Very what? Is she pretty? Is she beautiful? "Very . . . Ukrainian."

"Ah, Ukrainian girls also we have plenty. Every night you see them on street and on beach making sex for money."

"Not this girl."

The shopkeeper smiles diplomatically, and he leaves the shop in a foul mood.

Back at the pier he is surprised to find Emanuel surrounded by a small crowd, and at the heart of the crowd is Vitaly. Vitaly grabs Andriy by both hands, and embraces him like a brother, elbowing Emanuel out of the way.

"My friend. Good you are here. We have excellent business opportunity. Good work. Good money. You will be rich. You will return to Ukraina millionaire."

Andriy disentangles himself from Vitaly's embrace.

"What is this opportunity?"

"In factory. Twenty kilometers only. Good work, good money. All these people"—he waves his arm to include the dozen or so of unsuccessful fishermen he has recruited—"can have good employment. You and Emanuel also. Twenty pound an hour for you. Supervisor rate. You have transport. You bring trailer, put all inside, take to factory."

He must have read the doubt on Andriy's face.

"I give you money for petrol."

Still Andriy hesitates.

"And transport. How much you want?" He pulls a wad of notes out of his pocket. They are all twenties.

"But I have only Ukrainian license. To take so many people maybe I need special license."

"Is no problem. Only if vehicles is with seats for more than eight people you need passenger license. Now all modern transport is without seats."

This seems an odd arrangement.

"The trailer is not here."

"No problem. You fetch it. We will wait here."

By the time Andriy and Emanuel have returned with the trailer, the crowd has grown. Vitaly climbs into the front of the Land Rover beside Andriy, with Dog at their feet. Emanuel and three other passengers sit in the back, and some fourteen hopefuls squeeze themselves into the trailer. Those that cannot fit onto the bunks sit on the floor hugging their knees. Andriy notices that the Bulgarian lad and his friends are among them. He waits until Vitaly has peeled off five twenty-pound notes from his wad and handed them over before he will even turn the engine on.

It is money well-earned, for with such a weight on board, the trailer bucks and swerves all over the place and he has a job keeping it on the road. He has to drive mostly in first gear, with 100 percent concentration, to avoid overturning on a bend. They have been driving like this for almost an hour, on roads which are becoming increasingly narrow and difficult, before at last Vitaly directs him down a lane with a sign saying BUTTERCUP MEADOW FARMFRESH POULTRY and a picture of a little blond-haired girl, holding a bunch of buttercups in her hand and clasping a fluffy brown chicken to her chest, with a slogan beneath: PARTNERSHIP IN POULTRY. It all looks very nice.

But as they approach the entrance, a scene of wild commotion unfolds before them. What's going on here? The iron gates are open and police in riot gear are holding back a screaming, battling mob which is surging toward them, while a flock of crazed chickens is running around and around the yard squawking and flapping frenziedly.

"What is this, Vitaly? Where have you brought us?"

He puts the Land Rover into first and starts to nose his way forward through the gate. Suddenly he hears a high terrifying howl and a wild Chinese man wearing blood-spattered clothes and wielding a knife bursts through the police cordon and hurls himself onto the hood of the Land Rover, chicken feet spewing out of his pockets.

Who is this man? What does he want? His mad black eyes meet Andriy's for a moment through the windshield, his mouth jabbering urgently, then two policemen throw themselves on top of him and drag him, struggling, away. By the gate, two more policemen are wrestling with a big blond man wearing shorts, forcing his arms behind him and bundling him into a van. This is definitely not a good situation.

"Why does this Chinese want to kill us? What is all this police, Vitaly?"

"Is okay. Police on our side."

"But why police is here? What is going on?"

"All is because of troublemakers. Lazy Chineses refusing work. Police defend you right to work. We will show them good Ukrainian-type work. Good work, good money, eh, friend?"

Andriy is beginning to feel uncomfortable. To drive the overloaded trailer through this throng with all these police watching, when he is perhaps an outlaw on the run, and definitely has no passenger license, and still has that five-bullet gun hidden in his backpack—is this a good idea? But it's not just that holding him back, it's something his father had said that had stuck in his memory, repeating the words of the visionary blind man of Sheffield in his speech all those years ago. He's trying to recall—it was something about solidarity, the essential fellow-feeling of man—his father had drummed it into him—something about self-respect. Be a man—is this what he meant? That there are some things a man should not do, not for any amount of money?

He puts the Land Rover into reverse and starts to inch backward.

"No, no. Go on! Go forward!" Vitaly jumps up in his seat waving his hands and inadvertently steps on Dog's tail. Dog lets out a yelp, leaps from the Land Rover, and, drawn by a powerful smell of chicken, dives into the melee.

"Dog! Come back!" Andriy hits the brakes. "Come here! This chicken is not for eating!"

But Dog, seeing the challenge of the situation, wants to show them his true colors, and weaving in and out of the crowd with a few courteous woofs he soon has the chickens neatly rounded up in a corner of the yard, where they stand looking a bit surprised and clucking obediently.

Suddenly there is a bloodcurdling shriek and a small fierce figure, petite but voluptuous, breaks out of the crowd and hurtles toward them, arms flailing.

"Yola!" cries Andriy. "What you doing here?"

"I want home to Poland! This place is hell! All is cheating and lies!"

Then she spots Vitaly sitting in the front of the Land Rover and turns on him with her fists, pulling at him through the door, howling, "This is the one! This is root consul flexi dynamo!"

A policeman tries to drag her off, but she holds fast and fights like a fiend, biting and scratching, struggling against the policeman's grip and kicking him so hard in his sensitive parts that he is forced to let go. Emanuel grabs her by the arm from the back of the Land Rover and pulls her in. Then Marta runs toward them, and Tomasz, and they are hauled in too, and all the time the Land Rover and trailer are backing up gently and Vitaly is shouting, "No, stop! Stop!" until they come to a place where it is wide enough for them to swing round, and at the last minute Dog comes bounding up too, leaps into the back, and Andriy puts his foot down and they're away.

By the time they get back to Dover, Marta, Yola, and Tomasz have told Andriy and Emanuel about everything that happened to them, Vitaly has tried unsuccessfully to get Andriy to give the money back, and most people in the back of the trailer have been sick.

Marta regrets that she didn't manage to bring a chicken with her for their supper, but her views about food have changed in the last few days. After dropping off their passengers in Dover, they make their way back to their favorite spot by the carrot field, where she manages to improvise a delicious supper from white bread, margarine, and cold fish, supplemented with carrots and garnished with lemon slices and roadside herbs.

Yola and Tomasz are helping to peel the carrots, and Yola is telling Tomasz about her disagreements with Geta. Tomasz gazes with fascination into Yola's eyes, asking her to repeat the sounds she made in the toilet, which she does in her typical vulgar way, and they both fall about laughing like children. And Marta thinks, here we go again.

She remembers the last time this happened, when Yola met a nice man, a plump greengrocer, and it was all holding hands and giggling and stolen kisses. And then Yola took the man back to her house in Zdroj, and as soon as he met little Mirek, as soon as he took one look at the boy, he was out through the door again like a cornered tomcat. He didn't even take off his hat. He didn't even let go of the box of liqueur chocolates in his hand.

"I piss on your cabbages!" Yola shouted at his retreating back, but the words slid off him like butter off a hot dumpling.

It took Yola a long time to get over that. And you have to give her credit for this—she didn't blame Mirek. Not once.

"Yola," says Marta, lighting the gas for the stove, "why don't you show Tomasz your photos?"

"I'm sure Tomasz has no desire to see my uninteresting photos." Yola gives Marta a kick on the shins. Yes, her shins are already quite bruised.

"I would like very much to see your photos," says Tomasz.

So Yola has to get out the three photos she always carries with her. The pretty house in Zdroj, with its garden sloping down to the river and its orchard of plums and cherries. The four Masurian goats, a bit blurred, because they wouldn't keep still. And Mirek, sitting on a swing in the garden, that sweet smile on his big round face, his tongue sticking out, his cute pointy eyes wrinkled up with laughter.

"This is your son?"

"My beloved son, Mirek."

"I would like very much to meet him."

Early the next morning, Andriy wakes up feeling disoriented. There's something different in the trailer. He can hear whispering and giggling. What's happened to Emanuel? In the other single bunk, where Emanuel should be, Tomasz is fast asleep. At the other side of the cabin, the double bed has been pulled down, and in it are Yola and Marta. Andriy shuts his eyes again and pretends to be asleep. A little while later, the whispering stops, and Marta gets up and puts the kettle on. Emanuel, who had obligingly gone off to sleep in the Land Rover, comes to join them for breakfast.

It is midmorning by the time they get to the ferry terminal in Dover, and they are all in a rush. Contrary to what Vitaly had said, Yola, Tomasz, and Marta have no trouble exchanging their tickets. There are tears and hugs and exchanges of addresses as they say good-bye in front of the harbor.

"We will come again," says Tomasz.

"For sure," says Yola. "But not for strawberry or chicken. Now we are in Europe marketing, we can earn good money here. I will be teacher. Tomek will be government bureaucrat. Marta . . . what will you be, Marta?"

"I will be vegetarian," says Marta.

"One day Ukraina will be also in Europe marketing." She kisses Andriy on each cheek. "And Africa too." She gives Emanuel two little kisses, and he blots his eyes on the sleeve of his green anorak.

How hard it is to tear up old boundaries, and how easy to set up new ones. Andriy watches with a heavy heart as the ferry pulls away from the dock. In addition to the sadness of parting, there is the sadness of knowing that he is on the far side of this new boundary across Europe. It will be a long time before he can work freely in England; even in Russia, now, Ukrainians are illegals. Will Ukraine soon be the new Africa? He puts his arm around Emanuel's shoulder.

"Let's go."

They walk across the harbor, where a crowd is gathering to greet a ferry boat coming in. Andriy stops to watch, remembering his own arrival almost a month ago. Where is the innocent carefree young man with terrible trousers and a heart full of hope who disembarked from that boat? Well, the trousers are still the same.

A little ripple runs through the crowd. Two figures who had been standing together move away from each other in opposite directions. He spots a shaven shiny head cutting toward the terminal—Vitaly—and he remembers the £65 he still has in his pocket after filling up the tank with petrol. They'd better get going before he sees them. In the other direction a line of darkness opens up as the crowd gives way to a dumpy black-clad figure walking fast with his head down. Andriy knows at once that it is Vulk. His heartbeat quickens. Should he go up and accost him? Or should he be friendly and try to wheedle information out of him?

In the end he does neither—he just goes up and asks very directly, in English, "Please tell me, where is Irina?"

Vulk looks startled. He doesn't recognize Andriy.

"Irina? Who is it?"

Andriy feels a red-hot surge of anger. This monster who tried to take her didn't even ask her name. She was just a bit of anonymous flesh.

"Ukrainian girl from strawberry picking. You remember? You took in you car?"

Vulk looks around shiftily. "That Ukrainian girl is not vit me."

"So where she is?"

"Who are you?" says Vulk.

Thinking fast, Andriy puts his hands in his pockets, narrows his eyes, and tries to put a Vitaly-like expression on his face. "I am from Sheffield. I know someone who will pay good money for this girl."

Vulk gives him a canny look: This is a language he understands. "This is valuable high-class girl. I too vill give good money for it."

"I am expert in finding disappeared people. My friend"—he indicates Emanuel—"is very skill in track and footprint."

"Mooli bwanji?" Emanuel beams.

"And we have dog."

Dog woofs.

"If you find it you vill tell me?"

"How much you pay?"

"How much is pay other man?"

"Six thousand. Six thousand pound, not dollar."

Vulk whistles. "That is good price. Listen, ve vill make a business. I vill give three thousand, plus percentage of enning."

"What is enning?"

"Ven it is enning money, you vill get percentage. Good money, my friend. This girl vill be enning every night five hundred, six hundred, even more. Maybe even ve vill take it to Sheffield. Exclusive massage. Plenty up there. Executive elite VIP clientele only. English man like Ukrainian girl. Good clean no-boyfriend girl like this one, first time is man take it pay five hundred." Then he pauses, shakes his grizzled pony-tail. His face softens. "No. First time Vulk vill take it. I lose a money but I heff a loff. Hrr. Good loff."

He smiles a wet tobacco-stained smile. Andriy feels the blood beating in his head. He clenches his fists by his sides—this is not the time to lash out. He forces a smile.

"But this girl—this high-class girl. She will not stay with us. She will run."

"Aha, it vill stay, no problem. I heffa friend," he winks. "Friend mekka little visit to mamma house in Kiev, say to mamma Irina no good verk you family get big trouble. Maybe somebody get dead. No problem. Every girl stay ven I tell it this. In two three year ve vill be millionaire. And one more good advantage is this—ven it has time for rest, ven other man is not in, ve can enjoy."

Pressure is building up in Andriy's chest like a steam hammer. Control yourself, Palenko. Stay in control. His throat so tight he can hardly talk, he asks, "What percentage I get?"

"Fifty-fifty," says Vulk. "Better money in girl than in strawberry picker. Strawberry soon finish. Girl carry on. One year, two year, three year. Always good income. Little cost. No wage to pay, only food. And clothings. Hrr. Sexy clothings."

"Okay. Fifty-fifty is good business."

Vulk gives him his mobilfon number and describes a grassy picnic spot on the Sherbury Road, between Canterbury and Ashford. Andriy knows the place exactly.

"She is there?"

"Was there. I was look. Now I think she gone. Or dead. Maybe dog will find it."

"Where she can go?"

Vulk shrugs.

"Maybe London. Maybe Dover. I still looking. I heffa passport for it."

"You have passport of Irina?"

"Without passport it cannot go far. Maybe on other strawberry farm. Somebody telephone to me yesterday from Sherbury, near this picnic place. Ukrainian girl no pepper. Maybe is same one. I go look. If it is same one, I vill heff it. Or maybe other nice Ukrainian girl vill come to Vulk. Make loff. Make business. I vill give it passport. I heffa plenty."

five bathrooms

Sherbury Country Strawberries was altogether a different kind of operation from Leapish's ramshackle strawberry farm. The work was better, the pay was better, the trailers were better. There were facilities— a separate barn with a Ping-Pong table, a common room, a TV, a phone. Even the strawberries were better, or at least they looked more even in size and color. And yet each morning since I'd been here, I'd woken with a feeling of emptiness, like a big blank inside me where something vital was missing.

Maybe it was just the scale of the place—fifty or so trailers parked side by side in rows so close together that it was more like a city than a farm. You couldn't see the woods or the horizon, and in the morning it wasn't birds that woke you, it was lorries, and men clattering around with wooden pallets in the yard. You couldn't hear yourself think because people were always talking or playing their radios. My head was full of questions, and I needed a bit of peace and quiet.

No, it definitely wasn't that Ukrainian miner I was missing. There were plenty of Ukrainian boys here, and none of them was of any interest whatsoever. Okay, I know it seems snobby, but these Ukrainians were not my type. They just wanted to play pop music and talk about stupid things like who was going to bed with whom. Oksana, Lena, and Tasya kept saying, Hey, Irina, you've made a real hit with Boris. That pig. I've been keeping out of his way. Sex for entertainment doesn't interest me— I'm still waiting for *the one* to come along.

Mother must have thought Papa was *the one*. The sad thing is, she still does. Last night I phoned her from the pay phone, reversing the charges. I didn't want to alarm her, so I just said I'd left that farm and I was on another one. Mother started crying and telling me to come home, and how lonely she was. I snapped at her to shut up and let me be. No wonder Papa had left home if she went on at him like that, I said. I knew I shouldn't have said it, but it just came out. When I put the phone down I started crying too.

Today after work I was sitting on my bunk trying to read a book in English, but I couldn't concentrate. I'd been crying off and on all day for no reason. What was wrong with me? *Irina, you should phone Mama again. You should say sorry. Yes, I know, but . . .* I put on my jeans and my jumper, because it had already turned cool, and I walked out to the pay phone. I asked someone for some change. There were a few people milling about there. Then I saw him.

There was no mistaking him, even from behind: the fake-leather jacket; the ratty ponytail. He was standing at the top of the steps, knocking at the door of the office and peering in. My stomach lurched. Was my imagination playing tricks on me? I closed my eyes and opened them again. He was still there. Maybe everywhere I look from now on I will see him. *No, don't think like that. If you let yourself think like that, he's got you. Just run. Run.*

Dear Sister

I am still in Dover where I have become entrapped in the passages of Time but I have some tip-top news for you.

Yesterday while I was awaiting for Andree at the pier Vitaly that tricksome mzungu from the strawberry trailer suddenly appeared and started urging us to travel into a different town for the slaughter of chickens. Then a great Multitude thronged around shouting and calling out in tongues some yearned also to partake of the slaughter and some cursed Vitaly and despised his name. One man cried out that Vitaly is a <u>moldavian toy boy</u> and I committed this saying to memory for I wonder what it means. But when we went to the chicken place Andree made an outstanding speech about Self Respect saying there are some things you should not do even for money it was like Our Lord chasing the moneylenders from the temple. So the chickens were saved and we brought back with us Toemash and Martyr and Yola who had been hidden there and returned them to Poland. And I was very sad to say good-bye to them especially Toemash and his guitar.

In Dover we met the Spawn of Satan and Andree asked him the wherebeing of the beauteous strawberry picker Irina for he is beloved of this lady and he says we must find her before the Spawn can seize her and exercise his Foul Dominion over her. So speeding up her Salvation we drove once again through this country which is as green as the plateau of Zomba with many thickets of trees and flowering bushes crowning the hilltops. Then Andree enquired about my country and I told him our hills and plains are outstanding in beauty and our people are renowned for the warmest hearts in Africa and everything is broken. Your country sounds very much like Ukraine he said in a brotherly voice. I told him that in the dry season everything is covered in red dust. In Ukraine the dust is black he said.

Andree is a good man with a heart full of brotherly love. Although he has a woman's name and his English is feeble apart from Toby Makenzi he is the best mzungu I have ever met. Maybe he has an African heart also his dog. Also he is an outstanding driver for he delivered us from many perils aided by the intercession of Saint Christopher whose medallion I always wear upon my neck which was given me by Father Augustine with a prayer to bring me safely back to Zomba.

Sometimes I dream of the beauties of Zomba and the good Nuns of the Immaculate Conception at Limbe nearby who took me in after our parents

died and our sisters went working in Lilongwe and you my oldest proudest
dearest sister won your Nursing Scholarship in Blantyre and I was beloned.
Then good father Augustine became like a father to me and before I came
to England he spoke to me of the Priesthood with gentle words and
kindness saying I would make a tip-top priest and I could go to the
seminary at Zomba to learn the Mysteries which is very desirous to me for
I hunger and thirst for Knowledge. And he said you will say Goodbye to
Death for death is only of the body not the soul and you will sing in the
Choir of Angels.

But Goodbye to Death means also Goodbye to Canal Knowledge which is
an earthly delight and this is why I am turmoiled in my heart dear sister.
For I have a Decision to make.

So as we drove along I asked my mzungu friend Andree do you
understand the heart of God? He replied no one understand this and if
a problem cannot be solve why waste time to worry about it? Then he
brought us into the same leafsome place where we stopped once
before and we ate like the Disciples of bread and fish. But I was still
unsatisfied and I inquired Andree brother did you ever experience
canal knowledge?

After some whiling he said Emanuel why for you asking me this question?
And I put my turmoil before him for I said if I choose canal knowledge I
will walk in the valley of the shadow of death. Andree shook his head and
in a voice like a man possessed he said friend why you asking all this big
question? Why you always talking about canal? Why you always thinking
about death? You too young for this thought. Today is only one big
question for us—where is Irina???

I AM DOG I RUN I SNIFF MY MAN SAYS GO SEEK SMELLS OF RIBBON-
ON-NECK FEMALE I SNIFF I FIND A TREE PLACE WITH THIS FEMALE
SMELL BUT SHE IS NOT THERE I FIND STINKING MAN-FOOD PAPER
WITH FEMALE SMELL I TELL MY MAN HE DOES NOT UNDERSTAND
RUN SEEK SNIFF HE SAYS I SNIFF I RUN I AM DOG

Why is this useless dog running around in circles sniffing at old bits of paper and cigar stubs on the ground instead of following her trail? Does it mean she is no longer here? Andriy feels a cold breath on his heart. What was that other strawberry farm Vulk had mentioned—Sherbury? Maybe he should take a look there.

The turning to Sherbury is a few kilometers up the road. As the lane starts to climb, he slows down and eases carefully into first to take the hill. They pass the pull-off with the row of poplars, and there, down below, he sees their strawberry field, the prefab with its locked door, the men's trailer, even the women's shower screen he built. It all seems so familiar, and yet so distant, like childhood places revisited. At the bottom of the field is the gate where a different, more carefree Andriy Palenko used to watch the passing cars and dream of a blonde in a Ferrari.

If she is still alive and hiding, he thinks, maybe this is where she would come. He turns back and drives in through the gate, parking up by the prefab. The field looks neglected. It's obvious that no one has been picking these strawberries for a while; many are overripe and rotting on the ground. Weeds are springing up between the lines of plants.

Emanuel jumps down and fetches all the bowls from their trailer, and working up from the bottom of the field, starts to fill them with strawberries. For every berry he puts into a bowl, he puts one into his mouth. Should he try and stop him? Never mind. If he has a bit of looseness in the bowels later on, it's not the end of the world.

Someone has propped their men's trailer back up on its bricks, but it has a desolate and abandoned air—dead flies beneath the windows, cobwebs, a smell of must and staleness that he never noticed when they lived there. He looks at his old bunk, the dirty and sweat-stained mattress. He never noticed that either. The Andriy Palenko who used to sleep here was a different man—he has already grown out of him, like a pair of too-tight shoes. It has happened so quickly.

Hm. Here are some signs of recent activity: a couple of glasses in the sink with a faint whiff of alcohol in them and a used condom on the floor at the side of the double bed. Some secret lovers have been meeting here. He smiles. Taking the condom, he wraps it in some paper and puts it in the bin before Emanuel spots it. But Emanuel has swung himself up into his old hammock and lies there with a blissful look on his face, swaying gently. Just for a moment, Andriy stretches out on the double bed and gazes through the window up the field to where the women's trailer used to be. A misty feeling comes over him. He closes his eyes.

Holy bones! Suddenly it is a quarter past six! He shakes Emanuel awake.

"Come, my friend. Let's go!"

To speed things up, they uncouple their trailer from the Land Rover and leave it to collect later. Quietly, without telling Emanuel, he takes the five-bullet gun from his backpack and stows it in his trouser pocket.

The strawberry farm at Sherbury is only a couple of kilometers farther on. It seems more like a factory than a farm, a soulless industrial place with big packing sheds and lorries waiting to be loaded. There are no strawberry fields here, but behind a low wire fence is a field full of trailers, dozens of them, anonymous oblong boxes parked as close together as cars in a parking lot. He pulls the Land Rover into the yard and looks around.

The brick building at the end of the yard has some steps up to a door marked OFFICE. It is closed, but people are hanging around down below. He approaches them at random—"I am looking for a Ukrainian girl. Her name is Irina." They direct him to one trailer after another, jabbering away about who lives where, keeping him waiting. Come on, come on. Time is passing and they're getting nowhere.

Then he sees it—he is sure it was not there a few minutes ago—the gleaming black curvaceous dark-windowed chrome-barred leather-seated four-by-four, crouching half hidden at the corner of the barn like a predator waiting to pounce. A pulse starts hammering in his head.

"Emanuel—you start at that side of the field. I start at this side. Knock on every door."

There are Ukrainians, Poles, Romanians, Bulgarians, everybody seems to be here. Some people know Irina, some even worked with her today. Yes, definitely the same girl. Pretty. Long dark hair. Not sure which trailer she is in. Come on, come on, you idiots. Now all his pulses are hammering. He races frantically from one trailer to another. Eventually he knocks on the door of number thirty-six.

"Yes," says the girl, "Irina lives here. Irina Blazhko. But she went out somewhere. And Lena, too. Maybe twenty minutes ago."

"Lena went out for cigarettes," says another girl. "I don't know where Irina went."

They lead Andriy and Emanuel to the common room in the barn, where the cigarette machine and pay phone box are installed, but neither Lena nor Irina is there. A crowd of strawberry pickers has gathered, and now they're all milling around looking for the missing girls in the trailer field, the packing shed, the barn, the yard. There is an air of excitement and chaos. Everyone wants to know what's going on. Then he notices something that makes his heart stop—the black four-by-four has disappeared from the yard.

Is he too late? Where have they gone? Maybe they're already on their way back to Dover. Or maybe, yes—the same place they stopped for lunch. Good place for *make possibility*. That's where Vulk will have taken them. He tries not to think about what might be happening to the girls. Focus on what's possible. Just get there quick. He's glad he left the trailer behind.

"Let's go! Let's go, Emanuel! Dog! Dog!"

The useless animal has disappeared. He'll have to come back for it later.

Without the trailer to slow them down, it takes less than twenty minutes to get back to the grassy picnic place. He stops a few meters short of the turning, then inches forward, as slowly and quietly as he can. Yes, as he guessed, the black four-by-four is there, parked a little way up the track, beyond the ruined picnic table, pulled well in under the overhanging branches of a tree. He brings the Land Rover in, so they are blocking the exit. Wait—are you crazy, Andriy Palenko? This type's a killer. But the comforting weight of the gun on his thigh gives him courage. He jumps down silently. Emanuel jumps down too. Together, keeping close to the bushes, they sneak down the track.

As they get near the four-by-four, he notices that it's moving—it seems to be bouncing up and down rhythmically on its springs. He hears some muffled moaning and grunting from inside. The monster! The devil's bum-wipe!

They creep closer. The light has started to fade. The windows of the vehicle are of darkened glass and steamed up from inside, so at first it's impossible to see what's going on in there. Then he notices a centimeter gap at the top of the driver's side window. He presses up close, cupping his hands round his eyes. Inside, the seats have been pulled down into a bed and he sees a woman's figure lying there, naked, her pale breasts casually exposed, her head thrown back, her white knees spreadeagled. And between those fragile girlish knees Vulk's solid rump is hammering away, up and down, up and down.

"Stop!"

Rockets explode inside his skull. All his plans and tactics are blown away. All he can do is bang on the window with his fists, howling "Stop! Stop! Stop! Stop!"

The couple inside the vehicle stop dead. Andriy glimpses a gleam of purple as Vulk, still massively engorged, withdraws from the girl. Raising himself on his forearms, he flings back his head and bellows, "Yrrhaaa!" Then he flops forward onto the girl with a groan.

The girl lifts her head and turns her face toward the window, her eyes like empty wells, her mouth sagging open. But what has she done to her hair? He realizes in that instant that it is not Irina.

As she catches his eye watching her at the window, the girl's mouth opens wider. She screams. She cannot move; she is pinioned under Vulk's vast belly. She tries to raise herself, struggling frantically. Suddenly Andriy is aware of a tremor from Emanuel, who is standing beside him, craning to see through the chink with apparent enthusiasm.

"Emanuel! Go back to Land Rover! This is not good for you to see."

Emanuel turns to him with a cryptic smile.

"Canal knowledge!"

What has got into him?

Now the couple in the vehicle have started to scramble into their clothes, the girl is covering herself with her arms, her thin childish body trembling, and Vulk is trying to get a grip on his trousers, which are stuck on his boots around his ankles. But he can't do it—he just can't do it in the cramped space in the back of the four-by-four, so he opens the door, thrusts his thick legs out, and struggles into his trousers with a pained grimace. Andriy is waiting for him.

"What type of devil are you?" he shouts. His rage gives him courage—and the weight of the gun in his pocket. "Why for you take this young girl?"

"You bleddy idiot! I kill you!" Vulk's jaw is twitching, his fists clenching and unclenching as he wrestles to ease the zipper over his monstrosity.

"Where is Irina?"

"Not here. It is not here. You bleddy fool. You can see. This is another."

"Where is Irina? I know you been after her."

"Irina is running. Running from Vulk. All time running."

He half expects Vulk to draw a gun on him, but either he has not replaced it yet or he has decided that he needs nicotine more than an armed showdown, for he now gives up the struggle with his zipper, lights a cigar with shaking hands, and starts puffing away as though his life depends on it, sucking the smoke in through his teeth.

"Listen," he mutters, "if you find this Irina, I vill pay you for it. Good money."

Andriy feels a mixture of relief and disgust.

"Why for you want her? You have this girl now."

Vulk puffs, enveloping Andriy in a cloud of smoke, his stained teeth chomping on the cigar. His lips are pink and moist. He licks them with his tongue, a quick movement, like a snake.

"Irina is better. Better-class girl. No boyfriend. Hrr. I like it."

"You degenerate pensioneer. Why you not find nice babushka to fuck?"

"Young girl is good for old man." Vulk's snake-tongue flicks across his lips. "Mek him nice stiffy. Good business."

Wreathed in smoke, he resumes the tussle with his zipper, and breathes a grunt of relief as it slides up at last. Andriy stares, despite himself fascinated by the physicality of the man, those greedy eyes, that smile of possession, that gross bulk stretched tight as a drum above his trouser belt, the little flecks of dandruff like droppings of mortality on his collar. So this is how evil is embodied.

"Is it for love you want? Or business?"

"Loff? Business?" He grins. "Is same thing, no?"

This corrupted old devil—he doesn't understand the difference.

"Maybe you little puppy boy, you like it older?" Vulk sneers, lowering his voice to a coarse whisper. "If you vant I can find for you. Good voman. Matoor. Plenty titty. Better than this one. She mek you nice little stiffy."

Then he reaches into the back of the vehicle, where the girl is pulling on a pair of too-tight jeans, and gives her a slap on the rump.

"This my new girlfriend. Eh, Lena? You like Vulk?"

She shrieks playfully.

"Where is Irina?" Andriy leans forward and asks the girl quietly in Ukrainian. "Have you seen her?"

The girl looks no older than fifteen. Her eyes are completely blank, unfathomable. She shrugs. "You know, this Irina, she doesn't talk to nobody. She thinks she is better class of person than other Ukrainians." Her voice is girlish and breathy, with a strong Kharkiv accent. Her eyes shift sideways and downward, avoiding his gaze.

"Little sister, you come with me." He reaches out his hand to the girl. "This is no good for you. I take you back to strawberry place."

The dark eyes flicker upward briefly in a look halfway between fear and contempt.

"Who you are, Mr. Clever-Clever, sticking poky-nose in everybody's business?" For the first time he catches the faint whiff of vodka. "Who asked you to come here?"

"Sister, you too young for this type of game. You should be in school."

"I am seventeen. Older than you think." She has climbed out of the four-by-four and is buttoning up her jumper. She is scarcely more than a meter and a half tall. Her breathy voice has taken on a defiant edge. "And I know this game since age of twelve." In the dusky light, the dead pools of her eyes gleam darkly. "First with uncle. Then with others. You think you so clever. You think you know everything. What you know about life for woman in Yasnygor?"

He thinks of his mother, her face haggard at age forty-five, scrabbling to collect droppings of coal from the railway line near their house, of his sister drudging all hours to support her drunk of a husband, then preparing his evening meal when she gets home.

"Sister, only you know your life. But you can try to make it better."

"So I try. This my boyfriend." She strokes Vulk's ponytail, a ghost of a smile on her mouth. "He gives me money. He gives me new job. Better than strawberry picking. Eh, Vulchik?"

He wishes he could just grab her with both hands and shake her—shake that pathetic smile off her face, shake the deadness out of her eyes. What is happening to his country? It is becoming a human wasteland.

"Sister, this new job is only to make sex for money."

The smile flickers.

"Sex for money. Sex for no money. Which you think is better, eh, Mr. Clever nosy-poker?"

I AM DOG I RUN I SEEK YOUNG RIBBON-ON-NECK-SMELL FEMALE FOR MY GARLIC-AND-LOVE-PISS MAN I CAN SMELL HER SNIFF SHE IS HERE SHE IS RUNNING BIG SMOKE-STINK MAN IS RUNNING AFTER HER I BARK HAARR HAARR I JUMP I SNAP I BITE HIS LEG I BITE HIS ARM I SMELL HIS BAD BLOOD HAARR HAARR HE SHOUTS HE STOPS SHE RUNS AWAY I FOLLOW WOOF SHE STOPS I STOP SHE TURNS AND RUNS SHE RUNS I RUN AFTER WOOF WOOF SHE IS RUNNING WRONG WAY RUNNING TOO FAST I RUN IN FRONT OF HER I SIT NOSE ON GROUND WOOF SHE STOPS I COME CLOSER WOOF WOOF SHE

DOESN'T KNOW WHICH WAY TO RUN THIS YOUNG FEMALE IS MORE
STUPID THAN A SHEEP WOOF WOOF SHE TURNS AND STARTS TO RUN
ANOTHER WAY I RUN IN FRONT OF HER I SIT NOSE ON GROUND
WOOF SHE STOPS SHE TURNS ANOTHER WAY THIS IS THE RIGHT WAY
NOW SHE IS RUNNING THE RIGHT WAY I RUN BEHIND NOT TOO
FAST WHEN SHE STOPS I COME CLOSE SNAP SNAP SHE RUNS AGAIN
SHE IS RUNNING TO MY WHEELIE-HOME SHE RUNS I RUN I AM DOG

Dear Sister

I was blessed today with a joyful Opportunity to witness canal knowledge
thanks to that good mzungu Andree who cheered me up with brotherly
love fearing I had never seen this sight before when infact I have witnessed
canal knowledge more than once it being common in Limbe though not
with the Nuns.

When the Spawn of Satan cried out and cursed his upstanding manhood it
brought into my mind the time when Joel the one-eyed drover was
witnessed in the garden of Mrs. Phiri by seven boys from the orphanage
who had encircled the adulterers in the hot fever of their sin and hurled
mangoes upon them which were ripe and full of yellow juice. That also was
a joyful occurrence.

Then occurred the most outstanding occurrence for when we got back to
the trailer Andree was still heavyhearted and we came upon the dog which
was barking as if possessed and inside the trailer was the beauteous Irina
beloved of Andree. And Andree's countenance was filled with Radiance
and many joyful embracings followed. And Andree's eyes gleamed in an
unmanly way and Irina's also although off course she being a woman it was
not unmanly. No it was. It is very confusing. And my eyes also became
womanly.

I AM DOG I AM GOOD DOG I HAVE CHASED AWAY SMOKE-STINK MAN
I HAVE BROUGHT MORE-STUPID-THAN-SHEEP RIBBON-ON-NECK-
SMELL FEMALE TO GARLIC-AND-LOVE-PISS MAN HE IS HAPPY SHE IS
HAPPY NOW THEY SAY GOOD DOG I AM GOOD DOG I SEE FAT

PIGEON COME DOWN FOR BERRIES EATS BERRIES TOO GREEDY
EATING NOT LOOKING I JUMP SNAP DEAD I GIVE TO MY MAN
GOOD DOG SAYS GARLIC-AND-LOVE-PISS MAN GOOD DOG SAYS
MEAT-AND-HERB-PISS MAN I AM GOOD DOG I AM TIRED AFTER ALL
MY GOOD-DOG JOBS I REST HEAD ON PAWS BESIDE FIRE WITH MY
MAN I LISTEN TO THE SINGING OF BIRD IT SINGS IN BIRD-
LANGUAGE THIS IS MY FIELD BUGGERRR OFF THIS IS MY WOOD
BUGGERRR OFF FEMALE SAYS HOW BEAUTIFUL IS THE SONG OF THE
BIRD SHE IS MORE STUPID THAN A SHEEP THAT BIRD IS NOT GOOD
BIRD IF IT COMES DOWN FROM ITS TREE I WILL CATCH IT SNAP
DEAD EAT I AM GOOD DOG I AM DOG

Dear Sister

We feasted tonight upon bread and marrow gin and carrots of which we
had an abundance and a fat pigeon which was captivated by the dog and
strawberries which were even more delicate than before. We made a big
fire and sat on the hilltop from whence we could behold the beauteous
sunset (though not as beauteous as the sunsets of Zomba) and the bird sat
on the branch singing its cheerful song and the running dog was at rest.
Then we fell upon remembering our previous feastings in this place and
the songs we had sung and Andree said Emanuel sing something for us. So
I closed my eyes and opened my heart and sang the prayer for peace Dona
Nobis Pacem. And more unmanly tears were shed.

As the first stars prickled the ferment Irina said she was weary and she
returned to the small trailer which had been the women's dwelling place.
I guessed that there might be some canal knowledge between these two
so I went into the empty trailer which had been the men's dwelling and
it was very delightful for me to sleep in the hammock that I had made
there.

Before I went into sleep I prayed as every night for the forgiveness of my
sins and for the Lord to protect me from evil and to be reunited with you
dear sister. Then I fell to thinking about Sister Theodosia who was the
organist in the convent at Limbe who is fat and beloved of singing and who

taught me the prayer for peace which I sang this night and many other beauteous songs.

I was enraptured in thought of Sister Theodosia and her musics all the time beating the two pedals up and down with her two small feet which I recalled with great delight when the door of the trailer opened and Andree entered very silently in order not to awaken me although I was not asleep and Andree took off his clothes and lay upon his bed. And I thought that if canal knowledge had occurred between these two it was very speeded up or if it had not occurred at all Andree might be grievous vex. But Andree said nothing. So after some whilings I was smitten with a sinful curiosity and I asked whisperingly Andree did you commit canal knowledge? He whiled in silence then he said in a heavy voice go to sleep Emanuel.

Soon I deducted from the long drawn breaths that Andree was asleeping and I too was standing with one foot on the doorstep of Sleep. And as darkness stole me away I returned in my dream to the time before the orphanage and the convent and the mission house to the time when we lived in our small village beside the Shire River with our parents and our sisters and we spoke the Chichewa language which is still the language of my dreams.

Suddenly I was called back from the dreamworld by an outstanding disturbance which was aroused by the barking of the dog followed by infernal blazings of light and roarings of engines. Andree leaped from the bunk and banged his head uttering some blasphemies in his Ukrainian tongue for it was dark in the trailer with no lightings. I jumped from my hammock and opened the curtains and we saw the blazing was from the lights of a car. Then Andree put on his trouser and I thought that his manhood was upstanding but he had some large heavy item in the pocket and I also put on my trouser for I feared the Spawn of Satan was come for Irina.

Outside in the field was a pandimonium of barkings and shoutings and blazings and roarings but when I emerged from the trailer I saw it was not the Spawn who had arrived but Vitaly of whom I told you before and his accompaniment who was a mature woman of diminished beauty with blond hair arranged like a cockerel sitting upon her head. And she was

leaning her cheek on the shoulder of Vitaly in a rollsome way which made
me wonder whether I was about to witness another canal knowledge.

Vitaly!!! What you doing here??? shouted Andree.

I could say same to you!!! shouted Vitaly.

Then the cockerel-haired woman started to laugh rollsomely and she said
to Andree we meet again I thought I told you to beat it.

And Vitaly said yes beat it this place is no longer available.

And Andree said you beat it you devil's bum-wiper.

And the woman said looking all the while wantonly upon Andree who was
wearing a trouser but no shirt Boys Boys please there's no need to fight.

And Vitaly said Wendy this Ukrainian is a no-good.

And the woman said in a commodious voice it's OK puppet let's go back
home Lawrence won't mind he can watch.

And Andree said Lawrence the farmer?

And the woman said yes puppet he has just come out of hospital and he
likes to sit in his wheelchair and watch mind you it's the only thrill he gets
these days serves him right the philandering old goat.

Then the cockerel haired woman entered the car which was small and red
and like a precious jewel in appearance and Vitaly also entered the car. And
behold Vitaly was sitting in the driver seat. Vitaly took the keys for the car
from his pocket and started the engine with a fearsome roaring and with
more fearsome roarings turned the car around. And I saw that Andree was
watching Vitaly driving the car and his countenance was darkened with a
cloud of desolation.

Then we came back to the trailer and I saw Andree take the item from his
pocket and put it in the bottom of his bag and go back to his bed and soon he
was sleeping again. But I could not sleep on account of the disturbance and
after a while I was smitten with a sinful curiosity and I looked into Andree's
bag and I saw the item hidden there was a gun. And my heart began to
hip-hop like a bullfrog for a gun is the hand tool of Satan for bringing
Sorrow and Death into the world. And I took the gun and went creeping
into the wood and buried it beneath the prickly bushes for Andree is a good
man and I would save him from the possibility of committing a grave sin.

So, it has come to this. That mobilfonman Vitaly has a blond Angliska girlfriend and a red sports car. And what have you got, Andriy Palenko? An old Land Rover that needs a new clutch, a friend who is obsessed with canals, and a dog—well, actually, the dog is quite superb, there are no complaints about the dog. And a Ukrainian girl, nice-looking but showing not the least inclination toward you, which you have to admit is disappointing after all the trouble you've been through. You would have expected some reward, even just a little kiss.

For when you reached out your hand to stroke her cheek, her plump, curved, irresistible cheek, ripe like an apple, but you did it courteously, and in a gentlemanly manner, she jumped back as though you'd tried to violate her and cried out, "Leave me alone!"

Then she started to cry, and you would have put your arm around her, but you didn't want to provoke another outcry. Why is she behaving like this? Maybe she still thinks she's too cultivated for you. Maybe she just doesn't find you so attractive, Andriy Palenko. Maybe she is still thinking of her boxer boyfriend, or maybe she's dreaming of a smart mobilfon businessman type. Then she wants to go to bed, and you say you'll go back to the other trailer, thinking she will say, no, Andriy, stay with me. But she doesn't. She only says, let the dog stay with me. She prefers the dog! Well, what do you care? So you go back to the trailer not in a good mood. And just as you're about to go to sleep, Emanuel starts talking about canals.

The way he touched my cheek—it reminded me of Vulk. *You like flov-ver.* . . . My whole body froze. I tried to explain, to tell him what happened to me that night in the woods, how it feels to be hunted. But no words would come. I just started to cry. I was longing for him to take me in his arms and comfort me, make me feel safe. But he just looked annoyed. Then he went off to stay in the trailer with Emanuel. Why didn't he stay with me? I felt so lonely and scared, I asked if the dog could stay with m

even though I didn't like it so much because it stuck its nose shamelessly between my legs and fixed me with its doggy eyes.

In the middle of the night the dog started to bark. When I woke up and saw the headlights of a car blazing in the field, I was overwhelmed with despair. I thought it was the end. I was sure it was Vulk, come to get me.

My mind told me to run, but I couldn't. Suddenly I felt too tired of running, as though not just my bones but my heart was full of lead. I remembered how light-hearted I had felt when I saw my orange ribbon around the dog's neck. Then I saw our homey little trailer parked in the field. It's in the wrong place, I thought. This must be a dream—the honeysuckle air, the whole hillside bathed in that illusory mauve evening light. The door wasn't locked. Inside, it was warm from the sun, and there was an intense smell of strawberries, and there they were, ranged out on the table, six bowls full. Who were they for? It was like a fairy tale. I couldn't stop myself—I started to eat. But who could have picked them? I looked around. On the floor was a bright green anorak that looked familiar. And here, in the locker above the bunk, was my striped canvas bag! I looked inside. My nightie, my hairbrush, my spare T-shirt, some dirty underpants, even my money. It looked as though someone had rummaged through it, but it was all there. Even the pictures we'd stuck up on the walls: David Beckham, the Black Virgin of Krakow, a baby seal, a tiger cub, and a little panda. Mother and Papa. They were all here. Then, when Andriy and Emanuel turned up, I knew it wasn't a dream, and I thought, this is it. I'm safe at last.

No, I wouldn't run anymore. Instead, I crawled under the folding bed, like a hunted animal goes to earth, down into a deep place where it feels safe, and I curled up and pulled all the sleeping bags around me. After a while the noise died down and I must have cried myself to sleep. I can't remember what I dreamed that night. I can only remember it was a dream of emptiness and despair, as though my cup of life had drained to the bottom.

In the morning I was surprised to find myself still alive, and lying under the bed. The sun was shining through the window. I heard Andriy and Emanuel running up and down the field calling my name. When he said my name—"Ee-ree-na!"—it sent a tingle through me. Then the dog showed them where I was hiding, and we all started to laugh. We had breakfast—strawberries, and bread and margarine again. Then he said, "Today we are going to London to find Emanuel's friend, Toby McKenzie. Do you want me to take you back to strawberry farm, Irina? *Ee-ree-na*. Or do you want to come with us?"

"I will come with you."

Dear Sister

Today we set out for London with me sitting in front beside Andree and I was cheerful at this opportunity for further questioning but Andree said he could not drive and talk in English at the same time.

So I fell to thinking about this English language which sometimes seems like a fearsome slippery serpent sliding this way and that unleashing his scaly coils upon the tongue. Then my first English lessons fizzed into my memory at the orphanage school at Limbe with Sister Benedicta who was not English nor had ever been in England but was from Goa in India and inpartially Portuguese. Who herself had learned English from an Irish Nun who had somehow turned up on their faraway shore by whose exemplar Sister Benedicta herself became a Nun and voyaged to Africa because of the many lost souls here to be saved ours among them she said. Sister Benedicta forced education into us through choral chanting from scriptures prayers sermons and other uplifting objects of devotion in order to commit them to memory. Unlike Sister Theodosia who was fat Sister Benedicta was thin and stern with shining brown skin and darting eyes and she wore small gold-rimmed glasses that hung on a chain around her neck and she was quick to chastise us with her staff.

So being aged twelve years at the time and you dear sister were already away at Blantire I fell into wondering about canal knowledge. When I asked Sister Benedicta she shook her staff at me but Sister Theodosia told me to ask Father Augustine when he came from Zomba but Father Augustine said canal knowledge is Sin and the wages of sin is Death. And whenever I think of canal knowledge these words rattle in my memory.

Andriy is still feeling disgruntled after last night and in no mood for conversation with Emanuel, who is sitting beside him in the front seat of the Land Rover, smiling cheerfully and asking questions about canals. Where does this obsession with canals come from? And why was he so excited by that horrible business in the back of the four-by-four? Surely he's too innocent to be interested in such stuff. Or maybe he isn't.

And here's another thing that's bothering him: Why is Irina sitting in the back, when clearly as a woman she should be seated in front? It can only be because she doesn't want to sit beside him. Is he too uncivilized for her? Well, it doesn't matter, because soon he will drop them both off in London, Emanuel with Toby McKenzie and Irina at the Ukrainian Embassy, where she will get a new passport, and then he will be on his way to Sheffield and whatever awaits him there.

The clutch slips as he tries to engage second, and he has to do a quick maneuver to get straight from first to third. This place they are looking for, this Richmond Park—it seems to be nothing but a big field and a few trees. Where are all the houses? Finally, they are directed to a small row of houses on the south side. The house they are looking for, number five, is at the end of the row.

He can see even from outside the gate that it is the house of a successful businessman. Many windows, porticoed door in the center, double garage, et cetera. No doubt Vitaly will one day live in a high-spec house like this. And the car? Hm. The only car outside is a VW Golf, 2.0 GLS—not a bad car, features include convertible roof, leather seats, advanced sound system, et cetera, and looks like automatic transmission, unfortunate in high-powered car because you get better performance with a manual gear shift, but even so, quite a nice car. Yes, he wouldn't mind taking it for a run, but really he would have expected something more interesting with a house like this.

But how does Emanuel know such a wealthy man? For his friend strides up to the house with his piece of paper in his hand and a beaming smile upon his face, and rings on the bell several times. A woman appears at the front door, about the same age as Wendy but more beautiful, though her hair is brown, not blond, with some threads of gray, and swept elegantly back from her face. In fact she is quite like *Let's Talk English* Mrs. Brown, with neat waist and breasts, but her feet are bare with purple-painted toenails. This is so unexpected that he has to force himself not to stare at them. There is something incredibly sexy about those purple-painted toenails.

She looks at the three of them and Dog with surprise, and takes the piece of paper that Emanuel hands to her.

"Yes, Toby lives here. But he's out at the moment. And may I ask who you are?"

"I am Emanuel Mwere, and Toby is my brother. Two years ago he came into volunteering at Zomba, near Limbe, and our extreme friendship commenced at this time."

"Zomba in Malawi?"

"Yes, madam. Toby was volunteering in the school contagious to the mission center where I was learning to perform wood carvings, and Toby came to pursue a wood carving." Emanuel speaks carefully, as though his mouth is full of stones. His vocabulary is surprisingly sophisticated, thinks Andriy.

"Oh yes, I remember the wood carving Toby brought home. Exquisite. Did you do that?"

"Alas, no, madam. The wood carving pursued by Toby was the work of a much more talented carver. Our friendship springs from a different source. I once saved him from an evil occurrence, and we swore brotherhood together. My name is Emanuel Mwere. Did he not talk to you of me?"

"You saved him from evil?"

"Yes, madam. From prison incarnation. In connection with substances."

"Ah." A subtle look passes over her face. "You'd better come inside. And these . . . ?"

"These my friends from strawberry. Irina, Andriy. They are Ukrainian. And our resplendent dog."

Dog woofs and wags his tail. She bends down and rubs his head. Andriy can see that she is already smitten.

"I'm Toby's mother, Maria McKenzie. Come in. You must be hungry."

She leads them through a tall wood-paneled hallway into the kitchen of the house, which is bigger than their whole apartment in Donetsk, with a refrigerator the size of his grandmother's wardrobe, glass doors that open onto the garden, and a long wooden table in the center, on which are flowers in a vase and a bowl piled full of strawberries. Only the sight of the strawberries is strangely depressing. Then she sets a feast out for them—so many strange and delicious dishes, of leaves and herbs and grains and nuts, and breads, and vegetables cut into salads, tomatoes, peppers, radishes, olives, avocados such as he has only seen and not tasted before, with delicious yogurts and sauces, et cetera, which after their monotonous and restricted diet create such a pleasurable sensation in the mouth that he finds himself eating more and more, and then he has to restrain himself, because he doesn't want her to think he is starving, and he doesn't want Irina to think he has no manners, though what does he care what she thinks? Surreptitiously he looks across at her and sees that she too is stuffing herself as though she has not eaten for days, and even licking her fingers, which he did not allow himself to do.

But one thing is disappointing. Where is the meat? In a house like this you would expect a big fat steak, maybe some juicy pork cutlets cooked with garlic, or at least a tasty piece of sausage or some stew with dumplings. As though reading his mind, Maria McKenzie goes over to the cupboard and fetches a large tin marked STEAK IN GRAVY. The picture on the tin shows huge chunks of gleaming brown meat. His stomach purrs in anticipation. She opens the tin and empties the contents into a bowl. Then she puts the bowl on the floor, and before he can say anything the dog has gobbled it all up.

"Would you like some more?" she asks them.

"Yes, please, madam." He and Irina say it simultaneously. They look across the table at each other and laugh. Her cheeks dimple in that sexy way, and she doesn't seem so stuck up anymore. Maria McKenzie fetches some raw carrots from the refrigerator and chops them into fingers, with some celery and cucumber pieces, and a bowl of some delicious creamy, nutty sauce, which he eats with great pleasure. But his eyes meet Irina's and they exchange smiles again, because there is a bag of carrots in their trailer, and Dog is sitting in the corner with a satisfied look on his face and licking his jaws.

While they are eating, Maria McKenzie takes out her mobilfon and dials some numbers, and though she speaks very quietly with her back turned toward them, he can pick up what she is saying.

"Yes, from Malawi. Yes. Yes, he said prison. No, he said substances. Toby, don't lie to me. No, he doesn't know. He's not here yet. Okay. Okay. See you soon, darling."

She turns to her guests with a radiant smile.

"Toby says he'll be back soon."

The woman, Mrs. McKenzie, was very kind, despite having purple toenails like a witch's. In my opinion, nail varnish, if used at all on the toes, should be discreet. She offered me some strawberries and I forced myself to eat a few out of politeness, for how could she know the truth about her strawberries? Then she made me some special herbal tea, which she said would rebalance my positive and negative energies—it's a stupid idea, but the tea was quite nice. It was warm and quiet in the kitchen, and it smelled of baking. We sat on a sofa to one side of the huge enameled stove. You could hear the tick-tock of a big clock, and the snoring of the dog—sss! hrr! sss! hrr!—who was curled up in the cat's basket in front of the stove.

We chatted a bit. It turns out she has been to Kiev. She asked about my parents, so I told her my Papa is a professor and has written a lot of books, and I hope one day to become a writer too, and my Mother is just a housewife and a schoolteacher. Then I felt sad for Mother having such a boring life, and I remembered I had never made that phone call to say sorry.

"Would it be possible to telephone my mother?" I asked.

"Of course, dear."

She passed me the phone.

"Mother?"

"Irina? Is that you?"

At once she started on about being lonely and wanting me to come home.

I said, "Mama, I'm planning to stay here a bit longer. And I'm sorry about what I said last time. I love you."

I'd been dreading saying it, because I thought it would make me cry like a baby, but as soon as I said it I felt better.

"My little girl. I miss you so much."

"Mama, I'm not a little girl. I'm nineteen. And I miss you too."

There was a silence. Then Mother said, "Did you know your aunty Vera is expecting another baby? At her age!" She put on a scandalized voice. Aunty Vera is a source of much gossip in our family. "And a nice couple have moved into that empty flat downstairs. They have a son a bit older than you. Very nice looking."

"Mama, don't start getting ideas."

And we both laughed, and suddenly everything between us was normal and easy again.

Just as I put the phone down, the door opened and a boy walked in, about my age, wearing jeans cut off in that raggedy fashion below the knees and a black T-shirt with a skull on it. His hair was a *koshmar*—long and twisted in thin rats' tails all over his head—and there were some wispy bits of beard on his chin. Definitely not my type.

"Hi, Ma!" he said.

Then he looked at Emanuel, and their faces broke out in big smiles, and they hugged each other and shook hands in a peculiar thumb-twisting way, and hugged again. Mrs. McKenzie started to sniffle. Andriy and I looked at each other and grinned, and he squeezed my knee under the table. Then the cat came in and hissed at the dog, and the dog chased the cat around the kitchen, and Andriy shouted at the dog and he knocked the flower vase over, the water went everywhere, so he started mopping it up with a towel and Mrs. McKenzie cried out, "It's destiny!"

still dabbing at her eyes. Then the door opened again and a man came in, and he said, "Good Lord. What on earth is going on here?"

And the amazing thing is, he looked just like Mr. Brown in my school textbook. But where was the bowler hat?

"Darling . . ." Maria McKenzie's voice is so low and seductive that Andriy feels a distinct tremor in his manly parts, though she is speaking not to him but to the man who has just come in and is now slumped down on the sofa. "Darling, let me get you a drink. Whiskey? Double? On ice? Darling, these are some friends of Toby's. Emanuel here is from Limbe, in Malawi. Do you remember when Toby did his gap year in Malawi? Well, Emanuel is one of the friends he made. And now he's come all the way over here to visit us. Isn't that wonderful? And this is Irina, and Andriy. They're from Ukraine but they've been staying in Kent. And Emanuel has brought them along because they'd like to meet a typical English family."

"Well they've come to the wrong place, haven't they?" The man takes a quick gulp of his whiskey. "And what about the dog? What's the dog's name?"

"Sir, the dog's name is Dog." Andriy wishes he had thought of something more intelligent, but the man chuckles.

"Excellent. Excellent name for a dog. Crossbreed, is it?" His voice is deep and booming, like a foghorn.

"Sir, we know nothing of origin of this dog. It arrived mysteriously in night."

"Hm. That's interesting. Dog, come here. Let me look at you."

Obediently, Dog walks across and sits down at the man's feet, returning his gaze in a way that is both friendly and courteous. Andriy's heart swells momentarily with pride.

"Labrador collie, I'd say, with a bit of German shepherd in there too. Excellent cross. Best dogs you can get."

"Yes, he is very excellent dog." Though he has heard of the Angliski love of animals, still it seems strange that this man seems more interested in the dog than in any of the people in the room. "He is hunting also, and brings all type of creature for us. Many rabbit and pigeon."

Dog is glorying in the attention, wagging his tail, turning his head, and lifting up his paw. The man takes the paw in his very clean business-man hand and shakes it.

"How do you do?" Just like Mr. Brown! "Hm. Not a young dog. You say he arrived in the middle of the night?"

"Yes. When we are camping in wood. We think he is long time running, because feet is bleeding and he has scratchings on body."

"Fascinating. And he hasn't left you since?"

"No. He is all time with us."

"Hm. Remarkable creatures, dogs. Faithful to the end. Maybe he was kidnapped. Dognapped. Kent, did you say? Yes, they still go in for a bit of dog fighting down there, Sadly, in this day and age. They catch pet dogs and throw them to the fighters. Get their aggression up. Barbaric, really. Miners. Should be shot."

Andriy doesn't like the turn this conversation is taking. The man's left eye has started to twitch, and he is gulping the whisky. Dog reaches forward and rests his chin soothingly on the man's knee. The man seems to relax.

"Once, I had a dog. When I was a boy. Buster." He leans down and scratches Dog's ears. His voice is thick with emotion and whiskey. "Can't you take me with you, young man? When you go camping? Down in Kent? Hunting in the woods, with the dog? I'm quite handy with a shot-gun, you know. Hares. Rabbits. Pigeons. I can skin a rabbit. I've still got my Swiss army knife. Fetching wood. Making the fire. Damp matches. Smoke everywhere. Kettle boiling. Tea in enamel mugs. Baked beans. Burnt toast. The whole lot." He looks up at Andriy, his eyes watery and sad. "I wouldn't get in the way."

"Sir, of course you can come with us. But unfortunately we are just coming from Kent, and we are on our way to Sheffield."

The man drains his whiskey glass and groans.

"Supper ready soon, is it, Maria? I'll go and get changed."

As soon as his father has left the room, Toby lets out a sigh of relief.

"That stuff about the prison, Emanuel. It's better if he doesn't know."

"He does not know?" asks Emanuel.

"Sweetheart," says Maria McKenzie to Emanuel in that low seductive voice, "Toby's father is quite old-fashioned in some respects, although he is a very kind and loving father. Isn't he, Toby? But I think it would be fair to say that he has had some difficulty coming to terms with some aspects of Toby's personality."

"Yeah, Ma, he's so straight you could stick him in the ground and grow weed up him."

"Toby, your father is a very good man, and he works very hard for us. And if I had known you would get yourself into trouble in this way, I would never have let you go to Malawi for a year; I would have sent you to my family in Renfrewshire."

"Yeah, yeah, Ma. Is that the end of the sermon?"

"And if your father finds out, Toby," Maria continues, in her sexy *Let's Talk English* voice, "he will blame me for encouraging you to go. Because I was the one who said it would broaden your mind and help you to understand the developing world, and your father was quite against it, because he said there was quite enough underdevelopment around here without going to Zomba, especially in Croydon."

Andriy is beginning to have some doubts about this family. The woman means well, and she does bear some resemblance to Mrs. Brown, with her tiny waist and insatiable tea-drinking, but her ideas about food are bizarre. And what is the significance of the purple toenails? Of course it is well known that married women are sexually voracious, but to make love to a woman under her husband's roof would be asking for trouble, even though the man is drinking too much whiskey and talking strangely and setting a poor example to his wife. And this boy Toby—he speaks to his parents with disrespect, and Andriy wonders whether he will be a suitable mentor for Emanuel, who is young and impressionable and showing an interest in the wrong kind of sex.

"Croydon?" Emanuel exclaims. "I think we went through that place today!"

Dear Sister

Today I was reunited with Toby Makenzi and I will tell you the outstanding story of our friendship for the first time I encounted him was at Zomba. But now these mzungus have sown confusion in me because I can see no likeness between Croydon and Zomba expecting the mission house which is tip-top and built of brick. Now this Toby Makenzi had brought from England an outstanding soccer ball made of leather the likeness of which we had never seen. For when the poor boys of Zomba play soccer we must inflict a balloon and wrap it in plastic baggages which is easily prickled on the prickly bush and many soccer balls perish in this way. And seeing my cheerful countenance when I beheld the soccer ball the mzungu said Brother I am greatly desirous to attain some Malawi Gold and in exchange I will give it to you.

This Malawi Gold is so desirous to mzungus I think it is the main reason they come to our country. And I wonder if Toby Makenzi's parents did not know this why did they send their son here at all? It is regretful also that some of our policemen are corrupted and incarnate the mzungus in order to magnify their income when with much weeping and wailing and a payment of one or two thousand kwachas the mzungus are set free.

But the baggage of Malawi Gold I got for him exceeded any seen before in Zomba and the corrupted policeman who saw it demanded four thousand kwachas and this sum was out of Toby Makenzi's reach. Then I took pity upon him and went to the police and confessed that the Malawi Gold belonged to me and they freed Toby Makenzi and incarnated me in his place. But these policemen have no reward from incarnating a poor orphan boy for whose freedom no one will pay even a hundred kwachas so after four days they set me free after first smiting me numerous blows. And Father Kevin also did chastise me extensively.

And Toby Makenzi's expression was exceedingly mystical for he said Brother you have endured Blows for my Blow. And being filled with outstanding gratitude he said thanks mate if my Ma and Pa ever found out we'd never hear the end of it which I understood to mean that they would be unendingly grateful. And he gave me a desirous green anorak and a good pair of shoes which I still have to this day alongside the soccer ball and he said listen brother I owe you one if you ever come to England drop around at my place and my ma and pa will look after you. Then he wrote his name and address on a paper though it was spelled wrong and we shook hands in the traditional Chewa way of brotherhood.

But when I came to his place I was disappointing that the Ma and Pa had not been a praised of my Good Deed how I freed Toby Makenzi and the grievous blows I endured for his sake. For although I did not yearn for any reward still it would be joyous for them to know.

For this Pa Makenzi is downhearted and partakes exceedingly of whiskey and he takes the name of the Lord in vain. For when the Ma set down his dinner before him he cried out for God's sake Maria do we have to eat this rabbit food isn't there a decent piece of meat in the house? And after some whilings a tip-top fragrance pierced the air and Dog leaped to his feet barking joyously and the Pa said good boy come here I've got a bit for you too.

And when the door was closed again Toby said hey Emanuel did you bring any Malawi Gold with you? And I replied no Brother because I think in England police are less forgiving than in Malawi.

After his dinner Pa Makenzi said to Toby Makenzi so in what useless way have you been idling away your day son of mine?

And Toby said if you must know Pa I've been working on my project.

And the Pa said what project is that?

And Toby said it's about the representation of opiates in the media.

And the Pa clapped his hand upon his eyebrow and said son that will never lead you to gainful employment.

And Toby said Pa who's interested in gainful employment?

And the Pa smote his eyebrow once more and said is there any more whiskey Maria?

And Ma Makenzi said Toby don't talk to your father like that.

And after further excess of whiskey the Pa turned toward Andree and pleaded to let him accompany us on our huntings in the woods. And

Andree who is a very good mzungu maybe even better than Toby Makenzi
said in a calm voice that we were finished with the life of the woods but the
Pa would be very welcome if he wished to travel to Sheffield.
Then the Pa set down his whiskey and smote both eyebrows with his hands
and began to weep and the Ma said in a cheerful voice now I think it's
bedtime everybody would you like me to show you to your rooms?

I AM DOG I SLEEP MY BELLY IS FULL OF GOOD DOG FOOD MEAT I
HAVE WON THE HEART OF THE GOOD VEGETABLE-SMELL FEMALE I
HAVE SOOTHED THE MAN-DRINK-STINK MAN I HAVE CHASED AWAY
THE TROUBLESOME CAT NOW I SLEEP I AM DOG

Dear Sister
In this house of Toby Makenzi is a miraculous bath which upon touching a
switch swirls the water around as fullsomely as the Shire River though off
course without crocodiles and whiling in this bath I fell into a worry about
these good mzungus in their godless torment and wondered how to bring
them consolation.
For this Pa loves hunting and the life of freedom in the woods yet is
confounded by the city. This Ma loves the Pa but is confounded by his
whiskey drinking and blaspheming. Then I was smitten with a joyous
thought. I will give Pa Makenzi the fishing rod of the Mozambicans and
the red bucket. Thus he will hunt for fishes in the rivers and leave behind
the whiskey drinking and blaspheming. And what could I give to Ma
Makenzi? For everyone knows that a beauteous woman is hard to please
and I am a poor boy with nothing to offer. And I was smitten with another
joyous thought. This Ma is beloved of vegetables I will give her the carrots.
This thought along with the fullsome swirling of the water caused me to
open my heart and sing the song of praise which Sister Theodosia taught me
Ave Maria Gratia Plena. And this was also joyous for the Ma's name is Maria.

Andriy Palenko, how can you in all conscience go off and leave your young
friend Emanuel in the care of this abnormal family? What's the matter with

these people, in their massive many-windowed house? Two cars (yes, after the father arrived, he saw a nice fat Lexus squatting on the drive beside the little Golf), three high-spec computers, four televisions, all with flat screens, five bathrooms, four en-suite (yes, he made a little tour of the house). Et cetera. What is the point in all this stuff if it doesn't bring you happiness?

If his own family had had a tenth, no even a hundredth of all this wealth, everything would have been completely different—and would these people even have missed it? "A man needs enough," his father had said, "no less, and no more." But they hadn't had enough. Poor Dad. Yes, his father knew better than anybody that to go underground in those conditions was risky. But when you haven't got enough, that's what you have to do.

Andriy is lying stiff and fully clothed on one of the two beds in the room he is sharing with Emanuel, staring at the ceiling and trying to prepare himself for the conversation ahead. In the nearest of the five bathrooms, Emanuel is singing, filling the whole house with his exuberant music. Andriy has a sudden image of that moment in the cathedral; the pink open mouth, the closed eyes, the tears. The singing stops. There is a sound of water gurgling down a drain. Here he comes.

"Emanuel, my father was kill in coal-mining accident. Your father was kill in canal accident, yes?"

"Both killed. Mother and father."

"This is very terrible. To lose both parents at one time."

"Also my baby brother. This I cannot understand. To punish my little baby brother."

"Emanuel, this is not punishment, it is accident. Sometimes no person is to blame."

"But maybe my father is to blame for being unfaithful to my mother."

"And you think this canal accident was for punishment?"

"No no. HIV sickness was punishment."

Hm. There may be some vital connection you are missing here, Andriy Palenko. But it's no use worrying about something you don't understand. You've only got tonight to get your message across.

"Emanuel, my brother—do you know what is condom?"

"Of course I know. It is an abomination in the eye of the Lord. In Chichewa, we have a saying: *Only a fool eats the sweet with its wrapper*."

Emanuel is standing in the middle of the room, drying himself vigorously on a fluffy white towel, as though buffing his small, lean, knotty body into polished ebony. Andriy has never seen him naked before. He tries not to stare, but he can't help taking a surreptitious peep. Is it true what they say about the black man's manly parts?

"Condom will protect you life, Emanuel. With condom you can have plenty sex no problem. No virus. No organism. No HIV. No problem. After, you say prayer and God will forgive."

Mrs. McKenzie showed me to a room right up under the eaves of the house—such a pretty room, everything matching in blue and white, like in a magazine, and even my own little bathroom with a fluffy white towel warming on the rail and a new bar of scented soap still in its wrapper. I unwrapped it straightaway. It smelled spicy and expensive, not sweet and sickly like soap in Ukraine. I wondered if it would be rude to ask whether I could keep the soap when I left, or whether she would even notice if I just slipped it into my bag. After I'd showered I put on my nightdress, which looked crumpled and gray in that clean white and blue room, but I had nothing else. Then I sat in the armchair, smelling the soap on my arms and hands and wondering where Andriy was, and wondering whether he was wondering where I was. There's something very romantic about attic rooms.

Then there was a knock on the door. My heart started to beat like crazy.

"Come in."

But it wasn't him, it was Mrs. McKenzie.

"Hello," she said, in that soft subtle voice that was like the smell of the soap. "Can I come in?"

"Of course. Please."

She sat down on the edge of the bed.

"Have you got everything you need?"

"I like this room very much."

It was true—I felt as at home as in my own little bedroom in Kiev. Why is it that when you think happy thoughts, tears can suddenly come into your eyes? Sniffle sniffle. What was the matter with me? I don't know why, but all at once I found myself telling her about Vulk, and then the words just came pouring out: his creaky coat, his live-rat ponytail, his cigar-stinking car, his sly black hungry-dog eyes. When I tried to describe that night, the words got stuck in my mouth and made me choke.

Mrs. McKenzie said in her kind voice, "You know, yoga is very calming when you need to relax. Would you like me to show you?"

"No, it's okay."

In my opinion yoga is a typical Western fad, but I didn't want to offend her, and anyway I was still sniffling.

"Do you miss your mother, darling?"

"Yes, of course." Then suddenly I blurted out, "In fact I am missing my father. Since he is no longer living at home."

"He isn't living at home?"

"He is gone to live with someone else. Someone much younger."

As I said those words, I felt my face turn red. I didn't know if it was shame or rage. I felt so sad for Mama, all by herself in the apartment, talking to the cat, eating breakfast on her own and dinner on her own. Then I thought of the way she was always nagging him: Do this, Do that, do you love me, Vanya? When I have a husband, I will never do that.

"You really love him, don't you?" Mrs. McKenzie smiled.

"No. Not at all."

Then I laughed, because I realized that she was talking about Papa, but I was thinking about Andriy Palenko, and wondering what it would be like to feel his arms around me.

Suddenly there was a quiet knock, then the door opened. My heart jumped. But it wasn't Andriy, it was Toby.

"Ma, have you got any condoms?" he whispered.

Mrs. McKenzie didn't even turn her head.

"Second drawer down, my side of the bed. Take care not to wake your father."

"Thanks, Ma."

Hm. Interesting. Strawberry Flavor Ticklers. These are not like any Ukrainian condoms that Andriy has seen, though probably the principle is the same. But how will they demonstrate it to Emanuel?

"I suppose we could show him some porn." Toby McKenzie looks glum. "That might get him horny. I could download something from the net. Paris Hilton and friends. Busty Biker Chicks. You ever seen that?"

"Pornographia?"

"Busty Biker Chicks. Unbelievable."

"I think for Emanuel pornographia is not good."

"Yeah." Toby McKenzie nods. "He's a bit of an innocent, isn't he?"

Andriy is sitting with Toby McKenzie on the red sofa downstairs in the TV room. Everyone else in the house is asleep. Toby is drinking beer from a can. He offers one to Andriy. Andriy shakes his head. He needs to keep his head clear. Then he thinks maybe it's better to be a bit drunk in this situation. He accepts the beer and takes several gulps.

"Toby, this my friend Emanuel, I am worry for him after I go."

"Don't worry, mate, I'll look after him." His glibness is not reassuring.

"Like you say, he is innocent. Maybe better is for him to stay like this."

Toby McKenzie gives him a sideways look. "You want him to stay innocent? What you giving him condoms for?"

Andriy wants to say something deeply intelligent about how Emanuel must take the best of what the West has to offer while also keeping hold of the best from his own culture. But the thought is too complex for his limited English. Maybe the beer wasn't such a good idea.

"He is African," is all he can mumble.

"It's up to him, innit?" Toby scratches the roots of his long plaited hair, examining his nails for evidence of dandruff. "He's got to have the choice. Everyone's got to make their own choice. That's freedom."

"Sometimes we have freedom but we make bad choice. Look at my country Ukraine."

Toby McKenzie shrugs. "You make the wrong choice, you got to live with it. Look at my pa. Funny thing is, he thinks it's me that's making the wrong choice. He thinks it's a choice between working for the system or being a slacker. But it's not." He crunches the empty beer can in his hand. "It's just a choice between whiskey and weed."

This boy is not stupid. But why is he in such a mess?

"Okay, Toby, maybe you right. With condom he has choice."

"At least if he makes the wrong choice it won't kill him. Not like that bloody stuff my pa drinks."

"But how will we make this condom demonstration?"

"Maybe *you'll* have to demonstrate," says Toby.

Hm. This could be embarrassing. Andriy takes another gulp of beer. On the television screen in front of them a troupe of almost-naked female dancers are tossing their hair and thrusting their hips forward rhythmically. Despite their frenzied activity they are having zero impact on his manly parts. Will they be arousing for Emanuel? Unlikely.

Toby McKenzie takes the remote control and starts flicking through a few channels. There is politics, home improvement, a cooking program. Suddenly he stops. "That's it. Vegetables!"

Andriy struggles to picture some arousing scene with onions and cabbages. Really, these Angliski are quite original.

"My ma's got plenty of them. What size is he? Carrot? Banana? Celery? Cucumber?"

Andriy tries to recall that lean black-skinned figure toweling himself dry with a white towel.

"Not cucumber. No. Carrot, no. Maybe we try medium-size banana."

Dear Sister
I have been thinking much about those long ago days before the convent and the orphanage and the mission house at Zomba when we lived with our mother and father and sisters in our mud walled cottage on the banks

of the Shire River of the long days of my nakedness and river fishing and
gathering of mangoes. In those days I had a different understanding of
the world.

But when aged twelve I was beloned and taken into the orphanage by the
good Nuns there I discovered the Knowledge of Good and Evil. For Sister
Theodosia said that God is Love and the Maker of all Good things but
Sister Benedicta said that all the Evil that befalls us is a punishment for our
sins such as the sickness that took away our parents. And the everlasting
punishments that would happen after death she said were consideringly
worse than death itself with roasting fires and boiling oils and lumps of
scorched flesh torn off with pincers.

Then I fell to imagining the gruefull torments our dear ones would be
suffering in hell and often I cried in the night longing for your comfort dear
sister but you were away in Blantyre. Then Sister Benedicta chastised me
with her staff but Sister Theodosia taught me a prayer to sing to Mary
mother of Jesus who would enter seed on our behalf Ora pro nobis
peccatoribus. This is a song of such outstanding beauty that singing it would
set our loved ones' souls at rest even the peccatoribus and also my own soul.
The fear of these torments kept me away from any canal knowledge
despite my sinful curiosity. But tonight Andree and Toby Makenzi showed
me how I may be protected against orgasms that cause the deadly sickness
by clothing my upstanding manhood in a condom and in this way I may
enjoy canal knowledge without paying the mortal price. Then I recalled
that Father Augustine had said the condom is an Abomination in the Eye
of the Lord and although my body would be saved my soul would frizzle in
hell. And I said if I am going to frizzle for canal knowledge should I first
taste the sweet without the wrapper?

But these good mzungus showed me the use of the Abomination by means
of a Banana in such a cunning way that the Banana would frizzle and not
my own Immortal Soul. They took the Banana and clothed it in the
Abomination and Andree said now Emanuel when you are coming
together with woman you put it not upon Banana but upon your own
manly part. This caused me to smile then Andree unclothed the Banana

and ate it being Ukrainian and much beloved of Bananas. So by using a
Banana instead of my own upstanding manhood it would frizzle up in the
Fiery Pit and I would be spared.

For the life of the soul endures beyond the life of the body which has only a
brief flowering then is cast like grass into the oven said Father Augustine
who is a kind man with a big belly and crooked teeth and very short-
sighted. Then he put his arm around me and said don't worry boy your
parents were not bad people but they suffered from the frailty of our fallen
human condition. And seeing the questioning look still on my face he
sighed and said dear boy there are some mysteries in the ways of the Lord
which we are not given to understand but some among us believe there is
no evil without a purpose and we believe He only permits evil because it is
a test for our own Goodness.

But still I have been rubbing some questions over and over in my head
until they begin to smoke and burn like fire sticks and I pray feveredly for
His guidance as I contemplate the Decision I must make. For if I choose
the earthly delights of canal knowledge then I will never know the
heavenly Love nor sing in the Choir of Angels.

bendery

It had rained in the night. I could tell, because the air smelled different. I woke up early in my blue and white attic room, full of excitement and anticipation, because at last I was going to see London, the city of my dreams, and especially because I was going to see it with *him*.

It was strange, at first, being just the two of us in the Land Rover, him sitting at the wheel and me sitting in the passenger seat with the dog at my feet. What were we going to say to each other? I wanted to talk to him. *London is a very beautiful city. English men wear bowler hats.* No, not that stupid stuff. I wanted to talk about us, him and me. *Tell me who you are, Andriy Palenko. Do you love me? Are you the one?* But you can't say that. So we just drove in silence, crawling in the heavy traffic.

According to the map Maria had given me, we were on the South Circular Road. He had that fixed look on his face, concentrating on his driving. And I know this sounds strange, but although he was a Donbas miner I noticed for the first time that in profile he had a slight look of Mr. Brown about him. Then he said, still with that look on his face, as though he were talking to himself, "I wonder what happened to all the carrots?"

"Which carrots?"

"From the trailer. Didn't you notice? Two bags gone. Only six small carrots left."

"Only six? Maybe *she* stole them."

"To feed to her husband."

Then we both started laughing, and that broke the tension between us, so we laughed even more, till our sides ached. Then we drove on in silence for a bit, but now it was a different kind of silence.

Suddenly Andriy slammed the brakes on. "Devil's bum! Did you see that?" The Land Rover lurched all over the road as the trailer bounced on its bracket. "These Angliski drivers! Cut-throat bandits!"

I couldn't help myself. I burst out laughing. "Is that what they say in Donbas?"

"What?"

"Devil's bum!" I laughed.

He gave me a hard look.

"Do you think we're all hooligans in Donbas? Primitive types?"

"No, it's not that. It just sounds funny."

"And so what did you think when you saw all these uncivilized coal miners coming into your Kiev? All with Blue and White flags to protest against your Orange Revolution? All talking with Donbas accent? Did you think it is the barbarians' invasion?"

"I didn't say that."

"No, but I can see what you are thinking. Every time I open my mouth you start to grin."

"Andriy, why are you saying these things?"

"I don't know." He frowned again and clenched his jaw. "I should concentrate. Where are we going?"

"Kensington Park Road." Maria had looked it up for me and shown me on the map. "You have to turn left somewhere up here. About eight kilometers."

On Putney Bridge we got stuck in a traffic jam and then it was solid cars all the way, so by the time we got to Kensington Park Road the consulate was just closing. I pleaded with the woman behind the desk. I explained my passport had been stolen and I needed to get a new one. But she was one of those pouty-mouth types who looks as though she finds talking to people too exhausting.

"Come back Monday." She rolled her eyes and tottered off in her pencil-tight skirt, which in my opinion she did not have the figure to wear.

"Well?" asked Andriy, who was waiting outside, and when I told him, he said, "These new Ukrainians. They forget who pays their wages."

Then we went quiet, because obviously we had a decision to make.

"Do you want to go back to Richmond?" he said

"Do you?"

"It's up to you."

"No, you decide." I was being careful—careful not to upset him again.

"I'll do whatever you want," he said.

"I don't mind."

"Well, let's toss a coin. Heads we go back, tails we go on."

He found a coin in his pocket and flicked it in the air with his thumb, and it landed heads up.

"That's it. We'll go back, then," he said.

"All right." I looked at the coin, and I looked at him. "But we don't have to if we don't want to, do we?"

"I'll do whatever you want."

"I don't mind. But I don't really want to go back to Richmond, unless you do. I mean, they were nice . . ."

"Nice but crazy," he said.

We both laughed.

"Where do you want to go, then?" He had that Mr. Brown look on his face again.

"I don't mind. You decide."

This girl—he's getting nowhere with her. One minute she's smiling, then she won't talk at all, and then sometimes she laughs at him as though he's some kind of idiot. It's like the Land Rover gearbox: fourth gear and reverse are too close together. You're just going along nicely in third, and ready to change up to fourth, and suddenly you find you've slammed it into reverse and you stop dead or jump backward. Now she's smiling again, saying she wants to look around London and see Globe Theatre, Tabard Inn, Chancery, Old Curiosity Shop. What is this stuff? What does she think he is—an exclusive VIP tour guide? First he'd better find somewhere to park, because driving in this traffic with a trailer is no joke. He can't even get up into third most of the time, and that second gear keeps slipping out, so he's been driving in first, and they're burning up petrol fast, and he's going to need at least another tankful to get up to Sheffield. If he had the tools, he'd take a look at that gearbox. He has heard that the Land Rover gearbox is quite something. How would it compare with their old Zaporozhets? he wonders. Yes, that had had a similar gearbox fault.

When he was thirteen, his father had bought a second-hand sky blue Zaporozhets 965—the "Zaz," they called it affectionately, hump-backed like a kind old granddad. It was the first mass-produced workers' car in Ukraine. Real metal body—not fiberboard rubbish like the Trabant. He was the first person in their apartment block to own one. Every Sunday he cleaned and polished it out in the street, and sometimes he and Andriy would spend a couple of hours together, head to head under the hood, just tinkering. (Listen, boy, his father had said. Listen to the music of internal combustion.) His dad would tune the engine fine-fine, to make it run sweetly. Tut-ut-ut-ut-ut-ut. Those were good times. As the car got older, the tinkering sessions grew longer. Together, they ground down the valves and replaced the solenoid and the clutch. He learned something about car engines, but the main thing he learned was that all problems can be solved if you approach them in a patient and methodical way. In the end, the car outlived his father. Poor Dad.

This girl—he has tried to approach her in a patient and methodical way, but she is more unpredictable than a slipping gearbox. Will he ever get to the fine-tuning stage? Hm. He turns off onto a side street, and then another, following a narrow alleyway between two tall buildings. Here's a piece of land where something has been demolished, with a sign saying NO PARKING and some vehicles parked. This'll do.

"Let's walk?"

"Let's walk."

Now, for some unfathomable reason, she's smiling.

The weather is too warm. Despite the recent rain, the air is already dusty again. It smells of car fumes and blocked drains and the miscellaneous smells of the five million other people who are breathing it at the same time. He feels an unexpected excitement rising in him. This London—once you've gotten your feet on the ground, and you don't have to worry about those Angliski bandit-drivers—this London is quite something.

He is amazed, at first, just by the vastness of it—the way it goes on and on until you forget there is anything beyond it. Okay, he has seen Canterbury and Dover, but nothing can prepare you for the sheer excess of this city. Cars that glide as smooth and silent as silver swans, deluxe model, not the battered old smoke-belchers you get back home. Office blocks that almost blot out the sky. And everything in good order— roads, pavements, et cetera—all well maintained. But why are all the buildings and statues covered in pigeon droppings? Those swaggering birds are everywhere. Dog is delighted. He chases them around, barking and leaping with joy.

They come to a row of shops, and the windows are stuffed with desirable items. Minute mobilfons, packed with advanced features, everything compact and cleverly made; movie cameras small enough to fit in your hand; cunning miniature music systems, a thousand different tunes, more, at your command; wall-sized televisions with pictures of amazing vividness, imagine sitting back with a glass of beer to watch soccer game, better than being at the match, better view; programmable CD players; multifunction DVD players; high-spec computers with unimaginable numbers of rams, gigs, herz, et cetera. Too much choice. Yes, so many things that you didn't desire before because you didn't even know they existed to be desired.

He lingers, reads the lists of special features, studies them almost furtively, as if standing on the threshold of uncharted sin. Such a surfeit of everything. Where did all this stuff come from? Irina is trailing behind, staring into the window of a clothing shop, a look of unbelief on her face.

Food shops, restaurants—everything is here, yes, every corner of the globe has been rifled to furnish this abundance. And the people too have been rifled from all over—Europe, Africa, India, the Orient, the Americas, so many different types all mixed together, such a crowd from everywhere under the sun, rubbing shoulders on the pavements without even looking at one another. Some are talking on mobilfons—even the women. And all well-dressed—clothes like new. And the shoes—new shoes made of leather. No carpet slippers, like people wear in the streets back home.

"Watch out!"

He is so intent on the shoes that he almost stumbles into a young woman walking fast-fast on high heels, who backs away snarling, "Get off me!"

"What are you dreaming about, Andriy?"

Irina grabs him and pulls him out of the way. The feel of her hand on his arm is like quickfire. The snarling woman walks on even faster. The look in her eyes—it was worse than contempt. She looked straight through him. He didn't register in her eyes at all. His clothes—his best shirt shabby and washed out, brown trousers that were new when he left home, Ukrainian trousers made of cheap fabric that is already shapeless, held up by a cheap imitation-leather belt, and imitation-leather shoes beginning to split on the toes—his clothes make him invisible.

"Everybody looks so smart. It makes me feel like a country peasant," says Irina, as if she can read his thoughts. This girl. Yes, her jeans are worn and strawberry-stained, but they fit delightfully over her curves, and her hair gleams like a bird's wing and she's smiling, teeth and dimples, at all the world.

"Don't say that. You look . . ." He wants to put his arms around her. ". . . You look normal."

Should he put his arms around her? Better not—she might shriek "Leave me alone!" So they walk on, just wandering aimlessly through the streets, opening their eyes to all there is to be seen. Dog runs ahead making a nuisance of himself, diving in between people's legs. Yes, this London—it's quite something.

But why—this is what he can't understand—why is there such abundance here, and such want back home? For Ukrainians are as hard-working as anybody—harder, because in the evenings after a day's work they grow their vegetables, mend their cars, chop their wood. You can spend your whole life toiling, in Ukraine, and still have nothing. You can spend your whole life toiling, and end up dead in a hole in the ground, covered with fallen coal. Poor Dad.

"Look!"

Irina is pointing to a small, dark-skinned woman wearing a colored scarf like the women of the former eastern republics. She has a baby bundled up in her arms, and she is approaching passersby, begging for money. The baby is horribly deformed, with a harelip and one eye only partially open.

"Have you got any money, Andriy?"

He fumbles in his pockets, feeling vaguely annoyed with the woman, because he hasn't much money left, and he would rather spend it on . . . well, not on her, anyway. But he sees the way Irina is looking at the baby.

"Take it please," he says in Ukrainian, handing her two-pound coins. The woman looks at the coins, and at them, and shakes her head.

"Keep your money," she says in broken Russian. "I have more than you."

She takes the baby off and sidles up to a Japanese couple who are photographing a statue covered with pigeon droppings.

They have already turned and started to retrace their steps when Irina spots, in the window of a stylish restaurant where the tables are set for the evening meal, a small card discreetly stuck in one corner: STAFF WANTED. GOOD PAY. ACCOMMODATIONS PROVIDED.

"Oh, Andriy! Look! This may be just the right place for us. Here in the heart of London. Let's inquire."

What does she mean, "the right place for us"? How have she and he suddenly become "us"? Maybe that wouldn't be so bad, because really she is a nice-looking girl, and she has a good heart, she isn't one of these empty-headed girls who is only thinking about what to buy next, like Lida Zakanovka. But he doesn't know where he is with her. She keeps changing her mind. And he likes things to be definite. One way or another.

"You can inquire if you like."

"Don't you want to?"

"I think I will not stay very long in London. Maybe just one or two days."

"Then where will you go?"

"My plan is to go to Sheffield."

"Sheffield . . . where is this?"

"It's in the north. Three hundred kilometers."

Her smile disappears. Her brow wrinkles up.

"I would like very much to stay in London."

"You can stay here. No problem."

"Why d'you want to go to Sheffield?"

He stares in through the window of the restaurant, avoiding her eyes. He decides not to tell her about Vagvaga Riskegipd.

"You know, this Sheffield is very beautiful. One of the most beautiful cities in England."

"Really? In my book it says it is a large industrial town famous for steel-making and cutlery." She looks at him for a moment. "Maybe I will come too."

Why has she removed the orange ribbon from Dog and taken to wearing it herself? It looked much better on Dog.

"I thought you wanted to stay in London."

"Don't you want me to come?"

He shrugs. "You can come if you like."

"But maybe we could stay in London for a while, to earn some money. Then we can go and look at this Sheffield."

What's the matter with you, Andriy Palenko? You're a man, aren't you? Just say no.

The woman who ran the restaurant looked Andriy and me up and down. She had black hair scraped back from her forehead in a ponytail, a white powdered face, and red-red lips. Why did she put all that makeup on? It looked dire. She tapped on her teeth with a red fingernail. "Yes, we have a position for a kitchen hand, and we need someone presentable for front of house." She looked at me. "Have you done waitressing before?"

"Of course." I lied. "Golden Pear Restaurant. Skovoroda. Kiev." After all, what's so complicated about placing a plate of food on the table?

"Have you got a black skirt and shoes, and a white top?"

"Of course." I lied again. I never used to lie before I came to England. Now it seems I'm quite skilled at it.

It was agreed that we would start tomorrow, working split shifts from eleven till three, and then six till midnight. The pay was four pounds an hour for kitchen hands and double that for front of house, plus a share of tips and service, meals and accommodations provided. She said it all fast-fast, without looking up at us.

"We don't need accommodations," said Andriy. "We have our own."

"Well, the pay's the same, with accommodations or without. Take it or leave it."

I did a quick calculation in my head.

"We take the job," I said. "Without the accommodations."

He got quite moody when I asked to borrow some money to buy the waitressing clothes. "You have to think capitalist," I said. "See it as an investment." I promised I'd share my money and my extra tips with him. I'd seen a shop with a big sign in the window saying SALE 50% REDUCTIONS, and I couldn't wait to have a look. I would go in the morning on the way to work.

When we got back to the trailer, there was a metal barrier with a padlock across the entrance to the site, but that was all right because we weren't going anywhere. By then, we were starving hungry. Maria had packed a whole feast for us of her peculiar food. She'd even put in some tins of steak for the dog, but Andriy said that was ridiculous and the dog should go and catch some pigeons and sent him off outside and Andriy ate the dog's food.

There was an embarrassing moment when I had to go to the toilet, but fortunately it was dark by then. When I had to change into my nightie, that could have been embarrassing too, but Andriy very courteously pretended to be reading one of my books, even though he can't really read English, and when it was his turn to get undressed, I pretended to read the book. But I did sneak a look. Mmm. Yes. Definitely more interesting without the Ukrainian trousers.

I stretched out on the bunk that had been Yola's, and he crawled onto the bunk that had been Marta's. We didn't even fold out the double bed, because that would have meant we were going to sleep together. It was so quiet in the warm enclosed space of the trailer that we could hear each other's breathing. Then I started to wonder what it would be like to sleep together in the double bed. Because really he has very nice hands. Sun-browned, with golden hairs. And arms. And legs. And he is also very gentlemanly, with good manners, just like Mr. Brown, who is always saying please and excuse me and pardon. And I liked the polite way he talked to Emanuel and to Toby McKenzie's parents, and even to the dog, and the attentive way he listens to people. Including me. Okay, I admit he isn't very educated, but you can see he's no fool. But is he *the one*? When it's your first time, you have to get it right.

I lay listening to his breathing and wondering if he was lying awake listening to mine. Just as I was beginning to drift off to sleep, the dog came back and woke us up by barking at the door. Andriy got up to let him in and gave him a drink of water—slurp slurp slurp—and spread the old bit of blanket from the Land Rover down by the door for him to sleep on. The dog fell asleep almost immediately, whistling and snoring very loudly—sss! hrrr! sss! hrrr!—which made us both laugh. After that, I didn't fall asleep for ages. My heart just wouldn't slow down. I kept thinking of all the things that had happened to me since I left home, and about him, lying so close in the dark, and wondering what he was thinking.

"Andriy. Are you asleep?"

"No. Are you?"

"No."

"We'd better try to get some sleep. It'll be hard work tomorrow."

"Okay."

In the darkness, I could hear the faraway sound of the city, a restless throbbing hum that is never still, like when you hold a shell to your ear and hear the sound of the sea, even though you know it's just the blood rushing around inside your own head.

"Andriy. Are you asleep yet?"

"No."

"Tell me about this Sheffield."

"You know, this Sheffield is one of the most beautiful cities in England. Maybe in the whole world. But not many people know this."

"What is it like?"

"It is entirely built of white stone with magnificent domes and towers. And it is set on a hill. So you can see it from a long distance away—it looks as though it is shimmering and glimmering in the light as you approach."

"Like the Lavra monastery in Kiev?"

"A bit like that, yes. Go to sleep now."

I AM DOG I AM BAD DOG I RUN MY MAN EATS DOG FOOD GO RUN CATCH PIGEON HE SAYS I RUN I COME TO MANY-PIGEON PLACE EVERYWHERE PIGEON PIGEON PIGEON I JUMP I CATCH PIGEON I EAT STRINGY MEAT MOUTH FULL OF FEATHERS NO GOOD HERE IS MEAT SMELL GOOD MAN FOOD MAN SITS ON BENCH EATS BREAD WITH MEAT HE PUTS BREAD AND MEAT ON BENCH I JUMP I CATCH I EAT BAD DOG SAYS THE MAN I RUN I AM BAD DOG I AM DOG

Kitchen hand! How have you allowed this to happen, Andriy Palenko? Your definite plan was to drop them both off in London, then go on to

Sheffield. Now suddenly you are not just kitchen hand, but kitchen arms, legs, shoulders, back, feet, et cetera. The feet are the worst. If the floor wasn't so greasy you could go barefoot. Yes, when you get your first week's pay, you'll have to get some of those spacecraft-style sneakers.

During the split in their shift, they just wandered around the streets, which was not intelligent because by the time the evening shift starts their feet are already aching. The heat is intense in the kitchen, and the atmosphere frenetic. Do this! Fetch that! Faster! Faster! All the time his hands are wet and slimy from the strong detergent, his sleeves soaked, his feet skidding on the slippery floor, and each breath taking in a lungful of steam and grease.

The chef, Gilbert, is an Australian, a big beefy man with a terrible temper, but a magician in the kitchen, wielding the big knives, chopping and slicing like a wizard. This cooking business—Andriy had always thought of it as women's work, but seeing Gilbert go at a piece of meat with a blade, then fling it in a smoking pan with a hiss of burning—that looks quite interesting. Maybe he will even learn something. Gilbert has two assistants who are from Spain—or maybe Colombia—who fly around at Gilbert's command, and a team of choppers, stirrers, and assemblers. And there is Dora, the only woman in the kitchen, who does desserts. Then there are the kitchen hands—himself and Huan—who clear and scrape the plates, wash the dishes, mop up spillages, and hump big sacks of stuff when the others command—really it's like being a slave with ten masters, of whom Dora, who is maybe Croatian or Montenegran, and no beauty, is the worst.

As the evening wears on, there is less shouting from Gilbert and more shrieking from Dora. More dirty plates to clean. More soap and steam. He can already feel an itchy rash developing between his fingers. At least on the coal face you could set your own pace. When Gilbert slips outside for a cigarette, the Colombians sometimes let him taste one of the special dishes, but after a while his gut aches as much as the rest of his body, and all he wants is to sit down near the open back door, where occasionally a slight breeze stirs the soupy air.

Sometimes, as the double doors swing open, he catches a glimpse of Irina in the dining room, gliding from table to table—she has been put to serving drinks, so she seldom comes into the kitchen. She's done her hair in two plaits, which makes her look even younger, like a voluptuous schoolgirl in her black-and-white uniform. You can see the eyes of the men following her as she moves around the room. Who is she smiling at like that? Why is her blouse so low-cut? Why did she find it necessary to buy such a short skirt? When she bends over to pour a drink you can see . . . no, not quite. Look at the way that man is staring at her.

Long after the chefs and wait staff have gone home, the kitchen hands still have to clear up and mop the floor and get everything straight for the next day. Irina waits in the dining room, sitting on one chair with her feet up on another, picking at a dish the Colombians prepared for her.

It is almost one o'clock by the time they can go. The night is still and starry. Andriy breathes in huge gulps of the cool smoke-tainted air until he feels quite dizzy. They still have a good half hour's walk back to the trailer. He walks, putting one foot in front of the other, like a robot. Robot. The word means "work" in Russian. That's what he is. A machine that works.

"Not so fast, Andriy."

He realizes she's struggling to keep up with him.

"Sorry."

"Look, Andriy. This is for you. I can pay you back what I borrowed."

She reaches down into the opening of that absurdly low-cut blouse and pulls out a rolled-up twenty-pound note.

"Where did you get this?"

"A man gave it to me. A customer."

"Why?"

"I don't know why. He just did. I was serving his drink."

"I saw him staring down into your blouse. You look like a tart in those clothes."

"No I don't. I look like a waitress. Don't be so stupid, Andriy."

"Keep your money. I don't want it."

"No, you take it. It's for you. What I borrowed. Why are you being like this?"

"I said I don't want it."

He sticks his hands in his pockets, and thrusts his chin down, and they walk on in silence like that. Why is he being like this?

The way that old man looked at me made my skin crawl like maggots. He got out his wallet, took a twenty-pound note and rolled it between his fingers very ostentatiously, then as I leaned forward with his glass, he pushed it down inside my bra. I could feel it there all evening, stiff and prickly between my breasts.

The restaurant had been quite busy, with all the tables occupied and a few people waiting by the door, the waiters rushing from table to table trying to keep their cool, and Zita the manageress strutting around showing people to their tables with that lipsticky smile. He was sitting near the window, so probably no one else even noticed. Maybe I should have given it back. But I thought, I'll never see him again, and I can pay Andriy back straightaway, and that'll make things easier between us. Then Andriy got all moody, and that was the last thing I needed, because I have enough unpleasant thoughts to deal with tonight.

And the most unpleasant is this—that twenty-pound-note man reminded me of my Papa. Same build. Same rimless glasses. Same old-age-porcupine hair. He was sitting at a table on his own. I stared for a moment, startled by the likeness, then I caught his eye and quickly looked away. Probably this is how it all started—the business of the twenty-pound note—with that quick exchange of looks. But this is what's been bothering me—had my Papa been like that? Making a fool of himself over a young girl, peering down into her blouse?

Because the girl Papa left home for, Svitlana Surokha, is almost the same age as me—in fact, she was two years ahead of me at secondary school. She is one of those girls everybody likes, pretty, with fair curly hair like a starlet, and blue eyes and a turned-up nose, always laughing and making jokes about the teachers. Then at Shevchenko University, where Papa is professor of history, she was one of the Orange student organizers. And they'd fallen in love. Just like that. That's what Papa told Mother, and that's what Mother told me, crying into the night, using up box after box of tissues, until her nose was all red and her eyes were puffy and squinty like a piglet's.

Not a pretty sight. Really, no one could blame Papa for falling out of love with someone so middle-aged and unattractive who nagged at him all the time, and falling in love with someone so young and pretty and full of fun. "Fallen in love"—the pretty blond-haired student activist and the distinguished Ukrainian historian, drawn together by a love of freedom. What could be more romantic than that?

Of course, I felt sorry for Mother, with all her sniffling and soggy tissues. But really, everyone knows it's a woman's fault if she can't keep hold of her man. She just has to try harder. The worst thing was, even Mother knew it, and she did try harder, dyeing her hair and putting on bright pink lipstick and that silly pink scarf. But then she couldn't stop herself nagging at him in a really humiliating way. "Vanya, don't you love me just one little bit?" It only made things worse. *I'll* never make that mistake.

That Mr. Twenty Pounds—his appearance reminded me of Papa—an elderly respectable man, probably with a middle-aged wife and family tucked away somewhere out of sight. But the look in his eyes was the look of Vulk. Hungry eyes. *You like flovver . . . ?* Greedy eyes. The way the man watched me was not romantic, it was like a cat watching a mouse, concentrating on its every movement, anticipating the pleasure of catching it.

Had my dear craggy crumpled Papa looked at Svitlana Surokha in that way? Is that what men are like?

Andriy had his head down and that moody look on his face and he was walking too fast for me again, but I wasn't going to ask him to slow down. I wasn't going to be the first to speak. I didn't even blame Papa. I just felt a big empty hole of disappointment in the middle of my heart, not only with Papa, but with this whole man-woman-romance thing. You go through life waiting for *the one* to come along, kisses by moonlight, eternal love, Mr. Brown and his mysterious bulge, faithful beyond the grave; then suddenly you realize that what you've been waiting for doesn't exist after all, and you'll have to settle for something second-rate. What a let down.

So when after ten minutes of silence Andriy suddenly slipped his arm around me, I just pulled away. "Don't!"

And then straightaway I wished I hadn't, but it was too late. *Sorry, I didn't mean it. Please put your arm back.* But you can't say that, can you?

That's it, then. In a few days he'll collect his week's wages, then he'll be off to Sheffield. No point in hanging around here and making a fool of himself, chasing after a girl who has not the slightest interest in him. This London, it is exciting, it gives you plenty to think about, and to tell the truth he is glad he stayed here for a short time and tasted its bittersweet flavors. And it will be good to travel north with money in his pocket. But it's time to go. The girl will be all right. She can stay in the accommodations that come with the job, whatever they are, and she seems to be bringing home something in tips as well as her wages. Probably that's why she wears that blouse. Well, that's her business. It means nothing to him. She can sort out her passport, though she seems to be in no hurry to do this, and save up for her fare, and even buy a few nice clothes if that's what she wants. He doesn't have to worry about her. He will take the trailer, and Dog. He is quite looking forward to being by himself, on the road.

They are within a block of the place where the trailer and Land Rover are parked when they hear the sound of Dog barking furiously and an intermittent dull thudding noise. As they get closer the sound intensifies, along with a babble of shrill voices. He quickens his step, then breaks into a run.

As they turn the last corner, they see a horde of children surrounding the trailer, pelting it with bricks. Dog is barking frantically, dodging the stones, and trying to chase them off. Where did these little buggers come from? In the shadowless orange glow of the street lights the small figures are dancing about like a bizarre bacchanal. One of them has set a pile of sticks and paper under one end of the trailer and is tossing lighted matches at it.

"What you doing? Stop it!" Andriy races toward them swinging his arms. The children stop, but only for a second. Nearest to him is a raggedy boy with hair like a rat's nest. Their eyes meet. The boy picks up half a brick and lobs it at him.

"Yecontgitmeeyafacka yecontgitme!"

It falls short. Andriy runs at the little fiend, grabs him by both arms and swings him around, throwing him sideways. The kid staggers as he hits the ground.

"Fackyafackyafackincant!"

Andriy grabs at another kid, who dodges out of his way and starts to run, and another who wriggles out of his grasp, lithe as a cat, and darts off, showering him with spit. Even Irina is getting stuck in. She snatches one of the boys by the arm, and when he spits and swears at her she spits and swears back and gives him a hard wallop on the behind. Where did she learn those words? Dog snarls and launches himself at the boy with the matches just as the fire starts to catch on the paper. The smell of smoke drifts toward them. The children scatter, shouting and throwing stones behind them as they run. Dog chases after the stragglers, snapping at their heels.

The paper has caught fire and now the sticks are crackling under the trailer, sending smoke and sparks into the air. Dog is going mad. Quick as a flash, Andriy unzips his trousers and pees on the flames. There is a hiss and a bit of smoke, but not too much damage to the trailer. Why is she looking at him with that grin on her face? It was an emergency. Well, let her look. Let her grin. What is she to him?

He sits down on the step of the trailer and rests his head in his hands, surrendering to the fatigue. But she has to come and squeeze down beside him. Her arm, her thigh—where her skin touches his, it's like hot steel. This girl—why does she have to get under his skin? If it isn't going to lead to any possibility, why can't she just leave him alone?

The thought makes him feel bleakly irritated, both with her and with himself. And something else is bothering him—the look in the rat-boy's eyes as he swung him into the air. They weren't the sparkling mischievous eyes of a naughty kid having fun. They were blank dead-pool eyes—eyes that have already seen too much. Like the naked girl in the four-by-four. Like the Ukrainian boys on the pier. Why are there so many people in the world with those dead zombie eyes?

"Andriy?"

"What?"

"We can't stay here."

"Why not?"

"Those children—they'll come back while we're asleep. They'll set fire to the trailer with us inside."

"No they won't."

Why can't she just shut up and leave him alone?

"They might. And even if they don't come back tonight, the trailer won't be safe here. They're bound to be back."

"Well, we can move it in the morning."

He feels exhaustion like a trickle of molten lead seeping and solidify-ing inside his limbs. He must have pulled his shoulder swinging the boy, and there are other obscure aches in his back and legs. He needs to sleep.

"There'll be too many people around in the morning. It's easier to find somewhere now. Let's go now."

"Where do you want to go?"

"I don't know. Anywhere. Maybe we could find somewhere a bit nearer to the restaurant."

So he gets a bit of brick and hammers off the padlock on the bar gate. It comes off quite easily. In fact, she is right—driving around at night is better. He even gets up into fourth gear once, without going into reverse. He remembers a quiet side street not far from the back of the restaurant where there are sometimes a few cars parked. That will do for now. It is only a temporary place. Soon he will move on.

After that incident with the children, Andriy got even more moody. I tried to make jokes and cheer him up, but each day that passed he just got more grumpy and kept saying he would be going to Sheffield as soon as we got our first week's wages.

I already had about eighty pounds from tips left on the tables. I tried to share them with him, but he shook his head and said, no, keep it, frowning like a belly ache and saying he was tired of this job, and anyway he would soon be going to Sheffield. What was the matter with him? He wasn't still sulking about that twenty-pound note, was he?

So I went back to the shop with the sale and I bought a different blouse that wasn't so low cut. I thought that would make him happy, but it didn't. He said it was still too low, and my skirt was too short. Why was he being so boring? It's a nice skirt, only a bit above my knees, good cut, lovely silky lining, and reduced to less than half price just because the button was missing, which I soon fixed. Also it has a deep pocket, which is handy for tips. I saw there was no pleasing him. If he doesn't like my clothes, that's his problem. Why doesn't he just go to Sheffield, instead of hanging around getting on my nerves?

Next morning, I decided to walk over to the Ukrainian consulate to get a new passport. I still had some money left from tips, so I looked in on that first very expensive clothes shop. Really, the prices on the clothes—they just took your breath away. I spent an hour trying things, trying other things, looking in the mirror. I never made it to the consulate. There was one pair of trousers, thirty pounds, reduced from one hundred and twenty. They were black, low-cut, and tight-tight. Actually, they looked fantastic. I knew Andriy would really hate them.

I stopped by at the trailer, but Andriy had already left for the restaurant, and that's when I noticed that there was some kind of yellow and black label stuck on the windshield of the Land Rover. I peeled it off and put it in my pocket to show him. And there seemed to be something fixed onto the front wheel of the Land Rover, and also to the trailer wheel. That was strange. No doubt he would know how to get it off. We were busy that lunchtime so I didn't get a chance to talk to him. Anyway, he was looking so grumpy I just kept out of his way.

Then someone else came into the restaurant, and that made things even worse.

It was just before three o'clock, the end of the lunchtime shift, and some of the staff had already gone. There were only two customers left in the restaurant: a young couple finishing their meal. Then a man came in on his own and sat down at one of the window tables—the same one where Mr. Twenty Pounds had sat. I didn't recognize him at first, but he recognized me straightaway.

"Irina?"

He was young and dark, with very short hair. He was wearing a dark gray business suit, a white-white shirt with a big gold watch peeping out under the cuff, and a blue and pink patterned tie. Quite attractive, in fact.

"Vitaly?"

He smiled. "Hello."

"Hey, Vitaly! How much you've changed."

"What you doing here, Irina?"

"Earning money, of course. How about you?"

"Earning money too. Good money." He took a tiny mobile phone out of his pocket and flipped up the lid. "Recruitment consultant, dynamic employment solution cutting edge"—he did a little slicing movement with his hand—"organizational answer for all you flexible staffing need. Better money than strawberry."

Okay, I admit I was impressed.

"Recruitment consultant? What is that?"

"Oh, it just means finding a job for some person. Or finding some person for a job. I am always on look out for new arrivals to fill exciting vacancies."

"You can find a job?"

He pointed his phone at me and pressed a few buttons.

"I can find very first-class job for you, Irina. Excellent pay. Good clean work. Luxury accommodation provided. And my friend Andriy. I have a good job for him also. Near Heathrow Airport. Is he here?"

"He is working in the kitchen. Kitchen hand."

"Kitchen hand. Hm." He shook his head with a little smile. "Irina, you, Andriy . . . you make possibility?"

"Vitaly, why you are asking this?" I said. Then he reached up and took my hand and looked at me with his dark-dark eyes in a way that made me shiver. "Irina, all time I am thinking about you."

I blushed. It sounded so romantic. Was he serious? I didn't know what to say. I took my hand away, in case Andriy was watching.

"Vitaly, tell me about this job. What kind of work is this?"

"Very first class. Gourmet cuisine. Top-notch international company desperately seeking reliable and motivated replacement staff." His voice was deep, and the way he pronounced those long words in English sounded incredibly cultured. "Food preparation contract for major airline near Heathrow Airport."

Yes, ever since man first lifted his head above the mouth of the cave to gaze upon the heavenly stars, and thought how pleasing it would be to have one such star exclusively for himself, it has been the dream of man to get others to work for him, and to pay them as little as possible. And no man has been pursuing this dream more dynamically than Vitaly himself. He has spent the day trawling through the bars and restaurants of London looking for the right kind of people. The new arrivals, the confused, the desperate, the greedy. You can make good money out of people like that.

For as that brainy beardy Karl Marx said, no person can ever build up a fortune just by his own labor, but in order to become VIP elite rich you must appropriate the labor of others. In pursuit of this dream, many ingenious human solutions have been applied throughout the millennia, from slavery, forced labor, transportation, indentured labor, debt bondage, and penal colonies, right through to casualization, zero-hours contract, flexible working, no-strike clause, compulsory overtime, compulsory self-employment, agency working, subcontracting, illegal immigration, outsourcing, and many other such maximum-flexibility organizational advances. And spearheading this permanent revolution-ization of the work process has been the historic role of the dynamic-edge cutting-employment solution recruitment consultant. Not enough people appreciate this.

This is why despite the exclusive hand-tailored charcoal gray, pure wool suit, the state-of-the-art Nokia N94i nestled in his pocket and the genuine Rolex Explorer II winking boldly from under his cuff, he still feels sadly unappreciated. What you need, he thinks, is a girl to share your good fortune with—a pretty, clean, good-class girl, not a painted-up cheap-rent girl; an innocent girl, whom you can train in the art of love the way you like it; nice looking enough to attract envy from other men, but not so nice looking that she will run off with the next chancer with a Nokia N95ii and a Rolex Daytona. What you need is a girl who can reas-sure you that, really, you are a good man. A dynamic man. A VIP. Not a criminal. Not a loser. And here she is, the very girl you've been dreaming of, smiling sweetly as she pours you a second glass of chilled Sauvignon Blanc. Really, this is a very nice wine—one of the nice little perks of the business. And—here is the real tragedy of it—even as you gaze into the silky hollow between her lovely breasts, a businesslike voice in the back of your head tells you: You could make good money out of this girl.

For if you have grown up in the faraway Dniester valley in a provin-cial town nestled on a bend in the river that divides Moldova from the Republic of Transdniestria—where the only law is the gun, where your father and two of your brothers were shot down in the main street near your home for refusing to pay protection money, and your third brother was killed in the war of secession, and your mother died of sorrow at the age of forty-two when your house was razed to the ground, and your two younger sisters have been traded by a Kosovan wide-boy to a massage parlor in Peckham—if you grow up in a place like Bendery, it toughens you up a bit.

Ah, Bendery! Whose desolate Soviet—era concrete blocks conceal a feral heart; whose alleys smell of blocked drains and frying garlic; whose sunsets glow like fire through the burned-out windows of the buildings near the bridge; whose wide river laps in silvery ripples along those sandy banks where from time to time a corpse is washed ashore; in whose forests the ghosts still sigh; whose streets have run with blood. Ah, Bendery! His eyes go misty with bittersweet pain. He gazes at the opening of Irina's blouse. Once, he had a girl like this in Bendery. Rosa. The school librarian's daughter. She was fifteen and a virgin. So was he. Her eyes were dark and gleaming with promises. They met after school in a secret glade on the riverbank. Probably she, too, is in Peckham now.

Once, in a different kind of time, Vitaly had been the bright hope of his family, the student, the dreamer of great dreams, the apple of his mother's eye. He would most likely have grown up to be a lawyer or a politician, had he not lived in Bendery, and had he not come across that life-changing book, locked away in a school cupboard full of out-of-favor texts, some dating back eighty years or more, which the librarian was keeping hidden just in case any of them should ever come back into favor again. Probably they are still there.

He had just turned sixteen when Transdniestria seceded from Moldova in 1992 over the issue of language. Cyrillic versus Roman. He had joined the patriots, of course, along with his brothers, but his heart wasn't in it and he managed to keep out of the worst of the fighting, even though Bendery, which lies on the west bank of the Dniester River and is joined to the rest of Transdniestria only by a bridge, had been in the front line of the civil war. Two thousand lives lost, his oldest brother's among them, hundreds of homes burned out, theirs among them, over how a language should be written. Okay, he was a patriot as much as the next man, but he just didn't think it was an issue worth getting himself killed for. Some know-it-alls said it was really about politics—about whether it was time to say good-bye to their Russian-dominated past and cozy up with Westward-leaning Romania. And others said that it was just a tribal war between rival gangster families. Probably each person had his own reasons for getting involved, and some had no reason to but still did.

After the truce, when life got back to an abnormal sort of normal, he tried for a few years to make a go of it in the family construction business. He really tried. He worked all hours, humping bricks and mixing concrete, laying pipes and drains, hammering in doors and windows, and paying protection money all the while. But after his father and his younger brothers were shot dead in the main street of Bendery by a henchman of one of those gangsters for daring to question a hike in the protection fee, he realized that work was for losers, and the wily old grizzle-jaws was right (probably that's why those dangerous books had to be locked away) and if you want to join the elite, you have to learn to tap into other people's labor, and let them make you rich. Harvest the efforts of the others—the losers. It is the only way.

So he got in touch with that Kosovan phony-asylum-seeker wide-boy who had transported his sisters, and offered to get four girls for him in exchange for a passage to England. In the event, he could find only three, the two daughters of his impoverished former English teacher at school, who had been sacked for refusing to teach English in the Cyrillic alphabet, and a deaf-and-dumb girl who sold pickled mushrooms in the market. The Kosovan wide-boy got them all Greek passports, and Vitaly escorted them on the ferry to Dover, where the wide-boy, who was working under the name of Mr. Smith, took the girls off his hands and introduced him to his uncle, Vulk, who had once run a similar business in Slovenia and Germany, who introduced him to farmer Leapish, who made the mistake of introducing him to his wife (ha ha), who introduced him to Jim Nightingale of Nightingale Human Solutions. That's how it works in the world of business—you need contacts, and if you have the right contacts you can sell anything.

And now, look, only four months later, here you are, sitting at the best table in this expensive London restaurant, wearing a good-class expensive suit (the shaved head and gold chain with pendant knife belonged to a different phase, which may have given a wrong impression to some Angliski businessmen), with a genuine Rolex Explorer II, not one of those replicas that any fool can see is fake, enjoying a glass of reassuringly expensive super-chilled New Zealand Blind River Sauvignon Blanc while waiting for your client to arrive, taking a picture of this attractive and potentially very expensive girl on your expensive Nokia N94i, and facing the pleasant dilemma of whether to keep her for yourself or sell her on to someone else. You know a couple of guys who might be interested if you send them her picture.

For in Bendery, girls as pretty and innocent as this used to be two a penny, in fact you yourself deflowered several of them—that was after Rosa, after the war, after all the killings—and you've been thinking recently that spending so much money on the visibles, the suits, watches, phones, girls, is all very well, and probably an essential investment for creating the right brand image for the business, but if you want to be seriously wealthy, you can't just spend it all, you need to accumulate and invest, to build your capital, and property is hellishly expensive here in London. And you could really do with the cash.

Not enough people appreciate what a struggle it has been—what a lonely struggle—rooting yourself out of that nowhere town on the borders of an unrecognized republic that is really nothing but a strip of countryside with half a dozen little towns sandwiched dangerously between the east bank of the Dniester River and the western border of Ukraine, and establishing yourself as an advanced motivational human solution recruitment consultant here in the bona fide Western world; they don't understand how dynamic you have to be, and sometimes how ruthless, and how lonely it is not being able to trust anyone, no one at all, because every other chancer will take their opportunity to knock you down and steal your business, and your closest business partners are also your deadliest rivals.

For in the transition from the old world to the new, as that cunning old bushy-beard wrote, all fixed, fast, frozen relations are swept away, all that is solid melts into air, all that is holy is profaned, and a man has to face up to his real choices in life and his relations with others. For in this new world, there are only rivals and losers. And, of course, women.

She sidles up to him with that infuriating smile.

"Andriy. Vitaly's here. Vitaly from the strawberry field."

"Where?"

This is all he needs. The mobilfonman coming to taunt him as he stands with his hands in the sink.

"Here. Here in the restaurant. Sitting by the window."

"What does he want?"

"He says he has a job for us. A first-class job. Gourmet cuisine near Heathrow Airport."

Andriy feels the anger rising in his face.

"Irina, if you want to go with Vitaly, that is up to you. I have no interest in that job."

He gropes in the hot caustic water and grabs at a couple of slippery plates, noticing how red and raw his hands have become.

"He says the pay is good. And the work is clean. Maybe it will be better for you, Andriy. Better than kitchen hand."

"He knows I am kitchen hand?"

"I told him we were working to earn some money. At least go and talk to him."

"What else did you tell him?"

Really, it's not her fault, this girl. She doesn't understand anything.

"I don't know. What's the matter with you, Andriy? He is trying to help us."

"He is trying to help only himself." He dries his hands on a damp cloth. "Did you pour his drink for him, Irina? Did you let him look inside your blouse?"

"Stop it, Andriy. Why are you like this?"

"Did he show you his mobilfon?"

"Just go and say hello. He's your friend, isn't he?"

"I'll say what I want to say."

He stacks the slimy plates on the rack and kicks open the swinging door to the dining room. He looks around. Vitaly is sitting at one of the tables in the window. He is sipping wine and fiddling ostentatiously with his mobil-fon. Where did he get that fancy suit? Suddenly the street door of the restaurant bursts open and another man strides in—a tall man with a shaved head and an ugly scar across his cheek and lip. Poised by the kitchen door, Andriy watches, rapt, as the scar-cheek man spots Vitaly, moves across the room, and positions himself in front of Vitaly's table. Andriy is sure he's seen him before, but he can't remember where. Irina is in the kitchen, hiding out of the way. Now here comes Zita, looking around for Irina, who should be out there offering the new customer a drink.

The scar-face man says—his voice is so loud that everybody can hear—"Where is she?"

"She is somewhere here," Vitaly says. "Please sit down."

"You owe me one girl, dead-boy. You promise four, and you only bring three."

"Please, Smitya, sit," says Vitaly in a quiet voice. "We can discuss everything. Have a drink." He beckons to Zita.

"Those Chinese bitches you sell me. Neither one was virgin. I got burned."

Now Andriy remembers where he has seen him before. Vitaly holds his hands out in a gesture of placation. "Okay. We can make deal, my friend. I have proposition for you."

"Just show me the girl."

"In a minute. She is here. Sit down. I will fetch her."

Andriy has broken into a sweat. His body is taut with rage. If he had his gun in his hand he would just shoot Vitaly dead right now, he thinks. But he steps back quietly behind the half-open kitchen door where Vitaly can't see him. Irina has melted away somewhere.

The man with the scar looks around wildly. His eyes light on Zita.

"Is it this one? This ugly dog? Do you take me for complete cabbage-head?"

"Please, Smitya. We are civilized men, not gangsters. Let us talk business."

"You no play tip-tap with me." His scar is purple against his livid skin. "You forgotten who I am, dead-boy. You think you talk clever business? You forgotten how we talk business in here."

He sees the man draw a revolver from an inside pocket of his jacket. It all seems to happen very slowly. He sees a scarry smile stretch across his teeth. He sees Vitaly's face contort in fear. Zita screams. The man fires four shots: two at Vitaly, one at Zita, and one at the mirror behind the bar.

Bang. Bang. Bang. Bang.

The quick succession of blasts reverberates like underground explosions in the contained space. Andriy puts his hands over his ears. Around him there is a chaos of screams and shattering glass as Zita falls backward, Vitaly slumps forward onto his table, and the young couple eating their meal start to scream hysterically. The man turns, walks quickly back out of the front door, and disappears into the street.

In the stillness that follows, Andriy can hear Gilbert shouting from the kitchen, "What the fuck's going on out there?!" He can hear the female of the couple talking to the police on her mobilfon. He can hear Zita's long quivering moans as she examines the shattered mess of flesh, blood, and bone that was her left leg. There is no sound from Vitaly. He steps carefully over to where Vitaly has fallen across the table. Dark blood is oozing in a vivid widening stain into the white damask, along with some other grayish stuff that is bubbling out of a gaping double wound in his forehead. The eyes are open. The hand still grips the stem of the wine glass that has shattered in his hand. Suddenly, a strange music erupts from his body—a grotesquely cheerful jingle—di di daah da—di di daah da—di di daah da—daah! It rings for a few moments, then goes quiet.

Andriy stares. Horror rises up in him like bubbling gray matter—horror compounded with guilt. Should he have intervened? Could he have saved him? Was it his own unspoken anger that had summoned Vitaly's death to him? His first instinct is to laugh—he has to put his hand over his mouth to stop himself. His next instinct is to run—to run from death into the sunlight of the living world.

Beefy Gilbert takes control in an amazingly matter-of-fact way, telling the dining couple to shut up, sit down, and wait for the police, attempting to stanch Zita's wound with clean napkins.

"You can go if you like." He pulls Andriy quietly to one side. "If you're worried about the police."

"Is okay," says Andriy. Then he remembers the gun in the bottom of his backpack.

When he goes back into the kitchen, he finds that all the other staff have disappeared. Only Irina is still there, clutching on to the sink with both hands, as though she's about to be sick.

"Are you feeling okay?"

She nods silently. She doesn't look okay.

"You?"

"Yes. Normal."

"Where's everybody?" she asks. Her whole body is shaking.

"I think they've gone. They're all illegals. Apart from Gilbert. Someone called the police."

Gilbert shouts from the dining room for some ice. Andriy gets a bowl, fills it with ice cubes, and takes it out to him. In a space between tables, Gilbert is struggling to stanch Zita's wound, his big meaty hands amazingly deft at knotting the napkins into a tourniquet. The smell of cordite still hangs in the air. The young couple are gazing in stunned silence at Vitaly's forehead, which has stopped oozing and started to congeal, and at their own congealing dinners. The young woman is crying softly.

Suddenly, the front door of the restaurant opens. Andriy looks up, expecting to see the police or an ambulance crew, but in walks a big man holding a mobilfon in one hand and a bunch of flowers in the other. He looks like another diner in search of a pleasant meal who has opened the door and stumbled by chance across this terrible scene. But it isn't just another diner—it is Vulk.

Vulk stops in the doorway and looks around slowly, as if he's trying to make sense of the chaos. His jowly face reveals no emotion. Andriy backs away noiselessly, his heart pounding. Vulk walks over to look at Vitaly's slumped body and mutters something under his breath. Just as Andriy reaches the kitchen door, Vulk looks up. Their eyes meet. Vulk lunges forward. Gilbert bars his way with a beefy arm.

"Sorry, sir. We're closed."

Vulk tries to push through, shouldering Gilbert aside, using the flowers as a flail, but Gilbert is as big as he is. He blocks his way.

"Didn't you hear? We're closed."

"Hrr!" Vulk gives him another hefty shove and barges through to the kitchen. But in the moment's grace that Gilbert's intervention has bought him, Andriy has grabbed Irina, pulled her into the kitchen store-room, and, taking the key from the lock, has locked the door from the inside. Clack.

The storeroom is cool and smells of onions. The light switch is on the outside. In the darkness they wait and listen. She is shaking and whimpering. He grips her tight against him, putting his hand across her mouth to keep her quiet. He can feel her heart jumping around inside her chest. On the other side of the door, they can hear him still charging around. They hear a crash of plates and the metallic bounce of a saucepan rolling on the ground, and that voice, like a mad beast bellowing, "Little flovver!" The storeroom door judders and the handle rattles, but the lock holds. Someone—it must be Vulk—switches the light on from the outside, and for a moment they gaze into each other's terrified eyes.

"Little flovver! You vill never hide from Vulk! Everyplace you hide I vill find you!"

Then they are plunged into darkness again.

He holds her closer. A moment later he hears Gilbert.

"What the fuck are you doing? Get out of here, you asshole!"

There is more crashing and banging, and a yell that could be Vulk or Gilbert or someone else. Then the kitchen is suddenly quiet. They can hear a faint wail of sirens.

"Is he gone?" Irina whispers.

Andriy listens. "I think so."

As quietly as he can, he turns the key and eases the door open a crack. In the dining room he can hear voices, but no one is in the kitchen. He tiptoes through to the scullery end and the sinks. No one. No one in the cloakroom. He peers through the back window. The yard is empty. He picks up his backpack from the cloakroom and Irina's striped bag—ever since the incident with the children, they don't leave anything of value in the trailer—and makes his way back to the storeroom. The door is locked. She has locked herself in again. He taps softly.

"Open the door. Quick. It's me."

He hears the key turn in the lock. Clack. She opens it two centimeters and sticks her nose out.

"Is he gone?"

"Yes. Let's go!"

He grabs her by the hand and together they sneak through the kitchen and out of the back door. There is no one in sight. When they are in the street they start to run. The wail of sirens is everywhere. He has slung the bags over one shoulder, and holding her hand he pulls her along. The trailer is only a couple of blocks away. At least, he thinks it is. Maybe it's the next block. No? Maybe the next one? No, surely it was back there by those bins. They turn back. They are no longer running, but panting for breath as they walk. They go around the block a couple more times before they realize that the trailer has disappeared.

He sits down on the pavement and sinks his head in his hands. His legs, stretched out in front of him, have turned to lead. His heart is still thumping. The trailer and the Land Rover. Their sleeping bags. A few clothes. The carrots. Their water bottles. All gone.

"Dog! They've even taken Dog!"

But even as he is thinking of what he has lost, another part of him is thinking, you're alive, Andriy Palenko, and the mobilfonman is dead. His blood is turning sticky on his fancy suit, and yours is pumping through your body. And you held the girl in your arms and felt her body against you, yielding but firm, soft but lithe, tenderly curved. And now you want more.

And here's the problem: They all want more—the twenty-pound-note man, Vulk, Vitaly, and all their seedy cohort of clients—they all want what you want. To wash themselves in the sweet pool of her youth. This decent young girl, as fresh as the month of May. And she senses it. No wonder she trembles like a hunted rabbit. No wonder she jumps about all over the place. Leave her alone, Andriy. Be a man.

I AM DOG I RUN I EAT TWO PIGEONS MY MAN AND MORE-STUPID-THAN-A-SHEEP FEMALE ARE GONE AWAY I AM DOG ALONE TWO MEN COME TO TAKE AWAY OUR WHEELIE-HOME I BARK I SNARL I JUMP ON THEM I BITE BAD DOG SAYS MAN HE IS BAD MAN I AM BAD DOG I AM SAD DOG I AM DOG ALONE WHEELIE IS GONE MY WHEELIE-HOME IS GONE BAD MAN CATCHES ME PULLS ME INTO BACK OF WHEELIE CAGE WITH MANY SAD DOGS WHERE ARE WE GOING WE ARE GOING TO DOG'S HOME SAYS SAD DOG I KNOW THIS DOG'S HOME IT IS NOT A GOOD PLACE SAYS SAD DOG IN THIS HOME ALL DOGS LIVE IN CAGES SMALL CAGES AND ALL THE PLACE SMELLS OF DOG SADNESS AT NIGHT SAD DOGS CRY THEY HAVE NO MAN I WILL NOT GO TO THIS SAD DOG'S HOME I AM A RUNNING DOG MAN OPENS WHEELIE-CAGE I JUMP I RUN MAN RUNS I RUN FASTER I RUN FROM CAGE I RUN FROM DOG SADNESS I WILL FIND MY MAN NEAR THAT PIGEON PLACE I RUN I RUN I AM DOG

When he held me and pressed me against him in the storeroom and I could feel the grip of his arms around me, strong and protective, that's when I knew for sure he was *the one*. It was dark in there. I couldn't see anything. I could only smell and feel. I could smell onions, and spices, and the warm nutty smell of *him*, my face pressed against his chest, and I could feel our two hearts beating together. Boom. Boom. Boom. I was scared, yes, but *he* made me feel safe. It was so beautiful, like that bit in *War and Peace* when Natasha and Pierre finally realize that they're meant to be together. Except I think he doesn't realize it yet.

He grasped my hand as we ran, not in a passionate way, but it was still romantic. And I thought, even if it doesn't always last forever, all that man-woman-romance stuff, you still have to believe in it, don't you? Because if you don't believe in love, what else is there to believe in? And now I've found *the one*; it is only a matter of time until *the night*. Maybe tonight, even, him and me together in the fold-out double bed, wrapped in each other's arms in our little trailer home. Okay, I know it's not *War and Peace*, but so what.

When we found the trailer had disappeared and we had nowhere to go, he sat on the pavement with his head in his hands and I thought he was going to cry, so I put my arm around his shoulder. But he just said:

"Dog! They've even taken Dog!"

I love the way he really loves that dire dog. I was thinking that they had also taken my new thirty-pound trousers, which was annoying as I hadn't even worn them yet, but I didn't say that. Of course I also felt very sad for the loss of our homey little trailer, especially when I realized that tonight wouldn't be *the night* after all. I showed him the yellow and black sticker I'd found on the windshield, and he said, in quite a nasty voice, "Why didn't you show me this before?" Then he said, "Sorry, Irina. It's not your fault. Probably it was already too late."

I love the way he says sorry. Not many men can do this.

We sat side by side on the pavement, with nothing except what was in our bags. We hadn't even been paid our first week's wages. At least I had some tip money. How I was wishing I hadn't bought those trousers. Andriy said that we should get out of London and go to Sheffield straightaway, so I said I'd go with him. Sometimes you have to let men have their way.

We spent that night outside, huddled up on a bench in a square, not very far from our trailer parking place, because Andriy said the dog might come back. We put on all our clothes, and we found some newspapers and

cardboard boxes to put underneath us and two unused black plastic rubbish bags outside a shop which we climbed into like sleeping bags. And
though it got cold in the night, I think it was one of the happiest nights of
my life, feeling so safe with his arms around me, his body solid like a tree,
and all the brilliant lights of the city twinkling away, and up above them,
very faint in the sky, the stars.

We didn't get very much sleep because so many people came by to talk
to us—aged alcoholics, religious types, police, drug dealers, foreign tourists,
a man wanting to know whether we were interested in posing for some
photographs, another man who offered us a bed for the night in his luxury
accommodations, which I thought sounded quite nice, but Andriy politely
said, "No thank you." Somebody feeding the pigeons gave us the bread she
had brought, and also some cake. Somebody else brought us a cup of coffee.
It is surprising how many very kind people there are here in England. For
some reason, that thought made me start to sniffle pathetically.

"Why are you crying?" he asked.

"I don't know," I said. He must have thought I was really stupid. "Tell
me about this Sheffield."

"You know, Irina, this Sheffield, it is one of the great cities of Europe,"
he said, in that funny Donbas accent, but I didn't laugh. "It has wide-
wide avenues lined with trees, so there is always shade in the summer,
and cool water plays from many marble fountains, and there are squares
and parks filled with flowers, and red and purple bougainvillea grows
over the palace walls."

"Is this really true?" I asked.

"I think so."

"Tell me some more."

"And the inhabitants of this city are renowned throughout the world
for their gentleness and kindness and their welcome to strangers, for
they have learned the art of living in peace from their ruler, Vloonki, who
is a leader of great wisdom, who lives in a bougainvillea-covered palace
on top of the hill, and he is a visionary even though he is blind. When we
get to Sheffield, Irina, we will be safe, and all our troubles will be over."

I can't remember what else he said, because then I fell asleep, still with his arms around me.

When we woke up in the morning the square was full of pigeons, and Dog was there, sitting at Andriy's feet, wagging his tail.

He can picture them so clearly—the fountains. Was it in Yalta or in Sheffield? And the bougainvillea tumbling with such abandon over the walls, cascades of red and purple pouring down the stone. He had asked his father what it was called. Yes, probably that was Yalta. That was a nice place. In the old days, in the days of the Soviet Union, when a miner was somebody, and a miners' union representative was somebody who counted, there was a sanatorium at Yalta for miners and their families, where they went every summer. Surely they must have something similar in Sheffield? All the buildings were of white stone and they gleamed in the sunlight. That was a good time.

And you told her about the blind ruler, Vloonki, and his words of peace, and the warm welcome that awaits you in Sheffield. But isn't it time, Andriy Palenko, that you told her about Vagvaga Riskegipd?

Because now she wants to come with you, and she's a decent girl, a good-class girl, and she seems to like you. And even if she has some stupid ideas, and she can't make up her mind, still you shouldn't lead her on if you're going to abandon her when you get to Sheffield. You have to decide, one way or the other. So maybe this is the time to make a possibility with this girl, and forget about Vagvaga Riskegipd and Angliski rosi and red Ferrari, which is probably just a stupid idea anyway. Bye-bye, end of story.

And don't be troubled about Vulk and Vitaly and Mr. Twenty Pounds. You're not in that category. Because you're the man who will protect her and make her happy with your love. Sooner or later—it will be sooner, you can tell from the way she is looking around, smiling at every man who comes her way—some man will take her and have her for his own. And it could be you, Andriy Palenko.

four gables

So there we were, standing by the North Circular Road, heading for Sheffield. In front of us, a great torrent of metal—two torrents, in fact—was rushing in each direction, the cars gleaming black, blue, silver, white, as they caught the sun, wave after wave, as endless as a river pouring into the sea. In my opinion there are too many cars in England. Andriy was watching the cars like a man bewitched, following them with his eyes, turning his head this way and that. Once he shouted out, "Look, Irina, did you see that Ferrari?"

"Mm. Yes. Wonderful," I said, even though to me they all looked the same, apart from the different colors. You have to do that, with men, share their interests.

Poor Mama tried to share Papa's interest in politics, and became very Orange, and stood in the square chanting for Yushchenko. But he obviously shared more with Svitlana Surokha.

"Slavery begins when the heart loses hope," Papa had said. "Hope is the first step toward freedom."

And Mama had said, "I hope in that case you will learn one day to wash the dishes." You see? Mama only has herself to blame. She should have tried harder to please poor Papa. Maybe I will have to stand by the roadside, shouting for Ferrari.

"Andriy, tell me what is so special about Ferrari?" I asked

He looked very serious and furrowed his forehead. "You know, Irina, I think it all comes down to engineering. Some people say it is design, but I would say it is high quality of V12 engineering. Transverse gearbox. Dry sump lubrication."

"Mm-hm," I replied.

I like it much better when he talks about Sheffield.

Although it was early morning the sun was already hot, and the air had a bad smell of burning oil and warm asphalt. Despite the torrent of cars, it was almost an hour before one stopped to give us a lift. The driver was an old man, almost bald, with thick-lensed glasses. His car was also very old, with patches of rust on the doors. The seat cushions were squares of foam with raggedy knitted covers. I could see the disappointment on Andriy's face.

It didn't take us long to realize that his driving was very strange. He kept swerving from lane to lane, passing cars on either side. When he accelerated, his car groaned and juddered as though the wheels were coming off. Andriy was hanging on to his seat belt with both hands. Even Dog looked alarmed. Sometimes when we passed a car the old man thumped his horn Beep! Beep! Beep! and cried out, "That's another Gerry shot down in flames!"

"Why is he shouting at those cars?" I whispered to Andriy in Ukrainian.

"German car," said Andriy in a low voice. "Volkswagen. Bee-em-vay."

In my opinion, his driving license should be confiscated.

The man asked us where we were from and when I said Ukraine, he said, Ukrainians are fine people, and great allies, and shook my hand as if I personally had won the war, the car veering from side to side. Then he passed a Toyota, and he beep-beeped his horn and shouted, "Little yellow bastard!" which was strange, because the car was red.

"I wonder what he'll do when he passes a Ferrari," I whispered to Andriy, but Andriy said it wasn't possible.

Then quite unexpectedly we took an exit off the highway, whizzed around a roundabout, made a left turn, and suddenly we were threading our way along little country roads.

"Is this the way to Sheffield?" I asked.

"Yes, yes. Near Luton. It's on your way."

In front of us, an old blue Volkswagen Polo was driving along quite slowly. Our driver pulled up behind and started to beep his horn and flash his lights. The car in front kept going. Our driver revved up and pulled out to pass him. Andriy and I held our breath. The road was far too twisting to see what lay ahead. We had just started to pass the Polo when, out of a bend in the road, a large gray car appeared, coming toward us, traveling fast. Our driver braked. Then he changed his mind and accelerated. The car jerked forward past the Polo and he cut in sharply. There was a double screech of brakes. The Polo veered to avoid a collision and two wheels went in the ditch. The gray car skidded into the opposite shoulder. Our driver drove on.

"Got him!" he said with a look of satisfaction on his face.

I glanced back at Andriy. He had gone very white.

"We must get out of here," he muttered.

"Excuse me, please stop!" I yelled to the driver. "I need a toilet. Urgent."

The driver stopped. Andriy and Dog jumped out of the back with our bags and I jumped out of the front and we ran back down the road as fast as we could, until the car was out of sight. Then we sat by the roadside until we'd stopped shaking and got our breath back.

Now we were stranded on this small road going to nowhere, and there were no cars passing. Andriy said we should get back to the highway, so we started to walk, thinking we would wave our thumbs if a car passed, but none did.

We must have walked almost a kilometer when we came across the blue Volkswagen Polo we had passed, still stuck with two wheels in the ditch, and the driver, a young black woman, standing beside it, looking extremely annoyed.

"You need some help, madam?" said Andriy.

He sounded so gallant, quite like Mr. Brown. I was thinking to myself, that's good, soon we will have a display of sun-bronzed manly muscula-ture. And we did. The woman got into the driver's seat, and he went around to the front and pushed, and the muscles in his arms bulged like . . . well, like something very bulgy. And slowly slowly the car moved back onto the road. Mmm. I can't imagine Mr. Brown doing that.

The young woman offered us a lift. She said she was going to Peterborough, and even though it was the wrong direction, I said yes, because I didn't want to walk all the way back to the highway. She said she could drop us off on the A1, which is a major road going north, and that was good enough for me. Andriy and Dog went in the back again, and I sat in the front, next to her. She had a sweet turned-up nose and hair done in tight plaits all over her head that looked like neat miniature vegetable rows in a garden. I was very curious to touch it, but I didn't want to offend her. Her name was Yateka, she said, and she was a trainee nurse in an old people's home.

When he heard this Andriy got very excited. "Do you have a brother called Emanuel?"

We explained that our friend from Malawi has a sister who is a nurse but that he has lost contact with her.

"England is full of African nurses." She laughed. "More in England than in Africa. And I from Zambia, not Malawi, which is the next-door country." Then, seeing the disappointed look on Andriy's face, she added, "But there is one Malawian nurse at my place. Maybe she will know something, because Malawians tend to keep together."

So it was agreed we would go with her to Peterborough and meet this Malawian nurse. All this time we were driving along slowly—in my opin-ion women are much better drivers than men—and we had plenty of time for conversation, which was good, because Yateka was very talkative. It turned out she was not really a trainee, for in Zambia she had already been running a health center for six years, but to work in England she has to do a special adaptation training. She explained that there is a new rule that the National Health Service is not allowed to recruit nurses from Africa, so she must do her adaptation training in a private nursing home.

"This is a good rule for Africa, but a bad rule for us nurses," she said, "because my adaptation job pays only the minimum wage, not a proper nurse's salary. Then they make deductions. Tax. Food. Accommodations. Uniform. Training fee. Agency fee. At the end of the week, I have nothing left."

"I know about these deductions," I said. "We are strawberry pickers. Accommodations, food, transport; everything comes out of our wages. You know, I had not expected such meanness in England."

"Worst thing is the agency fee," said Yateka. "Nine hundred pounds I must pay for arranging this training place."

"Nine hundred!" exclaimed Andriy from the backseat. "This is more than we pay for phony work paper. These are bloodsuckers!"

"Nightingale Human Solutions. They are vultures, not nightingales."

"But is it worth it?" I asked.

"When I am in the National Health Service I will be able to earn fifty times more in England than in Zambia. This is a problem for Africa, because every African nurse wants to come in England, and there are not enough nurses to look after all our sick people at home."

"Same for us. Wages for strawberry picker in England is higher than for teacher or nurse in Ukraine." Andriy furrowed his brow in a very thoughtful and intellectual-type way, which is actually quite sexy on a man. "This global economic is serious business."

You see? He is quite intelligent, despite being uneducated.

"You come from Ukraine?"

"Yes of course. Do you know some Ukrainian people?" I asked.

Yateka told us that one of the old men in her nursing home was Ukrainian, and he was always causing a lot of bother with his peculiarities.

"I wish you would talk to him. Maybe he would listen if someone talked to him in Ukrainian."

"Of course," I said. "We would be happy to talk to him."

I was curious about these Ukrainian peculiarities.

It's happened again. He wanted to go to Sheffield, but somehow he's ended up in this place. Andriy is feeling vaguely annoyed with Irina, with Yateka, and with himself. Why didn't he just say no?

Four Gables Nursing Home is a large gray house on the outskirts of Peterborough, set back from the road behind a screen of gloomy evergreens. Yateka pulls into the parking lot and leads them inside. The first thing Andriy notices is the smell—sweetish and feral. It hits him like a blast of bad breath as soon as they open the door. Half a dozen old women in various stages of decrepitude are sitting in armchairs pushed up against the walls, dozing with their mouths sagging open, or just staring. "Wait here," says Yaketa. "I will look for Blessing." They sit down on a padded bench and wait. The air is heavy and stale. Irina gets into a strange conversation with an old lady sitting nearby, who thinks she is her niece. Dog goes off sniffing along the corridor on the trail of the strange smell, and disappears. After a while Andriy gets up and goes to look for him.

"Psst!" A skinny arm beckons him in through an open door. "In here."

He steps into a tiny room. That smell—it reminds him of the smell inside the rabbit hutch on their balcony in Donetsk. In the middle of the floor, Dog is sitting on a rug at the feet of a very old woman, who is feeding him chocolate biscuits from a tin.

"Hello, young man. Come in. I'm Mrs. Gayle. Your name?"

"Andriy Palenko."

"Polish?"

"No Ukrainian."

"Oh, splendid! I'm very partial to Ukrainian men. Have a seat. Have a biscuit."

"Thank you, Mrs. Gayle." Andriy crams the biscuit in whole, coughing as the crumbs stick in his throat—it is the first thing he's eaten since that bread last night.

"Have another."

"Thank you."

He sits down on a chair, then he realizes it is in fact a commode covered with an upholstered lid. The rabbit-hutch smell is all-pervasive.

"Take two."

She blinks. Or is it a wink? Her eyes are small and watery, sunk deep into their crinkled sockets. Her hands are thin and bent like claws. Will I be like this one day? Andriy wonders. It is inconceivable.

He remembers his grandmother's room at home, piled from floor to ceiling with heaps of musty clothes, the space for sitting becoming smaller and smaller. It was sad to watch her life shrink away. As she lost control of her bladder, the smell from the room became so intense that they could hardly bear to go in there. However much his mother had washed and scrubbed and sprinkled powder around, the rabbit-hutch smell just got stronger, until in the end she died and only the smell was left. A bit like the smell in Mrs. Gayle's room. He is starting to wonder about the commode he is sitting on. What is under the lid?

"My daughter put me in here, you know, after my husband died. She says I smell. In your country, young man, what happens to old people?"

"You know, usually they live with family, but sometimes they go into monastery. Woman-only monastery is very popular with Orthodox ladies."

"Hm! That sounds quite nice, a women-only monastery." Mrs. Gayle nibbles at a biscuit with what is left of her teeth. "Company. A roof over your head. No matron to boss you about. And the only man you have to worry about is Lord Jesus. . . ." She searches in her bag and pulls out a pack of cigarettes. "Who is probably much less demanding than a husband. Probably drinks less too." She roots through her handbag once more. "Have you got a light?"

"No, I am sorry. I not . . ."

"You'll find a box of matches in the handyman's room. End of the corridor, down the stairs, and it's on your left."

She gives Dog another biscuit, and he sits up on his back legs to take it. Andriy has never seen him do this before. The room is very hot and the smell overpowering. He is beginning to feel a bit strange.

"Go on." She gives him a little prod with her walking stick. "Don't hang about. The handyman's not in at the moment."

The handyman's room is a den of old bits of wood, furniture awaiting repair, defunct appliances, obscure machine parts, et cetera, and in a cabinet along one wall an interesting array of tools. Andriy pauses in the doorway. The handyman is nowhere in sight. On a table by the door are a package of tobacco, a large curved pipe, and a box of matches. He hesitates. Then he picks the matches up, puts them in his pocket, and goes back up the stairs.

On the door to the corridor is a NO SMOKING sign.

"Mrs. Gayle. Excuse me. Do you know about smoking ban?"

"Hah! You sound just like my daughter! She's always trying to stop me from smoking. Have to smoke in here—can't stand the stink. Have you got the matches?"

He hesitates. She pokes him with her stick.

"Come on, young man. Let an old woman have a bit of fun."

He hands the matches over. She lights the cigarette and at once begins to cough.

"My daughter put me in here because I'm a communist, you know." Cough cough. "Yes, I was incarcerated because of my political views."

"No! Can it be true? Do such things happen in England?"

"Yes. She's married to a stockbroker. A minor scion of the aristocracy. Vile man. Now I'm in here, and they're living in my house." Her left eye twitches.

"How is this possible?"

"Yes, I wanted to donate it to the International Workers of the World, but they got it off me. Made me sign something. Told the social workers I was mad." She has become so agitated that she gets another cigarette out of the pack and lights it, and starts to puff, even though the other one is still smoldering in the ashtray. "Do I seem mad?"

"No. Very not mad, Mrs. Gayle."

"But what they don't know is, I'm coming home. I'm getting married again, and I'm coming home." She chuckles. "Are you married, young man?" The eye twitches again. Or is it a wink? Andriy feels a moment of panic. He shakes his head. She takes a few more deep drags on her cigarette, coughs once or twice, and continues, "Yes, Mr. Mayevskyj in room nine. The Ukrainian gentleman. Have you met him yet?"

By now the little room is completely filled with smoke. It must be noticeable from the corridor. If someone catches them, they could be in trouble. Andriy reaches across to stub out the cigarette in the ashtray, but quick as a flash she grabs it first and sticks it in her mouth, along with the other one.

"No you don't, young man." She lowers her voice to a confidential whisper, puffing away on both cigarettes simultaneously. "He has an incredible sex drive for a man of ninety-two, you know. Yes, they don't know this yet, but we're getting married and we're coming to live at home."

"That will be nice surprise for your daughter."

"It'll be a surprise. I don't know about nice."

While I was waiting for Yateka and Andriy to come back, I heard someone calling out for help. It was the old man in room nine. He had dropped his hearing aid down the back of his chair, so I helped him find it. It turned out he was the Ukrainian resident Yateka had told us about. He put in his hearing aid and we got into a long conversation about Ukraine, the way it was when he lived there and the way it is now. Then he cleared his throat and embarked on a speech about malfunctioning hydraulic lifts and other engineering problems, and at the end of it he suddenly took me by the hand and said I had a very beautiful figure, and would I marry him.

I said teasingly that I couldn't marry him, because I agree with Tolstoy that a wife should share her husband's interests, and I could never be interested in hydraulics. "Oy oy!" he exclaimed, striking his forehead. "I have other interests too. Do you care for art or philosophy or poetry or tractors?" Before I could answer, he started to recite an obscure poem by Mayakovsky about love and destiny, but he got stuck after a few lines and became agitated and started shouting for his books. So I went to look for Yateka.

Yateka calmed Mr. Mayevskyj down, and brought him a cup of tea. Then she made some tea for us too, which we drank sitting out in the garden. It's strange because I didn't know any Africans in Kiev, but Yateka is the second African friend I have made in England. When I told her about Mr. Mayevskyj's marriage proposal, she grabbed my hand and laughed out loud.

"Now you understand what I mean by peculiarities," she said. "That poor old man. He has become more mentally unstable ever since they took his gearbox away."

"Gearbox?"

"He had a gearbox in his room. Did he not tell you about it? He said it was a relic of his beloved motorbike."

"Why did they take it away?"

"Matron said it was not hygienic to have a gearbox in the room."

"What is not hygienic about a gearbox?"

"I don't know," said Yateka. "But nobody can argue with Matron. You don't know what she is like."

"I cannot see the harm in a gearbox. I would let him have it."

Yateka giggled. "You would be the perfect wife for him. Maybe you should accept his proposal. It would make him very happy. And in a few years, you will have a British passport and an inheritance."

"Not all Ukrainian women are looking to marry an old man for his money, you know, Yateka." In fact, I was thinking these stereotypes of Ukrainian women are not helpful. Where does this idea come from?

"And why not? In my country if a young girl can make a good marriage to a wealthy senior it is good for the family. Everybody is happy. Sometimes nowadays the young girl can get AIDS, which is a terrible tragedy in my country. But this will not be a problem with Mr. Mayevskyj," she added quickly. "The only problem is his two daughters. These are not nice people at all. They have already intervened three times to prevent him from marrying."

"Is this true? He has had three fiancées?"

"Maybe they are worried about the inheritance."

"He has inheritance?"

"He told me he is a millionaire." Her eyes twinkled darkly. "And he has written a famous book. A history of tractors."

I could believe he has written a history of tractors. But I must say, he didn't look like a millionaire. Or smell like one.

"But maybe you already have a lover." She winked.

"Maybe," I said with a nonchalant shrug.

"You know, you can stay here if you like. There's a spare room in the attic which cannot be used for residents because of safety reasons. It's been empty for years."

She gave me another twinkly look. I could feel myself blushing. There is something incredibly romantic about attic rooms.

The Malawian nurse turns out not to be Emanuel's sister after all, though she does look a bit like Emanuel, thinks Andriy: very small and slightly built, with a round shining face. Her name is Blessing.

"I am sorry to disappoint you." She gives him a dazzling smile that also reminds him of Emanuel.

They are sitting in the nurses" room while Yateka and Blessing are having a tea break.

"But don't you know some other Malawian nurses?" says Yateka.

"You know, my cousin was in a nursing home in London that was closed because of a scandal—the proprietor was stealing the residents" money. Some of the other nurses there were from Malawi. They all lost their jobs. The agency found new jobs for them, but they had to pay another agency fee. Nightingale Human Solutions."

Yateka wrinkles her nose. It is a small plump nose, shiny like a stub of polished wood. Quite a nice nose, in fact.

"Would you like me to ask my cousin?" says Blessing.

"Yes, please. I give you telephone number where Emanuel is staying. Maybe you help brother and sister reunited." He writes the address and phone number of the Richmond house on a piece of paper and passes it to Blessing.

Another rather pleasant thought has started to nudge at the edges of his consciousness. He has heard it said that black women are incredibly sexy, but he has never before had an opportunity to find out for himself. Maybe here will be an opportunity for him? This little coupé-model Malawian nurse, she has quite an entrancing smile. And the other one— Yateka—see the way she moves, the curve of her shapely legs accentuated by those clumsy lace-up nurse's shoes, the sway of her buttocks in her slightly-too-tight uniform. You have to admit, there is something incredibly sexy about a woman in a uniform.

Stop! Stop this idiocy, Palenko! Here is a lovely high-spec Ukrainian girl sitting beside you, and still you are letting your thoughts chase about after other women. When the road forks, whichever way you choose, you can only go one way. Good-bye, Africa Yateka. Good-bye, Vagvaga Riskegipd.

Good-bye and God be with you? Or good-bye and see you again? Andriy Palenko, what's the matter with you? Good-bye is good-bye. End of story. And yet . . . And yet it's not really desire that makes that last good-bye so hard to say—it's curiosity. Never to know where the other road would have led you. Never to know what lies beneath that taut crisp uniform; never to know whether that long-ago kiss lingers in her memory as it does in yours. Never to know what would have happened when you met.

Irina's voice snaps him out of his reverie. She is talking about something incredibly interesting.

"I think there is only one thing to do," she is saying. "We must give Mr. Mayevskyj back his gearbox."

"Gearbox?"

"Yateka told me he used to keep a gearbox in his room. A beloved relic of an old motorbike. But the matron found it and took it away from him."

"Since then," said Yateka, "he has become unstable."

"It is enough to make any man unstable."

"I think if he had his gearbox again, he would behave in a more normal way."

"You are right, Irina."

Sometimes you have to let a woman think she is right.

I AM DOG I AM SAD DOG MY MAN IS IN LOVE WITH THIS MORE-STUPID-THAN-SHEEP FEMALE HIS VOICE IS THICK AND SOFT HIS PISS IS CLOUDY HE STINKS OF LOVE HORMONES SHE STINKS OF LOVE HORMONES TOO SOON THEY WILL MATE HE WILL HAVE NO MORE LOVE FOR DOG I AM SAD DOG I AM DOG

"I think Bill the handyman will know where the gearbox is," says Yateka. "Since Matron asked him to take it away."

"Down the stairs at the end of the corridor, then turn left," says Blessing.

Bill is back in his basement room, poring over an open newspaper. He is a short square man with a bald head and a clipped mustache. He looks up as Andriy comes in.

"They've nicked me bloody matches again. Those old birds. You can't trust 'em. Bunch of flaming firomaniacs. Who are you, anyway?"

"I am looking for gearbox of Mr. Mayevskyj. He has been asking after it."

Bill takes this as a reproach.

"It weren't my idea to take it off of 'im. I just do what Matron says."

Even as his mouth searches for a suitably annoyed expression, his eyes fall upon Dog.

"That your dog?"

"Yes, my dog. Dog."

"I used to have one like that. Mongrel. Called him Spango. Great ratter."

Bill settles himself back in his chair, and passes the newspaper he has been reading over to Andriy.

"What d'you think of them, eh?"

A young woman with bare breasts and blond hair is smiling at the camera. Andriy looks at the picture. The light in the basement is dim.

Actually, she looks very much like his last girlfriend, Lida Zakanovka. Could it really be her? He stares more closely. Did she come to England? Did she have a mole like that on her left shoulder?

"Nice, eh? Better than the missus. You should have seen the pair last Thursday. Magnificent." Bill gives a companionable grunt. "You can keep it, if you like. I've finished with it. Anytime you like, you can bring your dog down here."

"Thank you." Andriy folds the newspaper under his arm. He will have to look at it in daylight.

"Does he drink tea, your dog? Spango was a great tea drinker. Here, boy . . . ?"

Bill reaches for a mug with a few centimeters of cold brown tea left in the bottom and pours it into a bowl for Dog. Dog wags his tail and starts to drink, gulping noisily. Andriy watches, amazed. He realizes for the first time how little he knows about this dog. First he was sitting up for chocolate biscuits. Now he drinks cold tea, slurping and slopping as if in ecstasy. Where did this creature come from? How did he appear so mysteriously in the night? Why did he choose them?

Meanwhile, Bill searches in the corners of the room and comes back with a small, heavy package wrapped in an oiled cloth inside a plastic bag.

"This must be it. She told me to throw it away. But you can't, can you? Don't tell her where you got it from."

"Thank you. Dog likes your tea."

There is no one in the nurses' room when he takes the gearbox upstairs, so he pulls out a chair and sits down to wait. Something else is bothering him now. That mole—did Lida Zakanovka have a mole there? He unfolds the paper to take a closer look. Hm. Definitely it is like Lida. Holy bones! What is she doing in England? Here in the brighter light of the nurses' room, he can see clearly. No, maybe this one is more pneumatic. His Lida was more like the cabriolet model. To think he wasted four years of his life over her! What a fool he was. Lucky she never got pregnant. This girl in the photo is quite something. Good curves. Not too thin. But is it Lida?

"What are you looking at?"

Andriy jumps up. Yateka is standing behind him. She must have tiptoed in on those softie-softie nurse's shoes. She is frowning. Andriy jumps to his feet and quickly folds the newspaper. Did she see? Of course she did. That was a bit of bad timing.

"I have gearbox, Yateka." He smiles pathetically.

"You have it already?" Her face is severe. Her uniform is so crisp it almost seems to crackle. He can feel a blush creeping up his cheeks.

"Should I take to Mr. Mayevskyj?"

"Better wait until tomorrow. It is nearly his bedtime now. Too much excitement at bedtime can make him knotty."

"What is knotty?"

Her face relaxes. The smile comes back. "You know, that Ukrainian, he is always looking for a wife. Mrs. Gayle, Miss Tollington, Mrs. Jarvis. They all told me he asked them to marry. And they all three accepted. And now . . ." Yateka rocks back on her heels hooting with laughter; she laughs so much she almost falls over, and has to hang on to the door for balance. "And now also Irina."

"Irina?"

"Yes, he has asked Irina to marry him. I think she will accept."

"Irina?"

"It is a good marriage for her. British passport. And he has an inheritance."

"It is not possible."

Yateka smiles. "In love, anything is possible."

Then one of the buzzers starts going off, and Yateka grabs her bag and disappears silently on her softie shoes.

There was a gravel pathway leading through the rose beds down to a lower lawn, a secret place hidden away inside a circle of laurels, with a couple of benches and an old sundial.

"You and Andriy can sit down there," said Yateka. "I finish at seven o'clock. Then I'll show you the spare room."

It was still warm, but the sky was heavy with rain clouds, and no one else was in the garden. You could sense the storm coming, the leaves of the laurels were curling in the heat. Dog appeared out of nowhere and started padding along beside us, farting disgustingly. What had he been eating? Why couldn't he leave us alone?

Andriy sat down on one of the benches, and I sat down beside him. He seemed very moody. I was wondering whether I had done something to annoy him. Bad moods are not attractive in a man.

"I want to discuss a problem with you," he said. "Love problem. Man-woman relationship type of thing."

Oh, at last, I thought, and my heart started to beat faster. Then he said, "Mr. Mayevskyj, this old scoundrel, has proposed marriage to three old ladies, and all have accepted." He gave me a nasty narrow-eyed look. "Now I hear that it is in fact four. And that you also, Irina, have fallen victim to his charm. Is it true?"

What has that naughty Yateka been telling him? I shrugged my shoulders nonchalantly.

"Irina, you cannot go about smiling at every man who comes your way."

This made me quite annoyed. What makes him think he has the right to lecture me?

"I can smile at who I like."

Then he said, in a very primitive voice, "And if you do, you will end up giving full body massage to Vitaly's mobilfon clients for twenty pound."

I was shocked. Why is he saying such a horrible thing to me? I thought he was teasing, and now it seems he's serious.

"Vitaly is dead," I said.

"No, the world is full of Vitalys. You just don't see them, Irina."

"What are you talking about, Andriy?"

"The men you smile at, Irina—some of them are not decent types."

Oh, so he's still upset about the twenty-pound note, I thought.

"Mr. Mayevskyj is not a bad type."

"Actually he's quite a scoundrel." He frowned. "Are you going to marry him?"

"That's my business. I can decide how to live my life. I don't need you to lecture me."

"You are blind, Irina. You don't see what is happening in this world."

"For example? What don't I see?"

"This mobilfon world all around you. Businessmen buying and selling human souls. Even yours, Irina. Even you they are buying and selling."

"Nobody is buying and selling me. I made my own choice to come to the West."

I was thinking, if he is going to carry on like this, maybe tonight will not be *the night* after all.

"The West is no different. This Orange Revolution that you like so much—what do you think this was but a Vitaly-type business promotion? Who do you think paid for all the orange flags and banners, and the tents, and the music in the square?"

What on earth has got into him? I thought we were going to walk in the garden, and maybe talk about something romantic, that would be nice, and instead he starts prattling about politics. Maybe this is how it happened with Papa and Svitlana Surokha. No, with them it was probably the other way around—first the politics then the romance. Well, if he can argue, so can I.

"If we're going to talk about this, at least let us do so honestly, Andriy. Nobody paid my mother and father to be there. They went because they want Ukraine to be free from Russia. To have our own democracy—not one run from the Kremlin."

"To exchange one run from the Kremlin for one run from the United States of America."

"This is Russian propaganda, Andriy. Why are you so afraid of the truth? Even if the government doesn't change, the important thing is that we the people have changed. No one will take us for granted anymore. Once in a lifetime a nation makes a historic bid for freedom, and we have the choice to be participants or to stand on the sidelines." Was that from one of Papa's speeches, or one of Svitlana Surokha's?

"What use is freedom without oil and gas?" he sneered.

"With freedom, maybe we can join European Union."

"They are not interested in us, Irina. Only for new business possibility."

He lectures me in that ridiculous Donbas accent, as though I am the dimwit.

"And who do you think paid for the buses that brought you up from Donbas? Eh?"

"This is all Western media propaganda. You are naive, Irina, you believe anything that any mobilfonman tells you. You thought you were the actors, but you were only extras."

"You didn't walk, though, did you? You Donbas miner?"

"Hah! Now we hear the typical voice of the bourgeois schoolgirl!" His tone has become harsh and sarcastic.

"I'm not a schoolgirl!"

I don't know what came over me at that moment. I just wanted to hit him. I wanted to punch his smug stupid face. That ridiculous superior smile—what does he think he's got to smile about? I just wanted to get rid of that smile. I couldn't help myself—I lunged with my fist. But he caught hold of my wrist and held it. He wouldn't let go. And then he pulled me toward him, and then he grabbed me in his arms, and next thing he was kissing me, on the mouth, with his lips, with his tongue. And pressing me closer, so tight my breath was squeezed away, and my heart was beating its wings like a bird struggling to ride a storm. And the sky and the clouds were spinning and wheeling around my head until I didn't know where I was. But my heart knew I was where I wanted to be.

It is night time. The clouds have cleared, and through the pointed gable window above the iron-framed bed Andriy can see the hunter Orion, bright in the southern sky, his jeweled belt, his dagger, and nearby the starry faithful Sirius. On the floor at the foot of the bed lies his own faithful Dog, almost as starry, snuffling in his sleep.

Irina is in the bathroom at the end of the corridor, taking a shower. She has been in there half an hour. What is she doing?

So far, everything is as it should be. All satisfactory. You have moved up from second to third without slipping, and now all you need is to gather a bit of speed and gently engage fourth, without suddenly slamming into reverse. No, Andriy Palenko, it's more than satisfactory, it's fantastic. This is no Zaz, this girl, this Irina—so sweet, so lithe, one moment she melts like a snowflake in your hands, then she sears you like a fire, until you don't know whether you're freezing or burning; you only know you want more. And even though she doesn't yet know what's coming, somehow her body already knows it's yours; you can feel it, and so can she. Like a garden waiting for rain.

And although you can see there will still be many disagreements to negotiate—because this girl, this Irinochka, she's still young, and she thinks she knows everything; she has led a very sheltered bourgeois life, her experience is limited, and there's a lot she has to learn—and let's face it, she does say some very stupid things—still, you're in no hurry, you have eternity in which to reeducate her. And though she can be both stubborn and slippery, she's not unintelligent. Quite the opposite. She has already started to take an interest in Ferrari, and look how she came up with a solution to the gearbox problem. Yes, definitely you have made the right choice.

Andriy gazes through the window at the stars. Why is she taking so long? His mind drifts back over the events of the day, and for no particular reason he starts thinking: Room twenty-six, Mrs. Gayle's room, is directly below this one—two floors down. Is she still smoking down there? He thinks he catches a faint whiff of smoke wafting upward. The matches—what was that word the handyman used?—he should never have let her have the matches. Is there a fire escape in the attic? If that room were to catch fire in the night, how many of them would survive to see the next morning?

Then the door opens. Irina comes into the room, padding softly on bare feet. She is wearing nothing but a towel twisted around her hair in a turban and a small towel wrapped around her body. A very small towel. She walks toward him. Her legs and arms are rosy from the hot water and her cheeks are glowing. She smells wonderful. He murmurs her name.

"Irinochka!"

She smiles shyly. He smiles too. He reaches out his arms to her. His whole body seems suffused with radiance. Wait a minute—one part of his body is not suffused with radiance—the manly part. From there, all radiance seems to have completely disappeared. Why is this? What has happened to you, Palenko?

At that moment, Dog wakes up and sniffs the air. He growls, a long low growl. He sniffs again, then he starts barking madly.

I AM DOG I AM GOOD DOG I SNIFF I SMELL SMOKE MAN SMOKE FIRE SMOKE I SMELL FIRE PAPER FIRE WOOL RUBBER CLOTH BAD FIRE SMELL FIRE NOISE CRACKLE CRACKLE I BARK WOOF WOOF I BARK TO MY MAN WOOF WOOF WOOF MY MAN RUNS TO FIRE HELP HELP FIRE HE SHOUTS GOOD DOG HE SAYS I AM GOOD DOG I BARK HE SHOUTS BELLS START TO RING EVERYBODY RUNS ALL DOORS ARE OPENED ALL OLDIES START TO RUN SOME START TO PISS ALL THE PLACE SMELLS OF OLDIE PISS SMOKE FIRE AND OLDIE PISS ALL OLDIES STAND IN GARDEN TALK TALK TALK BIG RED WHEELIE COMES WHOO WHAA WHOO WHAA WHEELIE IS FULL OF WATER WHEELIE PISSES ON FIRE SSSSSSS FIRE GONE OLDIES LAUGH MY MAN LAUGHS GOOD DOG HE SAYS I AM GOOD DOG I AM DOG

Mrs. Gayle has been expelled from the home. The door of her room gapes open, and peeping inside, Andriy sees everything is black with smoke. The small rug where Dog had sat and eaten chocolate biscuits yesterday is a charred mess, and even the edges of her bedclothes are singed from the fire. Really, she had a very lucky escape. Good Dog.

Mr. Mayevskyj's room is farther along the same corridor. It is a small, untidy room, with books and loose papers spread over every surface, and it has the same all-pervasive smell of rabbit hutch and air freshener. Sometimes the rabbit hutch seems stronger, sometimes the air freshener dominates; and now the faint whiff of smoke adds its own sinister aroma.

"Oh, you darling!" cries Mr. Mayevskyj.

Andriy thinks at first he is addressing him, but the old man's gaze is fixed on the gearbox that Andriy is holding in his hands.

"This gearbox is from 1937 Francis Barnett. My first love."

"But not your last, Mr. Mayevskyj." Andriy tries to sound severe. "I have heard you have made many conquests among ladies at Four Gables."

"Yes, that is inevitable." The old man beams. He raises his hands as if in surrender.

He is completely bald, completely toothless, and his skin hangs in loose wrinkles; he sits in a wheelchair and his urine dribbles down a plastic tube into a bag at his leg. So this is his rival in love. Yet there is a such an untamed energy about him that Andriy can feel its magnetism.

"What a pleasure it is to talk in Ukrainian." He leans forward eagerly in his wheelchair. "Ah! Such a beautiful language, which can express both poetry and science with equal fluency. You are from Donbas, I guess from your accent, young man? And you have come all this way to return my gearbox to me? I wonder how it ended up there—these swindling Africans must have stolen it and traded it for vodka." He races on before Andriy can get a word in. "And this new young woman Irina is also from Ukraina. She is my latest love. What a beauty! Such a figure! A very cultured type of Ukrainian, by the way. Have you met her?"

"Yes, I have met her. She is indeed very cultured. But . . ."

"Stop!" The old man raises a gnarled hand. "I know what you will say. She is too young for me. But how I see it is this. To find wisdom and beauty in one individual is rare. But in a marriage, this combination is possible."

"You are thinking of marriage?"

"Of course. I think it is inevitable."

Inevitable? What has Irina been saying to him? Perhaps she is not as innocent as she appears. That smile—who else has she been grinning at? What a fool you are, Andriy Palenko, to think it was specially for you.

"But you have also proposed marriage to Mrs. Gayle and two other ladies previously. And all have accepted."

"Ah"—he waves his hands in the air and smiles gummily—"these were just passing fancies."

"Mr. Mayevskyj, it is not gentlemanly to offer marriage to so many women."

Mr. Mayevskyj shrugs with such a smug little smirk that Andriy feels an urge to punch the old goat on the nose. Control yourself, Palenko. Be a man.

"Women are weak creatures, and easily tempted, Mr. Mayevskyj. It is not gentlemanly to take advantage of their weakness."

"You see in our situation there are no other men for these foolish creatures to love." The old man is still smirking. "Apart from you, now, of course. And by the way I have heard certain murmurings in this direction also, young man."

"Murmurings about me?" Andriy feels a panicky quiver in his chest.

"There is one lady who says a mysterious Ukrainian visitor has proposed marriage to her. This same Mrs. Gayle, in fact. Formerly my fiancée. She was celebrating last night with whiskey bottle. She has already made announcement to her family."

The quivering in his chest becomes more violent. He can almost smell the rabbit hutch closing in on him.

"It is all completely untrue."

"This would be good marriage for you. Passport. Work permit. Inheritance. Big house," the old man continues with enthusiasm. "Only family may cause problem. Same like my family. Children nose-poking in parent's love affair."

Holy whiskers! This would be an original outcome to his adventure—he will marry Mrs. Gayle, Mr. Mayevskyj will marry Irina, and they will all live happily together in Peterborough, end of story.

"Mr. Mayevskyj, if there has been some misunderstanding about my intentions, I will do my best to clarify with those concerned. And you must do same. You must tell these old ladies that you have no intention to marry. If you refuse this, I will take away your gearbox."

"My dear Francis Barnett. We had many happy times." His lower lip puckers like a child's about to cry. "Is it so wrong to long for love?"

"Mr. Mayevskyj, you are old. It is better for you to love your gearbox and to leave ladies to their follies."

The old man gazes at the gearbox.

"Maybe I have been too dissipated in my affections."

Andriy takes some tissues from a box by the bed, cleans the residual oil from the gearbox, and places it on the bedside table.

"Now, you must promise me that you will tell these ladies that you have taken vow of chastity, and there must be no more talk of marriage. Next problem is where to hide gearbox so that Matron does not find it and remove it again."

Mr. Mayevskyj taps his nose. "This Matron is very nose-poking type. If she catches any hint of this gearbox, it will definitely be removed. Let me think. In this bottom drawer"—he lowers his voice and points to a battered piece of chipboard furniture—"I am keeping my specially adapted undergarments. However, since I am not permitted to wear them, no one ever looks inside. Maybe if you put it there, buried beneath, I will be able to take it out and talk to it from time to time."

Andriy opens the drawer. Inside is a jumble of grayish-white cotton and lengths of elastic sewn on with black button thread, some pieces of pink foam rubber, and a coil of clear plastic tubing attached to an empty yogurt container. Interesting. Andriy wraps the gearbox back in its oiled cloth and tucks it in a corner.

As he is closing the drawer he hears a screech of tires on the gravel drive below the window. He raises the blind. A huge black car has pulled up outside. An elegant streaked-blond woman with a horsey face is getting out of the passenger side; out of the driver's side comes a tall dark man who looks like—Andriy can think of no other way to describe him— a minor scion of the aristocracy.

"Good-bye, Mr. Mayevskyj. I wish you a long life and much happiness with your gearbox. Now it is time for me to return very quickly to Donbas."

I wish it would rain soon. Everyone is sweating and grumbling. You can feel the electricity in the air. I can even feel it in my body. A good storm will clear the heat and tension. Yateka has disappeared somewhere. Andriy has gone to give Mr. Mayevskyj his gearbox. I am sitting in the dining room, waiting for him to come back. I wish I could open the French doors onto the rose garden, but they are locked in case anyone should try to escape. Beyond the rose beds is the little gravel path that leads down to our secret garden.

Twice, he kissed me there yesterday. The first time was beautiful, like heaven, and I just wanted to believe it was real. The second time it was solid, like the earth, and all my doubts disappeared. Yes, definitely he's *the one*. I can still feel the imprint of his hands on me, hot and strong, as if he's already taken possession of me. And that melting feeling in my body. Last night, I thought it was going to be *the night*. Then that annoying dog intervened. Well, I suppose it was quite a good thing that it saved us all from the fire. But how much longer do I have to wait? I just wish it would come soon.

Who would have thought I would come all this way only to lose my virginity, not to a romantic bowler-hatted Englishman but to a Donbas miner? There are plenty of those where I've come from, but the strange thing is that in Ukraine we would probably never have met. We're from different worlds, me from the advanced Westward-looking Orange world, him from the primitive Blue and White industrial East, that old derelict Soviet world that we are trying to leave behind. And even if we had met, what would we have had to say to each other—a professor's daughter and a miner's son? Being over here in England together makes us more equal. It's as though destiny has brought us together. Just like Natasha and Pierre—they'd been acquainted for years, and yet it took a whole war and peace before they could see each other with new eyes and realize they were meant for each other.

I admit there are some things that frighten me. Will it hurt? Will I know what to do? Will he still love me afterward? Will I get pregnant?

You can't let these fears stop you. And there's something else that worries me, something so vague that it's not easy to put into words, and yet in a way it's the most frightening thing of all: Will I still be the same person afterward?

"What are you dreaming of?"

It was Yateka. She had crept up behind me and put her hands over my eyes. I knew it was her by her voice, but I said, "Andriy?"

"Aha!" she laughed and let go of my eyes. "You are dreaming about that naughty man."

"He is not naughty, Yateka. He is the best man in the world."

She gave me a funny look.

"You think so?"

"Actually, I think he is wonderful. Gentlemanly and thoughtful and brave. How he rescued everybody from the fire—that is quite typical of his behavior, you know. The only problem is his dog, but maybe eventually he will give it away. You know what I like best about him, Yateka? I like the way he says, 'You are right, Irina.' Not many men can say this."

"Irina, I think maybe the Ukrainian millionaire will be better for you. There's something about Andriy . . ."

"What?"

She gave me another funny look.

"What is it, Yateka?"

Then she laughed. "I think Ukrainian men are just like Zambian men."

What did she mean?

"Have you got a boyfriend waiting for you in Zambia?" I asked. "What will you do when you finish your training?"

"You know, Irina, I have only three weeks of this slavery left. After that, if I get a good report from Matron, I can work in NHS and earn good money. And I can do proper nursing work, not this minimum-wage toilet-cleaning type of work I do here. My dream is to train for theater nurse, or intensive care. And I will be free—free of Four Gables, free of Matron, free of Nightingale Human Solutions." She gave my hands a squeeze. "So don't worry for me, Irina. And good luck with your millionaire!"

Before I could protest, we were distracted by a sound of shouting outside in the driveway, and a few moments later Andriy came rushing in with a wild look in his eyes and blood pouring from his nose.

"Andriy, what has happened?" I put my arms around him—my own wounded warrior.

"Irina, I must leave this place immediately. Will you come with me?"

"Of course, Andriy. But why?"

"There has been big misunderstanding. Go and get your things. I will explain later."

I hugged Yateka.

"Good-bye. Thank you for your kindness."

"I'm sure you will come back," she said.

So there we were, back on the Great North Road, Andriy, me, and the dog. As usual, the river of cars was streaming past and nothing was stopping. Fortunately the rain hadn't started yet. Andriy still seemed very agitated, so I gave his hand a friendly squeeze.

"What happened? Why did we have to leave so suddenly?"

"It was all big misunderstanding."

"What misunderstanding?"

"Nothing. It's finished now."

"You said you'd tell me. Andriy, you promised."

"This old lady, Mrs. Gayle. She said I had proposed marriage to her. Then announced it to her daughter and son-in-law and told them they must move out of house because she is coming back. Then she celebrated with whiskey."

"Andriy, you have been lecturing me about smiling too much at old men, and now you are doing same thing exactly."

"It is completely different."

"In what way is it different?"

"It was misunderstanding."

"I cannot see any difference. You must have given her some encouragement."

"Irina, this is no laughing matter. These people are terrible, what barbarians. You cannot imagine what they said to me."

His face was like a thunderstorm.

Fortunately just at that moment, a car pulled up—in fact it was not a car, it was a van. Or a bus. In fact it was a bus turned into a trailer.

"Hi. Where you going?"

"We are going only to Sheffield," said Andriy emphatically.

"Great. Get in. I'm going up that way."

The driver was a young man about the same age as Andriy. He had small round glasses, some fluffy ginger curls on his chin that looked as if they were struggling to be a beard, and ginger hair pulled into a ponytail—a thick, curly ponytail, not like . . . In my opinion men should not have long hair. Andriy's hair is not too long. And it is not too short.

"My name's Rock."

In fact it was hard to imagine someone who looked less like a rock. He reminded me of a shy little snail traveling in his shell home. We introduced ourselves, and it was just as well we were soon on friendly terms, because the trailer went as slowly as a snail, and it was clear that the journey was going to be a long one.

nine ladies

i

It will be a miracle if we ever make it to Sheffield, thinks Andriy. This old single-decker bus must be fifty years old at least, with prehistoric transmission, only four gears plus reverse, on a long, angled gearshift, like the old Volgas. The engine drones like a swarm of bees, and when it picks up speed—the maximum is forty Ks per hour—the whole body shakes and vibrates. Even in Ukraine, to undertake a long journey in such a vehicle, you would call in the priest and ask for a blessing or two.

There is something else he notices—the smell from the engine. It is actually quite a pleasant smell. It reminds him—this seems strange—of the little restaurant on the corner of Rebetov Street. Fried potatoes. Irina sits up and sniffs the air.

"Fish and chip?" she says.

"Nearly," says Rock. "Actually, it runs on used chip fat—I converted it missen. Burns up t' excess by-products of consumerism. Not strictly legal, because you don't pay tax on it. But, as Jimmy Binbag said, the chips of wrath are wiser than the vinegar of instruction."

She is sitting next to him in the front, gripping the edges of the double seat. Andriy catches her eye.

"Are all Angliski drivers crazy?" she whispers, in Ukrainian.

"Seems so," he whispers back. "At least this one is not speed maniac."

"So where are you two from, then?" Rock relaxes into a steady thirty Ks per hour, resting his forearms on the wheel and rolling a cigarette at the same time.

"Ukraine. You know it?"

"Aye." He pauses to lick the paper. "We had some Ukrainians up in Barnsley. Miners."

"My father was miner," says Andriy.

"Snap," says Rock. "Mine too. Before he died."

"He died in accident?"

"Neh. Pneumoconiosis. Black lung."

"Mine died in accident. Roof falling down."

"Fuckin' roof fall. That's tragic. Sorry, pal."

"You still miner?" asks Andriy.

"Neh. They shut all t' pits round us. Anyroad, me dad said I were too soft. Said I should get educated, instead. What use is educated in Barnsley? I said. Anyroad, I went to college and did mechanical engineering. But then I thought to missen, in't engineering part of t' problem? So I decided to do this, instead."

Still resting his forearms on the wheel, he strikes a match and lights the cigarette. Puffs of sweetish smoke billow through the bus. "You still a miner?"

"I was. Before Father's accident. Now I cannot go back down. I cannot work underground. So I have no work. I come in England for picking strawberry."

"Aye, it's all crap. As Jimmy Binbag said, when t' toilet of capitalism is flushed, all t' crap rains down on them below."

He takes another deep puff and holds the smoke in his lungs. Then he passes the cigarette to Andriy. Andriy shakes his head.

"My father said, when miner goes underground, death may visit. When miner smokes, death is invited."

"Jesus! I bet that put you off! Anyroad, I thought they'd shut all t' mines in Ukraine."

"Many was shut. Then we open them again."

"You opened t' mines?"

"Miners did it. With our hands."

"Weren't that a bit dangerous?"

"Of course. Also illegal. Working in seam one meter tall. Thirty-seven degrees of heat. One hundred percent of humidity. No *ventilatsya*. No safety *vikhod*. No power tool. Only with pick in our hand we go back underground to cut coal. Then we sell it for money. You know, in this time there is no other work. We have to live."

"Holy fuck."

The swarm of bees drones on, soothing and purposeful. A few drops of rain spatter against the windshield. Irina sighs and stirs, her head heavy on his left shoulder. She is asleep. She hasn't heard anything. One day, he will tell her the whole story: the bright spring morning; the hole in the ground, gaping like a wound, where they lowered themselves into the earth; the stifling darkness that swallowed them up. Those first tremors. Then the long roar of the explosion. The shaking. The tumbling boulders from the roof. The voices shouting, screaming. Then the silence. Black dust. He moves his arm up and enfolds her, pulling her head onto his chest. Her hair flows over him like streamers of dark silk.

Behind the front seats, a curtain made out of an old sheet has been strung across the bus. It is only partly drawn and Andriy can see into the back, where all the seats have been taken out except four, which are arranged around a square makeshift table. In one corner is a low cupboard with a gas ring on top and some cardboard boxes in which clothes, food, and pans are jumbled together. The rest of the floor space is taken up by a double mattress, with some gray brown tousled bedding.

"You convert this bus youself?"

"Aye. It weren't hard."

"I would like to do something like this. Get old bus. Convert. Travel round world."

Would Irina come with him, he wonders, on a trip like this? And Dog? On the mattress in the back of the bus, Dog is snoring and farting in his usual vigorous way and Rock's dog, curled up beside him, is sniffing and sighing more delicately.

"I'm not sure Alice would make it round t' world."

"Alice is your girlfriend?"

"Neh, Alice is the bus. My girlfriend's called Thunder."

Hm. Interesting name for woman. Quite sexy.

"She is also miner?"

"Neh. They don't have women miners over here. Mind you, if they did, she'd be ace."

"Rock, if you not miner or engineer, what work you do?"

"Me?" Rock takes another long drag on his cigarette and adjusts the little round glasses that have slipped over to one side. "I suppose you could say I'm a warrior, like."

"Warrior like? This is your job?"

"Neh, not a job. More like a calling. Aye, an earth warrior. Defending t' earth from t' vile clutches of corporate greed." He starts to giggle.

"Hm. This is original."

"Aye, you see there's this ancient stone circle up in t' Peaks. Three thousand year old. And some greedy bastard wants to open up a quarry right beside it. So us warriors—we've made a camp there, up in t' trees. They can't blast the quarry without cutting t' trees down. And now they can't cut t' trees down, because of us"—he giggles again—"defending our ancient British heritage from tentacles of globalization, in Jimmy's immortal words."

This Jimmy sounds like an interesting type.

"But why for they make quarry in such historic place?"

"Greed, man. Sheer greed. All for export. Building boom in America. Turn muck into brass. Jimmy called 'em t' enemy within."

He has become quite agitated, staring all around him with anxious eyes.

"In Ukraine was same," says Andriy soothingly. "Everything was sold. Now is nothing left."

"Was it Ukraine where they had all them protests? Summat about t' election? Orange banners an' all that?" His voice has become calm again, almost dreamy.

"That also was greed. Few businessmen have got all public asset into its hand. Now they will sell to West."

"Andriy, you are talking complete rubbish!"

She sits bolt upright, rubbing her eyes.

"I thought you were asleep."

"How can I sleep when you talk such rubbish?"

"Is not rubbish, Irina. You know nothing about our lives in the east."

They have slipped into Ukrainian, and raised their voices. Rock watches them with a benign smile on his face, leaning low over the steering wheel. The bus is going incredibly slowly now, barely ten Ks per hour.

"I know what is good for Ukraine, Andriy"—she stabs her finger at him—"and it is not to be dominated by Russia."

What's got into her? Okay, so now it is time for reeducation to begin.

"Is not domination, is economic integration, Irina. Integrated production, integrated market." He speaks slowly and clearly. Can she, a young girl with a head full of feminine things, be capable of understanding such ideas? "Ukrainian economy and Russian economy was one. Without Russia, Ukrainian industry collapsed."

"Andriy, Russia has been robbing Ukraine under the tsars, under communism, now under economic integration. It is just a different name for the same thing. At least with Yushchenko we can build our own independent economy."

Her voice has taken on an irritating preachy note, which is not at all attractive in a woman. She should stick to womanly topics, not meddle her pretty nose in politics.

"Irina, the main people who have been robbing Ukraine are our fellow Ukrainians. Kravchuk, Kuchma, your Timoshenko—all of them billionaires. You know, when they closed coal mines in Donbas, there was

European money to help miners, for new industries to replace old. What happened? All money went into pockets of officials. New Ukrainian officials, not Russian. Mobilfonmen. Mines were sold, stripped of machinery, closed. No new industries replaced them. In desperation, miners went underground themselves to dig for coal. Can you imagine in what conditions? Can you imagine this for one moment, Irina?"

"There's no need to shout."

"I'm sorry." She is right. Shouting will not bring him back. "In one of these mines my father died."

"Oh, Andriy!" She puts her hands up to her mouth. "Oh, why didn't you tell me before? I'm very sorry. I'm so very sorry."

Tears brim up in her eyes, and there's such a look of pain on her face that he has to take her in his arms again to comfort her. He will have to go more softly with reeducation next time.

"It's not your fault, Irina. Please don't cry. You didn't kill him with your own hands."

She sighs. She buries her face in him. He strokes the dark bird's wing of her hair that settles against his chest.

Wait a minute—what's happening now? The bus seems to have slowed almost to a halt and is drifting slowly across the road. Rock is slumped forward over the wheel, sighing softly and still giggling a little. Andriy leans over, grabs the wheel, and tries to guide the bus back on course, giving Rock a hard dig with his elbow at the same time. Rock shakes his head, blinks, smiles, resettles the glasses that have almost slipped off his nose, then takes control of the wheel again.

"No stress, our lad. Time for a little nap."

At the next service station, he pulls off the road, parks the bus, drapes himself over the steering wheel, and in a few minutes he is fast asleep. Irina wanders off to find the restroom. Andriy sits in the bus, listening to the snoring sounds of Rock and the dogs, feeling impatience build up in him like steam in a cylinder. Will they ever get to Sheffield?

"What's the matter with him?" whispers Irina, climbing up into the seat beside him, looking bright-faced and relaxed.

"Tired from driving. You know, this old bus. No power steering."

He has a pretty good idea about the cigarette, but he doesn't want to alarm her.

Half an hour or so later Rock wakes up, scratches his head, shakes himself all over like a dog, and immediately goes off in search of something to eat. As he steps down out of the bus, Andriy notices for the first time how small he is—he looks like a curly-haired elf in his baggy earthy clothes as he skips off toward the service area. He returns a few minutes later with a bottle of water, an orange, a loaf of sliced bread, and four bars of chocolate. Andriy reaches in his pocket for some money, but Rock shakes his head.

"No stress. I liberated them."

He peels the orange methodically, doling out the segments one at a time between the three of them. Then he breaks up the chocolate bars and does the same. Then he carefully counts out the slices of the loaf. He seems to be in no hurry to go anywhere. Behind the little round glasses, his eyes have gone pink.

"I can drive if you like it," says Andriy.

"No stress," says Rock.

Half an hour later, when they have finished eating, he fills up the tank from a drum in the luggage box, hands Andriy the keys to the bus, and crawls into the back.

"Move over," he says, and stretches out between Dog and Maryjane. Soon, the three of them are snoring in chorus with the drone of the engine. In the front passenger seat Irina seems to have drifted off to sleep too.

Sitting behind the wheel, Andriy is doing his best to concentrate on the road. Well, for one thing, he was right about the steering—this old bus is even worse than the Land Rover. The gear movement is fiendish too. Fortunately, once they are on the road, there isn't much steering or gear-changing to do, nothing much to do, in fact, but to sit there and watch the kilometers slip slowly by.

The promised rain has not materialized, and the sky is still heavy and hot. It is early evening now, and the traffic has increased a bit. Not that it makes any difference to him—theirs is by far the slowest vehicle on the road. It is surprising, he thinks, that Sheffield doesn't seem to be getting any closer. Surely they would have seen a sign for it by now. On their left is a sign for Leeds. Is that not somewhere in the north? Then a sign to York. Well, at least they are in the right county. But isn't Sheffield supposed to be in South Yorkshire? Where has it disappeared to?

Irina wakes up, and reaches over to touch his hand.

"Are we nearly there now?"

"I think so."

"Tell me something else about this Sheffield."

"Well, you know, Sheffield is the first city in England to be declared a socialist republic, and the ruler, this Vloonki, is known throughout the world for his progressive policies."

"What are these progressive policies?" she asks, a note of suspicion in her voice. "Will I like them?"

"You will like the bougainvillea, for sure."

He leans across and kisses her, steadying the bus with his right knee.

Although Andriy is very handsome and manly, there are times when I wish he was not quite so primitive. How have I let myself fall in love with a man who is riddled with Soviet-era ideas? I hope that here in the West he will be able to shed some of his outdated misconceptions, but I wonder about this Sheffield. Will it turn out to be some kind of communist-style workers' paradise like Yalta or Sochi, with sanatoria and communal mudbaths everywhere? We will see.

Rock did not wake up for several hours. When he did, he was amazed to see how far we had come.

"You should've turned off on the A57. We've come way too far north. We'll have to turn around and go back again."

"You did not say anything about this," said Andriy rather grumpily. That is one of his bad points, I have noticed. He is inclined to grumpiness. I suppose he is desperate to get to this Sheffield.

Rock looked vague and apologetic. "It was that skunk," he muttered, staring into the back of the van, though I really don't see how Dog can be held responsible.

Anyway, the bus was turned around and off we went in the opposite direction, with Rock at the wheel once more. The light had faded from the sky. Occasionally a car or lorry thundered down the southbound highway, headlights blazing into the dusk. We must have been driving for an hour or so, nosing our way southward, Rock resting both hands on the wheel, staring straight ahead, without saying anything. The traffic on the road had thinned out. Once or twice a vehicle overtook us, its taillights dwindling in the darkness until there were two red pinpricks, then nothing.

Then suddenly he pulled off the road into a pull-off and announced, "I don't think we're gonna make it tonight, lads. Let's pull over for a nap and carry on in t' morning."

Andriy didn't say anything, but I knew what he was thinking. I could see the thundery look on his face.

"You two can have t' bed—I'll sleep on t' bench. Maryjane! Here!"

Maryjane bounded into the front, and Dog followed. Rock pulled two of the seats together end to end. He took off his T-shirt and jeans, threw them into a box with the crockery, and eased his pale little body into a khaki-colored sleeping bag like a larva crawling into its cocoon.

Andriy stepped outside and helped me down from the bus. We were in a pull-off, set back from the road behind a hedge. There was another trailer there too, all shuttered up, with a sign saying TEAS. SNACKS. The night was still warm and humid, the sky overcast, with no stars. I breathed deeply, filling my lungs, stretching my limbs and feeling them loosen. We had been sitting for hours. I wandered behind a bush to water the grass and I heard Andriy doing the same a little distance away, stumbling in the darkness, then the soft hiss of his pee seeping into the ground.

When he came back in the dark, he took me in his arms and pressed me up against the side of the bus. I could feel him, all hard, and his breath hot and urgent on my neck. I don't know why I started trembling. Then he held me close, until my body went still against his.

"Irina, we are two halves of one country." His voice was low and passionate. "We must learn to love each other."

No one has ever said anything so wonderful to me before.

He kissed my hair, then my lips. I felt spurts of fire running through my body, and that melting feeling when you almost can't say no anymore. But somehow I did say no. Because when it's *the night*, it has to be perfect—not on that disgusting mattress where Dog and Maryjane had been lying licking their parts. Not standing up by the roadside like a prostitute in a doorway. You can't imagine Natasha and Pierre consummating their love up against the side of a bus, can you?

"Not now, Andriy," I said. "Not here. Not like this."

Then he said something quite bad-tempered, then he apologized for being bad-tempered and I apologized for what I'd said, and he said he was going for a walk and I said I'd go with him but he said no, he wanted to go by himself. I stood at the side of the bus, waiting for him to come back and wondering what I should say to make him not be angry with me. Should I tell him that I loved him?

When at last we did crawl onto the mattress, the bedding was gray and greasy, with a sweaty doggy smell. I couldn't take my clothes off. Andriy thought it was out of modesty—he's such a gentleman—but it was really because I didn't want to feel those limp clammy sheets against my skin. He held me in his arms all night, my head tucked in between his chin and his shoulder. He didn't even notice the sheets.

In the morning, I woke to find my hands and feet were covered in red lumps. Andriy's were too. Rock was already awake, squatting by the gas stove boiling some water, wearing nothing but his underpants, which were gray and loose like the loincloth of an Old Testament prophet.

"Ready for a cuppa?" he said.

He was smoking a thin hand-rolled cigarette, which hung on his lower lip as he talked and puffed simultaneously. His body was stringy and very pale, with no manly musculature, just a sprinkling of ginger freckles and fleabites. I wished he would put some clothes on.

For breakfast we ate the remains of yesterday's bread and some wizened apples that were lurking in one of the boxes. Rock poured out the hot, weak tea, which he sweetened with honey from a jar. Andriy leaned over and whispered in my ear, "You are as sweet as honey."

A brown curl flopped down in the middle of his forehead as he said it, and for some reason I can't explain, I felt a shining bubble of love swelling up inside me, not just for Andriy, but also for Rock, for Dog and Maryjane, for the smelly old bus, even for the fleabites and the loincloth underpants, and for the whole fresh lovely morning.

It was still very early. Outside, the landscape was softened by a haze that lingered over the flat empty fields, clinging to the outlines of trees and bushes. The birds had already started to rouse themselves, chirping away busily. Dog and Maryjane were chasing around out there, tumbling and playing. Rock whistled, and they came running, their eyes bright, their tongues hanging out. They settled themselves on the bed, and we sat in front. Then Rock revved the engine, tearing through the misty silence, and we were off.

Sometime last night they must have turned westward off the Great North Road. The road they are on now is smaller, winding through a featureless agricultural landscape of large fields planted with unfamiliar crops and little settlements of redbrick houses. But what amazes Andriy is that there is already so much traffic on the road, cars, vans, lorries, people racing to get to work. A large black four-by-four cruises by. It looks like . . . No, surely there are dozens of such vehicles on the roads. He glances at Irina. She is sitting in the middle again, her left hand warm beneath his right hand. Her eyes are closed. She didn't notice.

A minibus overtakes them on a long straight stretch, and he counts some dozen men squashed together on the benches, swarthy dark-haired

men with brooding early-morning faces, some of them smoking cigarettes, gliding past them into the mist.

"Who are these men?" he asks Rock.

Rock shrugs. "Immigrant workers. Fragments of globalized labor,
Jimmy Binbag called them."

"Who is . . . ?"

"Whole country's run by immigrants now. They do all t' crap jobs."

"Like us."

"Aye, like you," says Rock. "Did you hear about that crash in Kent?
Minivan full of strawberry pickers. Six killed."

"In Kent?" Irina sits up sharply, her eyes very wide.

"Poor exploited bastards. Minions of faceless global corporations.
Not me. I've had enough of all that. Now I've turned warrior." He pushes
back the glasses that have slipped down his nose. "If only me dad could
see me now. He said I were too soft for t' pit."

"But you are defending stones and not people," says Andriy. "Why?"

"Coal, stone, earth—it's all our heritage, in't it?"

"What is mean eritij?"

"It's what you get from your mum and dad. Gifts passed on through t'
generations."

"Like underpants," whispers Irina in Ukrainian.

If I were a warrior, thinks Andriy, I would not be defending some
stupid old stones, but the flesh and blood of living people. In Donbas
too the mobilfonmen have taken over, and people have become dispos-
able, their precious lives thrown away through avoidable accidents and
preventable disease, their misery blunted by vodka. This is the future his
country has prepared for him—to be expendable. No, he will not accept it.

"What are you thinking?" asks Irina softly.

"I'm thinking how precious you are, Ukrainian girl."

The words feel strangely solid in his mouth, like lumps of undissolved
sugar. He isn't used to saying things like this to a woman.

They are still going westward. They pass through an ugly traffic-
clogged town, out onto a larger highway, then take a narrow road through

the fields, which are green and undulating but without the luminous beauty of the Kent countryside.

"All round here used to be pits," says Rock. "In t' strike, they blocked all t' roads to stop Yorkshire pickets coming into Notts. Scabby Notts, they called it. It were a battleground. My dad were arrested at Hucknall. That's all history now." He sighs. "No bin bags in t' dustbin of history, as Jimmy used to say."

"Who is . . . ?"

"Highway up ahead," says Rock. "Once we're over, we'll soon be home."

Beyond the fields, a few kilometers ahead, they catch glimpses of a huge road carved through the landscape, bigger even than the Great North Road, the lines of cars and lorries moving slowly, as close as colored beads on a thread.

After the highway, the road becomes narrower and starts to climb. The houses are no longer of brick but of grey stone, and the villages smaller and farther apart. As they climb, they come into a different sort of countryside, wild and heathy, with dark crags, copses of silver birch and conifers, and sweeping wind-smoothed hills. The sky is heavy, with storm clouds resting on the horizon. Rock is driving in first most of the time, leaning forward over the wheel, because the road is so narrow that if a vehicle comes the other way, one of them will have to back up to let the other pass.

"I like this landscape," says Irina. "It is how I imagined England. Like *Wuthering Heights.*"

"Peak District," says Rock. "We're nearly there."

On a steep narrow road between two woods, Rock takes a left turn onto a rutted dirt track that leads into a grove of silver birches. At the bottom, among the trees, another bus is parked. As they drive closer, two dogs run out of the woods and race toward them, barking. Maryjane pricks up her ears and starts barking too, and Dog joins in. Then three people emerge, following the dogs. Andriy studies them curiously—are they men or women?

Andriy was rather annoyed when he realized this was our destination. I think he had believed we would soon arrive in Sheffield. Rock had promised vaguely that he would drop us off in Sheffield the next day. Or the day after. To be honest, I was in no great hurry to reach Sheffield and I was curious about this camp. Maybe there would be a tent or little romantic trailer perched up on a hillside where we could spend the night.

But there was just a jumble of old vehicles at the edge of the woods, some of them propped up on bricks, and the only tents were crude tarpaulins stretched low over bent saplings. Then I looked up and my eyes blinked, because up there among the leaves was a whole spider's web of blue rope, stretching from tree to tree like walkways in the sky, and canvas shelters perched up in the branches.

Rock jumped down and ran toward three people—they must be his fellow warriors—who were coming out to greet us. He embraced them and introduced us. They were all wearing the same baggy earth-colored clothes. In my opinion, they did not have the appearance you would expect of typical warriors. The smallest of them, whose name was Windhover, had a completely shaved head. The two taller ones had the same twisted-rat's-tail hair as Toby McKenzie, though one of them had it pulled back into a ponytail. They were called Heather and Birch. Everyone around here seems to have these stupid names. In my opinion, people should be named after people, not things. Otherwise, how can you tell whether they are male or female?

Heather is the name of a small purple flower that is very popular in Scotland and it is also a woman's name, but this warrior Heather seemed to be a man, at least if facial hair is anything to judge by. Despite his feminine name, he looked quite chunky and muscular, with a thick brown beard that looked as if it had been chopped with nail scissors—maybe this is a warrior fashion. I was less sure about the other two. Warrior Birch was quite tall but seemed somehow insubstantial, with a soft voice and an apologetic manner. Warrior Windhover was smaller but seemed more ferocious, despite having no hair of any kind apart from eyebrows, which were dark and curved expressively over luminous sea blue eyes that stood out vividly in a pale bony head. As we followed them back to the camp, I noticed that Windhover and Birch were holding hands, so one of them must be a woman and one a man—but which was which?

To my surprise I spotted a wash line stretched between a trailer and a tree, just like at our strawberry field, and on it were hanging three pairs of warrior underpants, all grayish, shapeless, and soggy. And this amused me, because to be honest they did not seem like the kind of warriors who would bother much with laundry.

In a clearing among the trees a fire was smoldering, with a blackened kettle hanging over it and some logs set around it as seats. They invited us to sit, and Heather poured tea for us, which was grayish, smoky-tasting, and very weak, into cups that were also cracked, grayish, and smoky-tasting. Then Birch ladled out some food from another pot, and that was grayish and smoky-tasting too. It reminded me of the warrior underpants. If you boiled them and mashed them up a bit, they would look and taste like this.

They were talking among themselves. Rock was telling them about his visit to Cambridge, and they were asking various questions about laboratories, but I wasn't really paying attention, because I had spotted something in the trees. Up there among the leaves was a trailer—a little, round green-painted trailer, sitting in the crook of a massive beech tree, secured with blue rope, and a dangling rope ladder leading up to it.

"Look, Andriy," I said.

Rock said, "Aye, that's the visitors' trailer. You can sleep up there if you want."

Andriy gave me a look that set my body glowing from inside, and my heart was jumping around all over the place, because I knew for sure that it would happen tonight.

The bald woman, Windhover, has the most entrancing eyebrows—the way they lift enquiringly, curve suggestively, tighten into a frown, or rise up in arcs of surprise or pleasure. A woman's eyebrows can be a very seductive feature, thinks Andriy. She is talking to Birch, the eyebrows rising and falling in rhythm. Earlier, he saw them holding hands, and as they bent their heads together there was a little stolen kiss. To watch two women kissing is very arousing to a man. Were they doing it on purpose? He has never met a homosex woman before, but he has heard that they are incredibly sexy. Never until now has he had an opportunity to find out for himself. He has heard it said that their passionate nature, thwarted by the absence of a suitable man, turns in on itself and fixes on another of the same kind. But should a suitably manly man appear on the scene, with the skill and patience to unlock that passion, they say, the intensity of the ardor that will be unleashed is beyond description. There's no stopping these homosex women once they get going. A man has to keep a cool head or he could drown in the torrent of their passion. What's more, they say, the homosex woman will be profoundly indebted to the man who liberates her from her sterile inward-looking fixation, and will show her gratitude in an astonishing display of sexual abandon, et cetera, which he can only begin to imagine.

This poor hairless woman with beautiful eyes and seductive eyebrows, the thought of her mysterious body pale beneath its layers of dun-colored wrapping, hungry for the love of a good man, fills Andriy with intense . . . pity. And although of course he is completely committed to Irina and to their future together, still, he wonders whether Irina would object if as an act of kindness, he were to free this sad, confined creature from the prison of her thwarted passion.

Oh, don't be such an idiot, Andriy Palenko.

After our meal, Rock said, "Come on. Time to meet the ladies."

He led Andriy and me and a small pack of dogs back along the track, over the lane, and up a steep path through the wood on the other side. As we climbed up I stopped to look back at their camp, but it was hardly visible, the green-painted trailer and faded green tarpaulins hidden among the foliage. You could just see a wisp of smoke fingering up through the leaves. Warrior Heather, who had accompanied us, pointed out an outcrop of rosy-colored stone.

"That's the sandstone they want to quarry," he said. "Pretty color, isn't it? It was licensed in 1952. Now they want to open it up again. But we stopped them."

"You stopped it? With your camp?" said Andriy.

"Yes. We made them take it to court. The court threw it out. We should be celebrating, but actually it's rather sad, because it means the end of this camp. Some of us have lived here for five years. Isn't that so, Rocky?" His voice and manner of speaking were very cultivated, unlike Rock's low-class regional accent.

"Aye," said Rock, who had gone on ahead, and now stopped and waited for us to catch up. "Bloody sad. I've been here three year. Now I'll have to become a wage slave again. Earn. Spend. Buy crap. Surrender missen to t' vile clutches of materialism." He relit the cigarette that was dangling on his lip. "Some of them've gone up to Sheffield and Leeds already. Thunder, Torrent, Sparrowhawk, Midge. Working in t' call centers. Sweatshops of t' information age, Jimmy called them."

"Don't worry," said Heather. "Nobody'll let you near a call center."

At the top, we emerged on a wide stony plateau covered with heather.

Heather said, "Calluna vulgaris. Ericaceous. My favorite plant. Just smell it."

I stooped to pick a sprig, but he stopped me.

"It's protected. You've got to smell it in situ."

I bent down and breathed deeply. It smelled of summer and honey. I could see why he'd chosen this flower for his warrior name. The purple flowers were so small that in the distance they just looked like a mauve haze drifting over the hilltops.

Following a sandy track, we came through a small copse of trees, ash, beech, and silver birch, and found ourselves in a flat grassy clearing some fifteen meters wide. Set in the grass was a circle of nine stones.

In my opinion they were somewhat disappointing. I was expecting something bigger and more structured, like Stonehenge. These stones were crooked and uneven in size, like bad teeth. They did not look anything like ladies. No one who has seen the basilica of Santa Sofia or the Lavra Monastery at sunset, or even certain English monuments, would find these stones of interest. But then Heather said, "Iron age. Three and a half thousand years old. Forerunners of our great cathedrals."

I suppose that is quite interesting.

"You can listen to the spirits up here," said Rock. He flung himself down on his back in the middle of the circle, his arms and legs outstretched. "Sometimes, when I lie still, I think I can hear Jimmy Binbag talking. Come and lie down and listen."

So we lay, the four of us, in a cross shape, our heads at the center, our outstretched hands and feet just touching. I expected one of them to start chanting some weird stuff at any minute, but nobody did, so I just lay staring at the sky and listening to the breeze ruffling the grass. The clouds were heavy, their undersides purple with rain, with unexpected shafts of sunlight breaking through in bursts of gold and silver like messenger angels. I could feel the closeness of the others, *him* on my left and Heather on my right, and the silence of the stones. Then, in the silence, I started to feel the closeness of all the other people who had stood and lain in this place over thousands of years, staring at these same rocks and this sky. I imagined I could hear their footsteps and their voices in my head, not hurrying or shouting, but just the gentle chatter-patter of human life, as it has been lived on this earth since time was first counted.

It reminded me of my childhood, when my bed had been in the living room of our little two-roomed flat, and each night I fell asleep to the sound of my parents' voices and their quiet movements tiptoeing around so as not to wake me—chatter-patter.

The silence inside the stone circle is eerie. It hangs in the air like the huge hush in the cathedral, after prayers are finished. If you lie still, you

can hear the wind sighing in the grass like voices murmuring in your ear.
Andriy listens. Really, the sound is uncannily like the whisper of human
voices. What language are they speaking? The hiss of sibilants makes him
think at first that it is Polish—yes, it is Yola and Tomasz and Marta, talking quietly together. They are back in Zdroj. Marta is preparing a feast.
It is somebody's birthday—a child's. They are drinking wine, Tomasz
filling up the glasses and proposing a toast to—Andriy strains to hear—
the toast is to him and Irina, and their future happiness. Tears come to
his eyes. And in the background someone is giggling and whispering—
not in Polish now, but in . . . is it Chinese? Abruptly, the giggling stops
and turns to sobbing. The sobbing grows louder, and now he sees the
miners from the pit accident, struggling out of the mass of fallen rock,
reaching out for him with their hands, pulling at him, pleading. His
father is there among them, shrouded in that terrible black dust, already
formless as a ghost. He knows he has to run, to get away, but he is
pinioned to the ground. He can't move. His limbs have turned to lead,
but his heart is beating faster, faster. And just as it seems the panic will
overwhelm him, the sobbing turns into music, a voice—a man's voice—
deep and sweet, singing of peace and comfort, easing the pain and rage in
his soul with its promise of eternity. Emanuel is singing to him.

He awakes with a start, wondering—did Blessing remember to make
that phone call?

Maybe I was dreaming, because after a while I realized that the patter
was raindrops and the chatter was Andriy saying, "Wake up, Irina. Let's
go back. It's raining."

The others had already rigged up a large canvas awning between
the trees, and underneath it a fire was smoking. Heather was peeling
potatoes, and Rock was stirring something in a pot.

"Can I help?" I asked.

Rock passed me the stirring spoon. Then he disappeared.

"I'll get some more dry wood," said Andriy, and disappeared too.

"Where are the other people in your camp?" I asked Heather.

He explained that some of them had gone south to a music festival and others had found temporary jobs in nearby towns to earn some money. Unfortunately, since their victory in court the support of the local villagers had dwindled away, and soon maybe it would be time to close up their camp altogether.

"Where will you go?" I asked.

He shrugged. "There's always somewhere. Roads. Airports. Power stations. The earth's always under assault."

I thought how wonderful it would be to have some new roads and airports and power stations in Ukraine, but I didn't say so. We listened to the rain pit-patting on the canvas and the wood cracking on the fire. Somewhere, somebody was playing a guitar.

"Do you like cooking?" Heather threw a handful of chopped carrots into the pot. His fingernails were very long, almost like claws, and full of black dirt.

"Not much," I said.

"Me neither," he said. "But I like to eat. When we lived in Renfrewshire, my parents had a cook called Agatha. She was six feet tall and swore like a trooper, but she had a great way with pastry. One day she was making a batch of tarts when the oven exploded, and she was rushed to hospital where she died a week later of third-degree burns. That's enough to put anyone off cooking, don't you agree?"

"Of course." I laughed, despite the gravity of the story, wondering whether it was true. And I wondered how someone who spoke in such a cultivated way, and came from a house with a cook, could tolerate living in such a place, and eating such food, and having such dire fingernails. And I wondered whether he had a girlfriend, and whether she lived here in the camp, and what she thought of his fingernails. And I wondered whether he found me attractive, for he, like Rock, never stared or flirted or made personal remarks like some other men, so I felt completely comfortable in their company. Maybe they are only attracted to women of their own species.

Obviously the woman with beautiful eyebrows has her eye on you, Palenko—but does that mean you have to proceed? You have discussed the weather. You have discussed the stones. Is it time now to select first gear and try to engage? Or is there a time when you say to yourself, Okay. I have met the woman I love. That is enough. Bye-bye, end of story.

Andriy shovels the mush into his mouth, crunching on the chunks of almost-raw carrot, glancing up from time to time to check on the eyebrows. The rain is pattering intermittently on the taut tarpaulin, beneath which smoke swirls around the circle of faces. Windhover is seated next to Birch on the other side of the fire. Now her eyebrows are drawn together in contemplation. Such beautiful eyebrows. She is spooning the sludge into her mouth quite fast, and with apparent enjoyment.

In fact apart from the eyebrows she is not so attractive, he thinks. Her body seems shapeless and lumpy beneath its thick sludge-colored swaddling—not really a womanly shape at all. Perhaps . . . ? No, surely he could not be mistaken about something like that. Windhover does not return his look.

"This is nice, Heather," she says, completely ignoring Andriy. "What is it?"

"Lentil and carrot goulash." Heather looks pleased. "It could have done with some paprika."

Dinner was the same tasteless underpants-colored sludge as the previous meal, but this time it had pieces of chopped-up carrot in it. Another unpleasant thing is that this sludgy diet tends to make you fart, which was noticeable even out of doors, especially from the dogs. I declined Heather's offer of a second helping, while trying to seem enthusiastic so as not to hurt his feelings, because, okay, he's no Mr. Brown, but he is very kind.

After we had finished eating, Rock collected our bowls and scraped the remains of the goulash into them—goulash they call it! obviously they have never tasted the real thing!—and put it down for the dogs, who licked the bowls clean. In my opinion the hygienic arrangements at this camp are deficient, and I wonder why the authorities have not closed it down. There is nothing but a small stream for washing, and a much-too-shallow pit toilet, screened by a few branches, with a piece of wood to perch on above the disgusting festering *nuzhnik* of previous warrior dinners. Somebody has put up a scrawled notice saying *Beware of splashback.*

By now dusk was creeping up and the air was cool and damp. I took the bowls and went down to the stream to rinse the dog-lick off them (the others looked surprised—obviously as far as they were concerned, they were perfectly clean), and then I washed myself all over with Mrs. McKenzie's scented soap, because I knew tonight would be *the night.* Then I climbed the rope ladder up to the tree trailer.

The door was not locked. The trailer was much smaller even than the women's trailer at our strawberry field, and rounded like an egg. There was no room inside for anything except a folded-out double bed. I could not see how clean the bedding was, and I thought it was better not to look. I suppose one advantage of being in a tree is that the dogs cannot get up here. On a low cupboard by the bed was a bunch of dried flowers in a jam jar that gave the cabin a pleasant powdery smell. Some ends of candles were stuck into bottles, and there was even a box of matches. I lit a candle, and straightaway the little shell was filled inside with soft flickering light. Beyond the circle of light, the leaves at the window shifted and shivered in the dusk. Storm clouds had banked up along the hilltops. Down below, I could hear the voices of the warriors talking among themselves, and the strumming of a guitar. I stretched out on the bed and waited.

For some reason I found myself thinking about my parents. Had my mother lain and waited for my father like this on her wedding night? Was it romantic? Had it hurt the first time? Did she get pregnant? Yes, she did. The seed that was planted inside her that night was to grow into me. I had grown up sheltered by the twined branches of their love, nurtured until the seed sprouted into a tree—Irinochka—that could stand alone. Had he still loved her afterward? Yes, but only for a while. Temporarily. Provisionally. Until Svitlana Surokha came along. For the first time, I found myself feeling angry with my parents. Why couldn't they have just stuck together a bit longer, their love still entwining and sheltering me, while I learned my own first lessons of love?

I started planning a new story in my head. It would be a passionate romance, a story of enduring love, about two people who came from different worlds but after many diversions found themselves brought together by destiny. The heroine would be a virgin. The hero would have bronzed muscular arms.

The voices down below grew more animated and the guitar stopped. They were having a discussion, punctuated by bursts of laughter. Suddenly I felt the trailer lurch and sway in a most terrifying way. I sat up quaking. Typical, I thought, tonight—*the night*—the trailer will fall out of the tree. Then I realized the movement was the tug of someone coming up the rope ladder. My heart started to thump. A moment later, Andriy opened the door. He had a nervous smile on his face and a bunch of heather in his hand.

"I picked this for you, Irina." He sat down on the edge of the bed and handed me the heather, looking at me in that fixed, intense way. "You are beautiful like a green tree in May."

I buried my face in the heather, which still had the smell of honey and summer about it, because I didn't want him to see me grinning. On the scale of romance, I would say that was about a three out of ten.

Then he lay down beside me on the bed and started to stroke my cheek very gently. I could feel my body melting at his touch as he pulled me into his arms, kissing me with his lips and tongue, caressing me everywhere, and all the time murmuring my name. Mmm. Maybe a seven out of ten. The candlelight cast one shadow of our two bodies—blurring, looming, wavering on the curved ceiling. When he touched me down there, the unexpected intensity of my feelings made me cry out. Okay, at that point I stopped scoring. I don't even remember him undressing me, but somehow our clothes slid away and we were naked together, skin against skin, on the bed. The candle sputtered out and the canopy of darkening leaves closed in around us.

Suddenly there was a shudder of wind in the branches, and all at once the storm broke, heralded by a drumroll of rain on the roof, then blasts of thunder and a pageant of lightning flashes all around us like a carnival in the sky. Our little trailer bucked and heaved on its sea of leaves. The rain hammered on the thin aluminum shell and from time to time a razor of light would slash through the darkness. I was really afraid that our tree would be struck and everything would burst into flames.

"Don't be frightened, Irinochka," said Andriy, pressing me tighter against him.

And so we gave ourselves to each other that night in the storm.

Yes, it was very romantic. Yes, it did hurt a bit, but my feelings were so intense that I didn't realize until afterward how sore I was. Yes, I was worried about getting pregnant, but he produced something from his pocket that was rubbery and pink and smelled of strawberries. No, that was not quite so romantic, I admit, but it was thoughtful, and that also is a sign of love. Yes, he still loves me, because in the morning he went down on the rope ladder and came back with some bread and tea, and we spent half the morning lying in bed together talking about the future, and the places we would travel to after Sheffield, and all the things we would do. Then we made love again.

No, I am not the same person I was yesterday.

I AM DOG I RUN I RUN WITH MARYJANE I AM IN LOVE SHE IS A BROWN DOG FAST AND SLIM SHE HAS GOOD SMELL FEMALE DOG LOVE-HORMONES I SNIFF SHE SNIFFS ALL DOGS RUN AFTER HER BUT SHE RUNS WITH ME WE RUN IN STORM AND RAIN WE RUN IN MOONLIGHT WE RUN IN SHADOWS I GIVE HER MY PUPPIES I AM IN LOVE I RUN I RUN I AM DOG

Next day, before they leave, Andriy and Rock climb up the beech tree to resecure the trailer. One of the guide ropes snapped in the night, and the trailer is hanging at an angle, its axle wedged between two branches.

"That were a bit of luck," says Rock, "or a bit of bad luck, depending on which way you look at it."

"It was good luck," says Andriy.

It is early afternoon by the time they get on the road. Irina is sitting in the middle again, her profile inscrutable, her eyes sleepy, as the bus winds its way through narrow lanes and gray stone villages. He puts his arm around her, and she shifts and molds her body more closely against his. Her hair is loose and uncombed. He strokes it back from her face and watches her smile. This girl—she is quite something. Yes, Andriy Palenko, you are one lucky Donbas miner.

"So what takes you to Sheffield?" asks Rock.

The sun is high in the sky, a wispy mist steaming from the hills after the rain.

"Sheffield? Is twin town of Donetsk. My town. Is very beautiful, I think?"

"Sheffield? Aye, you could say that. If you've got an eye for steelworks. Or you could say it's not beautiful."

"The coal mining is still going there?"

"No, that's all changed. Used to be loads of slag heaps. Now it's just got slags." Rock pushes his glasses up his nose. "Barnsley were twinned with another town in Ukraine. Gorlovka."

"I been there. Is also in Donbas region. Not beautiful."

"Well, Barnsley in't noted for its beauty."

"I been in Sheffield once before. And I met Vloonki, who is noted for his wisdom and good heart. When we get to Sheffield, we will ask him for help."

"Vloonki?"

"The ruler. He is blind, but he sees everythings."

"Aw! You mean Blunkett!" Rock jumps in his seat and his glasses slip right off his nose and skitter across the dashboard. As he leans to grab them, the steering wheel lurches sharply and the bus swerves, skids sideways, and bounces off a boulder. "Bloody Blunkett!" Rock pinches the nose clip on his glasses to tighten it.

"Why he is bloody?"

"Class traitor. Sold our birthright for a mess of posh totty, in Jimmy's immortal words."

Sold what? Who is this Jimmy? Before Andriy can ask, Rock calls out, "There she is!"

They have been winding slowly upward for a few kilometers through a wild steep landscape of bracken, peat, and rock, more somber than the sandy heathery plateau of Nine Ladies. At the top of the rise the road levels out, and just as it starts to dip they see a city spread below them in the valley, a dense cluster of buildings in the center, glinting in the sunlight, thinning out to untidy scatterings of ugly new developments crawling over the surrounding hills.

"This is Sheffield?" Irina's voice is cold.

Andriy's heart shrinks with disappointment. Definitely this city is not upon a hill.

Nor is there any bougainvillea. The leafy outer suburbs soon give way to ribbons of brick terraces as they near the city center. Rock pulls onto a side road where many of the houses seem abandoned, their curtains drawn, their front gardens full of rubbish and weeds, and plastered with TO LET signs. How has Vloonki allowed his city to become so neglected? There is a distant taint of steelworks in the air that reminds him of home.

"Nowhere to park in town. We'll walk from here. I'm meeting Thunder at the Ha Ha."

They follow Rock through a urine-stained underpass up into the town center. The storm has chased away the clouds, and the day is hot and bright again. Here the surroundings looked neater, and the traffic had been diverted to make a pleasant quarter. Busy crowds throng the pavements, and there are shops, market stalls, even some new and stylish buildings. This is still not as he remembers it, but it is better than his first impression. Andriy's spirits rise. Fountains—yes, there are fountains!

And a square with a formal garden full of waterfalls, overlooked by a big Gothic building that seems vaguely familiar, and a modern citadel of glass and steel that should have been a palace, but sadly turns out to be only a hotel. He takes Irina's hand, twining her fingers between his. She smiles and points. "Look!"

In the fountains a horde of raggedy children, stripped down to their underpants, are running and splashing through the water. Just like Donetsk.

I AM DOG I AM WET DOG I RUN I PLAY IN WATER WOOF SPLASH RUN IN THIS WATER IS DREAM OF MY PAST-TIME PUPPINESS HERE ARE CHILDREN WET CHILDREN THEY PLAY WITH ME WOOF SPLASH RUN I AM HAPPY THEY TOUCH ME WITH SMALL WET HANDS GOOD DOG THEY SAY I AM GOOD DOG MY MAN IS WATCHING I RUN TO MY MAN I SHAKE WATER ON HIM SHAKE SHAKE SHAKE GO AWAY WET DOG SAYS MY MAN RUN AND PLAY I AM HAPPY I RUN I PLAY I AM WET DOG I AM DOG

On the edge of the square is a café with tables set out in the sunshine. A very tall girl with cropped blond hair runs toward them and gives Rock a hug. His nose comes just about to the level of her breasts, which are small and firm and barely covered by the straps of a faded orange vest. She too has a dog on a rope.

"I've got a few things to do," says Rock. "Got to surrender missen to t' vile clutches of t' missus. I'll meet you back here at six o'clock."

Irina announces that she will take a look at the shops. Andriy watches her vanish into the crowd, Dog padding along behind her, still wet from his splash in the fountains. Then he reaches for his wallet and takes out a piece of paper. He needs to find a telephone.

I was thinking about Natasha in *War and Peace*, how she and Pierre have their blazing moment of love, and all her beauty and passion flows into him, and all his intellect and strength flows into her, and they face the world together from their glorious tower of love. When you read it, tears will come into your eyes, I promise, unless you have a heart of stone. And then, after she has found *the one*, the passion slowly dissolves into a gentle everyday love and she becomes a solid housewife, devoted to their four children and interested in household and family matters. I wonder whether the same thing will happen with Andriy and me. Already I can see the first signs. For example I noticed today that Andriy needs some new underpants. The ones he is wearing will soon be in the same condition as the warrior underpants. This is not appealing in a man.

That's what was in my mind as I set out to find the street of shops and market stalls we'd come through earlier, because I had noticed they were selling such items—sexy styles in interesting colors, not the universal dark green baggy type you get in Ukraine. And some very small ladies' underpants made of lace. I thought if I could find my way back to that street, I could have a look. But somewhere I must have taken a wrong turn, for I found myself in unfamiliar surroundings, which seemed to be a commercial district, with redbrick office buildings and only a few cafés and shops, none of them selling clothing but cleaning products, stationery, office equipment, and other useless stuff. I must have been walking for almost half an hour, getting increasingly lost. The wet dog was following me, sometimes running on ahead, sometimes lagging behind or disappearing up an alley, sniffing at pissy lampposts all the time in his disgusting way.

The sun was still hot, but the shadows were lengthening on the pavement. There was nobody on the streets here, and a one-way road system, so the few cars were going quite fast. The dog had disappeared somewhere and I was on my own. I was trying to work out where I had gone wrong and find somebody I could ask the way when I noticed that a large gray car was crawling along beside me and the driver was staring at me and mouthing something. I ignored him, and he drove off. At the corner of the street a blond woman was standing smoking a cigarette. She was wearing ridiculous satin shorts and high-heeled boots. As I hurried toward her to ask for directions, the car pulled up alongside her and the man wound down his window. They exchanged a few words and she got into his car. Hm. Obviously I didn't want to hang around in this place. So I turned and tried to retrace my steps, walking quickly, when another young woman came sauntering up the road toward me on spiky high heels. She looked familiar. I stared. It was Lena. She spotted me at the same moment.

"Hi, Lena," I said in Ukrainian, reaching out to take her hand. "What you doing here?"

"What you think?" she said.

"I heard about the accident. The minibus. I was so upset. Was that at our farm?"

"I don't know what you talking about," she said.

Close up, she looked even younger. She had grown her hair a bit and put on white powder like a mask and a smear of very bright red lipstick that accentuated her babyish pout. It was smudged at the edges, as if she had been kissing. Her black stockings and high-heeled shoes looked absurd on her skinny legs. She looked like a child who had been trying on her mother's clothes and playing with her makeup. Apart from her eyes. There was nothing childish about her eyes.

"How are the others? Tasya? Oksana?"

"I don't know."

She had stopped, and was staring straight ahead, over my shoulder. I turned and followed the line of her gaze. She was looking toward the forecourt of an office block, where a number of cars were parked. Right at the back, half hidden behind a white van, was a huge black shiny four-by-four. I must have walked right past it.

I felt a terrible sick feeling rise up in me. My heart started up. Boom. Boom. Run, run, shouted my racing heart, but my feet stayed rooted to the ground. I looked at Lena, but her eyes were completely dead.

There is a telephone booth at the top of the square, near the café. Andriy fumbles in his pocket for change, puts a couple of coins in the slot, and dials the number on the piece of paper. There is a series of clicks, followed by a long single tone. What does that mean? He dials again. The same empty tone. He listens for a long time, but nothing happens. A blank. He was half expecting it. He sighs. This is it then. His journey's end. Vagvaga Riskegipd. A blank. Ah, well.

A middle-aged woman is sitting at a small round table on the pavement outside the café. He shows her the piece of paper.

"Oh," she says, "that's an old number. You have to dial 0114 instead of 0742. But you don't need that, because you're in Sheffield. You just put 2 before the main number."

He fishes a pencil stub out of his pocket and she writes it down for him.

He tries again with the new number. This time there is a ringing tone. After several rings, a woman picked up the phone.

"Alloa?" She speaks in the same broad regional dialect as Rock.

"Vagvaga?" He can hardly control the excitement in his voice. "Vagvaga Riskegipd? Vagvaga?"

There is a moment's silence. Then the voice on the other end of the phone says, "Bugger off." There is a click, followed by the dialing tone. He feels a stab of frustration. So close, yet still so far. Was that her voice on the end of the phone? He can't recall her saying anything at all to him that night. How old would she be now? The voice on the phone sounded crackly and breathless, like an older woman's. He resolves to wait a few minutes and try again.

When he goes back into the square the same middle-aged woman is still sitting at her table, drinking coffee. She has been joined by a friend, and their shopping bags are clustered around them on the ground. On impulse, he approaches her once more with his piece of paper.

"No luck?" She smiles at him.

"What is this name?" he asks her.

She looks at him oddly.

"Barbara Pickering. What did you think it was?"

He stares at the paper. Ah. His twenty-five-year-old eyes see what his seven-year-old eyes had not seen: Roman script.

"What is mean bugger off?"

She looks at him oddly again.

"That's enough. Bugger off now, will you?" And turning her back on him, she resumes her conversation with her friend.

He had meant to ask her for some change as well, but now he can't. He goes to the telephone again and puts a pound coin in the slot.

"Alloa?" the same woman answers.

"Barbara?" Barr—baah—rrah. Barbarian woman. Wild. Untamed. An incredibly sexy name.

"She's not here." The voice hesitates. "Was it you that called before?"

"My name is Andriy Palenko. I am from Ukraine. Donetsk. Twin town with Sheffield."

"Oh," the woman says, "I thought you was some nutter. Barbara's not lived 'ere for years. She's up in Gleadless now. I'm 'er mum."

"I met her many long times ago. I was first coming to Sheffield with my father for Ukrainian miners' delegation."

"Were it that big do at t' City Hall, wi' t' Ukrainians? I were there too. Bye, that were a night!" A cackling sound down the line. "All that municipal vodka!"

"Is she still live in Sheffield?" Andriy asks. Then he blurts out the question that has been on his mind ever since he had arrived in England—ever since he knew there was such a question to be asked. "Is she marry?"

"Oh, aye. Got two lovely lads. Jason and Jimmy. Six and four. Do you want 'er new number?"

"Yes. Yes of course."

He takes out his pencil stub. She says the new number slowly, pausing after every digit. Andriy listens, but he doesn't write it down.

I turned to run, but Lena was blocking my way. She had a horrible smudged smile on her face.

"Be careful," she said. "He has gun."

How could this be happening on an ordinary street in England in broad daylight? Even as I looked the door of the four-by-four opened and there stood Vulk, grinning at me with his yellow teeth, his arms outstretched in greeting. I could see no gun. If he had one, it was hidden in his pocket. Should I take a chance and run? In the brilliant slanting sunshine his dark backlit outline seemed like an apparition—a tubby grinning nightmare. I felt the same impulse of frozen panic. He started to walk toward me up the hill, quite slowly. His shadow slid before him on the pavement, hard-edged and squat. Behind me I could hear Lena muttering something. If I ran, would she try to stop me?

He was coming closer. "My darlink little flovver." He had taken off his jacket, and I could see the dark circles of sweat on his shirt under his arms. I thought he was panting for breath, then I realized he was whispering, "Loff, loff, loff."

I backed away, barging into Lena, and that is when he got out the gun. I stopped, transfixed. It was gray and so small it was hard to believe it could do any harm. He didn't point it at me. He just held it in his hand and played with it, twirling it on his finger, his eyes set on me all the time.

Then I noticed something at the bottom of the street, behind Vulk's back—people, movement. Suddenly, there was Dog racing toward us, bounding along four paws at a time, and a few metres behind, red-faced and breathless, was Andriy.

Dog is barking frantically. Andriy shouts at it to be quiet, but it jumps up, scrabbling at him with its paws, whining and tossing its head like a mad thing. Andriy picks up their bag and follows it up into the street.

It is half past four. The pavements are busy with shoppers making the most of the last hour or so until closing time. The dog runs ahead through the crush, weaving in and out between people's legs, then stopping to let him catch up, barking in an urgent, purposeful way. Now his heart is jumping around behind his ribs, because he realizes that Dog is desperate to take him somewhere, and that Irina has been gone for over an hour. Dog crosses a busy road and turns up a side street between tall brick buildings. The crowds have disappeared, and they are in a quiet business neighborhood, heading southwest away from the town.

Another right turn brings them to the foot of a long rising street of anonymous workshops and offices. One side of the street—the side they are on—is in bright sunshine; the other side is already in shadow. A hundred meters or so up ahead of them are three figures. Even as he races toward them, Andriy is taking in the whole picture. Nearest to them, with his back turned, is Vulk. He is walking slowly up the hill, waddling in that slightly splay-legged gait of people who are carrying too much weight in front. His bulky form fills the whole pavement. He has taken his jacket off and is wearing a dark blue shirt, tucked tight into the belt of his trousers. His ponytail straggles down between his shoulders. In his right hand is a gun, twirling casually over his forefinger. A few meters in front, facing them, stands Irina, motionless, her mouth open in a silent scream. Behind her, also facing them, is Lena, wearing black tights and a ridiculous pair of high-heeled shoes. Her lips are a scarlet gash. Her face is expressionless, completely blank.

"Stop!" shouts Andriy. "Stop!" He is fumbling in his backpack for the gun. Where is it?

Vulk turns. He sees the dog and Andriy running toward him, some five meters away. He raises his gun.

"Too late, boy." He sneers. "I heff it. Go back."

Andriy stops. In that moment of hesitation, Dog growls, bares his teeth, and launches himself forward. He has picked up such a speed in running that as he summons up all his strength for that final jump, as if to take flight, his heavy muscled mass hurtles toward Vulk like a missile—straight at the gun. Vulk pulls the trigger. Dog howls, a long keening howl. He seems to tremble in midair as blood bursts from his chest in a crimson shower, then he falls, but still with so much forward momentum that he crashes down onto Vulk, knocking him backward so that his head hits the pavement with a crack, the huge bleeding dog on top of him, whimpering to its death. The gun falls from his hand and skitters across the flagstones.

Irina has turned and fled, ducking into an opening between two office buildings. Andriy lunges for the gun, but before he can reach it, Lena steps forward and puts her foot on it. She bends down, picks it up, and points it at Andriy.

"Go."

He doesn't argue. He runs. As he rounds the corner into the same narrow sunless passageway, he hears a single shot behind him.

I will always think of Dog the way I remember him that last time, flying through the air like an angel of vengeance, stern and black, his teeth gleaming like rapiers. I looked into his eyes before he died. They were deep, velvety brown, and unfathomable. I had never noticed before how beautiful they were; for even an angel of vengeance has pity in its eyes. After that I forgot about his awful pissing and sniffing and eating habits, and all I remembered was the way he looked at me when he took flight. I often wonder what he was thinking. Did he know he was going to die?

Andriy was so upset, he wanted to go back for him, but I wouldn't. I said he was dead, and there was nothing we could do to bring him back. I just wanted to get away from that place as fast as I could.

A few minutes later we heard the wail of sirens and caught a flash of blue lights at the end of the alley. We found a gateway behind some bins that opened into a parking lot on the next street, and we headed away in the opposite direction, not running but trying to walk normally, trying to look as though we were just a young couple out for a stroll. Andriy had his arm around my shoulders, and I leaned against him. We were both shaking. I realized Andriy must have been frightened too. That was strange, because you always think that men are fearless—but why should they be?

We walked around and around for an hour or more. This Sheffield—it wasn't at all as Andriy had described it, palaces, bougainvillea, and all that stuff. Nor were there any workers' sanatoria or communal mudbaths. It was very ordinary. The shops had put their shutters up and people were going home. The roads were clogged with traffic. And maybe down a side street, somebody was lying dead. It could have been me.

"Where are we going?" I asked Andriy.

"I don't know. Where do you want to go?"

"I don't know."

I kept wondering about that last gunshot. I couldn't get it out of my mind.

Most of the time we stayed off the big roads and walked on the side streets, which were empty of people and still hot from the sun. You could feel the heat coming out of the bricks like an oven cooling, the trapped air heavy with dust and fumes. We walked, I don't know for how long, until we stopped shaking and our feet hurt and we started to feel hungry. In the end we found our way back to the café. Rock wasn't there, of course. We were more than two hours late.

The afternoon shoppers were gone and the place had filled up with young people, eating, drinking, smoking, talking, the clatter of cutlery and their shrill laughter bouncing and echoing off the hard surfaces so loud that my ears rang and my head started to swim. I realized then how hungry I was. We bought something to eat, I can't remember what, only that it was the cheapest thing we could find on the menu. We looked so shabby and out of place, me in my strawberry-stained jeans and Andriy in his Ukrainian trousers. The girl who served us was Byelorussian.

"Are you looking for a job?" she said. "They've always got vacancies. It's all Eastern Europe round here."

"I don't know," I said.

"No," said Andriy.

"We haven't decided," I said.

She brought us some servings of ice cream, which she said were for free.

"Is there a phone anywhere?" I asked Andriy. "I want to phone my mother."

The minute she said "Hello? Irinochka?" I burst into tears, and I had to pretend to be sneezing because I didn't want her asking what I was crying about. It would only upset her. I just wanted to hear her voice, like when I had a nightmare as a child and she would tell me that everything was all right. Sometimes all you need is a comforting story. So, still sniffling, I told her everything was fine, except that I had caught a cold and the dog had had an accident, and then she wanted to know why I wasn't wearing warm clothes, and which dog, and what kind of accident, and why I had left that nice family, so I had to make up another bunch of lies to keep her happy. Why did she have to ask so many questions?

"Irinochka, now I want to ask you something."

I thought she was going to ask me who I was with, or when I was coming home, and I braced myself to make up another story, but she said, "Would you be very upset if I found a new boyfriend?"

"No, of course not, Mama. You should do whatever makes you happy."

Mama! My heart flipped over inside me like a big wet fish.

Of course I was upset. I was upset and furious. You turn your back on your parents for one moment and they get up to all sorts of mischief!

"That's wonderful, Mama. Who is he?"

"You know I told you about that nice elderly couple who moved in downstairs? And they have a son . . ."

"But I thought . . ."

"Yes, we are in love."

First my father, now my mother!

When I put the phone down, I found my hands were shaking. The fish in my chest was flopping like mad. How could my parents do this to me, their little Irinochka? Outside in the square, dusk had come, but it was still warm. Andriy was standing waiting for me, leaning with his elbows on the balustrade watching the fountains, his outline supple and muscular, despite his awful trousers, one curl hanging like a brown question mark on his forehead. He smiled. Just looking at him made my body start to sing.

Would Andriy and I love each other forever? Love, it seems, is quite a slippery, unpredictable thing—not a rock you can build your life on, after all. I wanted it to be perfect, like Natasha and Pierre, but maybe that's just another story. How can love be perfect, if people aren't perfect? Look at my mother and father—their love didn't last for ever, but it was good enough for a while, good enough for Irinochka, that little girl I used to be. Of course when you're a child, you want to believe your parents are perfect—but why should they be?

"How is your mother?" asked Andriy.

"She's all right." I smiled. Yes, he wasn't perfect: He talked in that funny Donbas way, and he was moody, and he thought he knew everything, despite being riddled with out-of-date ideas. But he was also kindhearted, thoughtful, courteous, and brave, and that was good enough for me. "You know, Andriy, I discovered something just now. My parents don't need me anymore."

We leaned side by side on the balustrade, watching the fountains, and I started to think about the story I would write when I got back to Kiev. It would be a love story, a great romance, not something stupid and frivolous. It would be set against the tumultuous background of the Orange Revolution. The heroine would be a plucky freedom activist and the hero would be from the other side, the Soviet East. But through his love for the beautiful heroine, his eyes would be opened, and he would come to understand the true destiny of his country. He would be very passionate and handsome, with bronzed muscular arms; in fact he would be quite like Andriy. But he would definitely not be a coal miner. Maybe he would have a dog.

In the café, somebody popped a champagne cork, and an eddy of noise and laughter carried into the stillness of the square.

"Andriy," I said. He looked at me. His eyes were sad. A shadow had fallen across his face. "Are you thinking about Dog?"

He nodded.

"Don't be sad. You have me now."

I reached up and twined my finger into his brown curl and pulled his head down for a kiss. Yes, definitely the story must have a happy ending.

You have survived many adventures, and now you've reached your destination. You have escaped death a couple of times, and you have won the love of the beautiful high-spec Ukrainian girl. So why is your heart grumbling away like an old Zaz, Andriy Palenko? What's the matter with you?

He listens to the young people drinking in the café a few meters away—they live in a different world. Maybe he and Irina could stay in Sheffield and find jobs for themselves, and maybe he would even go to college and train to be an engineer. He would buy a mobilfon, not for doing business, but to talk to his friends, and at weekends they would come to a bar like this, and drink and laugh. But he could never be one of them. There are too many things he would have to forget.

She thinks it's because he's grieving for the dog, and she reaches out her hand to stroke his hair and whisper some little sweetness into his ear. Well, yes, you will miss Dog; there will never be another dog as superb as this one. But it's not just Dog. There's a special sadness at the end of a journey. For it's only when you get to your destination that you discover the road doesn't end here after all.

"Come on, Andriy! Don't be sad!"

She beckons. He follows her into the square. She skips down the steps, where water is cascading through stone channels and dozens of fountains are spurting like geysers out of the ground. There is no one there apart from a couple kissing on a bench. She takes his hands and pulls them around her back, pressing herself against him.

"Even though it was very exceptional, Andriy, still it was only a dog."

He holds her close. She is lithe and warm in his arms.

"Rock and the warriors dedicated their lives to saving some stones, Irina. You could say they were only stones, but it's what they represent. As their Jimmy would say, victims of global capitalism."

"Is the dog a victim of global capitalism?"

"Don't be stupid. You know what I mean." Sometimes her frivolity is irritating. "My father died . . ."

"But you are still alive, Andriy. Why don't you think of that sometimes?"

"Of course I do. And then I wonder why it was me who lived and not him."

"But you didn't kill him, Andriy. Do you think he would want you to be always miserable and brooding about the past? The future will be different."

He shakes his head.

"Andriy . . ."

"What?"

". . . your underpants are like the warriors'." She giggles.

"And so what if they are? You are always so mesmerized by superficial things, Irina."

"No I'm not." She splashes her hands through the fountain, spraying a wave of water at him that wets his shirt.

"Yes you are." He splashes back, soaking her hair.

"And you talk like a Donbas miner." She dashes handfuls of water at his face. "Holy whiskers! Devil's bum!"

"And what if I do? Should I be ashamed of that?" He rubs the water out of his eyes. "Now you sound like a bourgeois schoolgirl."

"And what if I am?" She gives him a shove that sends him stumbling backward into a jet of water. Her eyes are shining. Rivulets of water are running down her cheeks. In spite of himself, a grin breaks out on his face.

"If you are"—he sputters, snorting water out of his nose—"I will have to reeducate you." He grabs her wrist, and pulls her toward him.

"Never!" She lunges forward for another shove, slips on the wet stones, and slides into the fountain. As she grabs at him for balance, he slithers and tumbles on top of her with a splash.

"I will start now." He holds her down and covers her in kisses. "Bourgeois schoolgirl!"

"Donbas miner!" She wriggles out from under him, pinning him between her knees. "Riddled with Soviet-era ideas!"

"Orange-ribbon dreamer!"

"You think you know everything. Well you don't." She flicks her wet hair at him. Her clothes are soaked, clinging to the curves of her body. This girl, if he doesn't keep a cool head, she will drown him.

"Show me something I don't know."

"Here!" She presses him down on the stones, straddling him and pushing her tongue into his mouth. He gasps for breath. She is surprisingly strong, and as slippery as a mermaid. Water is everywhere, in his eyes, in his nose, gushing in shining torrents out of the ground.

And as they wrestle there in the jets of foaming water, a shadowy black dog appears out of nowhere, a mature, handsome dog, running through the spume, barking and splashing with them. Above their heads, stars are dancing on the inky floor of the sky.

But, oh, the water is so cold!

Dear Andree

I am writing to fill you up with my newses for today by the Grace of God I have received a telephone from my sister who with your help uncovered my wherebeing and a praised me of your address at four gabbles. And I feveredly hope one day my dear friend you will return to this place called Richmond where I await you with beatings in my heart. And also the beauteous Irina for I hope you two are now joined up in Holy Matrimony. My sister was full of questionings about my life in the dwelling of Toby Makenzi and his roilsome parents and she rejoiced to hear all has turned out benefficiently and we are blessed with daily manifestos of His Goodness. And I have given up my sinful curiosity of canals and turned toward rivers for I have become a Fisher of Men.

Each day at eventide the Pa and I together descend upon the river bringing with us the rod and red bucket of the Mozambicans and we spend two hours or more in contemplation of the slow moving waters of the Times. And sometimes in the evening when the river darkens in its mystery the power of Love is so great that I am minded to open my heart and sing. For the sunset upon these waters is beauteous to behold being painted pallid blue with delicious rosy cloudlings (though not as beauteous as the sunsets of Zomba) and I am confounded with admiration for His artistry. And through the mystery of our long conversions upon the riverbank the Pa himself has started to walk in the Way of the Lord and has abandoned his whiskey drinking and blaspheming.

And sometimes it has befallen that fishes come upon our rod. And now the beauteous Ma who prepared so many feastings of fishes for us has started to abandon her previous godless vegetarian ways and the practice of yogurt and is also coming into the Joyful Kingdom. Sometimes at eventide she walks to the darkening river with us to share our contemplation. And also that good mzungu Toby Makenzi for whose friendship I came into this land he has become a follower of the river. And I pray feveredly that before long the opiate will fall from his heart and he too will become aquatinted with Love.

acknowledgments

I would like to thank all the many people whose help, comments, moral and practical support have contributed to the making of this book.

First I must acknowledge two main written sources: Nick Clark, *Gone West: Ukrainians at Work in the UK* (TUC 2004), and Felicity Lawrence, *Not on the Label: What Really Goes into the Food on Your Plate* (Penguin 2004). Their thorough research was my starting point, but any shortcomings are entirely my own.

Many other people helped with specific information, including Ben Beneste, Cathy Dean, and Kate Fenton (dogs), Charles Gaskin (strawberries), Joyce da Silva of Compassion in World Farming, Richard Churcher (chickens), Dave Feickert (coal mining and trade unions), Sonia Lewycka (Malawi), and Simon Pickvance of Sheffield Occupational Health Project.

Thanks are also due to Bill Hamilton and everyone at AM Heath for encouragement and sound advice, to Juliet Annan and Scott Moyers for many helpful comments on the text, and to the team at Penguin for being so great.

Thanks also to the O'Brien family, who took me strawberry picking, to Bob and Doris Spencer at Gara Bridge, where we stayed in both trailers, and to Jos Kingston, who introduced me to Paddy, the original Dog.

Finally I would like to thank Beatrice Monti della Corte and the Santa Maddalena Foundation for a wonderful working retreat, and Judith and Pasquale Rosato, without whose generosity and kindness at a time of crisis this book would never have been possible.

A PENGUIN READERS GUIDE TO

STRAWBERRY FIELDS

Marina Lewycka

An Introduction to
Strawberry Fields

On a sunny hillside in Kent, in the Garden of England, a group of nine migrant workers from various parts of the world are picking strawberries for Mr. Leapish, the farmer. Housed in two trailers, and fed a daily diet of bread, margarine, jam, and sausages, life isn't easy for them. But the friendships they forge, and their dreams of love and hopes for a new life in the West, carry them along.

Nineteen-year-old Irina has arrived from Kiev, Ukraine, buoyed up by enthusiasm for the Orange Revolution, and full of dreams of a romantic and refined life in the West. Andriy, from Donetsk in Eastern Ukraine, has fled a harsher life—and maybe death—in one of its failing coal mines. Yola, the sharp-tongued but warm-hearted supervisor, has come from Poland with her gentle niece, Marta, to earn money to support her disabled son. Tomasz, also from Poland, is a latter-day aging hippie and Bob Dylan fan following his own dreams of freedom. With them are two Chinese girls and Emanuel, a devout young Catholic from Africa, seeking his sister, who is working somewhere in England as a nurse. The mysterious Vitaly, of unknown Eastern European origins, and a runaway dog round out the bunch.

Although the tone is often humorous, and the action moves quickly, there is an underlying seriousness in this modern tale of globalization, where people are expendable, and the worst exploiters are often other immigrants, traffickers in cheap labor and worse, who prey on the vulnerable new arrivals.

Author Marina Lewycka creates comedy from the language and cultural differences of this ragtag group, while never flinching from describing the horrors they encounter when they are forced to leave their idyllic strawberry field and embark on an adventure which takes them through an England that turns out to be very different from the country of their dreams.

Strawberry Fields is both a road story and a love story. As each one of the original strawberry pickers is forced to let go of some of their illusions about life in the West, they gain friendship, love, and a better understanding of their own nature. Before they can finally extricate themselves from the clutches of the gang masters and go their separate ways, the group has the bittersweet journey of a lifetime, tinged with hope, joy, tragedy, and love.

ABOUT MARINA LEWYCKA

Marina Lewycka was born to Ukrainian parents in a refugee camp in Germany shortly after World War II. She and her family emigrated after her birth to England, where she grew up. Her first novel, *A Short History of Tractors in Ukrainian,* has sold more than one million copies worldwide, has been translated into more than thirty languages, and was nominated for the Booker and Orange prizes. She lives in Sheffield, Yorkshire, with her husband, and has one adult daughter.

A CONVERSATION WITH MARINA LEWYCKA

The plot of Strawberry Fields *is a raucous one and you tell it with a good deal of humor, but the political issues you address are real. To what extent did you intend your novel to be social commentary, or an exposé of the trials and travails of illegal immigrants? Did you choose a lighthearted tone on purpose? How do you hope that readers will react to the political and social issues you bring up?*

Immigration is very much in the news in Britain at the moment, as it is in many prosperous countries, but it is always talked about in terms of statistics—so many thousand Poles, so many thousand Chinese, and so on. My modest aim in this book is to put a human face to some of those statistics, to tell the stories of a few of the people who find themselves adrift in the globalized labor market. We see the strawberries and the chicken pieces on our supermarket shelves, but we never really stop to wonder who put them there, or what those people's lives are like. My aim is not so much to raise social and political issues as to give readers an invitation for a few hours to see the world through someone else's eyes—someone who may have a very different background and culture from their own. That's really all that an author can do.

Your first novel, A Short History of Tractors in Ukrainian, *was hugely successful. How was writing your second novel different from writing the first one?*

Having written such a popular first novel made writing a follow-up very daunting. I was acutely aware that people would be watching to see what I did next, and there is also a nasty tendency, if someone has had success, to try to pull them down. So I decided to do something completely different. *Strawberry Fields* is much more of a fable or a fairy tale, and you have to read it in a different way from *A Short History of Tractors in Ukrainian.* But I hope I've captured some of the same directness and sense of fun that made my first book successful.

What was the inspiration for writing about immigrants? Did you draw on any of your own experiences growing up? Were any of the characters based on people you have known?

One of the things about being an immigrant myself is that I grew up with an outsider's perspective—although my own experiences were different from those of the characters in the book, I knew what it was like to be on the margins of a host society without ever quite fitting in. As a child, I picked peas in the Lincolnshire countryside with my mother, and though that was quite a harsh experience—the work was backbreaking and the wages were low—I don't remember the harshness. What I remember is being close to my mother, out of doors in the beautiful Lincolnshire countryside, and the banter and camaraderie of the other pea pickers. In *Strawberry Fields* I wanted to capture both the harshness and the beauty of that situation. Later, as a student, I picked strawberries, and I also worked as a waitress and a cook. Although I never worked in a chicken factory, I did work in a very disgusting sausage factory. I knew not only that this was a story that needed to be told, but also that I was the person who had to tell it.

All of the characters are partly based on people I have known—Irina and Andriy are modeled on people I met on my visits to Ukraine, and we have plenty of Polish people in Sheffield. I used to teach a lot of Chinese and Malaysian students, so that part of the story was in a way based on experience. My daughter works in Malawi and on one visit I met the young man on whom Emanuel is based. Even Dog is based on a real dog.

I must say that I also owe a great debt of gratitude to Geoffrey Chaucer in creating the characters. *The Canterbury Tales* is one of my favorite books, and once I knew that my story was to be partly based in Canterbury, and that it was going to be a road story, I thought it would be fun to include a homage to Chaucer. He is so clever at sketching in the characters and giving them distinct personalities in just a few phrases. All of my characters in *Strawberry Fields* have a *Canterbury Tales* equivalent. Sometimes it is quite clear—for instance Yola is a latter-day Wife of Bath—but sometimes the clue is just a reference to a detail of dress. You don't need to be a Chaucer fan to enjoy these characters, but if you are there is something extra for you. Actually, the real mystery character is Tomasz—I wonder whether anyone can work out which of the Canterbury pilgrims he represents.

Dog is one of the most sympathetic characters in the book, and he has a wonderful personality of his own. And your version of dog-talk is inspired. How did you decide to include Dog as such an important character?

The real dog, on whom Dog is based, was called Paddy and belonged to a close friend of mine who lived in Derbyshire. We would often go walking with him in the beautiful Peak District. My friend told me that he was a runaway who had arrived on their doorstep late one night, panting and bleeding. He was clearly running away from something, but being a dog he couldn't say what. I became fascinated with the dog's story and tried to imagine the adventures he'd had. I tried to imagine what it would be like to perceive the world primarily through your senses of smell and hearing. When I knew that my book was going to be about a pair of lovers on the run, I realized that they would also have to have a dog that was on the run.

I knew that he would perceive things mainly as happening in the present, and have only a hazy sense of the past, and little sense of the future. I knew that he would not be very articulate, but the one thing he would always be certain of was his own dogness. That's why he begins and ends every episode with the statement I AM DOG.

Irina may be the heroine of the story, but you give a lot of time to the voices and views of the other characters. While some of the characters speak in the first person, you tell others' stories in the third person. One character's story is even told exclusively through his letters to a sister. How did you pick each character's voice? Did you start writing with the idea of different voices in mind, or was it something that developed as you went?

When I started to write *Strawberry Fields*, I was going to tell it from the point of view of a single all-knowing narrator. But I found it seemed very lifeless, and I realized that the only way to bring the characters to life was to make them speak for themselves. With so many characters, I knew it could be confusing for the readers, so I made every voice distinctive in terms of person, tense, vocabulary and mode of address, and I took care at the start of every change of voice to flag up who it was who was now speaking. I personally hate to read books where I can't tell what's going on, so I tried to make it as plain as possible.

Strawberry Fields *includes a lot of information about agriculture, especially strawberry and chicken farming. Where did you get your facts from? Did you do a lot of firsthand research?*

I did get a lot of help from two farmers in Kent—a chicken farmer and a strawberry farmer—but their operations were far from the horrible exploitative situations I have described. For these, I turned for detail to an organization called Compassion in World Farming, which campaigns about the conditions in which livestock are kept, and they provided me with much detail about what happens on chicken farms, and were even able to send me a video. The trade unions who organize migrant workers in the United Kingdom were able to give me very precise details about the scams and hazards faced by migrant workers with a poor grasp of English. Of course some of the worst abuses, like those of the Morecambe Bay cockle pickers, have also been widely reported in the press over here.

When you write, do you develop special relationships with your own characters? Did you have a favorite in this book?

Although Irina is the first-person narrator of this story, she is very different from me—maybe she is more like I was when I was nineteen and convinced that I knew everything. I found her knowingness both irritating and amusing. And I was also a bit irritated by Andriy's constant pessimism. I thought they were a pair of opposites who really needed each other to be complete, and just had to end up falling in love. But they seemed so hopelessly contrary that I did find myself worrying about them when I was away traveling a lot, and not able to spend time with them. I would wonder how they were doing, and how I was finally going to be able to get them together.

Your characters, in general, don't have a very firm grasp of English, but they invent some wonderful phrases—devil's bum, poky-nose, and "make possibility" as a euphemism for sex, to name a few. What was your inspiration for these invented words?

I grew up among people who invented their own language as they went along, so I guess it must come naturally to me. The words someone chooses often say more about them than about the thing they are describing.

What are you reading now? What books have been most important to you over the years?

I've just started Orlando Figes's *The Whisperers,* about family life in Stalin's Russia. He is an extraordinary writer, who combines painstaking research with the psychological depth and empathy of a novelist. As a fiction writer, I find myself spending a lot of time reading nonfiction, to gain background material for my books.

I studied English Literature at university, but because of the options I selected, my knowledge ends around 1700. Shakespeare was hugely important to me, as was Chaucer, and Milton, and the Metaphysical poets. I also draw inspiration from Charles Dickens and James Joyce and, of course, the great Russian novelists.

Do you have any more projects in the works?

I'm about halfway through my third book. It's about an old lady who lives in a crumbling house in London with seven cats. But it's also an oblique discussion of the situation in the Middle East, and the dispute over Palestine and Israel. What makes me think I can write a comedy about something as deadly serious as this? I must be crazy

QUESTIONS FOR DISCUSSION

1. Each of the characters in *Strawberry Fields* has a very distinctive voice. All of the characters' stories are intertwined, but they each develop separately. How does the fact that each character's story and voice unfolds independently affect the narrative of the novel as a whole? Does it make it easier or harder to understand how the characters relate to each other?

2. Andriy and Irina are both Ukrainian, but they are clearly from different sides of the tracks. At the beginning of the novel, Irina looks down on Andriy, and Andriy thinks of Irina as stuck-up. But

as the story progresses, they grow to appreciate and even love each other. How did you react to their blooming romantic relationship? Do you think their adventures together allow them to put aside their differences, or did they create an artificial closeness?

3. All of the workers on Leapish's farm are migrant seasonal laborers, but none of them seem to know exactly what they have gotten themselves into. Was this initial setup believable? Did the following events make the story more or less plausible?

4. Vitaly is a strange character—first he seems to be one of the Leapish crew, but then he seems to turn against them, becoming a "mobilfonman." He coerces many of his less savvy friends into bad jobs in worse conditions. And yet, as we find out something about Vitaly's life, we learn that he has been just as much a victim of the system as those he is taking advantage of. Did you sympathize with Vitaly? Do you think he could have helped his behavior? How would you have acted in his situation?

5. In the novel's epigraph, Lewycka quotes Chaucer: "For myn entente is nat but for to pleye." The tone of the book is indeed lighthearted, but Lewycka brings up some very serious social and political issues. Does her political stance come across strongly? How did some of the situations she presents in the novel change your mind about real-world politics?

6. Like many novels, *Strawberry Fields* is about a journey. In what ways do the real journeys the characters take—from their native lands to Leapish's farm, to various parts of Europe, and sometimes back home—stand in for their emotional or psychological journeys?

7. Vulk is obsessed with "making possibility" with Irina. He is a frightening and revolting character, but he seems to have a genuine crush on Irina. Because of this, is he a sympathetic figure? What are some of the characteristics that would elevate him from the position of merely "bad guy"?

8. One of the stranger episodes in the novel occurs when Emanuel, Irina, Andriy, and Dog show up on Toby Mackenzie's doorstep. Toby's family seems stereotypical—an overbearing father, a repressed but kind mother, and a rebellious, drug-using teenage son. Was the author's description of the family funny, upsetting, or a combination of both? What about the immigrants' reactions to the family? In what ways was the scene realistic?

9. Discuss Emanuel's and Marta's religious convictions. Do their religious beliefs make them harder or easier to understand? Why do you think the author chose to include two devout Catholics from such different backgrounds?

10. Do you think the subject matter of the book works best as a novel? Would it have been more powerful as nonfiction—for example, an exposé of immigrant life?

11. What did you think of the characters' reactions to Western culture? Were their impressions accurate?

12. Which character did you relate to best and why? Was there any character you disliked? Did the story have a clear hero? A villain?

For more information about or to order other Penguin Readers Guides, please e-mail the Penguin Marketing Department at reading@us.penguingroup.com or write to us at:

Penguin Books Marketing Dept.
Readers Guides
375 Hudson Street
New York, NY 10014-3657

Please allow 4–6 weeks for delivery.
To access Penguin Readers Guides online, visit the Penguin Group (USA) Inc. Web site at www.penguin.com and www.vpbookclub.com.

A Short History of Tractors in Ukrainian

"Two years after my mother died, my father fell in love with a glamorous blond Ukrainian divorcée. He was eighty-four and she was thirty-six. She exploded into our lives like a fluffy pink grenade."

When an elderly and newly widowed Ukrainian immigrant announces his intention to remarry, his daughters must set aside their longtime feud to thwart him. For their father's intended is a voluptuous old-country gold digger with a proclivity for green satin underwear and an appetite for the good life of the West. As the hostilities mount and family secrets spill out, *A Short History of Tractors in Ukrainian* combines sex, bitchiness, wit, and genuine warmth in its celebration of the pleasure of growing old disgracefully.

"An amusing, astonishing debut . . . about how a family learns to let go of the past and live and love in the present."
—*The Atlanta Journal-Constitution*

ISBN 978-0-14-303674-6